Stand-In Hearts

J.C. NELSON

OTHER WORKS

GRIMM AGENCY SERIES

Free Agent
Armageddon Rules
Wish Bound
Soul Ink (novella)

OTHER NOVELS

The Reburialists

AS JAYCEE NELSON

Toys

Find other works by the author at
http://authorjcnelson.com

Stand-In Hearts

J.C. NELSON

AUSTRALIA

Print ISBN: 978-1-925825-73-2
eBook ISBN: 9781386155713

www.inkprintpress.com

National Library of Australia Cataloguing-in-Publication Data
Nelson, J.C.
Stand-In Hearts
400 p.   cm.
ISBN: 978-1-925825-73-2
Inkprint Press, Canberra, Australia
          1. Fiction—Romance—Contemporary 2. Fiction—Romance—Clean & Wholesome

Summary: Will Mathis takes on a job as a stand-in actor to pay back his debts, but he gets more than he planned with his gorgeous co-worker, Sonia.

First Edition: February 2019

Cover design © Inkprint Press.

For Radonna, who has always been my superstar.

ACKNOWLEDGEMENTS

This book is, like any book, the product of a community as much as any writer. Thanks to John, Abby, Leanne, Laurel, and Victoria, for sticking with me while I found the story I actually wanted to tell as opposed to the one I started with.

Liana and Amy, thank you for your patient prodding that got me to actually do something rather than talk about doing something.

All of you helped me find my way through this, and made the difference between "this would be a fun story" and "until next time."

Until next time…

CHAPTER ONE

In Hollywood, the key to survival is remembering what's real and what's not. The traffic, that's real. Everything else is fake, from the movie sets I work on, to the actresses falling in love with sweaty men in loincloths.

Los Angeles won't see the sun for another hour yet, but the eastern sky has shifted to dark blue, and the air is preparing to make the jump from cool enough to be uncomfortable to hot enough to make everyone miserable. I fiddle with the duct-tape my brother put over the tears in the vinyl seat of the truck and shuffle the mound of fast-food bags crumpled in the passenger floorboard, thinking of Seattle and what was. How much of that was real?

"Will? Earth to Will, come in, Will Mathis." Bradley glances my way as he turns his pickup truck into the studio parking lot. Bradley's my little brother in age only, since he's taller and wider than me. "You ready to represent my business?"

I am.

I'm not.

I have to be. "I'm always ready. And unlike you, I've never broken a security line and got thrown off the lot."

"It was a simple misunderstanding with the guards, and as long as I stay off studio property for the next three years, no harm, no foul." Bradley pulls at the tangles in his beard, like he does every time he's nervous. The beard is just about the only thing we have in common, dark brown and so thick it resembles a rat's nest attached to my face.

My ex-girlfriend (also my ex-accountant) Tamara loved me clean shaven, which is why for the last year and a half, I've avoided razors like I'm allergic to them. "I'm not going to panic, or break any rules. I'll be a good little peon."

"I'm not worried about you freaking out, I'm worried about you being Mr. Broody And Silent, when you need to be friendly. Work with the stage manager, figure out why he's sent back the last four staircase posts and what it's going to take to satisfy him."

Four staircase posts I carved myself in different styles, two of them completely by hand. Set carpentry isn't my first love, but art doesn't pay the bills. And if I could pay my bills, I wouldn't be crashing on my little brother's couch. I wouldn't be working for his company, carving pieces by the hour.

We wait in the studio drop-off line, which stretches around the parking lot and back out onto the street. You need a permit and an appointment and a vehicle of your own to park on set, so I'll be hoofing it.

Bradley taps his fingers on the steering wheel to pass the time, and before he turns it into a full-on drum concert, I turn on him. "Spill it, bro. What's eating you?"

"Word to my investment group is that everyone is on set today. You're going to be on the same soundstage as *her*."

Bradley's been looking to move from watching movies to making them for years, by way of financing people who actually understand how movies are made. The way he says it, I should know who he's talking about. Then again, Hollywood has always been his obsession. "Who is 'her'?"

"Kantina." He almost whispers her name, saying it the same way *everyone* says that name, like Kan and Tina are two separate words, or she's so gorgeous you forgot to finish what you were saying halfway through. "She's the reason we signed on to this project."

"Kantina's still making movies? She hasn't had an album in two years, and her clothing line—"

"She's making a sequel to *The Bride Becomes Her*."

Bradley's tried to show it to me five times in the last month. I like my films with more explosions of blood than outbursts of feeling. "You really think I'll just bump into her?"

"It's Kantina's movie. She'll be on set, and her autograph would be the pinnacle of my collection. God, I wish I could go with you, but if I get in trouble again, Tia says she'll have to post two bails. One to get me out, and one to get her out after she kills me."

There's only one thing Bradley prizes nearly as much as his wife of four years, and that's a celebrity autograph collection he's built up since we were sleeping in bunk-beds in the same room. "If I see her, and *if* I recognize her, I'll ask."

Bradley gives me the biggest grin as we pull to the front of the drop-off line. "Will, look for the hair. Brilliant red hair down past her waist, green eyes, tan skin. She might not be in makeup, and when you meet a star in real life, they look so different. But the hair's a dead giveaway."

"I'll ask." I give him a pat as I collect my duffle bag with five new staircase posts and hop out. Truth is, I know what Kantina looks like—at least, I've seen her on billboard ads for makeup and movie posters, and a commercial once for an animal shelter. But telling Bradley that would remove one of my few sources of entertainment.

At the studio gates, I pass through security, which consists of tired guards scanning the bags of tired people, all of whom probably have more interesting things in their knapsacks than carved bannisters and bits of old beef jerky. As I step through the metal detector, my phone chirps.

Another debt collector. You can tell those guys your ex-girlfriend stole your money. You can tell them she stole your heart. That doesn't stop the phone calls.

The backlots of the studio are a maze of warehouse-sized buildings with giant numbers painted on them. The gray walls tower above me, smooth gray, with curved tops, and palm trees in planters dot the sides. All around me, smokers light up for one last drag, the bitter smell of cigarette smoke joining hot blacktop and a sour underlying trace of garbage, like someone didn't close the lid on the dumpster.

Sleek white trailers nestle up to the concrete walls like puppies next to their mother. Already they shake from air conditioners failing to cool them down. Golf carts whizz by, carrying people too important to use their own two feet, while everyone else runs like the devil's two steps behind them.

Speaking of the devil, I've passed at least two people in demon costumes before I find Soundstage 52. It's really only different in the numbers, each of which is taller than I am. Under the sodium lights, the tan paint is purple and the letters black as the sky was when I got up. The wide double doors open into a cavern so cold the hair on my arms stands up.

I expected to see sets.

Instead, black curtains hang from the ceiling, leaving me nothing but a dimly-lit corridor and a desk where a cluster of men and women gather, most of them chatting into headphones. If you're supposed to dress for the job you want, most of these people want to be pizza delivery people. The men wear cargo pants with stuffed pockets and faded t-shirts, while the women seem to favor sweatshirts over tank tops and high socks.

"Excuse me?" I flag down a young man whose pantsuit sets him apart from the others as he balances a tray of coffee cups. "I'm Will Mathis, from Mathis Construction. I'm here to meet with Aaron Abrams."

He sets down the tray like his night job is waiting tables, then clicks the button on his headset. "Mr. Abrams? There's someone from set construction here to see you."

A moment later, an incoherent buzz has him nodding. "He'll meet you in Central Holding. That way." He points past the desk, like there's only one way to go, and then scurries off, throwing aside a curtain to cut through.

Turns out, there really is only one way to go. The heavy curtains and abrupt turns guard a single path straight into the interior of the soundstage—and what a mess. The whole place smells of paint and wood and burning plastic, and it's a nightmare of half-built walls, corners, or doorways. All the set pieces I worked on with Bradley were nearly complete rooms, but this leaves the carpenter in me baffled.

None of the sets have ceilings, which lets the lights overhead shine down, and we're not talking small lights. These are like search and rescue spotlights, and they'd kill someone if they fell.

Near the far right corner, another clot of people mills about in a rectangle marked off with yellow tape. The way they pace the line makes it clear this is where people wait, and so I stand and watch as the minutes tick by.

For my first time on a movie set, the place where movies are actually made, it's boring. Watching the people in Central Holding, it reminds more of a detention center, like the one I had to bail Bradley out of when he was seventeen.

"Will Mathis?"

I turn to find a slender man charging my way. He's at least thirty pounds thinner than me, and I consider myself fit at two hundred pounds to match my six feet. The black leather jacket he's wearing and faded jeans match his dusty work-boots. He offers me a calloused hand. "Aaron Abrams. You here to get the monkey off my back?"

"Sounds like you need animal control," I say, giving him a firm shake. "I'm here to find out what's wrong with the posts I carved for you. I swear, I followed the sketches you emailed perfectly. Show me what's wrong, I'll fix it."

"Follow me." His order comes with the tone of a man used to being obeyed.

Furniture lines the back side of the sets, Victorian tables and chairs stacked as high as the walls, and enough barrels for me to start a winery. The few whole sets I pass have a dusty, antique feel to them, but what looks like weathered oak flooring shows white pine, fresh metal straps and duct tape at the edges. Aaron twists past a six-foot tall clock face without hands, and when I follow, I find something that would give me nightmares if I were in charge of safety.

This set piece is two stories tall, built around a staircase, or at least, parts of one.

The top floor attaches to a metal ladder, the bottom to a stage base. What gives me the shivers is the banister railing, which is only held up by three posts, two at the top and one at the bottom.

"This is the centerpiece of the whole movie," says Aaron. "She goes up the stairs. She goes down the stairs."

"She falls off the stairs if she so much as leans on that railing," I say, giving it a test wobble. And shake it does. The existing posts are obviously my work, white pine carved so each casts an S-shaped shadow, but I would never have left something half-done when it could be done right. "This isn't safe. Give me a drill and a few minutes with some stud lumber and I'll fix it up."

Aaron shakes his head. "Leave it to the set carpenters. They get testy when other companies cut in on their work."

That's not how I raised myself to do things. I taught Bradley from the very beginning to do things right or not at all. But I can fight that war later. "You need what, fifteen of these? I brought several more samples, I could screw them into place and you could run tests."

"Leave 'em." he says. "You hit the concept sketches fine, did exactly what we asked, but light tests are showing some problems that might be easier to show than explain. Our director, Belion, he's all about light and shadows, and these aren't doing what we need. We need to be able to *see* the shape of the shadow on her legs when she's going downstairs. That's a close up shot. But they can't look awful when you can see more of the staircase. The top posts are good for long shots, but only the bottom one gives us the right shadow."

A short woman with jet-black hair rushes by and grabs Aaron. "We need to set up. Belion wants to get one more take in before lunch."

She's heavily built and looks like she's on the verge of a heart attack, gripping a tablet in her hands as she glances to me. "You here to fix the wiring?"

"Felica Slate," Aaron says, "meet Will Mathis. Will's going to fix the staircase banisters so we can shoot the stair shots. Will, take this woman's pulse and you'll find out why you never want to be the assistant director."

I dip my chin in deference to her. "A pleasure to meet you. I won't keep Aaron much longer."

"Mathis. As in... the head of the investment group?" Felicia raises one eyebrow.

Head? I have to keep my jaw from dropping, since Bradley told me he was a minor investor—and I took it more to mean he was doing the set work on the cheap. "Wrong Mathis," I say with a shrug. "Will Mathis as in 'lowly set carpenter.' As in staircase repair-man. I'll fix that for free, if you'll let me."

"Free?" She looks to Aaron. "Nothing is free in this town."

I look her dead in the eye and use the same words that won me clients in Seattle. "Those posts are my work.

Anything associated with my work is done right."

Felicia scrunches her nose like she's sniffing for a lie. "If you want to do something right, figure out what we can do about the shape of the posts. Then you can install them yourself."

Now this? This is the kind of problem that makes me smile, because I can fix this. "I'll make two sets of banisters. One for fat shadows, one for not looking awful. And if you need anything else fixed, call the shop and ask for Will. I'm looking for all the work I can get."

Aaron gives me a solid thump on the back. "How soon can you get them?"

"Let me get some measurements from this so I can make them taller. Both of the ones you like are custom, so you sign my work order and give me five days. Each of these—"

"Three days," says Felicia. "Get it done in three, and there's something extra in it for you. Now, Aaron, light #22, please. Will, I'll sign whatever you want and have someone show you out."

It takes six hours to cut each of these if I do it right, and that's the only way I do things. Maybe I just won't sleep for a few days.

While Felicia watches, I snap pictures of each style and scribble a few quick measurements, then follow her back into the maze. She pivots, one hand to her ear. "No, no, no. Tell him no. Roll up a newspaper and smack him on the nose. Oh, for the love of God—" She takes off again, and all I can do is follow and hope I don't get more lost than I already am.

Two half-built bathrooms and what I think is a wine-press later, we emerge, not at the exit, but at a scene where there are actual cameras, and actual people—and an actual fight. Felicia plunges into the mass of people arguing and anyone sane takes two steps back. "This argument is over. You, stand over there. You, back to your trailer. No one moves or says a word unless I say so."

She drags one unfortunate actor off and then pivots to point at me. "Stay put. Second crew on standby. Aaron, get it done."

The actors disperse—or at least change—and that's when I see the red-head.

Bradley said to look for the hair, but it's not like I could miss her as she comes sweeping onto the set, a Victorian kitchen table and window that opens onto a picturesque view of a concrete wall.

Red hair cascades down her back, not red like in the posters, but more a dark brown with golden highlights. Under the brilliant lighting, it almost glows, and it takes me far too long to stop staring and remember Bradley's request. Pen and work-request in hand, I have to remind myself how much I love my brother.

After all, I'm about to disturb an actress turned super-model turned singer. "Excuse me?"

She spins to look at me, and boy, was Bradley right about how different stars look in real life. Her face is narrower than I thought, but her eyes have those same deep green lines. High cheekbones and a rounded chin serve to accent the soft tan of her skin, which I'd always taken as darker, though the freckles show through.

She opens her mouth, and in a rich, melodic voice, asks, "Are you lost? Production's heading to 22 at the moment."

I blink—and stop my staring. "I'm sorry, ma'am. It's just—I mean, you're beautiful." My cheeks burn as I stumble over words and realize that maybe I've got more in common with my brother than I thought. "I mean, not like when you're on the posters, but *really* beautiful. They must do a lot of editing to make you look like that." She's not waif-thin, with an athletic build and well-toned muscles on her arms.

I cringe as my brain catches up with my mouth. "I mean, not that you need it. Oh, screw it. I just wanted your autograph for my brother."

She covers her mouth, and I can't tell if she's offended or hiding a laugh. "Are you serious?"

"Please." I don't take one step closer. I don't know Kantina, she doesn't know me, and I respect her personal space. Word of this will never leak out. "My brother is such a huge fan of yours. He says you're the most beautiful woman in the country, after his wife."

"But *you* say I'm not as beautiful as I am on the posters," she says, circling the table. "Because I haven't been edited."

There's a moment where my organs do a simultaneous triple flip, and I feel like I'm falling. Insulting pop royalty/ movie mega-star-models was not on my schedule for this morning, but I've managed it anyway. If this conversation were a plane, every engine would be flaming as it plummeted nose first. "You really don't need it—"

"Sonia, darling, where are you?" The female voice, with its soft Eastern European accent, sends a nightmare crawling down my spine.

The woman in front of me looks over her shoulder while I wrap my brain around the name I just heard.

Sonia.

Behind Sonia, like an angel, is the actual Kantina. Bradley was right—I couldn't miss her. Kantina's skin is a richer tan, her hair is more brilliantly red, her face perfectly round, with luminous green eyes that don't have gold flecks, eyes with pupils so wide it's almost inhuman.

I've been making a fool of myself with *Sonia*.

"K, this man here asked *me* for *your* autograph." It was a laugh she was hiding, and she's not hiding it anymore. "Also, he says I look different when I'm on the posters."

"In my defense," I say in a small voice, "I also said you were beautiful."

Kantina glides toward me. She has a presence, like the queen and a mixed-martial arts fighter all at once. She puts one hand on each of my cheeks and looks up at me. "She won't give you my autograph because Sonia is not me. And everything I create is a part of me. I don't give something so personal as a part of myself to someone I don't know."

I drop my gaze and turn away. "I'm sorry. I—I just saw you, Bradley said to look for the most beautiful woman on set, and I thought—I think, I'm going to leave now. Do either of you know my name?"

"No," says Kantina. "I have not had the pleasure."

I shake my head. "Good. How about we pretend this conversation never happened?" I glance away from Kantina to Sonia. "For the record, ma'am, you're not just beautiful. You're stunning."

Kantina gives me a short wave, almost pushing me away, and spins. "Help me rehearse, Sonia. There is yet another delay."

While Sonia whispers to Kantina, I stop to appreciate just how hot it is under these lights, because I'm sweating.

I haven't crashed and burned like that since high school.

Tamara was never that hard to talk to. Then again, look at where that got me. I owned my own wood-carving shop, I had commissions from around the world. Now I have a vinyl couch to sleep on and part-time job working for my little brother.

From a few walls over, I can hear Felica's voice, rising in volume and pitch. She's headed this way.

She emerges, trailed by Aaron and another man with platinum blond hair. He can't be less than sixty, and he wears gloves with the fingers cut from them, apparently so he can wave them better. He throws his hands up like he's being robbed and shouts, "He did not support my artistic vision."

"Belion," says Felica, in the tone of voice I'd use with a toddler, "you *cannot* keep firing people. I'm trying to make a movie. You may be the director, but it's up to me to get the movie done, and I *can't* if you remove half my staff."

"It is not up for discussion," says Belion. His accent reminds me of Russian, but it's like Russia by way of south Texas, since he draws out one-syllable words into two, if not three.

Felicia spins and jabs him in the chest. "You know what's going to happen when I tell our producer? He's going to explode on me. Then, he's going to explode on you. Aaron, can we move to shooting 113?"

Aaron looks around wildly, catching my eye and giving me a half-hearted shrug. "Not without the staircase."

"Right." The word escapes Felica as a white flag. "Everyone go to lunch while I put in a call to Central Casting."

Belion spins, sending his vest-cloak combination whirling like some sort of superhero, and stalks away.

"Ma'am?" I hold up the work order. "Could you sign this and point me in the right direction to the exit?"

Felicia spots me and sighs. "I'm so sorry. Making a movie is one set of—" She grabs Aaron by the goatee, yanking his gaze to look at me. "Do you see what I see?"

"A disaster in progress?" Aaron laughs, then goes quiet.

Felicia stares, and stalks toward me. "Will, isn't it?"

I nod, taking one step back as she comes closer. The lights are blinding, but I have the exact same feeling a piece of ham does when it's hanging from a hook.

"How tall are you?"

"Six feet flat in my stocking feet," I say.

She grabs my arm. "Turn."

I do, if only to get the light out of my eyes. "I'm sorry, I didn't mean to upset Kantina."

"Good luck with that," Felicia says, then continues like I said nothing. "Get Becton on set."

"He was gone for lunch before you called it. But you're onto something." Aaron joins her, arms crossed. "Right skin tone, right height, build. Pity about the hands, or he'd make a perfect double."

"Cut the beard, dye the hair, we could be filming again by the end of lunch," says Felicia. "Tell me, Will. Do set carpenters get much overtime?"

That's a joke. We're an offsite fabrication unit. All our stuff is brought to the studios by truck, except when there's trouble. "No, ma'am. I'm not even full time right now. I'm doing specialty work by the piece."

She pulls out a chair and pushes me toward it. "You told Aaron you were looking for all the hours you can get. How'd you like to work twelve to fourteen hours a day, union rate?"

Union rate isn't a definition, but I'm lucky to get four hours a day right now. Fourteen? That might kill me. But it would also get the debt collectors to stop calling. "For how long?"

"Every day we're filming, which might be the next eight weeks, since we are behind schedule," says Felicia. "Have you ever heard of a stand-in? They let us test the scene lighting without using the principals. Star contracts only let them work limited hours. Stand-ins have no such silly limits, and can make major money. For *standing* there."

Now I get where she's going. "*Might* be the next eight weeks means there's a catch—unless I'm fired like the guy before me?"

"I give it ten days at the most. What do you say? I'm on a schedule and I need a decision."

"But the staircase—"

"Can wait. I'll rearrange our shooting order. I need to be filming two hours ago." She tilts her head and glances back to her tablet every second, as if counting down.

But it's not even a choice. "I'm in."

Felicia turns and talks into her mic, then checks her tablet. "I'll have your contracts drawn up while you're getting ready. Sonia?"

"What do you need?" Sonia looks away from Kantina, then to me, like she doesn't understand why I'm still here.

"We found a way to keep filming," says Felicia. "Sonia Bracewell, I'd like you to meet Will Mathis. Will, this is Sonia, she's Kantina's stand-in."

She studies me for a moment, and I'm certain she's going to tell the rest of the tale. "We've met. He asked for Kantina's autograph."

Felicia shakes her head. "Like that's going to happen. Take Will to makeup, they'll know what to do. Will's going to be standing in for James Becton. Will, keep your eye on Sonia, do what she does."

Keeping my eyes on her is not the problem. Taking them off might be another thing entirely. I go to the slickest, funniest line I can think of, something to break the tension. "Hi."

Sonia glances to Felicia, one eyebrow raised, her hands on her hips, her lips pursed like she's trying to figure out if it's a joke. "Really?"

"Anything to keep to the schedule." Felicia glances at her tablet and grimaces as she studies it. "Get used to each other. You'll be spending a lot of time together."

❧

CHAPTER TWO

Soundstage 52 bustles with activity as I follow Sonia through the maze of sets, which she seems to know like the back of her hand. After hitting my head on yet another support brace, I try to slow her with conversation. "How do you know where you're going?"

"Not that hard if you're here when they build the first sets."

That's all she says with words, but her tense shoulders, the way she glares at fake fireplaces, tells me there's more.

"Did I say something to offend?"

Sonia pauses as she reaches a set of double doors and looks over her shoulder. "I'm not offended, I'm frustrated. This whole production has been a disaster, and now they're picking help from the set crew while Felicia gets a proper replacement from casting."

"They're not calling someone else. She offered me all the hours I want." We exit from the soundstage shadows, emerging outside on what I'm guessing is the back side of the soundstage. The sun is up now, and the air is well on its way to smoldering. Palm trees offer small dots of shade next to an army of white trailers parked at an angle. At the soundstage opposite us, someone I'd love to be friends with has a barbecue grill set up and the smell of searing meat makes my stomach rumble.

"That one is makeup," says Sonia, pointing to a door identical to every other door on the trailer. "To the left and right are changing rooms for wardrobe. And they're getting a replacement, Mr. Nine."

"I'm a nine out of ten?" I offer her a smile.

In return, she rolls her eyes. "No. You're stand-in number nine in eight days of filming. Trust me, they're getting a replacement lined up right now. I'll be back to collect you once the massacre is done." Sonia spins on her heel and disappears into the building, leaving me to puzzle out which of the five doors she meant.

After knocking on three, I find makeup, which I figure is code for getting my hair trimmed.

The Asian woman in charge of the makeup trailer looks up at me as I enter and points to the chair, which resembles a dentist's chair more than a barber's, with smooth white vinyl and a roll of paper covering. "We're running late. Is the beard natural, or can we pull it off?"

"I grew it myself."

"Pity," she says as I sit down in the chair. "I always enjoy pulling off fake ones."

What follows is less total makeover and more total humiliation. Within the confines of the trailer, the women treat me like a prop, not even introducing themselves before they begin cutting and dyeing.

Makeup makes my face feel thick, like I can't speak. When I finally get a look in the mirror, the me looking back could be a secret agent in a spy film. My normally-brown hair is now glistening black, and my beard is just enough stubble to prickle. "Is it supposed to look like this?"

"You're supposed to look like him," says one of the women, pointing to a head-shot hanging from a mirror.

That's James Becton, star of *The Man With a Million Tomorrows*. The last thing I saw him in was a wedding movie where he played the best man who ran away with the bride and six of the bridesmaids. "We really look that much alike?"

"No, honey," says one of them as she trims the back of my hair. "And hopefully you aren't an asshole like him, either. Now, next door, on my left, is costume. Get over there. I'll see you tomorrow morning, if you aren't fired."

I exit the trailer, thinking that this is how it feels to have my face frozen in carbonite.

A few minutes later, my dusty blue jeans and Born This Way t-shirt are changed for plain brown sweatpants and shirt. "This is the costume?"

"It's the right color, and that's what counts," says the man running the costume trailer. "Sonia! What do you think? Can we work with this?"

Sonia is sitting on the steps of the makeup trailer—and when she looks at me, my heart skips a beat. She doesn't say a word for far too long, just staring at me with her mouth slightly open. Then she smiles and nods. "He's fine—I mean, he'll do fine. Nine, come with me."

After we thread our way back through the sets, Felicia is waiting, surrounded by a swarm of production assistants. "Thank God," she says. "Aaron, he's up. Second crew, we need you."

The swarm of people around her disperse like rabbits. "You. Mathis. There," says Felicia, pointing to the kitchen set. "Go stand there."

It turns out, being a stand-in is less like being a model and more like being a mannequin who occasionally has to breathe. Aaron takes his place behind a camera the size of a small car and begins barking orders. "Move left. Move right. Head up. Eyes left. Turn shoulders."

It's like family picture day all over, except without my parents fighting and drinking just to get through it.

"Where's everyone else?"

Aaron stops his peering through the camera. "Setting up for other shots. Look down a bit, turn."

He calls out directions to the assistants, whose primary goal is to blind me with lights.

"Is Sonia going to be filming this?"

"Would you please stop moving?"

Aaron's tone leaves the please out. Even I can recognize a man engrossed in his work. "Will do."

"And stop talking. First rule of being a stand-in is that you shut your mouth. Don't move a muscle unless I tell you. Try not to blink."

I wanted hours, and I get them, but they're hard, primarily because I'm simultaneously surrounded by people and totally alone. After what seems like an eternity, Aaron looks up and shouts. "Someone get me Belion to check this."

Belion arrives shortly in a cloud of smug. "I have had a surge of inspiration, friend. We shall shoot 611 on this set."

Felicia clicks open her tablet and looks. "We don't need it yet. We do need dining room 309, 4, and 5. We've only got the actresses for those today."

"You will handle it," says Belion. "I will review tapes. Send me Kantina and James."

Felicia barks a few orders into her microphone and stalks away.

While I wait, I pace back and forth, wondering why Belion is grinning like a madman.

Then Kantina sweeps in, wearing a dress that looks absolutely ridiculous in real life, but will probably be amazing on film. It's white, with dozens of plastic beads sewn on to look like crystal.

On set, they click together like plastic silverware.

Behind Kantina comes Sonia, wearing a simple white dress without all the decorations.

Five minutes later, James Becton finally arrives. The Man With A Million Tomorrows could be my cousin, but never my brother. His hair is slick and black, his stubble shaved like it was measured, and he might work out with a trainer, but he doesn't lift sheets of plywood all day or carve with a hand plane. He doesn't offer me so much as a glance, focusing instead on Belion. "What is it?"

"I am deep in the throes of inspiration. We are shooting 611," says Belion. "You will rehearse while I make final adjustments."

"But of course." Kantina reaches out and takes James Becton's hand, then pulls him away.

Sonia remains, flipping through a tattered sheaf of paper. She scans the page, and looks up, her eyes wide. "Sir, could we have a moment?"

Belion's reaction tells me more in three seconds than a hundred questions. He seems genuinely surprised that Sonia's speaking, perhaps even more so that she's speaking to him. "What are you needing that could possibly be worth a delay?"

"A moment to go over this privately with Nine—Will. The new stand-in's not an actor."

"We are all actors," says Belion. "Playing the parts of our lives. First positions. Grips at the ready."

The grips move into place, ready to tune each and every light, most of them focused on an oil painting that resembles James Becton in a creepy way. It smells like fresh oil, as well, so they probably had it painted custom.

Sonia studies her sheet and moves to a set of masking tape marks on the floor, then points to mine.

They're inches away from her, and that's a generous estimate.

"Eyeline on each other," says Belion. "Right shoulder out to the camera. And hold."

I understand now why there's so many lights on us—this is a closeup, and every detail of the actress's face needs to stand out. Sonia's certainly does.

Her lips barely move as she whispers, "Tell me you have some sort of acting experience. High school play? Junior high?"

"I was in a play once." I wince as another light flares on, momentarily blinding me. "In third grade, I was a pine tree in Ms. Kitchen's production of 'We Love The Earth.'"

Sonia closes her eyes, and if I read her lips right (and I can't help but notice them), she's counting. After a pause, she says a little louder, "You're an actor now, Will. You're going to have to get comfortable acting."

"I'm a stand-in, and—" I freeze as Belion leans in and then goes back to ordering minor changes. I can't tell that he's fixing anything.

"Any moment now, he's going to call second positions."

"Which is?"

She closes her eyes, and when she opens them again, they're wider than I've ever seen them. "You're going to pivot on your right foot, lean in, and kiss me."

"Position two, and hold for closeup," says Belion. "Position two. What are we waiting on?"

Hell to freeze over.

Belion's voice cracks with aggravation as he asks, "Does he not know what position two is? Did he not read his scene guide? You will show him, Sonia, now."

Sonia steps away and offers me her copy. These aren't lines of dialogue, but details for a shot. *The Lord moves in. Closeup of Lady's cheeks as he cups her face in his hands, one on each side. Their kiss is fleeting at first, then cautious—then wild and hungry.*

"Who wrote this? One hand on each side is how I drink from a gallon of milk, not how I kiss a woman." My wave of the script slows as I realize exactly who wrote this. And that I've broken the first rule—never speak.

"Silence! It is a simple thing we ask," says Belion. "Position one, camera ready. This must be perfect for Kantina. Every shadow. Every highlight."

"Acting," says Sonia, as we step back to our spots. "It's about the character doing something, not you doing it."

The problem is, the character's doing what I want to.

There. I admitted it. My therapist said that was the first step to getting better.

Or getting worse, because now I can't stop thinking about kissing Sonia. "I don't just kiss women without asking first."

"If you do not have a line, you are not to speak," says Belion. "Camera one, focus check. Move to position two, and hold."

"Just do it," says Sonia, so close her breath tickles my cheek. "It's not like I haven't been wondering what it might be like from that first moment I saw you outside the costume trailer."

If she swung a baseball bat and hit me right between the eyes, Sonia couldn't leave me more stunned.

I lean in slowly, carefully, until my lips find hers.

She's as tense as I am for a split second, and then her shoulders relax, and she leans in, turning her head ever so slightly. Her arms were draped over my shoulders loosely; now she's clinging to me with such force I couldn't let go if I had to. There aren't lights overhead or cameras or any other people in this moment, there's only a connection I didn't see coming, like two power lines crossing.

There's no urgency, just a sweetness that can't be my imagination, and yet with every passing moment, her hold on me grows tighter, and we shift our heads together like we rehearsed it—except that there's no script for what I'm feeling.

"Hold!" says Belion—smashing through the daze and leaving us two people awkwardly embraced instead of lost in a moment that could go on forever. "Turn your head, Sonia. Nine, hands upon her face."

It takes me a moment to find my hands, which are both on her hips, even though I'm sure they weren't when I leaned in.

A moment ago, the spark between us could have started a dead man's heart.

Now she doesn't clutch me, maintaining a precise distance.

Before, we were catching fire.

Now, we're simply posing, like when my brother used to smash his Barbie dolls together and make kissing noises.

Belion calls for more overhead lights, has us adjust our heads up. I'm no longer looking Sonia in the eye, because that doesn't give the camera a clear shot of my profile, and her hair is tossed over her right shoulder so it doesn't hide everything about her.

"It will do," says Belion. "First crew."

I let go of Sonia and grasp the table for balance.

If I'm dizzy, she's lost, wandering aimlessly from the set, while I try to remember what it was I am supposed to be doing.

Someone taps my shoulder, and James Becton speaks before I can turn. "It's going to be difficult to shoot my scene with you where I need to be." In the light, it's clear now which of us is wearing faded brown sweatpants and which is wearing the actual Victorian costume with fancy sleeves and ruffles down his chest.

I step away, nearly hitting the camera. "I'm sorry."

"I don't care."

James takes my place, and I do my best to find somewhere people aren't moving, where lights aren't shining, and where men with microphones aren't crowding.

Just off set, Kantina perches on a barstool receiving a final touchup from a makeup artist, and Sonia stands right beside her.

Either they've turned up the lights, the heat, or both, and I keep catching whiffs of the shampoo Sonia uses. Or maybe I'm imagining it.

Kantina turns her head slightly to let the artist work. "Sonia, darling, are you well?" She reaches up and feels Sonia's cheek, just the way I was supposed to.

I wish it was me doing it.

"I'm—I'm fine." Sonia looks away. "He actually *kissed* me."

"Indeed, I saw. You must tell me, how was it?"

Sonia doesn't answer, though I want—I need—to know if she felt what I felt. Then she reaches up and touches her lips, her eyes closed. "It was..." She opens her eyes and looks up, past Kantina—and sees me watching her. In a flash, Sonia goes from unsettled to cool and calm. "You know, I mean, we were just setting the lights for your shot. By the way, hair has to go over your right shoulder, and lean your head back."

Sonia's body language has completely changed. She stands with shoulders rigid and avoids even looking my way.

"Ready on set!" Felicia shouts, and Kantina sweeps out to take up first position without so much as a thought. Only now do I see the difference in how they move, how they handle themselves. With Kantina, each step is precision, a performance in and of itself, while Sonia is relaxed and fluid.

James and Kantina move in to kiss, and someone's calling out timing. "Two, three, and shift."

His hands come up, hers brush his neck—

And James steps back. "Sorry, my bad. I was supposed to turn there, wasn't I?"

"Yes, darling." Kantina steps away. "I must hold, you will turn left. But I felt the timing was near perfect otherwise."

"Go again," Felicia shouts.

This is professional. This is how I'm supposed to be. They're pretending they feel something, when what I'm doing now is pretending I feel nothing. They shoot the kiss five times, stopping once for lip balm—and it's done.

"Set up for 612," says Belion.

Felicia shouts out, "Hold on that. Everyone but cameras, take five."

I can't find Sonia anywhere, but I know where she will be soon enough. In the meantime, I have another problem to fix. "Ma'am?" I say as I approach Felicia. "I'm sorry to bother you, but where do I get one of those sheets everyone is looking at? I don't know scene numbers or marks or any of that stuff."

She spares me one fraction of her attention before going back to her tablet, where she's doing some kind of scheduling. "Scene sheets are handed out at night after we wrap and I review what we got and what we didn't. Stick around by the production office tonight and I'll make sure you get your own copy."

If I knew what was coming, I could be prepared—well, at least better prepared. "Thanks. Any idea where I'd find Sonia?"

"Given that we're shooting 612 next, and Sonia is always one step ahead, I expect she's on the kitchen set, checking her blocking. Hold on." Felicia holds one hand to her ear, listening to her headset, then pivots like she's just spotted chocolate-covered espresso beans. "Go find Sonia, warn her it's a promo day. She'll know what to do."

"Where's the kitchen?"

"That way. Far corner. If you aren't at the corner, you aren't there." She half pushes me in the direction of a set that centers on a wooden wheelbarrow, which doesn't contain Sonia.

Neither do any of the three different bathroom sets I stumble across. But at last, I find a half-built kitchen, and Sonia practicing her paces, reading from the script as she checks off the marks on the floor.

"Hey." I keep my distance, so I can keep my focus, resting hands against the polished wood of the countertop. Though there's shouting in the distance, it fades away as I watch Sonia move with such calm and focus.

Until she glances up and spots me. Her cheeks flush red, complementing her hair. "Will. About earlier—"

"I promise I'll do better next time." Next time. I nearly choke on the idea of repeating that. Even the thought is like being strapped to the front of a roller coaster.

It wasn't my imagination earlier, she smells of coconut and lavender.

I've always considered fresh-shaved cedar to be my favorite scent—until now.

Sonia's still looking through me instead of at me, like she's lost in a memory, one that turns up the corners of her mouth. "You'll *do* better, but I *expect* better of myself."

"I have no idea what you could have done better."

"This is my *job*, Will. I do it professionally. I do it right. I don't get caught up in the moment." I'm not sure if she's convincing me or herself as Sonia bends over the kitchen counter, letting her hair fall forward and hide her face.

"Scale of one to ten, your worst kiss ever?"

That brings her gaze back, eyes clear and focused, a playful smile flirting at the edges of her lips. "Not even top ten worst. Once, a guy tried to stick his tongue down my throat during a light check."

The thought makes me shudder and wince. "There's not enough mouthwash in the world for that."

"Two tips: Brush after meals, and remember, on set, everything about it is planned to look spontaneous." She saunters around to me, script in hand, and plants a soft kiss on my cheek. "Like that."

After I remember to breathe again, I spurt out, "Was that spontaneous? Or planned?"

"A little of both," she says with a smile. "You're eventually going to have to relax around me, you know."

"I'm totally relaxed." I'm totally lying. "Besides, Felicia—Oh, crap. She told me to tell you it's a promo day. Does that mean something?"

If I pulled a gun on her, Sonia wouldn't turn so white. She's literally shaking and spins to look behind her, like she has x-ray vision that can see through the forest of sets. "We have to leave. Now."

"I'm not going anywhere. Felicia said I was to be ready, and if they want to shoot—"

"*I* have to leave. It's in my contract that I don't have to be present during media visits. Go back to Central Holding or stay here, Nine. I don't care."

I do.

The set we're standing in is just one corner of a Victorian kitchen, and while I'd bet the wine bottles on one wall are all empty, the cinderblock bricks that are the soundstage walls are completely real—as Sonia finds out as she steps around the kitchen wall and stops short.

"We're in the corner. I know that because it's how Felicia said to find you. You can see the soundstage walls if you squint and look up."

The rising echo of voices says someone else is on set, someone who doesn't know the 'shut-your-mouth' rule.

"I don't do media, press, or photographs. I don't like people taking pictures of me," says Sonia. She grabs my arm and pulls me closer. "One photograph, one video, can ruin a career. A life."

She knows her way through this set better than I do, but I know when someone has stopped thinking and started panicking, because I did it often enough in the first few days after Tamara disappeared. "We can go this way. There has to be an emergency exit along the back wall. But what's your deal with photographers?"

Sonia stares past me, frozen. Her lips mouth a single word—*please*—and then she ducks down, hiding up against the back side of a cabinet, her eyes closed.

I turn as a pair of reporters emerge from the side, ducking cables and booms. I don't even get out one word before the brilliant flashes go off.

❧

CHAPTER THREE

The set lights are already bright, but thanks to the camera flashes, I can't see anything but spots. I can only assume there's still a reporter and a photographer on set for some sort of media promotion, but I'm one hundred percent certain Sonia doesn't want to be seen by them. With the cabinet behind me, they have no idea she's there—and based on her reaction, I mean to keep it that way. "Hey, guys. You here for the documentary?"

"Allyssa Jones," says a woman. "From Entertainment Central."

"You're not shooting the documentary on set building?" I say, rubbing my eyes until I can make out the form of a tall black woman with short curly hair. "I have an entire tour planned. This whole set's almost all fir, but I can't wait to show you, she's got white pine where it counts."

The woman squints at me, which is only fair, since I'm doing the same to her. "This is a set walkthrough. Should you even be here?"

"Of course I should." I lean back against the cabinet top, painfully aware of how easily we might be found out. Just a slight move to the left or right and they'd spot the white dress train that stretches across the floor.

I don't claim to understand Sonia's response, but I recognize the same fear I've seen in Tia's eyes when her OCD is in control. And having grown up in the foster system, I know all about being afraid—and it's not something I'll willingly inflict on someone else.

The key to this diversion will be to make this set the *least* interesting place in the soundstage, and I've found a problem that digs at me. "I have to finish this—unless you want Kantina getting splinters. This here? Not nearly well sanded enough. I'll be talking to the boys at the shop about that when I get back. You have to use 400 grit, and me, I like a little oil for the sandpaper. Gives it that authentic look. Come here, feel this oil."

It really isn't sanded right, and there's a part of me that needs to see it done, but now is not the time. The two exchange a dubious glance, so I launch my counter-attack. "Now, if you've got time, I have six different types of stairs to show you—and wait until you see the banisters. Every one of them hand-carved by a master to give just the right shadow. And the trusses! Either of you a truss lover?"

"I'm sorry." The photographer, an older Asian man, lowers his camera and turns away. "I forgot to bring my... spare film."

"That's a digital camera, isn't it?" I ask. I can see the screen from here.

"No. Yes. I'm almost out of zeros and ones. Gotta save what I have left for the stars."

"We'll let you get back to your work," says Ms. Alyssa Jones, of Entertainment Central. She moves away, looking for her next set of victims.

Only after I hear Belion squeak a greeting from across the soundstage do I relax. "They're gone."

Sonia doesn't get up, so I take a spot beside her, sliding down to sit with my back against the cabinet.

"I'm not crazy," she whispers.

"I believe you."

She rubs her fingers together and wipes her eyes. "When I first started working with Kantina, I was so excited. Then she became this overnight star, and everything changed. She's the celebrity, but I couldn't go out to eat without tabloid after tabloid taking a picture of me and labeling it as Kantina. Kantina goes to the store. Kantina out jogging. Kantina out drinking."

"I don't see why that's your fault."

"My bad decisions were ruining *her* reputation."

This feels wrong on just about every level, but perhaps I have an overdeveloped sense of not being an asshole to others. "But… they're not pictures of Kantina. They can't print that, can they?"

"You're so sweet and innocent, like this town hasn't poisoned you yet. Of course they can," says Sonia, though the bitterness in her voice shows. "And mistakes have consequences that can follow you for years. One night after a hard day, I was out blowing off steam. I was angry, frustrated, and I didn't pay attention to who was recording, or what I said. The video was never publicly released, but the damage to my career was done. So I started avoiding pictures as a matter of habit. The more I controlled it, the better I felt—until the day I woke up and found my habits had taken on a life of their own. These days, I have panic attacks just thinking of people taking pictures of me."

I gently offer her hand a squeeze. "But you're a movie star. How does that work?"

"I'm a stand-in, and a body double. Even when people do see me, they don't *know* it's me. The public attention, the pressure, all of that goes to Kantina, and she just drinks it in. It's like she runs on it." Sonia draws up her knees and puts her head down. "Usually I get a warning, and I'll go wait someplace else. Instead, you had to run interference for my neurosis. I know it's not normal, and you're probably waiting to tell your family what a weirdo I am when you get home."

The fake cabinet back is gouging my shoulder, and it reeks of freshly cured stain and epoxy, so I sit forward and give her the same answer I always told my sister-in-law, back when she and Bradley were just dating. "Normal is a setting on the washing machine." Before I can second-guess myself, I plunge into a confession I hadn't planned on. "All of these people staring at me make me want to puke."

"Really?" Sonia looks up at me, and takes a deep breath. "You didn't seem affected during 611."

"That was before I realized anyone could see what we were doing, and there weren't that many. Aaron. You. Me. Belion."

"What about the camera operators? What about the grips? What about the assistants?"

There's a simple coping mechanism that's let me function this far. "Name one of them. Name a single camera operator."

She pauses, eyes unfocused. "There's... burrito guy. He's always eating a burrito, or putting it in his pocket to eat later."

"That's not his real name, so that doesn't count. See? They're basically part of the set. But ever since I realized people are watching me, my stomach does a triple flip. As a wood carver, my customers knew I'd get everything perfect. Now I want to freeze rather than make a mistake."

Sonia gives me a wide grin. "It's called stage fright. It hits everyone eventually, and we all survive. I'll talk you through it, maybe even give you some exercises once I untangle my sleeve from this edge. This cabinet is falling apart."

"I built the sides, and it's not going to collapse." I knock on the wood, which is plywood, not solid oak. "It looks good, but it's fake. Just like everything else in this town. You know, I passed three bathroom sets on the way here, and every last one of them has a fake toilet. They're foam."

"I found that out the hard way one day," says Sonia. "Trust me when I say you do not want to know how. Never understood it."

"Bradley says foam's light and easy to move. So what now? Do we just shelter in place?"

"No." Sonia stands up and pulls on me to follow. "I can get us out of here. The media will want time with James and Kantina. Once they're sequestered, the rest of us can get back to work."

I move around the counter to put some space between us, because what I need to ask her is easier when I'm not standing mere inches away.

Thinking in general is easier when I'm not mere inches away, and I give my brain the distance it needs to ensure I'm not making a huge mistake. "Can you help me? I'm not asking for you to do my job," I add quickly. "Just let me know when I'm doing something wrong. I'm a quick learner. You tell me to be quiet, I will. You tell me to stay near the set, I do. You tell me not to feel anything when I kiss you, and I'll work on it."

"I didn't tell you that last one," says Sonia. "I'm telling you there's a difference between a stage kiss and a real one."

Not for me. Not with her.

"Take my arm, and walk in circles around this set." Sonia offers it to me again. "If we're going to survive filming this, we've got to get to the point where you aren't terrified of being near me."

"Right." Terrified. Electrified. Same difference, right? I take her arm and let her guide us on a leisurely stroll around the kitchen set.

"Not everything is fake," she says as we duck under a tree limb covered in plastic vines. "Kantina is real. She's one of the most real people I've ever known."

"Sure she is. I've seen her. And I remember the rumors from a few years ago, about how she nearly killed a guy on set."

Sonia stops and puts one hand on my chest. "You see what's on the news. I see her day in and day out, for years. And don't make the mistake of assuming rumors are true. There's more to that story than you would believe."

I drop the argument, if not the notion. "I don't want to make any assumptions about you. You say I need to be comfortable around you, so tell me about yourself. Name? Birth date? Favorite type of cheesecake?"

"Margret Sonia Bracewell." She dips her head. "I go by Sonia for good reason."

"I don't know. Margie might fit you—" I duck her playful swipe. "Nope. Definitely a Sonia."

"I was born two months, four days after you were. Felicia had one of the PAs look you up to make sure you weren't a creeper."

"I'm near certain that's a violation of my privacy."

She grins as she looks at me sideways. "Do you want your privacy, or do you want answers?"

"Consider me an open book," I say with a bow. "Please, go on."

"I came to LA because I wanted to be behind the camera, not in front of them. I want to tell stories." As she speaks, Sonia's face lights up, and the smile that was playful becomes deeper, more natural. "I want to be the one making people laugh and cry and leave the theatre thinking they've learned something new about life—or themselves—or each other."

"How'd you wind up here?"

"I was on my second day as a production assistant, and an agent on set grabbed me by the hair. Literally, by my hair, and started going on and on about how I should keep growing it out. How I'd look just like a new client of his." Sonia spins, making her hair sail out and flick me. "Meet Kantina-From-A-Distance and Kantina-When-Viewed-From-Behind. Also, Kantina's hands, when she's not available, or on rare occasions, Kantina's shoulders."

"So are you her stunt double? Or her… what do you call it? Naked body person?"

"Body double," says Sonia, with a roll of her eyes. "Studio execs would die before letting her risk doing a stunt, and I'm not trained in it. I did sit on a horse once, if that counts. And Kantina does *all* her own nudity. That's her in *The Bride Becomes Her*."

"Never seen it." There. My dirty secret's out. Bradley won't stop blathering about how much of a travesty it is.

Sonia turns and looks closely at me, like she can spot a lie creeping across my cheeks. "You're serious? That movie was torture to make, but it's amazing. You should watch it."

I offer her my arm, and we continue our stroll in circles. "One day I will. Right now, I have better ways to spend my time. What could be better than this?"

"I can think of a few things," says Sonia, drawing us to a halt just as I'm getting comfortable moving in step with her. "This is a long shot," she says, gesturing at the scene around us, "and Belion's going for the back and forth, where the Lord wants to go to her, but he can't bring himself to. Where she wants to go to him, but her pride demands otherwise. They'll want to do light checks at each position."

"Does it end with a kiss?" I ask, determined not to freak this time. Sonia's got that something about her that makes me watch her every move, but I can pretend to be professional.

"Only if I improvised and threw one in." She points to a set of marks and takes hers, pulling her scene list from her pocket. "They're bantering here, back and forth. Mild innuendo is raised. Then you take two steps forward."

I do, narrowly missing a tan 'X' on the floor. "So this Master of the Manor, he wants to go to her?"

"Yes. One step forward for me, then a pause. They'll do another light check here. Her expression is the focus."

"So why doesn't he? I don't understand this guy at all."

Sonia looks up from her sheet. "Because he's *human*. He wants her, but he wants to keep his distance. Keep his reputation. He can't have both, and he's not ready to decide. You wait for me there, and when I don't come, turn—no, toward the camera."

"But... she wants him?"

"Debatable at first, and even if she did? She wouldn't say. He's attractive and charming, but they're so different. Accepting him might mean surrendering her independence."

"She's getting a bad deal, if it's costing her independence and all she gets is some man. Can't they just live together? Lord and Lady with benefits?"

Sonia drops her script and puts her hands on her hips. "*Love*. She's in it for love. Once she's sure he's the one, she'll risk anything for love."

"I can tell you from personal experience, 'anything' is a huge risk. What's my next move?"

"Depends," says Sonia, "on whether or not you want to live the rest of your life alone. If you do, you go on moping about some woman who obviously wasn't the one. Or, you let go, move on, and find someone better."

My cheeks blaze as the embarrassment wells up. "In the script."

"Right!" Sonia looks down at the floor. "Sorry, I wasn't thinking."

"Obviously you were, just not about the script. Where does the character go? I'm guessing he turns, or she turns, or they both turn. I swear, Belion should have cast ballet dancers to do this many turns. Where's the straight line walking? Where's the Irish line dancing?"

"There's not any in this revision. Though it would be great at the wedding." Sonia stops and leans against the counter. "The shot ends with him leaving. You turn, follow that set of marks. Last check will be right before they move out of focus."

I find my next X—and look back. "For the record, I'm not moping. Me, that is. I have no idea if the Lord of the Manor is, but I'm not moping. I already moved on. I'm already looking."

I lie so smoothly I almost fool myself.

"Right. Name one woman you've approached in the last month."

"Well, there's this one. She's smart, and funny when she's not scary, and she's beautiful, and I like the way she focuses. The way the other people around her treat her with respect."

This makes Sonia smile, and that might be the most wonderful sight in the world, so I add, "She's got this passion, and underneath her all-business exterior, I think she's kind."

"You seem to know a lot about this woman."

"Not enough."

Where her gaze was playful, now I can't help feeling pinned under her stare as she approaches. "So if you're so brave, why don't you talk to this woman? Ask her out? Trust me, I heard the things Felicia's production assistants said about you while Aaron was working."

I was taught not to lie by my parents, one of the few things I remember. And I've learned how much lies and deception hurt. "I made a mistake once. I trusted someone I shouldn't have. Someone who told me one thing and did another. So now, with every step, every time, every glance, I ask myself if I'm doing it again."

"You don't trust this woman," says Sonia, softly. "You don't know if you can?"

"Right. My brother says I should know better next time."

"I know a thing or two about that. In this town, even people you think you love will turn on you in a heartbeat. And those that don't love you? They'll do whatever suits them and leave you to pick up the pieces." She isn't focusing on me anymore. She's looking out past the set into the past, or the future. "Your brother is smart, Will. You should listen to him."

"What if I don't want to?"

"I can't answer without knowing more about this woman. Does she know you exist?"

I don't answer for a moment, despite our conversation being proof. "Evidence says yes."

"And is she interested in you?"

"I don't know, but I do have an idea." I look away long enough to catch my breath. "You could help me figure out what to say to her."

"What makes you think I know anything about this woman? Besides, that would be cheating," says Sonia, now so close her breath tickles. "You're going to have to do that all on your own."

"But I want to know that she at least feels *something*."

"There you go." Sonia puts one hand on my chest and looks up at me. "So you *do* understand how the Lord of the Manor feels."

She's right. I'm wrong, but that's something I can fix right now. "I've got the guts to ask her how she feels."

"No." Sonia stops me cold with a single word. "When it comes to this sort of thing, if you need to ask, you already know the answer. You know it here"—she traces one finger down my stomach, then up to my heart. "Or here."

My stomach's doing flips, and at this rate, my heart is preparing to exit my rib cage and head straight into orbit.

"Well?" she asks, leaning in.

What's to be afraid of? Everything. But just beyond fear—

"Sonia." Belion's voice cuts through my resolve like a knife. "It is good that you are rehearsing, but you must clear the set. I require time to meditate on the mood, and your lack of talent is distracting. Fetch my coffee while I cleanse my mind. You, other man, return to Central Holding."

Sonia looks at me, and for a moment, I think she's going to speak—and then she looks away and hurries off set.

I find my way back to the central area and wait until I hear Felica shout, "That's a wrap, folks." Moments later, she buzzes past, and then glances my way. "Will, come with me. Walk fast."

I do, and she has me sign one form after another. One makes me a member of the actors' guild, another says if I leak the details, I can be legally murdered, or something to that effect.

"If you don't sign your sheets, you don't get paid," she says.

"That wasn't twelve hours."

She gives me the sweetest smile, like she's talking to a toddler. "We've been here since six in the morning, which, incidentally, is when you'll need to be in makeup. Not in the parking lot, or on your way over. See you tomorrow."

"Sonia said you were going to replace me. That you'd probably already made the call."

"Sonia is smart, but she's not the assistant director yet, and I am. Tomorrow, we have a full slate to shoot. Long as you are saving me time and not costing me time, I'll keep you around."

I know from her tone I've been dismissed. "Have a good evening," I say as I leave.

"Hold up a minute." Felicia's tone says she's not happy. "I asked you earlier if you were Brad Mathis, and who do I see as your emergency contact? One of our chief investors. He's your brother?"

"Little brother."

"And he has you slumming it as his spy on set?" she asks, each word drawn out like a trap. "There are easier ways to get production updates."

With a heavy sign, I turn to face her. "Bradley may be my brother, but while he'll let me crash on his couch and skim from his fridge, he says I have to work my way up just like anyone else. He didn't build a multi-million dollar company giving handouts, not even to family. We live on a shoestring, we work hard, we earn our way."

Felicia's lips are drawn tight, but after a moment she looks back at her tablet and fiddles with the schedule. "Be on time. Be silent. Do a good job, or I'll make the call to replace you myself. That's just business, something your brother will probably understand. You're going to make sure he knows that, right?"

"I will."

It's not necessary. My brother looks before he leaps. He plans. Tia calculates and recalculates.

When I think about how I felt today every time I looked at Sonia, I realize how I need to separate my head and my heart.

But easy to think and possible to do are totally different.

CHAPTER FOUR

BRADLEY IS WAITING FOR ME AT THE DOOR WHEN I GET home, while Tia grates parmesan in the kitchen and the whole apartment smells like meat-lover's pizza with garlic and anchovies—the only true kind of pizza. "What happened to the hair, Will? And your beard? You didn't call for me to bail you out, but you didn't come back to the shop. So what gives?"

My stomach's doing a reasonable impression of a Doberman. "Pizza first?"

Bradley blocks my route to the microscopic kitchen-and-breakfast nook. "What did you always say when I broke curfew? Oh, right. Meat-lovers pizza is for people who can give me a satisfactory explanation. People who can't get pineapple on their pizza."

"Monster." I sit at the kitchen table, which is a card table Bradley found in the alley behind his apartment, and set my empty plate in front of me. "I have to make thirty new banisters for your movie, fifteen in each style. Also, I got a job as a stand-in. They dyed my hair to look like James Becton's."

Bradley's eyes go round, and he slaps the box down. "No way! That's amazing! Was it awesome? What was it like? What were they like? Did you meet her? What's she like?"

The living room is the size of a postage stamp, but every wall is covered in miniature glass-bead animals Tia collects, each meticulously dusted every week. I find a dolphin that's a brilliant shade of red and let the memories come back. "Beautiful. Smart. Focused. A little scary, but down to earth."

"What about the autograph?" Bradley freezes, watching me with an intensity I find a little troubling.

"Oh—you meant did I meet Kantina? Yes, I did. Yes, she's every bit as amazing as you think. No, she said she didn't know me well enough to give me an autograph." I shrug and reach for a slice of pizza covered in oily, fishy goodness. What did he expect? "Tia, slice?"

"Not of that garbage. Or at that table." She takes her hand-grated parmesan and sprinkles it on her own personal cheese pizza. It's easier on her OCD to have her own food she doesn't share with us, and besides, Bradley and I both detest plain cheese.

"Who did you *think* I was asking about?" Bradley mutters. He seizes a piece and pauses in mid bite, strings of cheese still clinging to his beard. "Oh, no, Will. I have the casting updates in email. Don't make me look over them all night. Is it the platinum blonde they cast as Lady Abernathy? Tia, back me up. No way, right?"

Tia puts down her pizza and sprays the counter with bleach, then studies the two of us. "How about some context?"

"Will, my brother, the man who spent the last two years of his life beating himself up about not recognizing his girlfriend was pretending, has eyes for an actress." He crosses his arms and waits for me to deny it.

"It's not like that," I say. "She's not…"

Tia comes over and puts her hand on Bradley's shoulder. "Will, maybe you should listen to Brad. The backlot people? Good people. Actors? Actresses? They say what they need to say. Trust me, I listened in on some of the funding calls. People will do everything for money."

Now I'm questioning every interaction. Every smile. Every feeling I definitely didn't have.

But one interrogation absolutely deserves another. "Since we're talking about not knowing someone," I say, not at all to divert from the point at hand, "when were you going to let your big brother know you'd become a big movie investor? I thought you meant you were giving them a deal on the set work, but no, you're one of the big shots—"

"Small shots, minor partner—"

I wave to the cramped apartment, a living room with a thrift-store couch and a shin-catching coffee table. "*Head* of the investment group? You live in a shoebox, and that isn't a truck you drive, it's a mobile mound of rust flakes. I taught you to live frugally, but that truck is beyond."

Tia shudders. She won't ride in the rust bucket, even when her meds are working. But she's the one who answers. "We live simply, Will. We built Mathis Construction here. We learned to live on what we had, and when we had more, we put it to use pursuing *our* dreams."

Bradley nods in agreement. "I'm not just building props for movies, I'm actually funding them. I may have fudged a little bit about how the company was doing. Business is booming, and the next time I have a full-time opening, we'll be working together, a real family business."

"You've made enough to buy into a movie?"

Tia frowns and swats Bradley. "You never told him, did you?"

The guilty look on Bradley's face says there's a detail here I probably should know. "Remember *Witchful Ways?*"

Memories come back to me, all right, of getting motion sick at the found-footage film which featured grainy, black-and-white video and a Victorian house that looked like it was going to fall in. "I remember watching a documentary on it. Shot on cell phones, camping in the woods, made for what? Fifty thousand?"

Bradley nods. "A little more. It pulled in sixty million gross before internationals, and twenty thousand of the funding came from us."

Now the pieces of the puzzle begin to click. "You're rich."

"*Were* rich," says Tia. "For a moment. We paid off all our bills. We bought the construction shop outright. We spent months and months planning and talking, and then we invested. I personally picked a movie that we're importing from Spain. Bradley went to lunch with the right people, and we've finally got our foot in the door."

"Why didn't you tell me?"

Bradley won't meet my gaze. "I wanted you to be proud. All those years you worked to send me to college?

You always said that halfway done wasn't done at all. We're halfway to making it big. And if you really owed anyone—"

"I do."

"We would help you," he says with a tone that says we've had this argument. "At least, we would have. Every penny we have, and most of what I can borrow, are tied up in this movie."

"How much did you lend them?"

Bradley doesn't answer me for far too long. "A lot. It's really important that this movie does well. Now, are you going back tomorrow, or do I need to have you sweep the shop?"

"Every day until I'm fired or they finish shooting. Twelve to fourteen hours, so hello, overtime." I offer him a fist bump, but Bradley isn't paying attention.

"Overtime that's coming out of my pocket, mostly." Bradley's voice contains a smile that says he approves. "I know you want to get back on your feet, but you don't have to work yourself to death. You'll always have a place here. We're family, man." Bradley doesn't look at me as he repeats the phrase I told him through all of our years growing up in foster homes.

But I have bills to pay. Debts that are legally not mine, but are morally my fault because I failed to see the obvious. "I'm a big boy. I can take care of myself."

"This movie is going to be amazing. And when it blows up the box office," he says, handing over another pizza slice, "the Mathis family is going to do very well." That look in his eyes means the matter's settled. I used to fight him, but even when we were kids I didn't win, and after a moment, he lets it pass. "Now, tell me everything, twice.

Also, I might want to get up early and hear this again before you go into work."

I recount the day, blow by blow, and if I leave out how it felt to kiss Sonia then, it's an honest mistake, or at least, an honest decision. But after I put a fresh piece of duct tape over the rip in the couch and stretch out under a crochet blanket, every moment replays in my mind. I know Bradley's right about actresses, but what I know and what I felt don't match up. Tomorrow, I tell myself, I'll be the best stand-in ever. I'll be professional. I wouldn't be so foolish as to let my heart get tangled up again, would I?

FELICIA SAID I WAS TO BE READY TO WORK AT SIX. THAT meant I had to be there even earlier for makeup and costume. To get to the studio at five o'clock in the morning, I have to be up and out the door at four, and I'm only one of hundreds, probably thousands of us crawling through traffic, then streaming through security. I've got a lanyard with my picture on it and an extremely distant idea of where the soundstage might be, but at five thirty sharp, I'm lined up and waiting at the makeup trailer.

Today I came prepared to work, with two bags of homemade peanut butter granola, a water bottle, and comfortable shoes instead of steel-toe work boots. Not too far back in line, I spot Sonia. It's not cold, but I have goosebumps on my arms, and now for some reason, my tongue is choosing not to cooperate, particularly not if I head in her direction.

Not that I'd do that. The way she's focusing on her phone, body turned out from the line, head down, says she's a woman who doesn't want to be disturbed. She's fierce, almost frowning, and unlike most of the people here, there are no bags under her eyes, though I think she'd be beautiful regardless.

I'm not sure I slept at all, wondering what I imagined yesterday, what was real, and what was an act. Without any makeup whatsoever, I do a passable zombie imitation until you put a coffee pot in front of me.

By the time I'm trimmed, caked, and swaddled in a brown sweatshirt and sweat pants combo, the real stars arrive.

I always figured they came by limo, but it's golf cart for Kantina, and a separate golf cart for James Becton.

I don't look either of them in the eye, and do my best to blend in with the crowd. I may have arrived by chance, but I want to stay by doing a good job, and the less attention I get, the better. Every hour here is another chip at the weight on my shoulders, and I won't let this chance pass me by.

"Oh, Sonia, look." Kantina's voice sends a shiver down my spine as it grows louder. "It is that 'Will' you were speaking of."

Given how badly my last attempt to speak to her went, I pretend to have found nuggets of gold in my granola, locking my gaze on the bag—until I can't.

When I look up, it's into Kantina's eyes. Even without makeup, she's without a doubt the star of the show, giving me a broad smile that shows way too many teeth.

I force myself to speak, rather than wondering how she can stand the lights with her pupils so large. "Morning."

Beside her is Sonia. Standing together, I again see how foolish my mistake was. They're so similar, and yet, Sonia is a person I'd meet on the street, or bump into at the grocery store, and Kantina... Well, normally she and I wouldn't cross paths once, let alone twice.

Bradley's warning echoes in my head, but I can't be impolite. I don't want to be. "Sonia, good morning."

"You exaggerated, my dear," says Kantina. "They did not ruin his looks with the dye, they merely changed them, and that beard is a thing better gone. He is still every bit as handsome as you claimed, perhaps more so. How do you feel about it, William?"

"The hair?" My voice comes out a whisper. LA mornings are never cold, but I'm near shivering as I churn through what I think I just heard. Sonia said I was handsome? *Before* the makeover? "I don't mind. I don't really see my own hair, most of the time."

Kantina pulls a strand of her own—flaming red with golden highlights—over her shoulder. It stretches past her waist, and has always been her signature. "Men," she says, as though that one word explains everything.

I tear myself away from her unearthly beauty and back to Sonia. I rub my chin in what I hope is a sophisticated manner and ask in a voice that's hopefully not shaky or excited, "What exactly did you say about me?"

Now it's Sonia's turn to look away. Her gaze is locked on the sheaf of paper she's holding, but her cheeks are the same color as the reddest streaks in her hair. "K, we need to get into makeup."

"Of course," says Kantina. "It would not do to be late."

Late is what all the people who didn't show up early will be, since Kantina heads straight into the makeup trailer, with Sonia at her side the whole way.

Can someone fake blushing? I don't think so, but what do I know? Part of me smiles, that part of me that doesn't worry about the phone ringing, or the commitments I've made, the debts I owe.

Sonia really did think I was handsome.

And in that moment, the rising feeling in my stomach pivots. She *said* that. But Tamara complimented me every day, and I was the one stuck explaining to everyone how my business bank account was as empty as her drawers in my apartment.

Tamara was a natural actress, able to play the part of a loving girlfriend. She was also a crooked accountant, and I hope wherever she's holed up, she's happy, because she took money from companies that don't ever forget, and one day, the past is going to catch up with her.

I'm more concerned with the present. With the suppliers who I owed money and couldn't pay.

My little brother has a thriving business, a good reputation, and a solid career. Starting today, I can earn that, too.

Once everyone's out of makeup, we gather inside the stage, where Felicia stands with her hands behind her back, surveying the crew. "Morning, everyone. We're going to get back on track today. We've got an aggressive schedule, and we need to nail it. Let's roll on 221."

I'm rapidly discovering that the assistant director is the one who runs the show. Belion Androse may be the director with his name on the poster, but Felicia is the one making it happen.

"Morning," I say to her. "What would you like me to do?"

Felicia snags a production assistant and points her to me. "Fix him."

A few minutes later I consider myself fixed, with a clear set of instructions on how to handle checking in every morning and night, as well as a read-by-rote warning that if I tamper with the monstrous electrical cords that line the floors, my death is my fault. "Where do I go?"

"221," says the production assistant. She's a college grad with stars in her eyes and bags under them. "It's at the manor front door."

That would be perfect—if I had some idea of where it was. The solution, however, is simple—I look for the place where people are arguing.

There, Aaron Abrams is making adjustments at a set that seems to be focused around a pair of oak doors ten feet tall. It's not oak, because I can smell the stain from here, and the grass is an astro-turf green, and crunches under foot if I take a step in any direction. Between the grips shouting to each other and the circle saws running as carpenters work one set over, I don't know how they'll film anything.

Sonia's already there, standing just inside the open door, and carefully avoiding me.

"Morning," I say to Aaron. "What do you want me to do?"

Aaron glances my way. "I thought they replaced you last night."

"Sorry to disappoint, but no."

"You're late." He points to the set. "Take your mark, set your eyeline to the right at shoulder level."

"What?"

Aaron stops, turns his full attention to me, and then points to a grey piece of tape on the floor. "Your mark. Stand there. Look right. The right hand—"

"Got it." I trudge over to stand near Sonia, who hasn't so much as acknowledged my existence. "Standing on the tape."

It's called 'standing in' for a reason, and it's because I'm primarily standing today. The oak doors, close up, are made of foam. They scratch and crumble flakes of paint off where the doors touch when Sonia opens them wider or shuts them. I could have built real ones, but I'm a carpenter, not a set designer.

A few minutes later, Aaron waves. "That's it, we're set up. Ready for first crew!"

Sonia rushes off set, and I follow—right up until she grabs Kantina and begins to whisper. I tell myself I'm not disappointed that she's making it easier to keep my distance. I tell myself a lot of things.

One take later, I'm back on the set, trying to decipher the marks. I could summon a demon with the twisted set of numbers on the set floor. "Which one do I move to?"

Aaron wipes his head. "You were watching rehearsals, right? Do what he did. If you screw it up, I'll let you know."

"Oh, for God's sake." Sonia shouts from just behind the camera. I can't see her because of the lights, but I don't think the frustration in her voice is an act. "He wasn't watching, so cut him a break. Nine, you walk slowly to the counter corner, then turn back, like you left something important behind. Like your copy of the scene."

"I didn't get a copy of the scene," I say as I walk toward the counter, cursing myself for not having a copy.

"Cut the banter," says Aaron, from behind his camera. He calls out a few adjustments to the lighting grips. "Hey, Nine—I mean, Will, stop a little earlier. Yeah, stop there and look back. No, too far. You're supposed to be looking back at someone longingly, not breaking your spine."

Sonia moves off camera, standing just a few feet from where I started. "Look at me."

Gladly. She moves like a boxer, not a ballet dancer, every step determined and with a purpose that says she'll flatten anything in her way. I can respect that. "This good?"

"Quiet on set, please. I'm trying to work here." Aaron goes back to fiddling with controls and barking orders. "Next point."

"Turn," says Sonia. "All the way around to me. Like you're going to come back, if you weren't afraid I'd punch you in the jaw."

"Would you?"

"Not when a kick would work better. I do a kickboxing workout three days a week when we're not filming."

I can tell she works out. I mean, I would have been able to, *if* I were studying her. Which I'm not, at this exact moment. Two seconds ago? That's in the past, it doesn't count.

"Final post," says Aaron.

Sonia points to the spot on the floor just past where I started out. "Come back to me."

And I do, dangerously aware of how close we are. Of how she could knock me out with a kick or a glance. The floor seems safer than her eyes.

"Eye line on Sonia," says Aaron. "Jimmy Becton doesn't

win awards for studying his shoes, and you're here to make him look great."

Her eyes have brown, not gold, scattered in with the green, and the smallest wrinkles at the corners that must bunch up when she laughs. I'd say she's concerned, maybe worried, or the slightest bit afraid, if I knew her well enough to read her emotions.

The way she looks back at me has me imagining so many conversations we could have, or dinners, or maybe hiking in a park.

"I said, that's good." Aaron's voice shatters the moment.

Sonia breaks our staring contest, turning away.

"Clear the set, get first crew. Nine, you need to relay blocking changes."

Sonia grabs my arm. "He means you need to tell James about the changes. Stop earlier, look back." She retreats, and two steps back the shadows swallow her. She might as well have drifted into the ether by the time I hopscotch over the cords.

Relay the blocking. I can do that.

When James Becton arrives on set, I head toward him with purpose. "Aaron made a few changes to blocking—"

"I was paying attention. Now, if you'll excuse me, I have to work." He turns and takes his place on set.

But where I'd expect Kantina, Sonia is standing, just like she did for me. Except that any sane man who looked back and saw a woman staring at him the way she's looking at James would run the other way. Her mouth is squared off, her shoulders tense, eyebrows furrowed. I expect she looks like this when she's kickboxing, except that she probably doesn't detest the punching bag this much.

Belion arrives within moments, his white hair brushed back over his head and slicked down with gel. Those enormous black glasses he's wearing could be either stylish or ridiculous. I'm voting ridiculous. "Silent on set. James, it is time to become Lord of the Manor."

"Cameras rolling," says someone.

Felicia looks to the side, then nods. "Action."

I've finally heard the famous lines. I expected more, but the way this crew works is like a group of surgeons.

James Becton starts off with his gaze distant. He saunters through the kitchen, then pivots two steps on to look back.

"What are you doing?" Belion shouts. "You have not run from her. You cannot possibly return if you do not first run."

James nods. "I was thinking, would the Lord really want to get—"

"You are the actor," shouts Belion. "The paintbrush with which I paint my work. Does the paint brush say 'I do not like this color' to the artist?"

James grimaces and looks down. "Sorry, Belion. I was told the blocking changed."

"By who? No one is changing anything about this movie without first consulting me." Belion glances toward the camera, as if he suspects exactly who made the changes.

"My stand-in."

"Who?" says Belion. "Why did you listen to this person?"

"It was a mistake. Can we start again from the top?" James asks.

I fight down the urge to defend my reputation in spite of the sour taste the fake blame leaves. This isn't a team of surgeons, it's a group of siblings looking for someone to blame. I move as far away from the set as possible while ensuring I can still hear if they shout for the second crew.

Six takes later, James finally makes it to coming back to Sonia. But I can't help noticing he doesn't quite finish the blocking, stopping at a safe distance.

"Set up for 318," shouts Felicia. "Second crew!"

This time, I'm smarter. I keep an eye on Aaron and follow him through the soundstage to a set I recognize. Bradley was building one corner of this when I arrived from Seattle.

It's a bedroom—well, it's two walls and a monster poster-bed. Like every other bit of furniture on the set, it's stained cherry red and has a canopy of silky gauze. Behind it is a chest-of-drawers Bradley worked on himself, with polished brass handles that match the fake lanterns hung from the silk-green wallpaper. The entire set looks ancient and smells like fresh construction, right down to the spray-foam used to tack the mirrors in place, and the double sided tape holding crown molding to the top of the dresser.

In keeping with the whole 'getting smarter' theme, I watch this time as Kantina and James join each other on set. Where I always believed Kantina moved with absolute elegance, on set she's careful, controlled. It takes someone of her calibre to make the ridiculous dress she's wearing look even half-way respectable. It's dark brown with a floral 'S' emblazoned on the stomach, and every inch of it looks like it has needlework stitching, like hand-spun lace, except it doesn't move in the slightest as Kantina does. All in all, I'm surprised she can breathe in it, with her stomach sucked in and her hair braided in a tight cord that coils behind her head.

I can't hear what's said between the two from this distance, but judging from looks I'd say it's professional, to the point, and done with little dressing. They are, after all, rehearsing.

After two takes, I understand. She sits. He stands behind her at the corner of the poster bed. Nonsensical dialogue is exchanged. She looks down, he turns and takes a dress from the drawers and tosses it on the bed as if he doesn't care if she wears it or not.

"Second crew!" Felicia shouts.

I'm on set moments later, standing in exactly the right spot, while Sonia takes up residence on the corner of the bed, one arm draped around the bedpost. She does everything with such precision and care, I can't help wondering if her personal conversations are the same. It wouldn't hurt to fish a little.

"Why do you think he takes the dress out, if he doesn't care if she wears it or not?" I ask. "If he doesn't care, why wouldn't he just say, 'There's a dress here. You're a grown woman who knows how to open drawers all by herself?'"

"Because," says Sonia without so much as glancing my way. "He *does* care. That's the point. He's imagining how she would look in it. He's hoping she'll put it on."

Aaron steps out from behind the camera, then looks through the viewfinder once more. "This is good, Nine, let's go through the motions."

"I have a name. It's Will," I say.

"Quiet on set," says Aaron. "Move slowly, please."

I do, mimicking exactly how James moved, how he turned. But the dresser drawer won't open. "It's stuck."

Well, it's sort of stuck. Just a small tug—and the drawer face comes off in my hands.

The dresser was originally a wooden monstrosity Bradley bought at a flea market. While I helped him stain the body, I had no idea the drawer faces were simply glued on—and this one wasn't glued well. I'll have to fix it—and any other corners my little brother might have cut.

"Crap!" Aaron shouts. "That's the wrong drawer. He opens the second from the bottom."

I give it a pull, and sure enough, the second from the bottom drawer opens with ease. There, tucked inside, is a feather boa cape still in the plastic packaging. "This is the dress? No wonder she says no."

Sonia's out of position now, standing just beside me. "That's a prop. They replace it with the real one when it's time to shoot."

"That's good. It wouldn't cover much, and it's a bit over the top."

"I don't know." Sonia unsnaps the package and shakes it out. "I mean, maybe I wouldn't wear *just* this, but I could pull it off."

Just the boa. The image is gone as quickly as it came, but now I'm the one blushing for even imaging it. "No. I mean, a dress too. I mean…"

Behind the camera, Aaron's yells for help have become a ferocious argument. "We have four more scenes to shoot here, and he just broke the set."

"I can fix it," I interrupt, desperate for something I *can* think about. "I'm a carpenter. It's what I do." As I press the drawer back into place, the decorative trim taped to the top sags —and falls, smashing into the crystal lined up on the makeup stand next to it.

"What on earth is going on?" That's Felicia. Her angry voice, the one I hoped not to hear, and it's aimed squarely at me. "Clear the set while we figure out how to fix this."

I put the drawer fronts on the bed and step out of the light. Felicia's waiting for me. "You see that plastic chair? Sit there. Don't move. Don't touch anything. We had six scenes to film here, and you just broke it."

"I was trying to—"

"Stop trying." She turns her back on me and focuses on Aaron. "Exactly what are we going to do now? Can you set up for the bridge?"

"We're most of the way already. You want me to call you when I'm set?"

"Yes." Felicia turns and shakes her head. "There isn't much he can break there. I'm going to make a call to casting. Sorry, Will, but you're costing me more time than you're saving. You can finish out the day, but you're not coming back tomorrow."

"I'm sorry. Give me some glue, and if you just..." My heart sinks as I recognize that look of determination, a woman who's made up her mind. Dignity demands acceptance, even if my mistake has cost me the best chance in two years to work my way out of debt. "Don't worry. My brother will understand."

CHAPTER FIVE

I DIDN'T HAVE HOPES OF BUILDING A CAREER AS AN ACTOR, but I need work so badly it hurts. And now, with one mistake, I've broken the set and am in the running for shortest career ever as a stand-in.

Once Felicia leaves, Aaron motions for me to follow him to the next set. "Don't take it personal, getting fired is practically part of the job description for stand-ins. Look on the bright side, we still need that staircase built."

I nod. "That I can do without screwing anything up. You want me to head to the shop and start on it?"

"You could," says Aaron, "but it isn't going to help us make up today's scenes. While Felicia's arranging for your replacement, Sonia will get you a copy of the script. We're supposed to pan across the bridge in time with the dialogue. I personally don't care what you say, but Belion… Well, you don't improvise with him. Even if you're not coming back tomorrow, he'll make you regret it."

I made this mess. It may have been a mistake, but it was my mistake, and I'll own it. What did I tell Bradley whenever we moved to a new foster home? *Make the best of it.* I couldn't appreciate then just how bad the best could be. I shake my head, blinking just in case my eyes are sweating. "I thought stand-ins just stood there. Next I'm moving, reading lines. I don't have to appear naked, do I?"

That, at least, gets a laugh from him. "Nope. Even if you were still around, James has a model who serves as his nude double."

I'm still trying to figure out if he's joking when we reach the bridge. It's just as fake as the rest of the sets, consisting only of the white wooden railing that looks real and a wide plywood platform in front of a green screen.

Sonia's waiting there for us.

Despite the crushing weight of failure that makes it hard to breathe, I force a smile into my voice. "Tomorrow," I say to her as Aaron and I approach, "you get to work with Ten, who will be much more professional than me, because he'll be an actual actor."

Sonia sets aside her script and gives me a fleeting smile. "Don't take this the wrong way, Nine, but the sooner we get this movie wrapped, the better. I'm sorry it didn't work out, but if I was sad every time someone was canned from one of Belion's productions, I'd never be happy."

"What makes you happy?"

Sonia stops checking marks, looking up at me like I just asked the circumference of the Earth. Her answer comes slowly, as if she has to chase it down. "Relaxing on a summer day by the pool. Reading at night before I go to bed. Going jogging with my neighbor's dog when we're not filming."

I don't consider myself an expert, but what she's saying feels real to me, so much it makes me want to ignore the warning bells in my head that say I already made this mistake once.

"What about you, Nine? Now that your film career is over, what dream will you chase?"

Her question hits me in the gut, hammering home once more that I've blown a real opportunity, my chance to get back on my feet. "I once owned a store in Seattle that sold wood carvings. I'm going to re-open it one day." Even thinking about it brings a smile to my face—and a tinge of sadness for what I lost.

"Move to the far side and take first position," says Aaron. "We've got three cameras to set, so hold it there."

On the way across the bridge, Sonia says, "Your business got hit by the recession?"

"More of a natural disaster." Tamara's brother called her 'Hurricane Tamara.' She left my bank account dry and my mailbox flooded with bills. "But I can turn things around. The shop front is still there, and I can make new pieces to sell."

She stops and glances my way. "I hope you do, Nine. Maybe someday I'll come visit your shop and buy a ring box."

Only then do I notice the gold band on her finger. "You're married?" My skin crawls as I realize I've been flirting with a married woman.

"I'm not married." She slips the ring, turning it so the swirls engraved in the gold catch the light before setting it at the foot of the bridge. "I wear it so men don't bug me, but it comes off for shoots unless Kantina is wearing one too, and even then, it'll be a matching one."

"Ok," says Aaron. "Let's do a basic check. Nine, face me. Sonia, you know the drill. Follow blocking, keep your eyeline high, shoulders twisted inward just a bit."

Together, we stride out across the set. She keeps one hand on the rail, while I don't have a rail—or a back half of the bridge.

"Start over," says Aaron. "There's an ugly shadow between you and I need to fix."

We return to the far edge of the fake bridge—and she offers me her arm. "You're supposed to be escorting me. Lock your arm in mine. Step closer." She flashes me a smile. "Don't be so afraid, I don't bite often."

I take her arm, and she meshes fingers with mine, showing nails that are filed short and smooth. "You might not bite, but you look like you have a wicked left hook."

Sonia tilts her head to one side in feigned embarrassment. "I do."

"Slow," calls Aaron. "Paul, Marty, pull in and let me check your views as well."

I don't remember the last time I went strolling with a woman, but I like to imagine it as something people do comfortably, without much thought. Me, on the other hand… How do I reconcile the urge to avoid getting hurt with the way I feel when she smiles at me? The contradiction is like an ache in my chest that makes every moment sharp.

"Relax," she whispers. "Seriously, what's wrong? Are you upset about getting canned? If so, you'll never make it in Hollywood. Recasting is a fact of actor life."

I shrug my shoulders a little, but it doesn't do anything to release the tension. "I take pride in doing things the right way, and I did about as wrong as you could imagine.

I had a chance to pay off some bills, and I blew it. One accident, and I blew it."

Aaron steps out from behind a camera and holds up his hand. "Lean in just a tad, Sonia. Head back. Nine, don't move a muscle."

She rests her head on my shoulder, and I couldn't move if I had to. While Aaron barks out orders for adjustments, I remind myself we're nothing more than a couple of props that have to be occasionally fed—and speaking of eating, my stomach rumbles.

"Look, Will. I can read your body language, and I swear you're afraid of me," says Sonia. Then her mouth curls up in a wicked grin and her eyes gleam. "Is it because we're so close together? Because I can tell you, this is nothing. If we were lighting some of the bedroom shots, you'd have to get used to it."

I can imagine. I can only imagine—and imagination by itself is more than enough to make me blush and look away. "I won't have to get used to anything, because today, I'm getting replaced." That's the first time I've found a positive spin on what's otherwise a definite disaster.

If I stop and think about the bills I won't be paying, I might not pull myself out of that spiral. But I might as well enjoy the time I have.

"Ok, first positions," says Aaron. "I need to bring in Belion to check this. You two are going to have to wait for lunch."

It's already noon. Holy crap, half a day gone and we've only shot one scene and ruined one other.

"We're good," says Sonia. Then, under her breath, she adds, "No matter what, you're always good. You can hit the catering table later. It's questionable when they put it out, it's questionable now, it'll be the exact same level of questionable two days from now."

I dig in my pocket and pull out the bag of granola. "Hungry? I make it myself with real peanut butter, not that store-stuff."

"Starving." She grabs a handful, then helps herself to the bag. "I always say I'm going to bring something to eat and keep it in my trailer. I never do."

It takes me a moment to connect actors and their movie set trailers, even though I passed so many on the way in. I can't help studying the curve of her neck, the profile of her face, so I'll remember. "You have a trailer. Do I have a trailer? I always wanted a trailer."

Sonia swallows another mouthful of granola and says as she chews, "When we're done filming, I'll show you mine. It's in Kantina's contract that I'm her stand-in, and that I get a place of my own."

"So the answer to the question 'Your place or mine' is always 'Yours'?"

"You'd have to ask me to find out."

That sounds like an expression of interest, and if I were half as smart as I like to think, I'd be silently reminding myself she's a professional pretender, not panicking over what I should say.

Across the set, production assistant earphones buzz as someone makes an announcement. The camera operators, who've been slouching by their cameras staring at their phones, snap to attention. Belion comes charging onto the set, practically on fire with rage. "Can you believe it? Can you believe it?"

If he's in funk over me breaking a drawer and some glass, he might take it out on everyone around him—

including Sonia and Aaron. I move to intercept him—and find she has my arm in a lock.

"Don't move a muscle, don't say a word," she whispers through gritted teeth. "He's always like this. Keep quiet, do what he says, get through it."

I can't be sure if she's talking to me or herself, but I can take her advice.

"We needed both of them," says Felicia, who's trailing behind him. "We've only got Becton through the end of the day. After that we're going to shoot the dinner sequence. How am I supposed to do that without the dinner guests?"

Belion's eyes are wild as he stomps to the edge of the bridge and surveys it. "That fool of an actor improvised, as if his own imagination could surpass my genius. I did not fire the woman, she chose to leave in support of him. Now, are we going to film a romantic stroll or are we going to debate the past?"

"First, we need to make some changes." Aaron's statement almost comes with a question mark on the end of it. "When they turn, we're not getting him in the shot. Move to center, please."

With forced grace, Sonia strolls, her grip on my arm still tight enough to cut off the blood-flow to my fingers. That's what's causing the tingling where she's touching me, I'm sure. At the bridge center, she pauses, and leans back to me.

Aaron looks up from the camera and points. "See? Is that what you want?"

Belion stands, one hand on his chin, the other on his hip as he surveys us. "Sonia, turn outward. You must not face to him so easily. You, other man, hand on her hip. She must not escape you."

I blink as I make sure I heard right. "You want my hand where?"

"He is speaking?" Belion looks back at Aaron. "Why is he speaking, and it is not the lines?"

"He's the temp from yesterday," says Aaron. "Felicia's replacing him. His name is Nine. I mean, Will."

"William." Belion moves his entire jaw as he says my name, like it won't quite fit in his mouth all at once. "We have simple rules here. Words spoken on set are the words of creation. Of love, of life. You do not speak what is not written. If there is nothing written, you do not speak. Do you understand?"

As I open my mouth to answer, Sonia digs her nails into the underside of my arm. Instead, I stare off into the distance.

"Hand on hip," says Belion. "Hers, not yours."

I slip my right hand over and rest lightly it on the curve of her hip, barely touching.

"See?" says Belion. "Now, there is fire between them. Now, there is creation."

What he takes as fire I'd describe as awkwardness, because I don't dance with strangers, and I don't touch women without permission, and I'm doing both at the moment.

"Can we move the primary angle to the right, get them both clear?" asks Aaron.

"Yes, yes. This is a minor detail." Belion waves his hand. "Are we done with the bedroom footage? I wish to review it."

Sonia doesn't need to squeeze my arm this time for me to know that's bad.

"We had an issue with the set," says Aaron. "It's being repaired as we speak."

"What kind of issue?"

Aaron tosses his head side to side in a way that makes me think he's trying to figure out a lie that will work. "It got broken during light check."

"*By. Whom?*" Belion spits each word.

Aaron can't even look at me as he points my direction. "Him. It's not his fault, he was helping us fill in for—"

"Not his fault?" With every word, Belion's voice rises higher. "William, come here."

Sonia releases her grip on me and steps away like I've got chickenpox.

They're all terrified of him, and it's at that moment it hits me that I have no reason to be. After today, I'll never see him again. I've picked myself up off life's concrete before. I'll do it again. And though I grew up in fear, as an adult, I have a simple rule not to go through life afraid of anyone.

With that, I take a deep breath, blow it out and let the tension that's infected me drain away. I pull out the bag of granola and take a few bites, because, after all, I'm hungry. Then it's time to stride down the bridge to meet him, leaving Sonia behind. "We seem to have gotten off on the wrong foot. Let's start again. Hi. I'm Will. It's good to meet you."

"I wish I could say the same. Why do you hate me so much, William, that you sabotage my life's work?"

I shrug. "I don't hate you. I don't *know* you well enough to hate you." He's a short man, and this close, I tower over him, but I'm doing my best to go out in style and with class.

"You are jealous of my genius, William. Of my art. I know this."

That takes the words right out of my mouth. I'd been planning on explaining. On cajoling. Flattering. Begging for him to please, please let me stay. But in this one moment, the misery and sadness I've carried for two years, the self-loathing at yet another mistake and missed opportunity, boils into anger. But not the type that has me screaming and using my fists. Forget style and flush class, I want to hit him where it hurts.

Everything I know about directors comes from Bradley, but something he said about them comes to mind; that every director lives in fear of being forgotten. "When I found out you were directing this movie, I asked my brother who you were. He looked you up on the internet and said, 'That's the guy that works for Kantina.'" I tilt my head. "Have you made any movies that *don't* star her? I sure can't think of them."

"Get him off my set," says Belion as the veins on his forehead bulge out. "Never let me see him again."

"One more thing," I add as he shakes with rage. I hold up the copy of the script Sonia gave me. "This dialogue? It's *awful*. This isn't the language of creation, it's what a drunk person screams after they fall down the staircase and hit their head." I nod to Aaron. "It was good meeting you. I'm so sorry for the accident on the set. I'll change my clothes and see myself off the lot. Sonia, I..."

I can't find the words to explain.

I want to ask her to dinner. Or lunch? Or breakfast? It's not the smart move, but maybe I'm not as smart as I like to think. Or maybe I just like getting burned.

Before I can collect myself enough to form a coherent thought, Belion tears the script from my hand. "You have *defiled* this. What are you, a plumber?"

"A carpenter, actually, a really good one. Though not even I could build a support to prop up that ego of yours."

"*This* is the problem," he says. "This is why the scene did not work correctly. There can be no fire between a carpenter and an actress, even one of her lowly talent. None."

I bristle at that. "Excuse me? Sonia's amazing. And for your education, I had an international business carving wood sculptures. I was an artist too, but the difference is, I didn't treat people like garbage to make myself feel better. Give me some time, and I'll carve a new stick to replace the one that's shoved up your ass."

I regret not asking for Sonia's phone number, or giving her mine, but I know when I've burned a bridge, and this one is doused in napalm and covered in matches.

Maybe it's better this way, because it sure feels good to be the one laying down the trash instead of taking it for a change. "By the way, about the film's title, the word is 'manor.' M-A-N-O-R. Lady of the *Manor*, not 'manner.' They're pronounced exactly the same. You think you're being all artsy, but it's a stupid pun."

It's not often that I get to revel in the glory of putting someone in their place, but this feels like wiping clean the last two years. I could get used to it.

Belion doubles over, coughing.

When he stands up, his face is red, his eyes bulging. There's a brilliant scarlet rash that wasn't there moments before, streaking down his cheeks and across his forehead. "That stench… is peanuts," he wheezes. "I am allergic!"

"Medical!" Aaron shouts. "We need Medical."

My moment of triumph has turned to a horror that leaves my stomach cold and my mouth dry. I can't find words for what I want to say, and despite how I feel, running away from a situation I created has never been in my nature.

Within minutes, Belion is whisked off in an ambulance, still wailing about how the shot they gave him hurts.

Sonia and I stand shoulder to shoulder, wordless as the chaos around us spreads—but soon enough, the moment I've been dreading comes. Felicia, flanked by two studio guards, approaches.

I expect her to shout, to yell. Instead, she speaks softly, her voice controlled as she says, "Will, you can't leave until we're done looking into this. You're going to go with these men."

She's scarier when she's not yelling.

"He can wait in my trailer," says Sonia.

"Shorter walk than going to the office," says one guard. "Let's do that instead."

Felicia sighs as I pass her. "You broke the set. You broke the director. Will, you're busting my balls. Your brother is going to be pissed at you."

I follow Sonia out of the sound studio, with both guards in tow. Past the makeup trailer are two extravagant travel trailers, white with black stripes down the side and gold lettering, easily as long as a tractor/trailer. And just past that is an actual semi, whose trailer sports six separate stairs and doors.

Sonia stops at one and says, "You said you wanted to live an actor's life of luxury. Check it out."

The inside reminds me of a jail cell (and I should know: I spent some time in one before the banks corroborated my story about Tamara taking the money). The difference here is there are fewer drunks.

The simple rectangle has just enough space for a twin bed, a chair, and what I'll generously call a desk because otherwise it's just a cracked plastic wart in the middle of the room.

"Like what you see?" Sonia has followed me up the stairs and is standing right behind me. "Build a career as an actor and all this could be yours."

"I was picturing something like the huge ones we passed," I say, taking the seat so she can have the more comfortable bed. Outside, the security guards wait.

"Those are for the big names. Kantina has a shower in hers. And a kitchen. And a chef, who cooks her dinner every night."

"You should spend more time there." I shake my head. "I think I'm going to be spending time somewhere else shaped very much like this. You think I'll look good in orange?"

Sonia reaches over and squeezes my hand—then doesn't let go. "Accidents happen, Will. Even I didn't know he was allergic, and I've been forced to learn almost every quirk the man has. You didn't mean to do it, and you didn't say anything all of us haven't thought ten times at least. You're going to be remembered as a hero."

"Felicia would say otherwise."

"Do you care?"

"No." The answer is easy—and wrong. I don't like lying, not even to people I don't know well. I shrug. "A little. Yes. It's not just my pride. Truth is, I needed this job. I needed the hours, because my business in Seattle went belly up, owing a lot of people a lot of money."

She doesn't recoil, or draw back her hand. "Why don't you declare bankruptcy?"

"And hurt a bunch of other small businesses just because my accountant was crooked? No, that just spreads Tamara's damage out to people who don't deserve it."

"And you do?"

"Yes. I should have seen through her sooner, but when you want to believe, you do." Like I'm doing right now. Cursing myself, I let go of Sonia and stand up to stretch. "There you go. Two days and you know everything important about me, Ms. Sonia Bracewell."

"I think there are more important things to know," she says. "Like, for instance, are you married?"

It wasn't so long ago that I was dating, and this I recognize as at least minor interest. "Why do you ask?"

"So I can notify your wife if they lock you up," Sonia says, face completely deadpan. "I'll be needing to put your emergency contact number into my phone. Just in case there's an emergency."

She wants my number. I sit up in the chair as a combination of panic and delight make my hands unsteady. This is the silver-lining in an absolute hailstorm. "No to married. Thank God everything blew up before we got to that stage. Would I have married Tamara? I don't know. I think we both knew what we had wasn't for life. As a matter of fact, if she's ever caught she'll *have* something that's fifteen to life. Also not dating, and haven't been looking."

The review of my past takes the wind from my sails, and I lean over on the useless desk. But then I realize Sonia's watching me. "That could change."

"Really?" She gazes up at me under thick eyelashes. "Under what circumstances, Mister Thankfully-Not-Married?"

"I can't really say just yet. I'm still dependent on my brother for a place to live—"

Sonia puts one hand to her chin, and I suspect she's about to tease me when she stops focusing. "What did Felcia mean about him being mad?"

"His name is Bradley Mathis. He owns the…" I pause, because Sonia isn't really in the room with me anymore.

She squares her shoulders and takes in a deep breath as she looks back to me, her eyes wider. "Bradley Mathis. Head of *Mathis* construction? And the investment group holding our bridge funding for this movie?"

"I guess?" My stomach had been twisting itself into knots with anticipation of something new and different. Now I've swallowed a cannon ball, since all I can do is try and defuse whatever this is. "Bradley's been investing for the last few years. They import movies from Europe, and he's got a new title from Spain coming soon. I guess it makes sense why his company is building the sets. Enough about my brother."

Sonia turns away, one first clenched. "Will… It's not—it's just—do you know what people say about actresses who have relationships with investment partners? Do you know what they call us? They call us whores."

"Bradley's the one with the money. I've got nothing—"

"You have influence with him." She says it without so much as a hesitation, like it's a fact. "I have a rule about on-set relationships, because they always end in disaster. That rule goes double for producers or investors. If I went out with you, in the eyes of people who know, I'll forever be the actress who used more than her talent to make sure the movie got made."

Sonia's face might well be cast in bronze for all the emotion she's showing as she heads to the door. "I'm sorry, Will. I'm sorry." Then she's gone.

Then I wait, wait, and wait some more. As the hours pass, I doze on the bed and wonder if in Hollywood they take you straight to jail, or if I get a phone call. Bradley won't expect me until late, and probably won't think anything's wrong until tomorrow morning.

It's well after eight when someone knocks on my door. Sonia's door. The door. Felicia steps through, looking about five cups of coffee from a breakdown. "Will."

I sit up and ready myself for the bad news.

"We've reviewed the tapes—"

"What tapes?"

"Those giant metal contraptions with men sitting behind them are cameras," she says like I wasn't aware. "They feed to the monitors whether we're filming or not, and the set mics picked up everything. We know it was an accident. I've already talked with Belion. They'll be releasing him from the hospital tonight. Come with me."

I do, following her out and back to the wardrobe trailer, where I exchange the brown sweatpants and shirt for my blue jeans and sneakers.

"Sign out, please." Felicia hands me the form, and I do. Then I take my lanyard off and pass it over.

She shakes her head.

"But I'm fired. Belion said so."

Felicia doesn't meet my gaze as she answers. "You *were* fired. Now you're not."

Hope for a second chance to prove I can do this thrills through me—and dies as my more cynical side kicks in. "If this is about my brother, I promise you, he's not going to second-guess your decisions—"

Felicia silences me with a stare. "Will, there's an all-crew meeting at six a.m tomorrow. Belion has an announcement he wants to make. You will be there."

Now I get it. "The munchkin wants to can me in front of everyone, doesn't he?"

"We were running light and sound checks for that shoot. Every crew member with a mic heard what went down. Every person near a monitor saw it. The video leaked out on the internet ten minutes after it happened." The way she says it, I've just lit the fuse on a very large bomb. "I have it on good authority it's going to be a feature clip on the late show."

Normally, I'd tell Belion where he could stick my lanyard. But while I won't be back, Sonia will, and now I regret that my bravado made her life more difficult. "If I show up, and he gets to humiliate me, he'll ease up on the rest of you?"

Felicia nods her head in a yes/no manner. "He'll be his normal level of intolerable. You come for fifteen minutes of tantrum, I'll sign off on twelve hours. Deal?"

"Deal." I offer her my hand. "And I'm sorry. I thought my days were long. Yours must be worse."

"I still have to call the producer and explain what happened. Not just your accident, or Belion's ambulance ride, I get to tell him that earlier today, Belion fired two other supporting actors before he got around to you. Eddie's going to flip, since he arranged those two personally as a favor."

Directors, producers, all of these are a jumble of titles. "Who's the producer?"

"The one with connections to the money to get the film made. He may not have the cash personally, but he knows people like your brother's investment group. He's the one with the final say. Eddie Gellar's been in this business four decades and he doesn't take anything from anyone, not even Belion."

I give her a thumbs up for anyone who doesn't put up with Belion's attitude. "I like this Eddie guy already. Will he be there tomorrow to wave goodbye?"

Felicia chokes back a laugh, but it's worry that creases her forehead for a moment. "Oh, God, no. I mean, I hope not. I give him nightly updates, he gives us the freedom to get our work done without standing over us. See you tomorrow morning, Will."

I head toward the gate. Humiliation is something I've had first-hand experience with, and I can take it like a pro.

Bradley might be right. Maybe I shouldn't have gotten involved with an actress. But given her declaration and me being fired, it's probably safe to admit I wouldn't mind seeing her one last time.

CHAPTER SIX

By the time I walk through the door of Bradley's apartment, I'm in no mood to explain to him what happened. If he wants to, he can watch the video of me exploding on Belion.

Turns out, he already has. Three times. "What happened to representing my company?" Bradley asks as I sit at the kitchen table and devour a container of what's either soup or milk gone bad. Honestly, I'm too hungry to check and too tired to care.

When I don't answer, his frown deepens into a scowl. "I didn't know you had that kind of trash talk in you, bro. Did you just lose me the set work on a movie I'm investing in?"

It takes every bit of restraint I have not to shout. Instead, I focus on the cigarette burns from the kitchen table's previous life, and try to release the tangled net of worry that keeps tripping me. "No, I did not, and thanks for asking if I'm okay. They still want two sets of banisters. The catch is, I have to report to work in the morning so Belion Androse can fire me in front of the crew." I shrug. "Also, I hear I'm going to be on the late night show."

Bradley nods. "Eddie knows a gal who knows a gal who arranged that. People will be talking about this movie and it's not even time for the marketing blitz. In that regard, you did good."

"I'll be in the shop by noon to start working on the bannisters."

Bradley crosses his arms as he watches at me. "You're going back to see her, aren't you?"

"Who? No, I'm not." Am I?

"I'm not familiar with the entire crew, and we don't get a good look at her, but pause... here." He holds up the phone. "Right before you go all righteous-warrior, you look back over your shoulder. I've seen that look before, Will. With you-know-who."

Since when does my little brother know me better than I know myself? The urge to fight for the sake of fighting rises. "I cut a deal with the assistant director. I get paid for a full day just for letting him work out his anger management issues. And since I won't be working there, I think you don't need to worry about me getting in over my head with an actress."

I don't know why I'm so upset, and frankly, I'm just a half-step from letting Bradley know what Sonia said, about how she wouldn't even consider dating me because I was related to Bradley. Instead, I channel the frustration inward. "Night, little bro." I barely bother wiping off the makeup they caked on my face before climbing onto the sofa and doing my best to die.

At five in the morning it destroys my slumber, but I can't help but feel positive as I roll off the couch and slide my suitcase out from under the coffee-table. Sure, I'm going to get yelled at, but if I can find Sonia and tell her how it really is between Bradley and I before the verbal beat-down begins, it'll be worth it.

What I mean is, find Sonia and tell her it was a pleasure working with her.

At the studio gates, I tense while security checks me over—probably for lethal snacks—and then relax as they pass me through. I didn't bring anything today, since I'll be back at the shop by noon, if not sooner. The walk to the soundstage is dark and lonely—the only other people are actors who are in makeup that makes them look like some sort of orc. Green, ugly, and joking with each other about how they're going to lay siege to the coffee stand.

I fall in behind them and march my way to 53, where they turn off—and I continue on alone, heading for the makeup trailer. That's where Sonia will be. That's where I'll be, for a minute.

But Sonia isn't in line, and that makes me sick. Did Belion try to have her fired, too, because of my stunt? Can that even be done when she has Kantina's loyalty?

Then, in the crowd, I see a flash of red hair, and move toward it. She turns to look at me, and I'm once more face to face with Kantina. I don't have time to be star-struck. "Morning. Do you have any idea where Sonia might be? I need to set something straight with her before the all-crew meeting."

"William, I am surprised to see you here. Come, darling. Walk with me as you did with Sonia. I will take you to her."

"I also need to find Felicia." I offer her my arm, and can't help but think how Bradley will never believe me about this. And how I couldn't care less. "Sonia's not going to get in trouble because of what I did, is she?"

"We are all in trouble. You may hear of difficult actors, but a difficult director is by far the worst." Kantina stops and glances to the side. "Ah, they were here earlier. She is a gifted woman, talented at the details of production."

Kantina's accent blurs the words slightly. It's easy to understand why people listen raptly.

But I've been listening to the words so closely I can't tell who she means is a gifted woman. "Who, Felicia or Sonia?"

"Both."

Since I only have minutes left, I might as well ask one question that's been bugging me every time I listen to her. "How come you don't sing the same way you talk? I was listening to one of your songs on the way home last night. You could be a different woman."

Kantina stops and sings the refrain from one of her chart-topping hits. *If you'd only love me the way that you love her.* William, it is a skill, like an American accent, or an English one. I learned from Edward Gellar himself, when I was a young woman."

I'm standing next to someone with a reputation and a presence that practically draws your eye—and yet, I'm looking for someone else with every corner we turn as we resume our death-march.

"There, darling." Kantina points to a heavy double door up a set of metal stairs. "That is the production office. Are you certain you are ready?"

"I don't run from my problems or my mistakes. And thank you." I mean it. "Thank you for putting up with my questions, and my awkwardness. And once I'm fired, I promise I'm going to watch every movie you've made. One day, you're going to give my brother an autograph."

She laughs and pulls on my arm, yanking me closer as we climb the stairs together. "I would have to get to know him. My movies are my life. Some are good. Some are bad. All are me, sharing parts of myself with the world." Kantina doesn't knock, she simply opens the door and strides in, dragging me with her.

Felicia's there, wearing the same pantsuit from last night, but with a new pizza stain. Her hair's no longer pulled back, she has bags under her eyes and a death grip on the coffee mug in front of her. Sonia's there too, wearing a plain black shirt and pants that hug her hips. She doesn't need jewelry or makeup to look stunning. Opposite them stands Belion Androse, dressed in royal purple from head to toe. He's only slightly worse for wear. His face may be puffier—or maybe I just despise him a little more.

"Good morning," says Kantina, in a sing-song voice that says she knows it isn't.

Belion hasn't even looked my way yet.

In fact, none of them have.

They're all staring at the table, at a phone, a phone I'm guessing is on speaker. "No *you*, listen up," says a man with a deep western drawl. "I ain't amused by your shenanigans at all. You're making me look like a fool in front of people who gave me the money to make this movie. Felicia's got it right, that a movie's like a business, B. You can't run a business if you got no employees."

"Do you not care for my life? For my vision? For my art?" Belion holds his hand over his heart as he speaks—and then he spots me, and I think he's actually gagging before he manages to puke out words. "What is *he* doing here? He was to be held in front of the crew. We are needed elsewhere, Edward. A movie is not like a business, it is like a ship, and I have let this one sail too far." Belion steps away from the table. "Have a good morning, Edward. We will film many scenes today."

But I'm not watching him. Maybe I can't read body language as well as Sonia, but Felicia hasn't moved, hasn't even blinked. As a child, I learned to know when Dad was about to slip into one of his rages, and the way she's staring at the phone sets every hair on my body tingling.

Edward clears his throat and lets out a long, trailing cough. "Now, hold on there, B. I need you to say it with me. Who's in charge of this business, or this ship, or whatever other ridiculous metaphor you want to use?" The man's voice deepens and loses a bit of its accent.

"Edward, you are bringing investors with money," says Belion. "But I am bringing the art. So we share."

"Close," says Edward. Edward must be Eddie Gellar, the producer—and Bradley's gateway to movie investing. "We *were* sharing. Then you fired twelve people in ten days, including my niece and nephew, who I'm going to have to make it up to. So here's how it's going to go. If it doesn't have to do with a shot, you don't get to decide it. No more casting. No more costumes. Leave that to the other folks. From now on, the only thing you're going to do is work your art-y magic, and make a film that brings in a ton of money for everyone."

"What if there are differences which make art impossible?" asks Belion, gazing at me with unadulterated hatred. "Then, I must have no choice but to fire them."

Nothing but silence comes from the speaker. Then Eddie clears his throat. "Kantina, you there, woman?"

"I am, darling. How may I assist?"

"You got my number, right?"

She leans over and speaks directly into the phone. "I do, but I have told you, I do not feel the same passion for you."

"Oh, I wasn't asking 'bout that," says Eddie. "Felicia, you too. Belion's got to learn who's in charge, and you two are going to keep him honest by calling me if he so much as sniffs in the wrong direction. B, you're a pain in the ass, but I get that's part of the whole 'art is my toilet paper' schtick you got going."

"Is there a point?" Belion says, his voice nearly a shriek. "My art has made you a rich man."

"True," says Eddie. "B, pick one person. One more you want to show the door."

"Him," Belion shouts without taking a breath—or his eyes off of me. "William Mathis. The man who tried to poison me. I can work no magic with a carpenter. I will have him escorted out immediately."

Eddie clears his throat in a way that makes me think he didn't need to cough. "That's the boy on the video, ain't it?"

"Yes." Belion drags the word out into several syllables, and at the end, he sounds like a hissing snake.

From the phone there's a tapping sound, like someone fiddling with a pen. "All right, B. You want him gone?"

Belion shouts, "You know I do! What is this game?"

"This isn't a game. Until you finish principal photography, he's the only one you *can't* fire. Every time you look at him, you remember who calls the shots. Boy, are you there?"

I can barely raise my voice to answer. "Yes sir—I'm sorry about the set, and I'm sorry—"

"You're wasting my time," says Eddie. "The way I see it, this is at least partly your fault. I hear from Felicia you wanted hours, didn't you?"

"Yes sir." I sound like I'm sixteen. Feel like it, too.

"Your brother's the junior investor on this project. The one that runs the set construction company, ain't he?"

I manage to squeak out an affirmative.

"Thought so. Well, since you helped get us into this mess, you're going to help get us out. You better show up every day ready to be the best stand-in to ever pin down a piece of concrete. You screw this up and I'll make sure your brother never gets in on the ground floor of a movie again. For that matter, he won't build a doghouse, let alone a set piece, for as long as I live. Now." With that one word, his tone shifts, and he reminds me of a cheerleading squad. "Enough being grumpy. Make me some money, folks. Felicia, I expect to hear from you tonight."

The line goes dead.

The room goes silent.

Belion stalks from it, shaking with rage as tears stream down his face. Kantina follows, her face a roadmap of worry.

"What just happened?" I say, still unable to find my full voice.

Felicia looks up at me and sags into a chair at the table. "For my money? Eddie's looking for a reason to shut down production, that's what happened."

"Eight weeks," says Sonia, her voice empty. "We were eight weeks from being done, and now, I'm never going to be rid of him." She looks up at me, her brows furrowed, her hands clenched in fists.

Before I can begin to understand what Sonia means, she bolts out.

I glance to Felicia, who is staring at a cup of coffee like it holds the answer to all her problems. "Why is she so desperate to get rid of me?"

"Not everything is about you, Will." She flicks me a glance. "As a matter of fact, most things in life are not about you."

That leads me to the question I should have thought of first. "You think Eddie was serious about his threat to hurt Mathis Construction?"

"Eddie Gellar doesn't make threats, he makes promises. He's got fingers in every pie, eyes and ears on every set, and favors to call in from everyone. How's your brother's business doing? I hear through the grapevine he borrowed every penny he could to buy in, so can his business afford a minor break in work? I figure Eddie'll live ten to fifteen more years at most."

"No way." Guilt surges through me. I called Tamara a hurricane, but it's me that's doing all the wrecking here. Bradley's built a business, built a dream, and now my big mouth could cost him everything.

"Then I suggest you get yourself down to makeup. We have scenes to shoot, and so help me God, Will Mathis, we're going to get them done. You may not have been an actor two days ago, but you are one now."

I don't waste time on snappy comebacks or morose musing.

If I do my part, we can make a movie.

I can pay off the bills that have haunted me for years.

I can keep my brother's business safe.

But it's one last thought that puts me to my feet and on my way to makeup: I've built a life of doing things right or not at all.

And Sonia? I'll show her I've got what it takes. As an actor, I mean, nothing else. It's that last bit—nothing else—that I have to remember most.

CHAPTER SEVEN

In the minutes it takes me to reach the makeup trailers, I've gotten an idea of just how welcome I am on the set. Production assistants scurry away, lighting people find something to fiddle with, and the other actors act like I'm a mobile cactus, stepping to the side.

The way the makeup ladies look at me, you'd think my beard was forked and my mustache had curly tips for me to twiddle while I plot.

The lead makeup lady looks back to the others and says, "Oh, no. It's him."

For the record, that's not an encouraging greeting.

While they re-apply foul-smelling dye to my beard and trim it, I learn that Belion is taking his frustrations out on the crew by being even more demanding than before. It doesn't take a genius for the crew to put two and two together and come up with me still having a job and Belion being pissy.

In wardrobe, instead of brown sweatpants they have me put on an ill-fitting long-sleeve shirt that buttons right up to my chin. It's made for someone six times my size and hangs off me like a tent, so they use safety-pins in the back to make it work.

By the time I'm decked out in pants that have puffed-out knees, it's already six-thirty, and I'm late.

I don't know where I'm supposed to be, but I know who I'm supposed to be with. I snag the nearest production assistant. "Where's Sonia Bracewell?"

The assistant leads me through the sets to where Sonia's sitting on a bare tree trunk, wiping her eyes. There's no branches at the top, no stump at the bottom, just a trunk with metal poles holding it up off the ground. I'm guessing it's enough for what will be in the shot. Aaron stands on a ladder, watching the shadow as he twists a light to aim at Sonia's feet.

I wait for Aaron to look down, and present myself. "Show me where you want me, I'll be there."

He bites his lip and then responds. "You're either the luckiest son-of-a-bitch or the most unlucky. I can't make up my mind, but I guess we'll find out."

I don't want to guess, but today, with the hindsight that comes from yesterday's disaster, I have a plan.

I watch Sonia.

She's a pro at this, having survived and thrived for nearly a decade. When she's near the camera, I'm near the camera. If she's watching monitors and taking notes, I watch monitors and take notes, even if most of them are sketches of her face in profile.

If she notices me watching, she doesn't say.

When we light scenes, I keep my mouth shut and my eyes focused wherever Aaron says. When we clear the set, I'm first off and hovering a few feet back from wherever Sonia goes. The only downside to my cunning plan is when I almost follow her into the women's bathroom—which is a mistake I make only once.

The hours spin by, and soon enough, Felicia calls for lunch.

Outside, there's a tray of not-quite food. Slices of lunch meat and cheese, and stacks of crackers line one tray. On another, in ice, are shrimp cocktails, what I believe is probably either a clam or some sort of amputated tumor, and a container on ice filled with rubbery black jelly I suppose is caviar, which I poke at.

"Careful, Will. You don't hate your stomach enough to eat that," Sonia says softly, sliding up beside me unannounced. "That's only brought in because of James Becton's contract. Better you get in the habit of avoiding anything that's his."

"I thought you weren't willing to be seen with me."

"Doesn't seem like I get a choice in the matter, now." Her tone alone could reverse global warming. "Given what the production assistants are saying about Belion's mood, this is going to be a hostile set, Will. If you need a break, there are lawn chairs out the side exit that are almost always empty." With that, Sonia leaves, carrying a plate of nothing but meat.

No matter where I go with my plate, the empty seats vanish as people claim to be saving them. I can't blame them, since being seen sitting with me could be taken for support, and I'm guessing Belion's assistants know I'm not his favorite person.

In the end, I follow Sonia's advice and sit outside. The lawn chairs are so hot they burn, but the heat is nice. There's a gentle breeze bringing in the chemical stench of spray foam, and a bunch of actors are dressed as a marching band. Given how they play, they should stick to acting. I scoot a chair under a palm tree planted in a plastic trash-can on wheels, devour my chemical-flavored lunch, and relax. The shade feels nice, and at least I can hear if someone shouts that it's time to assemble for scene setup.

But I'm not completely alone. After several moments, I notice the man in the wheelchair sitting two palm trees over. He wears an oxygen mask and what I think was once a fine silk suit, and is probably in costume for the orcs-versus-mafia movie being filmed one soundstage over.

He glances my way and nods.

I return the favor.

That's all the conversation either of us needs or wants, and as soon as I'm done with lunch, I brush myself off and head back inside to wait. When the camera men begin to assemble, I'm there—except, I can't find Aaron.

"Where is my second crew?" asks a voice that makes my skin crawl. Belion. He's standing near the camera, tapping his foot as he watches me.

I won't be anything less than professional, so I approach, but keep silent.

"Good, good," he says. "I am thinking, we will be working together so much. The problems we have been having have been because I did not personally handle important details."

I'm not often physically afraid, but any sane man would recognize that Belion can make my life difficult. Still, every minute he spends making my life difficult is a minute he isn't making someone else miserable. Someone like Sonia.

So we do a dance of sorts, where Belion tells me to move to a spot, and I do it, and he tells me I've done it wrong. The first hour it's frustrating. The second, it's annoying. The third hour, I've grown immune to his rants—and the fussy way he pulls at his goatee says he can tell.

Near four p.m, I get my first chance to bend over and stretch when Felicia steps in for a word with Belion. "We've shot the entire church sequence. Are you ready here?"

"Yes, yes," says Belion. "Bring in first crew."

No reference to how we've wasted half a day on the same scene, which isn't even shot yet.

While Belion gives James final directions, Felicia pulls me aside. "How are you holding up?"

I lean back, attempting to remove the crick in my back without dislocating my spine. "This is worse than yesterday. We haven't done anything but practice sitting on the fence in different poses. It's been four hours, and there's a permanent crease across my butt. It's a disaster."

Felica taps her tablet for emphasis. "No, it's perfect. With Belion preoccupied with taking out his rage on you, I've gotten more filmed today than we did in the previous week. That's going to make our favorite producer very happy." Felicia whacks me on the back hard enough to make a rib pop. "Chin up. Belion's got zero attention span. He'll get bored after a while, and move on to punishing someone else." She pushes me gently toward the chairs, but I won't be able to see the monitors from there.

"Felicia," says Belion, "You will handle this shot now that I have prepared everything. I have something planned which requires William."

The slightest pangs of unease twist their way into my shoulders as I fight to keep the crazy scenarios in my head at bay. He can't have me executed. He can't *harm* me.

I hope.

Felicia gives me a behind-the-back thumbs-up and salutes Belion. "I'm on it. Will, you are *so* lucky to get to work with our extremely talented director."

Belion presses his hands together as if accepting the greatest compliment of his life, then plods away, glancing back to make sure I'm following. "William," he says as we pass the front door set, "this is my life you are seeing. This is my kingdom. My crown."

His kingdom is half-finished, totally fake, and would fall over if someone so much as breathed on it wrong. "I believe that."

"You have come into my kingdom and brought disrespect for the very art we practice."

I know about art, too. My wood carvings are every bit as much art, just a different form.

"It is unfortunate, this misunderstanding between Edward and I, that leaves you trapped in this job. But I have spoken with him at lunch, and it turns out there is still a way for me to be rid of you. If you quit of your own choice, then Edward will only be displeased with you, not I." Belion stops and looks my way with a sly smile. "Do you understand?"

"Better than you think." I make a point of tilting my head down to emphasize my height. "I was listening to that call. I'm not the one trapped, you're the one stuck with me. And I'll do a good job, no matter what you throw at me. I take pride in that."

"Do you?" asks Belion. "Before, you were a lowly carpenter. Now you are an actor. I will expect of you what I expect from all my actors. No more, not one bit less."

We've circled the soundstage, following a trail marked out in yellow warning tape, passing the row of half-built bathrooms and heading down the center aisle from which other sets branch off. In one corner, set carpenters are using torches to give a fireplace realistic soot marks, and making the whole area smell like burning pine in the process. Belion hums as their torches roar, and with each moment, my trepidation rises.

"I make it a point to know my actors, and I have learned so much about you. It is good that we are going to communicate now," says Belion. "I admit, you brought me shame with your tirade. People mocking my art, my passion. Wine was my only consolation."

"Right." My attention's more focused on Sonia, who stands near Kantina, pointing out marks on the floor.

"Let us see how it feels when you are the one being mocked, William. You see, I found the production assistant who uploaded that video, and I have explained to him in detail how I am not angry with him. No. In fact, he is going to do me a favor, in return for forgiveness." Belion points to the set. "Now, let us prepare to film."

Only now do I notice the additional chairs drawn up behind the cameras. The production assistants lined up.

"Have you dreamed of fame?" asks Belion.

I'm more of a backstage person, myself. "Other people can have the spotlight, I don't think I really deserve it."

"False modesty is no better than naked ambition. Today, you have no choice." Belion holds out one arm, in a sweeping line. "William, I have brought each of our production assistants. They will be studying our work this afternoon and evening to help us. They will be listening, and watching our every word. Recording it all. Every mistake. Every miscue. Tonight, you will be the punchline."

I've always been a perfectionist, convinced I can do things right, certain that the right way to do something is the only way to do it. It started when we were children, and I was convinced that if I was perfect, my parents would return. Then, if I was the best, someone would adopt my brother and me. It carried through when I turned eighteen and took custody of Bradley.

I built a career on quality and pride in a job done right. The idea of taking my failures and packaging them up for someone's amusement makes me want to vomit. Fear that claws its way into my stomach without so much as saying hello. The absolute certainty that this can only end badly.

Belion gives me a wicked smile as he opens his arms toward the set. "Tell me again, who is trapped here, William?"

CHAPTER EIGHT

THEY'RE WAITING FOR ME ON SET, WAITING TO FILM ME making mistakes and share them with the world. I have to take my position, but I can't remember how to move.

I'm lost somewhere in my head, attempting to figure out how a job standing became a job moving, then speaking—and now, getting one chance to nail the shot. Of course, if I blow it, they'll probably pick the worst take to share.

Fear isn't a rational thing, it's a beast that sinks into you and doesn't let go.

My feet are a thousand miles away, walking me to first position, and all I can think about is how I must sound, how I must look. What's going to happen when—not if— I make a mistake. It's either freezing in here, or I'm burning up under the lights, or maybe it's both.

My heart begins to pound in my chest like a debt collector at my front door. Fear arrives as a tingle that begins in my fingers and rises up my arms, constricting each breath. Then fear is joined by panic that makes it hard to understand what anyone's saying or doing. Sure, they're talking, but what they're saying can't break through the voice inside me that says, *If you aren't perfect, you'll be separated.* When I was a child, it was from my parents. Then from my brother. I might be an adult now, but the fear still lurks.

"Look at me. Open your eyes and look at me, now." That's Sonia's voice, and for one brief moment, I pierce the panic's hold—and she's staring at me, her lips pursed. "It's just stage fright, Will. Don't look around, don't think, just breathe."

"First positions," says Belion, and I shuffle mindlessly to my spot on the marker. I need to think about anything except the inevitable. If I quit, Eddie goes after Bradley's business. If I stay, I'm abandoning the principle that's always been my guide.

Aaron calls for adjustments to the lights, while I focus on breathing.

"It is good," says Belion after making no discernible changes. "Second positions."

I don't remember what second position is, until Sonia glances down with a slight nod—and I see my marks. Two steps forward. Two steps closer.

"Ready for lighting transition," says Belion. "Run it."

A light I hadn't noticed, one on a track, winks on, then shifts to the right. For a brief moment, it makes me forget there's a dozen people watching.

"Do not move your head!" Belion shouts. "Do not move at all. Do not speak, except for the lines I have given you. The language of creation."

The problem is, I don't remember any lines. I can feel each and every gaze on me.

There's a reason my workshop in Seattle was closed-door, why I never let anyone see my work until it was polished and perfect. Where before I thought the set was spaced out, now the half-wall behind seems to close in on me, and the camera might as well be an inch from my face, leaving me no room to even take a breath. What Sonia calls stage fright has become stage terror, and if the ache in my chest says anything, it's that it will soon enough progress to stage petrification.

"Ready for second transition," says Aaron. "The candle's coming back, and we need to be able to see her face. Sonia, go."

"You think me a fool?" asks Sonia. "That I cannot see what is happening? Your subtle plot, your plan to make me flee? You should flee."

"Nope," Aaron says. "That looks horrible. Belion, do we need to change angles?"

Belion circles the set, smiling as he looks at me. "No, no, bring it in closer, and Sonia, you will turn your head like so—ah, there. Light and dark, the audience will see them both in Kantina's face."

He clears the set and nods. "Again with the effect."

And again.

And again, until at last the two agree. Belion sits back in his chair, like he's bored. "From her last line, lighting at full. Sonia, you will make certain my Kantina knows all that is required. Now, let us focus on William."

"Of course." Sonia looks back to me, and this time, I catch that moment where she shifts, changes, and becomes—well, someone else. "You should flee."

I would, if I could remember how my feet work. This is the point where I'm supposed to speak, I get that. What I don't get is exactly how I'm supposed to know my lines— or how my lips are supposed to function with everyone watching, waiting for me to make a mistake. *Say something,* screams one urge inside me. *Get it right or don't do it at all,* says my life's experience.

"Again!" Belion practically screams. "It is an easy line, is it not? While she is in shadow, you begin the speech with, 'I do not wish to flee. The Lord of the Manor is not so easily broken.' Again."

This time, I manage to mumble the first part. Only after Belion holds up his hand does my tongue loosen enough for me to speak a few more words under my breath that are much more recognizable. Everyone makes mistakes, I get that. But I make mine in private, where I can practice, get better, and then present to the world a Will people might like.

"Hold," says Belion. "Assistants, if you will, can you identify what is wrong?"

"He didn't project," says one.

"He didn't look in the right place," adds another.

"Or say any of the right lines."

Each is a gut-punch to my pride, to the part of me that says, *If you were better, Mom and Dad wouldn't have left. If you were smarter, you'd have recognized Tamara was fake.*

But I have to pay the bills she left behind. I have to keep Bradley's business safe. Which means I have to endure.

Belion paces back and forth, pulling at his beard like he can make it grow by doing so. "And the lighting is timed to my masterful dialogue. But we are understanding, are we not? We will simply repeat until we get it right. Each of you pay attention to William's every action, and help him make it right."

Now I know what it's like to have every shred of dignity scraped away.

On the fifth time through, I manage to speak enough of the lines to get Belion ranting about how I've mangled his dialogue. I can hear the words in my head, but every time I go to speak, there's a loop of realizing I've already ruined the shot, and in the time it takes for that, I've done it again.

Shot after shot, failure after failure blends together. I don't really snap out of the haze until Felicia drops by interrupting to shout, "One more time through, then we're wrapping for the day. I'll have scene sheets by production."

I've almost made it.

"Again." Belion isn't even looking. He hasn't changed a light-bulb or adjusted a shadow in a dozen takes. Even his production assistants aren't watching. They're all playing with their phones or dozing, except for the one closest to Belion, who's been taking notes the whole time.

"You should flee," says Sonia without feeling.

The light flickers by, though I couldn't care less.

"The Lord of the Manor..." I can't bring myself to finish. "Really, really needs to rest."

It's at that moment that movement off camera catches my eye. Belion has sat up in his chair, and in his hands, he hold a cellphone. "That will do nicely," he says as he types.

One by one, the crew slip away—but not Belion. He waits, tapping his phone. "According to the website of a business you once ran, you take pride in what you do, William. In the quality of your work. Tonight, everyone who laughed as you berated me will see the truth about you. Tomorrow, you are the mockery."

Dad used to say that you could tell what kind a person a man was by how well he did his work. I don't even want to think about what this says about me. The thought of people watching me make one mistake after another is almost enough to make me ill. "I'm going home."

"This is wise. In the morning, we must film a great scene, William. It is the Master of the Manor's speech to his servant. Your website says you are a master craftsman, but I wonder, is this how you want the world to know you? If you were to fall ill, it would be no one's fault." He pauses, watching to see if I'll bite, before handing me a notepad filled with incomprehensible scribbling. "If you must come, I hope you will at least come prepared. This was truly sad."

I'm prepared, all right. Prepared to break his nose. But the resulting mess might break my bank account, and honestly, I'm already broke.

So instead I slink away, exchanging my costume for sympathetic glances, and waiting in Central Holding for the ride I booked to pick me up. Judging from the traffic alerts, I'll be here a while. A worn leather couch disgraces the back of the square, and I lay back on it and close my eyes for what feels like a blink.

"Hey, Will."

I look up to find Sonia standing there, out of makeup, and dressed in a short-sleeve aqua shirt and matching shorts. If it were anyone else, my tongue would cooperate, but it's her, so all I can manage is a weak, "Hey, yourself."

"You didn't pick up your scene list from Felicia. Also, I nabbed a current copy of the script."

I take them from her, letting our hands touch one more time, and nod. "I've got good news and bad news. The good news is you won't have to worry about protecting your reputation while associating with someone who knows a financer. The bad news is, I'm not feeling well. Probably going to call in sick. I'm fairly sure I'll be able to get *those* words out. Stage fright doesn't happen over the phone, right?"

Sonia shrugs. "Some days this job is rough. What did Belion mean about your reputation? You're a set carpenter."

I slip out my phone and pull up the website, the last vestiges of my business. There are pictures of my work, videos from different galleries, and, oh yes, my poorly-thought-out claims about being a master artist.

"These are beautiful." She flicks through the pages. "Seriously, K would love the dancing woman. How long did that take?"

"Sixteen months. It was single piece of drift wood. I spent half that time polishing it alone." If I were doing it over, perhaps the face would be slimmer, like Sonia's, or the chin more pointed, like hers, and the hair would cascade down past her shoulders.

"I can't imagine spending that long on one piece."

"I can't imagine not. I don't want people judging a piece until it's done. Until every knot and bump is carved and smoothed, until every grain matches how I dream of it. That's what I've always done—until today."

I sit up, because the weight of failure on my chest is suffocating.

"Stage fright passes." She sits down on the leather couch, just close enough that I'm uncomfortable, but not so close I think she's coming on to me. "Funny, I didn't figure you for the kind to give up."

My phone buzzes, and after reading it, I can't help but laugh, because the alternative is to cry. "That's my brother. Apparently the same person who uploaded the video of me tearing up Belion just added an 'acting fails' video staring all my failed attempts at delivering a single line, mixed with the video from my website about how I pay attention to detail and quality." If this is being famous, then famous feels like being rolled in dog turds, as best as I can tell. "If I can't do something right, I don't do it—"

"Don't quit." Sonia's squared her shoulders toward me, her arms crossed.

"I'm a good carpenter. I'm a great wood carver, and I'm a lousy actor. There's no harm in understanding what you're good at and sticking to it."

"Yes, stick to it." Her eyes widen, and she beams me a smile I can't look away from, even though I can tell what's coming is a pitch. "Stick to being a stand in, and if you don't like how you did today, then *do better*. Standing in is harder work than people realize. We run the lines. We check the blocking. We do the grunt work so the principals can make the money shots." She puts her head back and sighs. "And some days, it just sucks. But we still get it done."

I lean on the couch and stare at the ceiling. "Belion suggested that if I were sick, Eddie wouldn't be able to complain about replacing me. I think I'm coming down with something. If I could manage to get a line out, I might have a prayer, but not with him yelling and everyone staring and recording. You know, Felicia promised me this job was just standing there."

Sonia laughs and scoots over to lean against me.

I freeze, holding in the breath I'd taken, as her arm brushes mine.

"Let me share a secret about Hollywood with you." She looks me straight in the eyes as she speaks slowly. "Promises that aren't in writing are worth less than toilet paper, and 'trust me' is how you spell 'screw you.'"

"If it's always changing, how do you do this job every day?"

"Filming isn't always like this." She takes my hand and gives it a squeeze that gives me goosebumps. "Belion isn't normally involved in every shot. He's only doing it because Eddie's using you to put him in his place and he's pissed."

I'm speechless for a moment, but only because I want to savor this feeling. She's holding my hand, and for something so simple it feels like I'm being launched into orbit. I'd rather stay in this moment, but I have to be honest. "Your producer threatened to blackball my brother, but I'm going to call him up and beg him to let me quit. I'll apologize. I'll promise to never set foot on the lot again. I may be a pitiful actor, but I have life experience as the role of 'man who bit off more than he can chew.' I think I can sell it." I hold up my lanyard and hand it to her. "Speaking of Bradley, wait until he finds out what it's really like on this set. That will be enlightening."

"Don't." Sonia stands up and looks around, her face clouded with worry. "Do you not understand? Eddie's got half a mind to shut us down anyway. Your brother makes a call, and the other investors will revolt. If that happens, Eddie's not going to let bygones be bygones."

"So I just come back and let Belion continue to burn what's left of my pride to ashes?"

She studies the concrete as she answers. "I'm sorry you're caught up in this, but you don't have a choice either."

I think I've spotted a flaw in her argument, probably there because she's trying to encourage me. "Explain something to me? If Eddie wants to make money, why would he shut down production on a movie?"

"This is Hollywood, and Hollywood accounting almost breaks the laws of mathematics. The hard way to make money off of movies is by making a good one." Her voice gains volume and strength as she speaks. "The easy way to make money is to lose money on another film. The studio can write off the losses and wipe out the tax on the movies that succeed."

"So Eddie means for this movie to fail?"

Sonia gives a half-hearted shrug. "No, but if it does? He'll not only break even, he'll come out smelling like roses. Surely you've seen movies and you have no idea why anyone agreed to make them, right?"

"*House of Party Freaks Five: Return of the Freaks*," I say. "Bradley and I loved the first two. After that... not so great."

"They're producing another sequel," says Sonia. "Even though the last two didn't make a dime in the conventional sense. So yes, Eddie would shut us down. I know about wanting to do the best job you can. I know more about embarrassing videos than you would believe. But you have to come back."

She's so certain. I wish I shared a fraction of her confidence. "I'll think about it tonight. I have to talk it over with Bradley, though. I'm sorry, but he needs to know."

Whatever answer Sonia wanted, that wasn't it; she stands and stalks away like a woman on a mission.

According to the app, my ride is still an eternity away—but I can waste a few of the minutes walking to the front gate.

I fade into a crowd of extras and actors, just men and women going home from their jobs, and follow the flow toward the front gate.

But as I approach, a golf cart wheels up and cuts me off.

Sonia gets out and blocks my way. "Trust me, you want to take a ride."

Though I told her I'd think about it, what I want most is to go back to carving staircase bannisters in a quiet shop, in the company of people I know and love.

Then I look at Sonia, waiting behind the cart wheel. The part of me that wants to leave this madness behind can't compete with the part of me that wants to be sitting beside her, even if it's on a Hollywood lot instead of a picnic at the beach. I climb onto the cart, and she wheels it around like an expert, dodging people as she drives us back all the way to Soundstage 52. This time, however, she wheels past the entrance to the soundstage, and turns at the back. There, a full-length travel trailer waits, with lights on.

"Come." Sonia pulls at my hand, and lures me one step at a time, until she opens the door, and I follow her inside.

The interior is exactly what I imagined a star's trailer would look like. The walls have glitzy silver wallpaper, the lighting is soft amber, and there's a full kitchen—with a chef cooking—across the room.

Sitting in a walnut rocking chair is the queen of entertainment herself, Kantina. "William," she says. Unlike when Belion calls me that, it's less derision and more precision. Like calling me 'Will' wouldn't aim her words or her gaze closely enough.

"Ma'am?"

She rises, the yellow knit dress she's wearing complementing the dark tan of her skin. "Sonia told me much about today's filming."

"She tell you Belion recorded every mistake I made? Or that he posted the video on the internet?"

"Yes, darling. She told me all of this. I am so sorry."

Sonia makes herself at home, picking through the cabinet and coming out with a box of cookies, which she proceeds to eat while sitting on Kantina's white couch. All I can think of is how she'd never get the chocolate chip stains out.

"I remember my first day of filming," says Kantina. "I was terrified."

"Sure you were." I stifle the snort because it's rude, but I know better than to believe what she's feeding me. "Supermodel? Singer? Afraid?"

"Now." She tilts her head side to side. "Then, I was a young woman of nineteen, fortunate to have a contract for three movies when most had none. But knowing I wanted to act and doing so were different. I could barely bring myself to speak for fear of what I would do wrong."

"Like me?" Something fails the sniff test about this story.

"No," says Kantina. "I was never as awful as you were today. But, I have something for you that may help."

She goes to a bookshelf, and from a collection of geodes, picks up something dark green. When she returns, she holds out her hand. "Take this."

It's no magic feather, though I could use one of those. Instead, it's a stone frog, jade from the looks of it, and it's old, scratched and chipped. "Can I fly if I hold it?"

"I do not suggest jumping off a building to find out. Instead, perhaps you could do as I did, and carry it in your pocket," says Kantina. "When the fear rose within me, I would squeeze it. The discomfort helped break the cycle of worry. It helped ground me, to focus on where I was rather than what might be."

The darn thing *is* sharp in places, painful almost. I still might not be able to deliver the lines, but at least I wouldn't be able to sink into a cycle in my head. "Thank you, but I'm not sure I'll need it."

"You wanted my autograph for your brother, did you not?" The way she has her head cocked, she knows my answer as well as I do.

"Yes. You can keep the frog, I'll take the signature."

"I think we are not nearly so familiar as that," says Kantina. "But he is the fan, is he not?"

"Totally."

"Ah. And I know that Edward is using this movie to educate him on the finer points of contracts. Did you know your brother did not even think to ask for a seat at the premier?"

"I doubt that. He's funding a huge chunk—"

"And failed to be specific. Do not doubt Edward sees this as a teaching moment, that an investor must make their demands clear." Kantina nods to Sonia in some secret agreement. "I take it your brother has never been to a movie premier? Walked the carpet? Been first to see a new work enter the world?"

"You take it right." But I see where she's going. "You can arrange that? Bradley's probably kicking himself over not demanding tickets, and Tia might just be a bigger fan than he is."

"Stay through principal filming," says Kantina. "Do not quit, and I promise you will both be my guests at the premier. I do not break my promises, William."

I look back to Sonia, who's stalking the last cookie in the tray like a lion on the Serengeti. "Sonia? You willing to work with me?"

"Work, yes," she says. "I'm sorry about earlier, Will. Felicia gave me some good advice and helped set me straight."

"Indeed," says Kantina. "She said, 'Put an ice-cube in your panties and do your job.'"

Sonia stops, mouth still wide open.

I can't stand to wallow in her embarrassment, so I return my gaze to Kantina, even though her eyes are so wide it's downright creepy.

Premier seats. There are few things I think Bradley will love more. Today's been awful, but I want the money for myself. I want the experience for my brother. I want to watch my brother and his wife gawking at the premier. Also, it would be nice if my mistakes didn't totally destroy his business. "I suppose the video is already out. Can't get much worse, can it?"

"Darling, when I was on tour in France, I became ill, and vomited into a man's lap while we were filming a music video. My sickness has more views than my most recent single." Kantina holds up both palms in a what-else-can-you-do gesture. "It will pass. In a few days, your name will be forgotten, if that's what you desire."

"Can I count on seeing you?" Sonia speaks up as she tosses aside the empty cookie package. "I don't want to train someone new, Nine, and I—" She shifts her hands restlessly. "I like having you around. The only thing you need to ask yourself is, 'Can I do one more day?'"

It's not so much Belion I'm up against, it's myself, my fear, and I want to believe I can find a way to make it through. For money. For my brother. For the chance to see if Sonia and I have something going or not, I answer. "I can."

CHAPTER NINE

WHEN I GET HOME THAT NIGHT, BRADLEY'S WIFE, TIA, GIVES me a sympathetic pat on the back before she locks and re-locks the door. They've watched and re-watched the video of me failing for the last hour. There's even a speak-along segment where the viewer can root for how far I make it before messing up. Bradley shared it on his profile and tagged me in it, so the few friends I have can see my failure. Not that I have many friends—most of them were Tamara's, and after I posted a picture of the warrant for her arrest, her mom and dad dropped me.

"Will!" Bradly shouts, standing up and rushing to meet me. "Come in. We're about to take a family picture."

"Fine. Afterwards, you and I need to talk." I decided on the way home it's not fair for me to keep Eddie's threats a secret when it's my family's money and business on the line. I stand to one side, and we both put one arm over Tia, while she snaps a picture with a selfie stick. She waits for the Polaroid to develop, shaking it dry, and then turns it over and writes the date, time, and names. When it's finished, she hands it over. "What do you think?"

"I look good. My brother could use a shave. You are gorgeous as always." I turn the picture over to read her caption. *Will Mathis. Bradley Mathis. Tia Mathis. Not pictured—Baby Mathis.*

I glance to her belly, and then back as she smiles at me and says, "You're going to be an uncle!"

She's short, but the hug she wraps me in is strong enough to nearly crack my ribs. After I get my breath back, I pat my brother on the back. "Way to go. When?"

"February," says Tia. "Though my sisters were always late. Our little family is going to get a little bigger."

As they kiss, I look around the one-bedroom apartment and wonder how and where, and the logistics of this. Then it hits me that my brother is going to be a father. That he's going to have a baby to care for.

"What'd you want to talk about?" asks Bradley, his arm still wrapped around Tia's shoulder.

It no longer matters what people think about me. What matters isn't a what, it's a who: the people in this apartment, for whom I would walk through fire—or a film lot. My hands shake and my eyes sweat, as I draw them in for another hug. "It's nothing."

"Such a frown, Will," says Tia. "I'm the one giving birth."

"Just taking my responsibility as an uncle seriously." I put on a smile, one I hope hides the ice clawing at my stomach, and join them to celebrate with sparkling cider and pre-natal vitamins for all.

After we clear the dinner off, Tia taps the table. "Sit."

I join her, even though the way Bradley's squirming, this is going to be uncomfortable.

"Bradley and I did some digging," says Tia. "I knew I recognized the woman's voice on that first video. Bradley and I did some digging, and Will, I think there are things you need to know."

Bradley shifts in the chair as he pulls at his beard. "During the pre-production calls with the investors, I actually thought she was one of the directors. The woman wasn't just passionate, she was desperate to get this film made."

I listen in silence, uncertain of what to think, even less willing to contemplate the doubt and fear swirling inside. "Probably because she's Kantina's stand-in. Work for Kantina is work for Sonia."

"Don't get defensive." Tia waits for me to look toward her. "It was more than that, Will. I've listened to you mope about how it was your fault you didn't find out about Tamara sooner. I've listened to you talk about how all you wanted was someone real. And Will, as your sister-in-law, I have to tell you, I don't think you're seeing this clearly."

Bradley nods. "You didn't know how much I invested in the movie, but I guarantee you, she does. This woman pretends to feel things for a living, bro. It's her job, and she's good at it, or so I hear. You can't trust her."

"I didn't—I don't—" I can't. What they're saying makes sense in so many ways. I just don't want to believe it.

Tia gets up from the table and puts a hand on my shoulder before she leaves. "You know what the difference is between a good actress and a great actress?"

I shake my head.

Bradley takes Tia's hand as he speaks to me. "A good actress makes you believe she feels what she's acting. A great actress makes you believe she's not acting."

It's all I can keep in mind, until far past midnight. In the dark and cold morning hours, I can't deny the logic of what I've heard, which gives me no choice but to deny what I felt.

The next morning, I'm done getting slathered with makeup in record time and, according to my scene guide, ready for humiliation, since I'm supposed to deliver a rousing speech and I couldn't get two lines off yesterday. I see zero point in us being in this scene, since there's zero lighting changes, but a job is a job.

The jade frog rests in a cloth bag pinned inside my sweatpants. It rests against the side of my thigh, cool and sharp.

But when I arrive on set, Belion isn't waiting. People aren't cowering.

Sonia's waiting near Central Holding, and when she sees me, the smile on her face makes me giddy at the same time my stomach sinks. "Looks like someone decided they could do one more day."

Someone spent the entire night thinking about my brother, his wife, their business, and their soon-to-be baby. "I can do all the days."

"That's the attitude. We're filming on 518. Carpenters just put it together. It's a rowboat." Sonia snags my arm, holding until I look at her. "Can we talk?"

"Talk," I say, though I suspect it's not banter.

"About us."

Definitely not banter. "There's an 'us?'"

Sonia opens her mouth to speak several times—and each time stops, until, "When I thought we wouldn't be working together—I mean, when I didn't know who you were—"

I hold up a hand as an act of mercy, because she's saving me as much as herself. "It's fine. You and I can start over, just two co-workers, getting their jobs done." The sting inside feels like I just snapped a guitar-string in my soul. "No expectations, or need for apologies, no anything."

"Thanks, Will. See you on set," she says, her voice quiet—and she walks away.

I let her, though it's the last thing I want to do. Turns out, Sonia's not the only one who knows how to pretend.

There's no water around the row boat, which kills all the fun I imagined. There was no water at the bridge either, so I suppose I should have lowered my expectations, and for what it's worth, there actually *is* a complete rowboat, one that might once have seen water, before someone screwed it to the floor, so that's something.

Aaron's already at the set when I arrive and greets me with a nod. "How's our director's least favorite stand-in?"

"He's doing fine, thanks." I relax, leaning on a camera while I wait. "At least you're not avoiding me like his production assistants."

"Belion needs me, and I have to be able to talk to you to do my job. Go have a seat in the Titanic."

Sure enough, that's the name someone's stenciled on the back of a boat that's no more than five feet long. This whole production feels like a sinking ship, so I suppose it's appropriate.

"Wrong seat," Aaron says as I sit on the back. "If I have to get any of you on film, I want it to be the bits that are plausibly deniable as James Becton. Shoulder. Hair. Not even that if I can help it."

"Gee, thanks." I shift to the right so the nicked wooden side of the boat presses against my side.

He gives me a thumbs up, and then turns to the camera. Friendly Aaron disappears in that instant, replaced by pure-business Aaron, until he's sure he has the camera focus right. "Look at it this way. You get paid way more when I can't avoid having you on film."

That's something worth smiling about—until Sonia enters from the side. She's wearing a white dress that's more lace than actual fabric, with pale yellow shoulder straps and a skirt that blossoms out and whispers as she walks. "We ready?"

Aaron points to the boat. "You know the drill. Look away from him. Nine, eyes on her shoulder, chin up, keep your head off to the side like you broke your neck."

"Why?" I lay my head over.

"Because I want her face in frame, not the back of your head. It'll look right in the finished shot."

With my back to him, he can't see my face. So I let my tongue loll from the side of my mouth and roll my eyes backward.

Sonia glances my way—and bursts into laughter. "Oh, my God—"

"Don't move," Aaron bellows. "Eyes away, Sonia."

She turns her face back so the light catches her profile just perfect. "If you could see his face—"

"Flirt later," he shouts. "Film now."

"We're not flirting," Sonia and I say together, as though we practiced it.

"Are we ready?" Felicia's voice comes from behind me. "Or are these two flirting again?"

"Still," says Aaron. "And we're good to go. First crew, on set. Nine, don't you move a muscle."

Sonia hands me a copy of the script as she leaves the boat—and a moment later, Kantina takes her place. She smiles at me. "Good morning, William."

"Morning," I say, still not willing to look her in the face. It's the eyes, I'm telling you. Her pupils are always creepily large, like they're going to siphon out my soul.

Kantina films her scenes with absolute grace and effectiveness, nailing several on the first shot. My hair does its part, or at least, I think it does. Possibly part of my ear, too.

While Kantina films a shot of her standing on the shore, I watch the monitors.

Her hair really is a character of its own, given how much attention is paid to how it flows, flips, or hangs. As Sonia joins me off camera, I nod. "Her hair should get separate billing on the poster. 'Starring Kantina's Hair—and Kantina.'"

"Little hint. If you can't see Kantina's face on the poster, you're probably looking at *my* hair, since the darker tones adjust better and she's got better things to do with her time. And my hair is offended," she says, though her tone says otherwise. "Seriously, it's a chore to care for, and it's always in the way, but you *will* show proper respect for the hair."

"My apologies." I press my hands together and bow my head. "Forgive me, hair."

"Never." She swings the tail like a whip, striking me.

Her hair smells of sweet coconut. "That shampoo is delicious."

"I buy it by the case." Sonia takes a seat and pats the one beside her as Kantina does yet another take at what the script calls a monologue and I call a rant. She's whipped herself into a fury that leaves me amazed she's not ranting to someone.

"Is this what working on movies is usually like?"

"Sometimes. There's always an asshole on set, but when it's the director, it gets worse. And believe me, when someone gets on Felicia's bad side, she can be one too."

"I prefer the term 'boss-bitch,'" says Felicia without looking back at us. "The boom mics are picking up every word you two say. Unless you want your flirting broadcast to the entire crew, pick some other time and place to do it."

"I'm not flirting." Sonia turns away, her cheeks made even redder by the light from her hair.

"Me either," I say, more as a reminder to myself of what a bad idea this is. Flirting doesn't hurt people, and if both people are interested, it's fun. But what comes after flirting can leave a trail of wreckage. Businesses. Hearts. Lives.

"Nine, head to the bedroom set, you're needed," says Felicia. "Sit across from her, read your lines."

At the thought of reading the lines, my throat constricts—but I press against that stupid frog until it digs into my thigh and find the right spot in the script.

I follow Sonia back to the now-repaired bedroom, and consult the script. "I didn't know James was in this scene."

"James Becton isn't even in the state, which accounts for some of my good mood this morning." Felicia points to a line. "Welcome to your roll as 'meddlesome mother-in-law.' Sonia, you're filling in for Father Joseph."

"Ready. Don't need the pages." Sonia takes a place on the set, just out of camera view.

Kantina's sitting on the edge of a bed—the same set I broke earlier—and brushing her hair.

"Will, kick it off. Steph, I want clicks when his line ends and Kantina, you go from there. We'll splice and dice." Felicia waves. "Roll cameras, and action."

"What do you know?" I say. "The love of a woman springs from the heart, from a well no man has seen, but they taste and come back eternally."

Sonia shakes her head. "Nonsense. It is from a mind quickened, a hand held, a breast warmed."

Someone clacks a piece of plastic, and Kantina's eyes go from unfocused to laser sharp. "My mind was already quick before he came. If there's a well in my heart, it is mine to drink from alone, I—"

"Cut." Felicia shouts. "K, you missed a word. 'There *is*.' You know how Belion is about the dialogue."

Kantina frowns. "I am sorry. I was lost in her, but I will not make the same mistake again."

I wipe my mouth on my sleeve to get the taste of the dialogue out of my mouth. With Belion absent, I can risk a question that's been brewing for a bit. "What does he do to get in the mood to write this? Hit himself with a frying pan?"

"Probably." Sonia stifles a laugh. "You *never* change what he's written. Ever."

"You two can improvise." Felicia gives us a wave. "I don't care what you say, I'm going to cut you out anyway. You can recite lines from *Pretty Woman*, for all I care."

"I don't want to distract," I say. "I'm ready."

Sonia holds out a hand. "Distract? Kantina? I'll bet you dinner you can't make her break character. She's in her own world when she's filming."

"You're on." I might have to borrow money from Bradley to pay for dinner if I lose, so I won't lose. I wait until Felicia calls for action, and lay it down. "You want to know where love comes from? A bottle. Two people get drunk at the same bar, have a good time, and bond over hangovers."

Sonia pauses, as her eyes grow wide. "Bull. Love develops because two people share common interest. Love is like—"

"My mind was already quick before he came." Kantina's not even aware of our conversation, far as I can tell. "If there is a well in my heart, it is mine to drink from alone. I will guard it. "

According to the script, my next line is supposed to be about how love creeps in like the shadows, how it rises like the tide. "You want to know what it's like? It's like two people who say they love each other. Then one day, one of them comes home and there's cops waiting. And there's questions. And there's empty rooms in the apartment and empty places in my—their soul."

Kantina twists to look at me. "But Mother, what will the Church say of this?"

Sonia doesn't even bother looking at Kantina as she answers. "No, love is a series of relationships where you commit yourself and find out you were just a sad substitute for the one they really wanted. Every time you swear you won't do it again, and every time you figure out too late that you dove in head first again. One day, you realize it's never going to happen."

"Exactly." I'm not sure if Kantina had a line here, but I couldn't agree more. "You get smarter. You carry a stick and you keep an eye out, and if Cupid so much as pops up over a hedge, you whack him like a piñata."

"Perfect," says Sonia, offering me a high-five.

Honesty gives me freedom, lifting the weight from my shoulders and making the world seem brighter as I put a pin on what exactly went wrong, and how I can avoid it again. "Next time? Next relationship? It'll be something I enter with my eyes open. When I'm dead certain I know exactly who I'm getting involved with. When I'm sure I'm not falling for an act. It'll be an agreement. A decision."

Sonia nods as she gives Kantina a smug smile. "Exactly as it should be. I couldn't say it better myself."

"You are both fools," says Kantina, glaring at each of us in a way I don't see noted in the script. "These are the desperate proclamations of wounded hearts, but the way to heal is not to stop loving. You cannot believe this, William. And Sonia, I have known you far too long to accept such nonsense."

That makes me stop.

Do I believe it? Do I really think I can steer my heart away from the rocks? Would I, if I could? "Look," I say, holding up both hands in my defense, "I'm not saying—"

"Cut!" shouts Felicia. "Kantina, what was that? And Will, Sonia, when I said you could ad lib, I didn't mean you could improv a group therapy session. Screw it. Let's wrap for lunch. I need to process and edit."

"You owe me dinner," Sonia and I say at the same time.

"I'm the one—" We stop together.

"Call it a draw?" asks Sonia.

Kantina rises, ties her hair back, and sweeps away after giving me the evil eye.

I can't hold back a shudder, because when a woman looks at you like that, it's trouble. "She's pissed."

"No," says Sonia. "I've seen that look before. She's plotting."

"Can you talk her into leaving me out of her plots?"

Sonia shakes her head as she follows after Kantina. "I can't even talk her into leaving *me* out. You don't have a prayer."

At lunch, I could probably find someplace to eat, but I wouldn't get to nod to Mr. Wheelchair, or watch people go by wearing the weirdest costumes.

As I sit down, he rolls a few feet out to make sure it's me, and nods.

Mission accomplished, I tear into my sandwich.

"You know what I like about you?"

His question comes out of the blue, and my mouth is full of sandwich, so I simply shake my head.

"You seem to be learning. For instance, you're doing a better job at keeping your mouth shut." He rolls back and continues watching the bustle of the lot.

"Thanks." I return to eating—until I realize he's still staring. "Can I help you?"

"You could introduce yourself."

"I could, but you just said the thing you liked was that I didn't talk." I wipe my mouth on my sleeve, leaving a mustard stain on the brown cloth.

"True." He nods to himself. "But now that I've indicated I'm interested in conversation, the polite thing to do is talk. Don't they teach manners anymore? Though I suppose it's not that important that you introduce yourself, since I already know who you are."

Of course he does. I stand up and scoot my chair over so we can share the shade of a single trash-palm. "I do have a reputation. Let me guess. You saw the videos on the internet?"

"Loved every second of both. Someone really doesn't like you, and I know a thing or two about that. So, William Mathis, it's good to meet you in person." He offers me a handshake, and his hands are bony but surprisingly strong.

"So, like you said, I'm William Mathis, but I just go by Will. You're Wheelchair Guy. At least, that's what I've been calling you."

That makes him laugh so hard he takes a breath from the oxygen tube, then puts one hand on his chest. "What? You thought this was a prop?"

"Everything is fake in this town."

"You seem real enough," he answers. "Not too bright, but real. You know my name, Will. We've talked. On the phone."

"Phone?" I don't have mine, but if I did, there's a name I'd be searching for, a picture I'd need.

He answers, his voice a deep southern drawl. "Glad to meet you, partner. My name's Eddie. Eddie Gellar. I'm your producer, and depending on how you look at it, guardian angel, or worst nightmare."

CHAPTER TEN

Eddie Gellar is Wheelchair Guy, who apparently really does use a wheelchair. The way he hunches makes his nose look longer and overgrown eyebrows bushier, and he gives me a wild grin. "Surprise!"

I am. My mind spins as I attempt to chart a course out of this disaster. All I can think is that Felicia, Ms. Assistant-Director-On-A-Mission, is *scared* of this guy. So I swallow to unglue my tongue from my mouth, wipe my sweaty palms on my pants, and give him the least aggressive response I can think of. "You want some of my sandwich?"

"Nah." He leans back. "I can't have white bread, according to my doctors. Bad for my health." He points to the oxygen canister. "You know what else is bad for my health? Being old."

"Sir, if this is about the job, I promise I'm doing it. My brother—"

"What?" He tilts his head and looks at me sideways. "Oh… Right. I don't watch over production, boy, though I did deliver some bad news myself earlier. Now, I'm just remembering what it's like to be an actor again. That's *all* I'm doing."

"Sorry." I go back to my chips, and check my phone twice to make sure I'm not late. And also to see how early it will be safe to leave.

"So, how is it going on set?"

"What?" I turn to him, trying to stifle the annoyance. "You *just* said you don't want to—oh, and now you do?"

Eddie's eyes twinkle as he answers. "You catch on quick. I don't want you bringing it up, but if I did, it would be rude not to answer my questions. You're not in a position to have bad manners. So?"

"I don't know what happened before I showed up on set, but this? It's a disaster. The director, Belion—"

"I know who he is, kid. Now, dish."

"Belion has the most ridiculous rules ever. We're not supposed to talk on set unless we're saying lines or a director gives us permission. James Becton is an asshole who blames other people for his mistakes, and I swear Sonia will kick him in the nuts if he gets too close. The assistant director's going to either have a stroke or a heart attack, and half the time, I'm not sure Kantina lives on the same planet the rest of us do."

Eddie puts his hand to his chin and thinks. "Everything sounds normal to me. Continue."

"What else is there to say? It's your business, you said on the phone. Why on earth would you let them behave like this?"

Eddie's eyes wrinkle as he smiles at me. "Because this whole industry is hoping lightning strikes. And when you get Belion, James and Kantina together, lightning strikes more often than not. I don't know if it's because they want to kill each other or screw each other, but I don't care as long as the films keep raking in the cash."

That was the best of my dirt and it didn't even phase Eddie, so I follow it up with the only thing I have left. "Belion hates me."

He nods. "He sure does, on account of me keeping you around just to twist his nuts. That man really can't stand you."

I glance at my watch. "I should get back on set."

"Boy, are you trying to avoid me?" He raises an eyebrow, daring me to answer wrong.

"Yes. You're the most connected producer I know of. Not the biggest name, but Bradley says you talk and people listen. And speaking of Bradley, you threatened—"

"Promised. A threat is something you might do. A promise, you keep."

That's not better. In fact, it's worse on most levels, but I can use his terms. "You promised to run him out of business if I quit. Why?"

"Keeps you motivated, doesn't it? Hey, you want some free advice?"

I shrug. "Everyone seems to have it. Why not?"

He holds up a hand and counts off three fingers. "The number one person you do not piss off is the assistant director. If Felicia pulls this movie off, she's going to be sitting in the big seat next time. Second, James and Kantina are too big to care about Belion's attitude. Kiss up to both. If they tell you to read lines, you read them. They say go mini-golfing, you best putt on over there. If they say put on a duck mask—"

"I'll quack."

That brings a wide grin, one that shows every last one of his perfect, white teeth. "The friendlier you are with them, the easier your life on set will be. Now, I know what it's like to be hated by a director, and it's ten times worse if you can't get away from him. I'm going to make a call, and you, you're going to keep your mouth shut, which I suspect you know you'd better do."

"Yes, sir."

"Cut that out," he barks. "I get too much of it already. Now, you better get on in and get ready. Oh, and Will, my third piece of advice? Not an order, just a thought. You know how Kantina feels about that woman she works with, I forget her name."

"Sonia." Like anyone could ever forget. From the way he nods, I suspect he didn't either.

"That's her! Yeah, I think if you hurt or offended Kantina, she'd be a professional. She'd work with you perfectly well, do her job. But you hurt her friend? If you're lucky, she'll knock out a few of your teeth like she did a few years ago. If you're unlucky, you might be found in the desert, buried up to your neck. That is, assuming you were ever found at all." He waves to the door. "My lunch is over, so your lunch is over. Exit stage left, son."

I want to, but not before I have an answer. "What makes you think Sonia and I—"

"Call it a hunch. I listen to production tapes at night, watch the feeds when I can't sleep. You'd be surprised how often some camera's pointed the wrong way and picks up stuff meant to be off screen. We get it all sorted out, but based on what I saw, I was thinking—"

I should be watching my tone, but he's hit a nerve, one I need the anger to deaden. "I don't care what you saw or heard, there's nothing going on between us. First of all, I'm not dumb enough to fall for an actress who knows how to manipulate me, and even if I was, Sonia's not interested in a relationship with me either."

"Huh," says Eddie as I walk away. "I wonder if anyone told her that."

Eddie's comment rankles, but I really do need to get back to work.

Sonia was very clear about how she felt. If he's suggesting she really is attracted to me, I don't know what to think. Even considering it sends my stomach in flips. I didn't survive one fake person to fall for someone who makes a living pretending to be someone else.

Since my scene guide is useless, I go to find Sonia, wondering if I should share news of my encounter. Then again, he told me to shut my mouth—and could really put the hurt on me if I don't.

When I do find her, she's waiting outside the producer's office, leaning over so she can listen by the door.

She spots me and holds up a hand for me to stay back, or silent. I do both, until she creeps away. "You hear that?"

The argument inside wouldn't be muffled by a vault door, let alone the thin steel.

"Yes. Are we being shut down?"

"No." Sonia pulls me along to get us further from the door. "That, Nine, is the sound of reshoots. Every so often, the directors present a partial reel that tells the story. Most of the time, the execs wait until we're done to meddle. This time, we're getting a solid dose of 'Fix this' before we've even gotten principal photography done."

I wait for her to explain more, and when she doesn't, I finally give her a prompt. "Help a poor boy out. What does this *mean*?"

"It means we'll have to shoot straight on through Thanksgiving. In fact, no telling if we'll film around Christmas. Every film does reshoots. Some big, some little. We won't know until they come out the door."

"What do we do?"

She points to the couch in Central Holding. "We wait."

And we do. The whole crew knows what's happening within minutes, and the result is a death-watch where everyone gathers. Their morbid fascination overrides the fear of being seen near me.

As the minutes turn to hours, I begin to idly wonder how long a studio can pay people to do nothing. Sonia goes from sitting on the couch, to laying with her back against my side. She dozes, while I study every line, wrinkle, and minute scar.

Part of me wonders why she isn't waiting with Kantina. Lord knows I'd take her trailer over the vinyl couches.

Our first clue someone is coming is the way the production assistants scatter like birds in a field. They rush down the hallway, practically leaving a trail of flying papers.

I have no idea what Sonia's dreaming about, but the smile on her face makes me reluctant to wake her. I give her a gentle squeeze on the shoulder. She opens her eyes, then jerks herself upright, looking at me in confusion—and then blushing once more.

"They're coming," I say, pointing to the production office.

"Right." Sonia stands, stretches, and shakes her head. "Look ready to work because you *are* ready to work."

Kantina leads the way—and this is the first time I've seen her flawless face marred by worry. She gives me a smile that would reduce any fan to a gibbering puddle, then looks to Sonia. "Why did you not wait in my trailer, darling?"

"Will was here, and I—I didn't want him to feel alone."

Kantina raises one eyebrow, then waves for Sonia to follow. The two fall in and retreat, speaking in hushed tones.

Belion and Aaron come next, but I might as well be a piece of styrofoam for all the attention they're giving me. The two are arguing over the essence of light and shadow, and all I can tell is that they've tapped the essence of frustration.

At last comes Felicia, with a flock of production assistants following her like chicks with a hen. She's not even looking at her tablet—and that worries me.

"Ma'am?" I ask. "What should we set up for?"

Felicia looks up like she's about to bark at me—and then sighs, shaking it off, and comes to take a stale donut from the box on the table. "Nine. Welcome to Hollywood."

"Every time someone says that, it's because something awful has happened. Or is happening. Or is about to happen." I leave the last bit open, hoping she'll fill me in.

"As much as I enjoy watching Belion entertain himself with you, I can't tell you what to set up for next because I don't *know* what to set up for next. 'Not what we were hoping for' is hard to fix." She consoles herself with a donut, something I can totally understand.

"Reshoots?"

"Well, we'd need to actually have them shot to reshoot them, but restructuring, yes. Which I can't even do until our *master* director figures out how to salvage it."

"Will?" Sonia calls to me as she approaches. "Don't bother her, come with me, I'll explain everything."

"He's not bothering me," Fiona says. "What's bothering me is I've got fifty percent of a film and no way to get the other fifty on schedule."

Kantina approaches and looks down at my spot on the couch until I move. She settles herself like a cat, smoothing her dress once she does.

"So," asks Sonia, "what was their actual complaint?"

"The whole film," says Felicia. "I have no doubt Belion will come up with something different. What I doubt is that he's going to come up with something I can actually make work. We aren't going to have James again for five weeks."

"Please." Kantina speaks, but not distant. She's focused on Felicia with a cloud of despair I haven't seen from her. "I have faith in you. You are a talented director—"

"With no leading man, and zero ability to bring in someone new. We're done."

Felicia's response kills the argument, the movie, and any hope I had left.

CHAPTER ELEVEN

FELICIA'S DECLARATION THAT THE MOVIE IS DONE HANGS IN the air like a death proclamation—until Sonia puts one arm around my waist, pulling me closer. "I have an idea."

"No. Not him. His acting"—Felicia looks to me—"is awful. Sorry, Will. You're a great carpenter. Love all three of the banisters, but the bobble head in my office has the same emotional range you do. Maybe if we had a few months to train you, but we don't."

I don't mind her being honest. If it involves Sonia putting her arm around me, I love whatever the idea is. It's the best idea ever.

After an awkward moment, Sonia crosses her arms and waits for anyone else to speak. In the silence, she begins. "All right, then, if this is supposed to be a sequel to *The Bride Becomes Her*, why aren't we shooting it like one?"

"Darling," says Kantina, "Felicia was not there. Perhaps you could be so kind as to explain?"

"Fine." Sonia paces as she speaks. "Belion was certain about Kantina from the moment we started filming *Bride*. But James? I think he planned to replace him the whole time. That's why you so rarely see the Groom."

"He planned to replace America's Super Spy? The Man With A Million Tomorrows?" Felicia's tone is one that says she barely believes it. "You have a bridge you want to sell me as well?"

"Believe it," says Sonia. "He's the Man Whose Studio Ran Out Of Time And Money To Get Someone Better."

"It is the truth," says Kantina. "James has grown in many ways since those days."

Sonia picks up immediately. "So what if we don't have him? Shoot around the bastard. He can voice over in the places we need to hear him, but this movie's not about him. It's about the Lady. It's about Kantina, and we can know everything about the Lord by how she reacts."

Felicia doesn't answer—she's leaned over, hand on her forehead. "Side shots. Rear shots. Center Kantina." After a moment or two, she looks up. "I need time with Aaron first. He'll know if this is even possible. Then, if—and that's a big if—I have to get permission. This is way above my pay grade, more producer level. This kind of thing will come better if it comes from Eddie himself. Tell me something, Sonia. Why are you not on my side of the camera?"

"I'm always on your side of the camera when we roll." The way Sonia answers says she's practiced this response.

"You know the business," says Felicia. "You understand the mechanics that make the art actually work. Isn't it time—"

"For you to make a call? Yes." Sonia brushes herself off. "I'll go run lines with Kantina. Will…"

"Can go wait in his trailer," Felicia says, her eyes narrowed. She's not happy, and her displeasure is directed at Sonia, when I'd rather it be at me. "Eddie mentioned it after the reshoot discussion. We don't have one free," she adds to me, "so you and Sonia will share. I figure you two ought to move in together anyway, given how much you're eye-boning each other."

Sonia's mouth falls open as she gapes at Felicia, but what comes out isn't angry, it's embarrassed. "Kantina," she says, turning away. "I'll be waiting for you in *your* trailer. You're shaky on the third act lines, and I'm sure some of them will survive."

Only after she's left does Kantina turn her attention to me. "What do you know, William? You were almost a star."

Her presence is still unnerving, but in the same way I'd get used to working under a thousand pound anvil, she no longer leaves me tongue tied. "I don't need that to be happy. But I am moving up in the world. Got a trailer and everything."

Kantina tilts her head. "What *is* it you want, William? Money?"

I shrug. "Money wouldn't hurt, but I want it for what I can fix with it. Fame? You can keep that. I'm happy the way I am."

"Completely happy?" She gazes at me through long lashes, like she knows the answer.

I hold her gaze steadily. "I'm getting there."

"Women would be attracted to you, or men, if that is your desire. Surely this, at least, has some appeal?"

That brings a laugh I can't control, one that nearly doubles me over. "Oh, my God. My woman-finding skills are about as bad as they come. To do worse, my next girlfriend would need to harvest my organs and sell them on Craigslist." I straighten. "Mind answering a question?"

"Ask anything."

"I hear it's good for me to kiss up to a few specific people. The assistant director, the leading man, and the leading lady. James isn't here. Felicia I've got covered by doing whatever she says. You—"

"You wish to kiss up to me?" Kantina says it in a soft voice. "How bold of you, William. I suppose, if that is your desire—"

"No! I didn't mean it like that, I..." The way she's holding her hand in front of her face, she's smiling. "You *know* what I meant."

Now she drops any façade, giving me a true grin that shines like a million watts. "I do, but I could not resist. Sonia is correct—you are so very cute when you are embarrassed."

My insides do a gymnastic routine, but it's not for Kantina. "She said I was cute?"

"She says many things. You should ask her yourself, if you want to know what they are."

Her answer leaves me in a whirlwind of doubt and confusion. Ask her myself?

I will. I'm an adult, with conversation skills better than those of a two-year-old. "My brother says I should be wary of Sonia. That she could have ulterior motives, if she was even interested in me. You tell me I should talk to her. Ed—someone else—says different. I just want to know the truth."

Kantina pauses, her lips pursed, deep in thought. "Sonia has told me of your previous relationship, and how you were deceived. I think you have learned from the mistakes of your past, William. I think you want to be sure you know someone before you bare your heart. But I think most of all, that if you do not know the answer for yourself, it does not matter what I say. Now, I must go."

MY TRAILER IS QUIET, AND EMPTY, AND BLAND, WITHOUT so much as a picture of a tiny turtle eating a strawberry to grace the walls. It smells like it hasn't been open since the last time I was in here, so I prop the door open regardless of the heat, lay back on the spongy foam mattress, and plug in my phone. I'm getting paid to sleep, and I always do a good job at what I get paid for.

It feels like I've only blinked—and someone bangs on my door, then a mousy production assistant pokes her head in. "Mr. Mathis? You're needed in production."

"It's just Will," I say, standing up.

She doesn't meet my gaze. "I'm not really supposed to talk to you. But the AD's waiting."

Assistant director, aka Felicia, one of the people I'm supposed to make happy. I practically sprint to the soundstage, and find my way to production as fast as humanly possible.

Sonia's already there, re-arranging notes on a whiteboard while Felicia watches. She glances up from the whiteboard to see me, and looks away before I can tell if she's happy. "That should do it."

Felicia shakes her head and points to the board. "You're too ambitious. I'm a slave-driver and I couldn't get these done in this order. Think about how many takes 106 is going to require and make a few adjustments."

Felicia looks back to me. "Nine, how are you liking the star treatment?"

I stand like a soldier, hands folded behind my back. "I'm ready to do whatever it takes, ma'am."

"Ma'am?" The way she scrunches up her nose makes me wince. "Just how old do you think I am?"

"Don't answer, Will." Sonia shoots me a warning gaze I didn't need.

Felicia turns away from the board and appraises me. "Whatever it takes, Will Mathis, may be filming straight through the Thanksgiving holiday. You can be thankful you have a job. You can help save this turkey all in one. We need a sizzle reel to sell the new cut."

I can handle the hours. "You say 'sizzle,' I hear 'Kantina.'"

"The man understands," says Felicia. "That looks better, Sonia. Except you're still overbooked by twenty percent. Try again."

I watch Sonia go over her post-its again, then focus on my job. "What do you need me to do?"

"A decent job. I know I said standing in was standing around, but job requirements change. You're a poor actor, and that wouldn't be a problem if this wasn't an acting job, on a movie set. So I've arranged for you to take lessons over the next few days while we sort out this mess." She waves to the door. "Go home, Will. Get some sleep. Eat something that doesn't come from a can."

"Yes, ma'a—" I cut off. "Yes, Mom— Oh, crap—"

Felicia stifles a snigger. "That one, I like. Someone get me another quad espresso, and start me a conference call with Belion and Aaron. Sonia, you should go home too."

Sonia doesn't look up. "I've almost got this. See you in the morning, Will."

So I do as I'm told, and head home. I have plans that involve drinking a six-pack of beer and watching a movie, maybe something starring Kantina, but from the moment I finish my dinner, my eyelids turn into solid lead, and it's all I can do to make it to the table. Bradley and Tia are out on the town, seeing some monster movie in 3D, but all I really want to watch is the darkness—and dream of what might be. What can never be, and who it can never be with. Dreams, at least, I'm allowed.

Once, I would have been embarrassed at crawling into bed before nine. Now, at seven-thirty, I lay down and die to the world for another night.

Felicia didn't give me any idea of when I was supposed to be there, so I show up at five thirty in the morning just like usual, but instead of heading to makeup, I snag a production assistant as he passes. "Can you ask the AD where I'm supposed to be? I'm—"

"I know who you are." He backs away, shaking his arm like I'm dripping with bees, and flees the moment he's out of reach.

A few minutes later, I spot a trio of PAs standing together. They're not even being discreet as they argue over which one of them has to deal with me. At last, the one I grabbed to begin with jams his hands in his pockets. "You're in Props & Recovery, room 118. You can find your way there, right?"

"It would help if you showed me. I can find my way back after I've been there once."

He mumbles something I interpret as 'start walking.'

So I do. We take the long way around—I'm guessing so he can avoid walking through the set, but as we pass the row of trailers, a cart pulls to a stop.

"William." Belion's voice makes my skin crawl. "I am pleased to see you. And who is your friend?"

"I'm not his friend," says the PA. "I wouldn't even be walking with him except that Director Slate said I had to help, I swear."

Belion fixes the man with a stare. "What is your name?"

"David, sir. I just want to learn to make great art like you. I haven't said a word I didn't have to."

"Wise," says Belion, as he strokes the patchy beard he can't quite pull off. "I think you will have a long and healthy career, David. Find me when you are done, and you may assist me personally today."

Belion rolls away, leaving a cloud of smug that's choking.

David looks like a man who's been asked to escort a skunk, and frankly, I would rather wander than continue to inconvenience him. "Listen, kid, just point me in the right direction."

David nods down the rows. "It's the building that looks like it's falling in. 118 is first floor—"

"I think I can handle that part." I trudge off through the early morning.

The guard at Props looks at my lanyard and doesn't so much as register my existence. He's more like the sphynx, if it came with a taser. The inside is crammed with parts of sets. There's marble columns made with fake marble, ivy arches with real marble and fake ivy, and a styrofoam boulder the size of Bradley's truck.

118 is less of a room and more of a storage closet in the rear of the building. But when I open the door, melodious laughter sweeps out—and the heavenly scent of coffee.

Inside, the lights are bright and across the middle of the room, someone's arranged a line of movie theater chairs with high backs and arm-rests folded up. The air smells of bacon, and standing at a dusty table, eating from a plate of bacon, is Kantina.

She's dressed in a tan wrap that reminds me of a toga, except that it doesn't look stupid, and I always thought togas did.

"What are you doing here?"

"William!" she says, waving to me. "Come in, it is early, so we may eat and relax. I heard of this wonderful idea and I could not wait to see you."

I'm more than a little awestruck—and worried. Kantina must have better ways to use her time. "I don't understand. Shouldn't you be helping them sort out the movie?"

"I will be," she says, offering me a plate that contains a donut wrapped in bacon. "It is in my contract, that I am to be consulted on all story changes. I came only to say I believe you can do anything, given the right motivation."

"Oh." I take the bacon. "That we agree on."

"Listen to Sonia as she teaches you," says Kantina. "Do as she says. Learn from her."

I'm not sure my brain has passed the word 'Sonia' yet.

Then Sonia sits up from the row of chairs, and wipes the crumbs of a donut off her chest.

I wasn't prepared for seeing her. For the way her hair is braided all the way down, and the khaki vest and shorts she wears that make her look like the world's most beautiful tour guide.

I'm not prepared for my pulse to roar or the room to spin just a bit as she holds up a script. "Morning, Will. You ready to get started?"

CHAPTER TWELVE

IN THE BACKROOM OF PROPS, YOU COULD HEAR A STYRO-
foam boulder crunch before I speak. "You are way, way too
smart to be stuck teaching acting to a carpenter. You
should be in the room with Felicia, helping fix the movie."

Sonia blushes, and looks down. "If Belion knows the
idea was mine, he'll fight it tooth and nail. If he somehow
concludes that he came up with it, everything is easier."

"And I'm here… why?"

"We have to convince the investors this new shoot is
going to work. Kantina is her best when she's got acting
to play off. There's going to be a live set visit to show
investors it's worth continuing."

"James Becton—"

"Not going to happen, Will. He's double booked, and
no executive in their right mind would prioritize this
movie over the other one he's working on." She rises and
moves around the chairs, closing in on me. "The focus of

the scene is going to be on Kantina, but you *have* to do your part to convince them, or we'll done before we ever start."

Speaking of Kantina, she left—I'm not sure when, because I couldn't take my eyes off Sonia. I wrap my finger around Kantina's frog as Sonia comes ever closer, and take a deep breath. "No pressure."

"I need you to learn from me. I can't make you an award-winning actor, but I can make you every bit as good as James Becton, and Kantina will do the rest." Sonia's not six inches from me, and her breath tickles my chin as she speaks. "Do you trust me?"

The part of me that thinks wants to ask how I can, and the part of me that feels has already made its decision. Bradley warned me Sonia seemed desperate to get the movie made, and my gut says he's not wrong.

I know there's so many reasons not to trust her, and only one I should.

Because I *want* to.

"I do." The words hang heavy in the air, an admission too dangerous. "What do we do? I'm picturing some training montage where we play 'Eye of the Tiger' and you have me practicing my reading and running in place."

"No." Sonia turns and pats the chair behind her in a way I recognize as instruction. "Acting is about compassion. It's learning and understanding not just what a character does, but why, and then showing that without ever saying a word. It's body language as much as spoken word, and like anything, it's a skill that can be learned. Sit."

I'm intimately aware of every motion as I settle onto the warm flannel cushion, which feels like the movie theater seats from my childhood. Every muscle tenses even though I want to relax.

Sonia picks up a sheet of paper and hands it to me. "First off, we're going to do some reading. Practice is worth more than a thousand hours of me lecturing, and at night, you'll need to watch movies and study how great actors work."

I bounce up and down, raising my hand like a kindergartener waiting to be called on. "Oooh! I have an idea. *The Bride Becomes Her*. Kantina's great, right?"

"No to your idea, yes to she's a great actress, and learning to act from that movie is like learning surgery by starting out with brain surgery." Sonia takes a seat opposite me. "Just read, Will. Relax. Put yourself in the mind of your character, and it's okay to have fun."

Fun isn't the word I'd use for the chill that sweeps through me each time she looks my way. Then I look at what she's printed, and the rich taste of bacon turns to dust in my mouth. "Romeo and Juliet?"

"One of Shakespeare's greatest romances."

"Negative." I close the script and throw it on the floor. "This isn't a romance, it's a tragic fable, the moral of which is 'teenagers make consistently bad choices.' And it's creepy."

"You. Are. Defaming. The. Bard," Sonia says through gritted teeth.

"You have a sister, right?"

The question catches her off guard. She pauses. "Yes."

"Older or younger?"

"Younger," says Sonia. "Do you have a point? Or are you scoping out your next date?"

I give an innocent shrug. "No to wanting to date your

sister. Scoping out my next date remains to be seen. Look at it from my point of view: Juliet is thirteen years old. Romeo is older, probably eighteen. Would it be romantic if I came creeping up on your house and knocked on the window of your thirteen-year-old little sister?"

Sonia snatches the script from me and flings it across the room. "You've ruined that play for me."

"You're welcome." I duck as she hurls her copy after mine, narrowly missing my head. "I know a romantic movie we could read from."

Sonia stops going through the stack of paper and looks at me. "Is it *Die Hard*? Because if it is, I'm going to throw another, larger script at you, and this time, I won't miss." She stops and takes aim.

"Sorry." I look down. "Just slipped my mind. I'll let you know if it comes back."

"Romance." Sonia flips another script over in the stack. "Think romantic."

"Got it!" I smile at the thought. "Perfect movie."

"Is it *Die Hard 2*?" she asks, hefting the rolled up script.

"It is not."

Suspicion plays across her face, and she doesn't drop the paper. "If you say *Mad Max*, you're getting hit twice."

"Sorry, slipped my mind again. You know, reading is boring. Don't actors get to do explosions and the sword fights?"

"Sword fights?" Sonia asks, her mouth open, her eyes wide. "You can barely take stage direction and you want to do combat choreography?"

From a dusty bin, I seize a cardboard tube that contains half a dozen movie posters and spin to point it at her. "*En garde!*"

"Will, don't do this," Sonia says, grinning as she holds her hands up.

"I won't hurt you," I say, advancing. "Just going to make you walk the plank. The sharks, they might nibble."

Sonia kicks off one shoe, then the other, and loosens the ties at the bottom of her pants so they look more like a karate gi than leggings. Then she unbuttons the top button of her blouse—and the next—and pauses before adding a third. "Walk the plank, Will? Really?" Then she bends forward, knowing full well what it does to my view. "Is there no way I can persuade you?"

I have to tear my eyes away before answering, because right now I could be outwitted by a tic-tac-toe playing chicken. "Let me think... Tempting, very tempting. I would love to let you go, but my shark friends? They're hungry, and I do have a reputation to keep up."

In a single move, Sonia rolls to the side and comes up wielding a movie poster roll of her own. "Oh, Will. I was head choreographer for the drama department in college. You are in so much trouble."

Bradley always used to say that discretion was the better part of valor. He said that right before he ran away— which is what I'm doing.

"You won't get away so easily," Sonia shouts from far too close behind me as I bust out the door of 118 and charge down the hall.

I think this building was once a soundstage, and the small rooms in back were production offices. The center of the building is still open, but piled with dusty props, some covered with cloth, others left open. But there I find what I was looking for—a set piece from a crumpled van, perfect for leaping up on—and then spinning.

Sonia walks with purpose, her cardboard tube dragging along the floor as she approaches. "I didn't think you for a coward, Will. Come here and take your lashes like a man."

"Never. I have the high ground," I say. That's what they say in the *Swords of Justice* movies. I know this because I've watched all three of them, and the high ground is apparently the best place to swing a sword when you're out for justice.

But Sonia doesn't come charging up. Instead, she seizes a foam brick from the remains of a wall and throws it—with startling accuracy—right at my forehead.

"Hiya!" I shout, swinging the sword straight down to deflect it, then duck the next, spinning, leaping—and in a single swing, she whacks me upside the head so hard I see stars.

With another whack, my knee buckles, and I fall to the ground. "Ouch!"

Before I can get the word out, the carboard tube bounces off the back of my shoulders, and again off my thighs.

"Ready to surrender?"

"Never—" I don't even finish the word before she smacks me again—and that is just uncalled for.

But, although I may not be a fancy sword-fighter, I *am* a scrambler, and while Sonia does a spin, raising the sword up high, I lunge forward, grab her by the waist, and heft her into the air. "Take that!"

From upside down, with no balance, her swings are little more than love taps as I spin us around and around until I'm ready to hurl—and then, with a flourish, deliver her back onto her feet. "I surrender, my lady." I kneel before her, head bowed, and can't help laughing.

We're both covered in sweat, and I've got a layer of dust on me as thick as the foundation I'm forced to wear for filming. But when I stand, Sonia lurches forward, and I catch her.

She's warm to the touch—and speaking of touch, her lips graze mine as she looks up at me. We both freeze.

Was it an accident or intentional? I don't know and don't care. As long as neither of us moves, the moment will go on—but Sonia steps away. "This concludes the lessons on sword fighting. I think you've got it down."

"I don't know," I answer. "Maybe you should test me again. Just to make sure."

"Work first, play later," Sonia says sheepishly as she returns to 118.

There, she snatches two more scripts. "This will do nicely. *Casablanca*. You'll love it. It has Nazis in it."

"*Indiana Jones and the Last Crusade* does, too, and..." I don't dare finish my sentence. Based on the look Sonia gives me, if I do, this will be my last crusade. I'll be found dead under a foam boulder. "Who am I?"

"Rick. I'll be Ilsa, and this is from the original stage version." Sonia opens her copy, wipes the sweat from her forehead, and looks my way. "Shall we?"

We shall.

In short order, I learn a few lessons that aren't on the syllabus, but they become ridiculously true. First off, acting—acting *well*—is much harder than I thought. Secondly, Sonia is as harsh a teacher as I could ask for.

By lunch time I'm already exhausted—not physically, but emotionally. It shouldn't be possible—I'm not the one bidding the love of my life goodbye—but there's a strange power in the words that leaves me hating the playwright for every poor choice Rick makes—and every right one.

At lunch, Sonia heads back to the soundstage, and I'd bet every dollar I can spare that she's reviewing the plans. She comes back even less talkative, and spends the next six hours teaching not just acting, but over-acting. "If someone brushes against you, you're thrown back. An insult can start a blood feud. You need to make me feel what you're feeling."

And those are the kinder things. By the time she calls it, I can barely summon the energy to drag myself home.

When I walk in the door, Bradley's already cooking dinner. "Now, Tia. Now!" he shouts.

From the back bedroom comes the rousing beat of 'Eye of the Tiger.'

Now I regret texting Bradley to tell him what I was doing. With my remaining strength, I slump on the couch and lay back. "Acting is a pain. I would rather do pushups and chin-ups and run laps than read through *Death of a Salesman* ever again."

Tia returns to setting the table and gives me a smile that says what she's imagining doesn't match up to reality. "But you're learning from an actual actress. On an actual studio lot."

"Can I help?" I stand—and stop. Once more, I've forgotten the rule of Tia's household: Tia does things her way. She sees a doctor once a week to work on her need to lay everything out exactly so, and everyone else lets her be.

She adjusts the forks for the fifth time. "Tell me what it's like."

"Hot. There's air conditioning, but it doesn't do much. And bright. She brought in these lights to get me used to them. And she yells a lot more than I thought she would."

The look of envy that passes between Bradley and Tia makes me happy and sad and envious all at once—and my emotions are already worn out.

"I heard Eddie was on set to deliver news about the reshoots," says Bradley. "Funding is on hold until after the new script is approved. If it's approved."

'If' is a terrible term, one that leaves a gnawing ball of worry in my stomach. "How does that happen? Do you vote? Do you—"

"Don't," Bradley says, with surprising authority. "You're my brother, but this is business. Eddie noted that since you're employed on the set, I can't talk to you about… well, anything when it comes to that."

"Fine!" I throw up my hands. "We'll convince you. You'll see."

"I'm rooting for you." Bradley brings me a plate, since the card table for two is cozy as it is. "After all, we need this film to be a success."

"It will be. I'm going to make sure of it." I'm just grateful they let me crash here. "When I get paid, I'm buying you both dinner."

"When you get paid," says Tia, with a wink, "you'll do what's right."

What's right? Right is paying off the suppliers who sold me hardwood—hardwood I never saw, but that isn't what counts. I don't want to waste time or energy thinking about Tamara and her lies. I don't have it in me to feel guilt at the moment. As I finish my dinner, I become increasingly aware of how Tia watches every bite. Dirty dishes are one of her triggers, and at last, I set the fork, tines in, on the center of the plate—and duck as she lunges, grabbing it. "I'm sorry. I just need to get this to the sink."

Who am I to judge? Tia's obsessed with ordering her house just so. I'm probably still under surveillance by the FBI for my ex's crimes. Sonia's terrified of people taking her picture.

My goofy little brother is the most normal of us all.

And Tamara's a criminal. I forgot that one, even though it's been part of my litany every time this comes up. Maybe I've finally managed to pry her lose from my mind. She absolutely doesn't have a place in my heart anymore.

"We're going to binge watch some *Doctor Who*," says Bradley, as I lay back on the couch. "That a problem?"

I shake my head, already drowsing. "Tardis away. Or Tardis ho! Or go-go-gadget-Tardis." I go-go straight to sleep, setting a pattern that repeats for the next three days. The daylight hours are spent being drilled, yelled at, and cajoled by Sonia. The evening hours are spent with me passed out on the couch. I don't know if I'll ever be as a good an actor as I am a carpenter, and it's unlikely I'd ever match my woodcarving, but acting has its upsides, mostly the company. It's thinking of the company that sends me to bed every night and wakes me up before the alarm.

FRIDAY DAWNS, AND WHEN I OPEN THE DOOR TO 118, there's a plate with two cupcakes on the corner table.

Sonia lights candles on each, and there's a bundle of balloons floating in the middle of the room which read 'Congratulations.'

"On?" I take the cupcake offered, savoring the scent of almond extract and vanilla, and the rich chocolate frosting.

"A little bird told me you didn't pick up your paycheck. Would you like to see it?" Sonia's holding something behind her back.

"Please?" I pucker my lip and summon fake tears by thinking about my dead pet tarantula. "I'm so hungry, and just a little food would—"

"Enough, ham." She hands me a white envelope.

When I read the check inside, the shakiness in my hands won't stop until I sit down and lean over. "How much do you usually make?"

"Union says a hundred and eighty per day, but thanks to Kantina's interference, you're being paid closer to my rate, and I'm not making much less than stunt performers. Think about it: we pull a forty hour week in the first three days, Will. Everything else is overtime."

This was the payoff Felicia hinted at. The one she promised. Being a carpenter for piece work wasn't going to let me pay off the bills, but at this rate, I could dig my way out of the hole Tamara left. I'm a combination of shaky from relief, numb from shock, and afraid that this is some sort of fever dream.

When I speak, I'm afraid my voice trembles. "I'm ready. Let's work."

"Today," she says, "We're going to read from an awful, awful script so you can practice."

I take her daily handout. "*The Lady of the Manner*? Is this the revised script?"

"This is more like the version Belion used to pitch it. If you can stomach these lines, you can handle anything. Now, my Lord, take thy place."

I find my blocking notes and arrange the chairs to form a mock table. "My lady, my heart bursts when thoughts of you—dear God, this is bad."

Sonia's standing inches away, which ought to make me nervous. "So… here's a secret. Imagine them being spoken by Elmer Fudd."

"My wady…" I break off, laughing. "That's supposed to help? Oh, I know!" I grab a balloon, untie it, and take a deep breath of helium. "You are truly the flower of a thousand gardens, my lady," I say in a voice like a chipmunk. "Verily, my love has grown for you."

"Verily." Sonia takes a breath from my balloon. "Who are you to speak of truth?"

Her voice, already high pitched, now sounds like I'm being berated by a squeaky flower, and it triggers a fit of laughter I can't stop. "This isn't helping."

"I disagree," she says, still squeaky. "I'm feeling a thousand percent better."

"It's not helping me choke down the dialogue."

Tears stream down Sonia's face. "Stop it. You remind me of him when you're whiny."

I thrust my chest out and imagine myself as an angry little man. "Bow before my artistry! Bow! This is my royal command!"

"Stop!" she says between gasps. "Oh, God, I can't breathe."

"I'll summon a squirrel to do mouth-to-mouth."

When she shoves me away, her mouth gaping, I stop. "It's not that funny."

Sonia doesn't answer until she draws a ragged breath. "You have no idea how much I needed a good laugh. My stomach hurts."

I place one hand on her back, waiting for her gasps to slow. "Mine feels fine. You should laugh more."

"Read." She thrusts the script at me. "Mr. Chipmunk, read. Get through it before lunch and I've got another surprise."

"We'll go get dinner?"

Sonia turns, now serious. "Felicia's going to walk me through the revised scene list, so I can understand why she thinks it will get approved."

"I thought we had longer. I'm not ready. Please."

That kills the smile on her face. She bites her lip before answering. "It's not up to me, and you're doing so much better. If I could get you to let go of your inhibitions, you might actually be good, one day."

"My inhibitions are the only thing keeping me going." They're the only thing keeping my distance from her. "What about you? I'll drop mine if you drop yours."

She studies her script. "My inhibitions, Will? Or is there something else you want me to drop?"

"I—" My cheeks turn hot as I catch her meaning. "I didn't mean—"

"Will." She's covering her mouth again. "I'm messing with you."

I can only hope my nervous laugh hides how unsettled I am, and how hard it is to get thoughts of her out of my head, thoughts that keep circling.

"Earth to Will?" Sonia says. "Tired already? You'll need to put in a few hours to earn a break."

"I didn't expect acting to be so exhausting. I go home, eat, and crash."

Sonia nods along. "Emotional energy is as vital as physical energy. When you pour yourself into a part, you take it on. Even the words become part of you. You didn't think actors worked?"

My shoulders sag as I recall the tumult of emotions. "We're not even in costume, we're just reading a play, and yet it grabs me. I didn't expect something completely staged to feel so real."

"Our emotions don't ask us if it's a play. The way we feel? That's never fake."

"How do you feel when you look at me?"

She opens her mouth, and just for a moment, I think she's going to answer. "I feel like we have a lot of work to get ready, and not much time to do it. Page eleven, line four, you start, and this time, work on getting both the feeling and the enunciation. If we can't understand a word you say, it doesn't matter how well you say it."

I know better than to fight—at least, not head on. So I dive in for one more pass at *Death of a Salesman*, which I don't consider even remotely romantic, but Sonia's shot down every suggestion I've come up with, including *Avatar*, *Terminator*, *Die Hard*, every *Godzilla* movie, and *Indiana Jones and The Last Crusade*.

But when we break for lunch, someone's waiting in the dusty outer storage bay.

"Sonia. Nine." Felicia's voice gives her away. She's fiddling with what looks like a rocket ship control panel. "We've got a proposal out that we think is going to get accepted. I need Nine in makeup."

"Now?" I ask, almost in shock.

"Now," says Felicia. "Ten minutes ago if I had my druthers, but I didn't expect Eddie Gellar and his key investors to show up unannounced. Belion's presenting storyboards but they want to see Kantina sell it."

I look to Sonia—and her moment of hesitation tells me everything I need to know about how she feels.

"Give me a minute for a pep talk, and I'll have him over as soon as possible." Sonia's dead serious as she points to the door. "Do you at least have the script for what we'll be doing?"

Felica shakes her head. "Belion will have it ready as soon as possible. You get thirty seconds."

Once Felicia leaves, Sonia looks back to me. "I'm sorry, Will. I wanted more time to prepare you."

"I have no script."

"Very common," says Sonia. "You read it once, you rehearse it once, you film it. You're ready, Will. Kantina is the most talented actress I've ever worked with, and all you have to do is not distract from her."

"Your pep talk sucks," I say, heading to the door, but before I can get there, she cuts me off.

"That wasn't the pep talk."

Before I can open my mouth to ask, we're kissing, softly, lightly, in a moment that I cling to, savoring the feeling of flying with my feet still on the floor. "I believe you can do it," Sonia whispers in my ear. "Go prove me right."

CHAPTER THIRTEEN

I KNOW HOW A CONVICT FEELS ON HIS WAY TO THE DEATH chamber. The makeup ladies apply anti-perspirant to my face to stop the sweat that's pouring off me—and I'm not under the lights yet. This time, instead of brown sweatpants, I change into a tight-fitting suit that the costumer literally sews me into, stitching the buttons that won't quite hold because my chest is broader than James Becton's.

Inside the soundstage, the air-conditioning is set to arctic levels. Steph, Felicia's mousy production assistant, follows me from just a few steps away, like she's afraid I'm going to bolt.

It's tempting, but I can't help thinking about Sonia's pep talk.

At the Titanic, Kantina waits, wearing a dress I can only call stunning, silken white with pearls stitched into the weave in a way that circles her waist, looping around her neck and crossing her cleavage in the plunge of her dress. Her hair is done in braids pinned tight against her head. "William," she says, not sparing me a smile. "I hear wonderful things from Sonia."

"Really? Because there are high-school students with more experience. If I mess this up..." My will to speak drains away as I consider the consequences. An entire movie crew looking for work. Kantina's come-back project destroyed. Sonia's work wasted. "I said I'm a perfectionist, but I'm never sure if how I'm acting is the right way or not."

Kantina nods. "If it is authentic, then it is right. No one can tell you what another feels. You decide in your heart, and convey it with every action, every glance, every word. Are you ready?"

I haven't found speaking this hard since the first time we met. "I'm ready."

A low whistle from behind me has me turning to see Felicia dressed in a black pantsuit that makes her look two-parts millionaire and one part psychopath. "Will, is that you, or did someone fly a better-looking version of James Becton in?"

I bow before her and do my best imitation of James. "I'm suave and debonair, ma'am, so very suave. Tell me you have the script."

Felicia holds out two pages, one for each of us. "K, you need to make this work. I'll try to delay ten minutes so you can rehearse, but no promises."

Kantina reads the words silently, mouthing each word. "Go," she says, glancing up at Felicia. "William and I will be here."

Only after Felicia leaves do I wipe my face again, and grip Kantina's frog like a lifeline.

"Do you understand your lines?" Kantina's voice is slow, quiet. I think she might be afraid I'll startle.

"I understand them." It's like I can hear Sonia speaking over my shoulder. *Understand what's being said. Then understand what's* really *being said.* The first is easy, if you can read English. The second takes more than brains; it takes heart, to empathize. "I definitely understand."

"Then let us rehearse. Do not hold back, William, throw your soul into it, and I will not fail you." Kantina reaches out with a gloved hand to take mine, but my heart doesn't thrill like I expect it should.

We step into the boat and take our places—right as the already-bright lights become unbearable.

I start to blurt out, "We didn't—"

Kantina's gloved hand shushes me. The look she's giving me says this is not the time or place to complain.

"Gentlemen, ladies," says Felicia, "We appreciate your time and attention, and I think you'll be impressed. We've truly uncovered the essence of the story here."

Whatever she says next, it's lost on me, because among the group of men following Eddie Gellar stands my brother, dressed in a finer suit than I've ever seen. His beard is combed, and—to my amazement—trimmed.

He catches my gaze, and the look of pure shock on Bradley's face is the second greatest thrill I've had today.

Felicia glances our way, and I recognize it's time for me to work.

As I glance back to Kantina, she's waiting for me.

"Lights?" asks Felicia.

Aaron calls out, "Ready."

"Cameras rolling," comes another voice. "Hold on, we're not tracking on two."

While they scurry to fix the problem, my mild case of nerves is escalating past what a single stone frog can handle.

"William," says Kantina, her voice a whisper. "May I make a suggestion?"

I close my eyes and clench my script so hard it twists. "Anything."

"Do you have a target for your emotions?"

Sonia taught me this, too. How we find a memory, or a face to evoke the emotion needed. I nod, trying to recall how it felt with Tamara.

Kantina leans over so close I feel the air when her lips move. "I have so rarely had to say this, darling, but perhaps you could imagine I were someone else?"

Off to the side, Sonia is standing, watching us.

I couldn't say these words to her, but I can't not think of her now that it's in my mind.

"Cameras ready!" Felicia shouts. "Roll in three, two, one, and… action."

Kantina's eyes, once sharp, now drift wide and unfocused. No inhibitions, Sonia said. Embrace the moment. Focus on the core of the emotion—and I know in that moment, it could never be Tamara, not now. Not ever again, and if I'm being honest, maybe never before.

But that doesn't leave me empty. It leaves me with room.

"Do you know, my lord, my greatest fear?" Kantina asks—or maybe she's not Kantina, not now.

No inhibitions. No fear of what might be. Only what is. "I know your fear, my lady, because it is my own. You fear you will never find the other half of your heart."

A tear crawls down Kantina's cheek. "It is more cruel to find the half you can never have. For no one can live without a whole heart."

"If I give you mine and you give me yours, then between us, one heart is all we need." I know inside what the Lord is feeling. I know the emptiness. The fear. The longing that can only be resolved by a single deadly question. "Will you, my lady?"

Kantina's answer isn't a word—it's shown on her face, as she looks up at me—maybe not me, not in her mind, but in my world, I'm not speaking to her. The joy that ripples across her face spreads in a way that leaves me breathless, and at last she opens her mouth—

"Cut!" shouts Felicia. "Fantastic job, K. You nailed it."

Kantina lets out a breath and wipes her cheek, then stands as Felicia comes in to point to the boat. "Cue the tipping scene, the shivering heart-to-heart in the lake, the moment of abandonment. They reunite at the bridge..." Felicia looks back to the group of women and men. "And... well, does anyone have any doubt how it ends?"

Eddie Gellar rolls forward in his chair, rubbing his chin with his hand. "But can you film it?"

"Of course." Felicia dips her head to him. "I have schedules laid out. Aside from the lake shots, most of this will be on set, not on site, to keep budgets tight."

Eddie nods and his assistant rolls him back. "It's a better show. This is what I had in mind at the beginning. But now, we need some time to think it over. To talk it over privately. I'll be in touch soon."

"Let me walk you out." Felicia rushes after them. "On the way, I'll give you the storyboards for the staircase—"

"Stay." Eddie's one word halts her. "I said I'll call. There's a fine line between persuasive and pushy. Make sure you know which side of that line you're on."

"What about him?" asks Felicia, giving Belion a glare.

Eddie rolls a bit closer. "You let him make his own bad decisions." With that, he pivots and leaves.

Belion follows anyway, bragging about the genius he's brought to fruition.

"Are we going to shoot more?" I ask as Felicia returns to the set.

"We're not authorized to." She steps over the side of the boat and plops down where Kantina was. "Go shower and have them cut you out of that suit, Will. Kantina, Sonia, a word?"

As the crew disbands, I slink away, a hazy mix of emotions that reminds me of the slurry of ice cream at the bottom of a caramel sundae. For one moment, I felt like I connected with someone I wasn't, a character I let shine out.

But it wasn't enough.

When I emerge from the shower, the lights on the soundstage are off. I unlock my phone and shoot Bradley a text. *Level with me. What did you think?*

Bradley doesn't respond for a good ten minutes. *I'm proud of you, Will. Never dreamed I'd see you do something like that. Also, I voted against continuing production. It'll hurt, but better to cut our losses and run now. It's just business, bro.*

At some level, I expected it. At another level, his text hits me like a hook to the gut, driving the air from my lungs, and stinging my eyes with tears.

On a hunch, I head toward Kantina's trailer, where the lights are on, and with some hesitation, I knock. If Sonia's here, I want her to find out from me. She shouldn't have to wait.

"Will?" Sonia's voice comes from the trailer window. "Hey, tell the guards to stop looking for him. Will, come on in."

I can hear the tears in her voice, and don't bother to wipe my face as I step inside. But Sonia's not there. Instead, Felicia is sprawled out on the couch, clutching a bottle of whiskey to her chest like a newborn baby. She raises her head enough to look at me and lets out a laugh.

"You heard?" I say.

There's a blur of motion, then someone slams into me, wrapping me in a hug that squeezes the air from my lungs. Sonia's impeccable makeup is smeared across my shirt as she looks up. "Thank you. Thank you so much."

"What?"

I momentarily let go of Sonia as she releases me just enough to be able to look me in the eye. "Will, Eddie called five minutes ago. The investors voted four to three to release enough money to continue shooting. We did it."

Shock hits me in waves. Relief. Laughter. I wipe the tears away.

"I told you he could handle this," says Sonia, sticking out her tongue at Felicia.

"It wasn't me," I say, my voice light, like I almost can't recognize it. "It was Kantina. Where is she?"

"Probably parading around her bedroom naked," says Felicia, taking another swig from the bottle. "You did good, Nine. Before, your acting made my eyes bleed. Now, you're probably a thousand times better."

"So," says Sonia. "About my idea—"

"No." Felicia's statement leaves no room for argument. "I said my eyes aren't bleeding, not 'We can replace the A-list leading man with a set carpenter.' I still want to go in the bathroom and vomit, though that may be the whiskey. Will, don't give up carpentry yet."

I grin. "Not planning on it."

"K?" Sonia calls to the back of the trailer. "You dressed? Will's here."

Kantina emerges in a pink tank-top and yoga pants, unwrapping her hair from the shower cap on her head. "William, have you heard the good news?"

I nod. "I have. Ladies, I want to go home and punch my brother in the arm for voting against me. Kantina, Felicia, is there anything I can do for the two of you? Bring you coffee tomorrow, perhaps?"

Felicia shakes her head. "You know my production assistants?"

"Yes," I say, waiting for the obvious continuation.

"I appreciate the offer, but every time you do something a PA is supposed to do, I have to skip feeding them at night."

It's a joke, one I'm too on edge to handle. "Someone with more experience than me said I should kiss up to you, James, and Kantina."

"Good advice, but what I want from you is one hundred percent availability and zero percent drama. That's all the kissing up I require." She looks to Kantina. "You want anything from him?"

Kantina nods, slowly. "William is obsessed with kissing me. He said so earlier."

"I said kissing *up*. I told you kissing *up*. It means—" I stammer as I back away—and then almost gasp as it hits me. "You're doing it *again*."

"See?" says Kantina, looking to Felicia. "He turns so red."

"I do not."

Sonia's eyes are crinkled as she laughs at me. "You're turning redder right now."

"I am *not*," I say as my cheeks grow hot. "I was told to—*help out*—the AD, the leading lady, and the leading man to make my own life easier. I never said anything about kissing Kantina."

"I know, William. We are just having such fun." Kantina smiles, and then looks to Sonia. "Should I do it anyway? Once I do, he will no longer wonder what it is like."

"No!" Sonia says, far too loud. Then she pauses, and steps back, as she stares at the ground. "I mean—it's just—you're the leading lady. You set the tone for everyone else. You have to be professional."

"Professional?" Felicia pulls long and hard on the bottle, coughing as she swallows. "That's the word least likely to be used for this movie. Whatever threesome you all have planned to get rid of this tension, make it quick and be ready tomorrow."

Tension. That's one word for the feeling that rests like a blanket across us. Kantina and Sonia are having some sort of stare down. I've never believed women can communicate by blinking, but whatever's being said doesn't use words. At last Kantina speaks. "I'm sorry, darling. Why did you not say something sooner?"

"Would it have mattered?" Sonia asks.

"The concerns of your heart are always mine as well."

"If we have to talk about this, let's do it alone," Sonia says. "Right now, I'm going to walk Will out to the front gate, where I'm sure he has a ride waiting—"

"I don't—"

"Or a *cab*, which I have distinct *feeling* will be waiting. K, don't you move a muscle." Sonia turns me toward the door with way more force than I would expect from someone her size.

Outside, the afternoon heat is just starting to settle in to evening cool, and stage hands are rolling new props in as the actors go home.

We pause to let the front of a spaceship pass, and then an actual tank rolls by, and I can't help staring. "This place is unreal."

Sonia shakes her head, and nudges me forward with her shoulder. "Everything you see here is just window dressing. You said reading was exhausting: that's because you're opening yourself up to the story. The props? The costumes? They're just enough illusion for people to accept the promise of a story. To open up their heart and make a connection and feel something they might not feel every day. Something they dream about."

"Like True Love?" I'm not mocking her. I know better, and I'd like to think it's real, even if experience points to the contrary.

"Everyone's looking for it. Even if they don't know it, or even want to, deep down, they are."

"Even you? You're still looking?"

She pauses before answering, which tells me everything. "I meant other people."

"You said everyone. Am I included in everyone?"

"I'll make another exception for you, Will Mathis. We're the only two not looking for true love." We stop at the gate, even though there's a cab driver holding a sign with my name on it. Sonia studies the asphalt long enough to count every pebble. "Kantina says if you aren't looking for true love, it's because you already found it. But I say you and I can be not-looking together."

'Together' is a word that holds bitter memories for me, but tonight, for just one scene, I had the glimpse of an idea, a thought, a feeling so terrifying I can't say it out loud. For the briefest moment, I wondered if maybe I wasn't looking, not because I didn't want to find someone to love—but because I already had.

CHAPTER FOURTEEN

THE NEXT FEW WEEKS TEACH ME HOW MUCH OF A BLUR LIFE can be when fourteen out of twenty-four hours are spent working. I'm there at five thirty, and we film until six in the evenings on the easy days. On the hard days, after the principals are done, Sonia and I light the next day's scenes. When she isn't an inch away, it's a foot, and when she's more than a foot away, I wonder what she's up to.

Some nights I spend in the trailer because I'm too tired to limp to the gate. I shower off in the morning by sneaking into James's unused trailer. The travel-sized soaps there carry absurdedly manly names, like 'angry hand-grenade,' for otherwise flowery smells.

I do my best at acting, but mostly Kantina takes my one-sided performance and turns it into something golden. I'd say she eases up on the teasing, but the reality is I'm probably just too tired to notice.

Evenings are for quick dinners and collapsing into bed. Mornings and days are filming—and Sonia. If I'm not on set, we're running lines. When I am on set we're checking lighting.

Lunches, if there are lunches, involve pacing back and forth in my trailer, rattling off the lines for our next shot.

Today, as I finish my last line, Sonia intervenes. "Enough. Stop. If we don't eat now, we won't be until after filming."

"I heard Felicia talking this morning while I was waiting for my scene list."

Sonia hands me half of a questionable tuna sandwich. "I was in the room, Will."

Of course she was. "What's happening?"

"Daily shots look good, but we need to pull off something big to make the daily reels more impressive. Felicia is thinking the balcony scene."

"Not with that staircase." I would have had fixed it by now, but that would involve having some days, nights, or weekends off. If there weren't a bank on the edge of the lot, I wouldn't even deposit my checks, which I only do because I need to pay bills. "I'll have Bradley assign it to someone else. What day is it?"

"Thursday, I think," says Sonia. She checks her phone. "No, Sunday. Thursday was when the blacksmith set caught fire." She lays back on the bed. "At least, I think it was. What are you doing for the holidays?"

Holidays. It takes a moment for me to realize she means Thanksgiving. "Do we have time off?"

"Felicia originally planned to film through, but she's taking her husband and all four kids to Florida, and without her, I doubt much will get done."

Time off would feel foreign. Empty. I don't know what I'd do with the hours if I had them. "Bradley and Tia are staying here, so I'll eat with them, but they're gone at Christmas. Going home to see her family."

"Me too," Sonia says. Her shoulders slump, her voice filled with what I think of as dread. "I haven't seen Mom and Dad in a year, and if I don't go home, they'll come and get me. Kantina insists."

"Kantina insists they'll come and get you?"

"That I get time off." She rolls her eyes at my lame humor. "Come on. Let's see if we can be done before eight tonight."

Belion is waiting on the wine cellar set, with its empty barrels and mugs filled with grape juice that I sneak sips from. His rants barely bother me now. He gave up on arranging my audience when he realized I'd bid my reputation and stage fright adios and good riddance, and I'm not pushing the issue.

"There is no passion," says Belion. "We should be showing them clips that leave their glasses fogged, their hands sweaty."

Felicia doesn't even look at her tablet before answering. "That can wait for James. We have him after Christmas solid. Can't have a sex scene without the primaries, and you do not want Nine trying to fill in for James on this."

Vaguely, in the back of my mind, memories of Sonia saying we'd have to film bedroom scenes come flitting back.

I've gotten to be an expert at sitting across from Kantina, looking the other way from Kantina, turning my back on Kantina, and probably a few more. My left shoulder is going to need its own talent agent at this rate. But... I lean over to Sonia. "Is he talking about..."

"Yes." Sonia sounds more bored than excited. "Let me destroy any fantasy that might be forming there. Let's say you're filming the second sequence, where K's straddling the Lord of the Manor. Sounds hot, right?"

It's a trap, and I'm learning to step around them. If a woman asks if you think something might be hot about another woman, the only answer is... "No?"

"Yes," Sonia corrects, leaning in close as though she's sharing a secret. "It sounds hot. But then imagine you holding that position for hours while they shoot a single take over and over. In between, the makeup artist sprays you with cooking oil so you look sweaty enough." Sonia pauses long enough for me to process that. "And neither of us is heavy, but I promise you, after the first hour, your hips will be aching for a break. Oh... and there's a director, and a dozen cameramen, and the grip, and everyone else on set watching, because, let's be honest, who doesn't want to see that?"

It's sounding less sexy and more horrible by the moment. "And it's scripted?"

"To the quarter-inch. You think the kisses were choreographed, wait until you see this." Sonia gives me a half-hearted smile like she's sorry she crushed my idea of what it would be like.

"Tell me Kantina isn't going to be—"

"Naked? Not for the shots you'll do. She does her own body work, but they'll clear the set of pretty much everyone for that." The way Sonia says it, this is completely normal.

As Kantina approaches, I ask Sonia, "James has a body double, doesn't he?"

Sonia puts one arm around me and looks to Kantina. "He wants to know if James has a body double."

Kantina stops, her mouth open in surprise. "I'm sorry, William, but you will have to tolerate me."

"I didn't *mean*—wait." One glance to Sonia, and my suspicions are confirmed. "You're kidding with me. Again."

"He's getting smarter," says Kantina to Sonia. "You'll have to watch out, or he'll know all our secrets."

With deep breaths, I calm my nerves, and remind myself it's just a job. Even if I had imagined it being fun instead of terrifying, Sonia's explanation would have cleared that up. "I'll do my best, and I swear, I will act professional."

"I'm sure you will," Kantina says. "But you are correct. James has a standing contract with a professional model who serves in his stead."

I didn't realize how nervous I was until the laughter erupts from me. "Oh, thank God. Those are some scenes I'd rather not stand in for."

Kantina looks from me to Sonia, her eyebrow cocked. "You did not tell him? Of course you did not." She shakes her head and looks back to me. "You will still get your chance to be 'professional,' William. But with her."

WHILE BELION SHOOTS A SERIES OF SHOTS WITH FEAST-goers that must be done today, I'm pacing back and forth in the small side area where I used to eat lunch with Eddie Gellar, while Sonia watches. I don't know if Eddie's done shooting or he died, but he hasn't been here for weeks. "When were you planning on mentioning this to me?" I ask Sonia.

"About thirty seconds before we started filming," she says. "This kind of thing weirds people out. Normal people, that is. I'm an actress. Tell me my role is to eat a cockroach, I'd probably do it on camera."

"I'll be fine." I may not be. "Questions. Will you be dressed?"

"Yes." She laughs like the idea is ridiculous. "You'd see more of me at the pool than when we're filming. Particularly because my skin in certain areas is not the same tone as Kantina's."

"And I *will* be dressed."

"That's totally up to you. But I recommend it. That way if you go out at lunch you don't have to put on more clothing than you already have."

Why does the idea of being near her freak me out even worse than the idea of filming with Kantina? "I can do this."

"This is why I said you needed to get comfortable around me. It makes both our jobs easier. See?" She pulls me into a hug. "We're closer right now than we will be while filming, and you're not stiff as a board."

"Give me a moment."

She flinches, and spurts out, "I didn't mean it like that."

"Look who else turns redder when they're embarrassed," I say. The tables have turned. The script's been flipped, though right now, I'm about to flip out and flip a table at the thought of what comes next. It's not like I haven't imagined what it would be like to lay in a tangle of arms and legs, wrapped around her so close I can feel her heart beat—but that is exactly the problem.

THERE'S NO LESS EMBARRASSING WAY THROUGH WHAT comes next. One of the bedroom sets is now lit like there's a search party going in at any moment. The bed is turned around, the monster headboard removed so they can get a better shot of the heroine in the throes of passion.

And passion, for certain, is lacking.

Wardrobe fits me with a pair of swim-shorts labeled "flesh colored" and I suppose they are, if the flesh in question is something found dead alongside the road. If I found my stomach the color of these shorts, I would drive to the emergency room immediately.

The soundstage is largely empty—the swarms of PAs are milling outside the studio doors, and Aaron is adjusting lights himself without grips, only Felicia and Belion to guide him.

"I'm ready," I say, as I approach the set. "What do I do?"

"Wow. Just…wow." Felicia sets down her tablet and looks me over from head to toe. "Can anyone remind me why we had him wearing a shirt before? My God, Will, you're built."

I shrug off the compliment. "Wood carving builds muscle tone. You want someone that looks sculpted, find a body builder. You want muscle built from work, I guess driving nails gets it done."

"Modesty isn't warranted in this case. New rule: All of Will's costumes include him shirtless." She pauses and turns to her lone production assistant. "That was a joke, Steph. Do not write that down. You know, Will, a few set photos leak, and you could be hammering a lot more than nails. I'm happily married, but I promise you there's a ton of women who aren't." She points to the bed. "Giddy up, cowboy, once touchup is done."

Touchup is an Asian American woman who works with brutal efficiency, using a spray bottle and a paint brush to make certain every inch of exposed skin on my body is painted with olive oil. While she works, she chats about how best to clean it off (paper towels), and if it bothers her that she's effectively drawing on me, she doesn't show it. I get the feeling this is a day-to-day occurrence for her.

Once I'm properly glistening, the PA snaps pictures of me that will be used for color adjustment.

Then Sonia enters the set.

She was right: the outfit she's wearing shows less skin than many a swimsuit, but I'd attribute that primarily to it being designed to keep her top from having a wardrobe malfunction. It's like a swimsuit top with a deep plunge of cleavage—and a set of heavy laces to keep it together.

While touchup works on her, Ila, the male model who will be doing this for real, stands at the head of the bed, chatting with me.

If Felicia thought I had muscles, she must have been drooling over him. Ila admits he spends every minute he isn't on set in a gym. Were I a man to feel intimidated, his bulging muscles would do it.

Felicia looks to Belion and exchanges a few words. When he nods, she whistles. "All right. So, we're going to set lighting for the primary shot. Do not move. Do not breathe. Do not speak. Do not so much as blink if I don't tell you. Aaron, you take point."

"Will do." Aaron steps forward and gestures to the bed. "Nine, you're there, and I want touchup after you're in position. Sonia, same story, and keep your hands off the chest. That's about all we'll see from him, so don't leave prints."

The bed's mattress is cardboard, because a real mattress would sag. After a few moments, it's uncomfortable, and the situation even more so as Sonia deftly straddles me, keeping her weight off my hips. All I can do is beg my body not to react to being so close to her, since this is not the time or place for arousal, and I will burst into flames from embarrassment if that happens.

Touchup paints me again, then gives Sonia the same treatment repeatedly.

"Hair," Aaron calls. "You really want it down for this?"

He and Belion argue for a good ten minutes, by which time, my hips do, in fact, hurt not from the weight, but from the rock-hard mattress-substitute I'm lying on.

I shift for just a moment—and earn half a dozen shouts.

"Do. Not. Move," Felicia says. "Touchup, now."

Sonia mouths the word, 'careful.'

I will be, if only because it will get us done quickly.

Again and again, they move the lights and spray me. I have enough olive oil on me to bake a pizza, and still the touchup lady finds new places to spritz.

Belion finally throws his hands up. "Pull it to one side. It must be seen, the hair is her essence."

Aaron shakes his head, then motions. "Sonia, left side, please."

She pulls her hair over, and now it pools by my arm, sticking to my chest.

"No good." Felicia says. "First off, it's clinging, second, it doesn't even look good. We're not filming the Lord of the Manor in bed with a mop. Check the monitor."

While Aaron and Belion argue, and touchup murders another olive tree just to make me look greasy, Felicia studies the set. "Sonia, what do you normally do with the hair?"

"What do you mean?"

"What do you think I mean?" Felicia looks over her shoulder to the arguing men. "How do you keep it out of the way?"

The heat from the lights might be my imagination. Ditto the way this bed feels like it's made of iron. But what I'm not imagining is the blush that colors Sonia's cheeks. She mumbles her answer.

"Sorry, didn't get that," says Felicia. "Try again?"

"I pin it up, or tie it off and toss it up at the top of the bed. You'll have to ask Kantina if you want to know what she does."

"What about letting it hang down?"

Sonia shudders and looks like she might puke on me. "No. No. No."

"I'll take that under consideration." Felicia stalks away, and after a few minutes, returns. "Listen up, gentlemen. Neither of you have enough hair to cover your heads, let alone be a problem. I have it on good authority the lady would pin her hair up. Trust me when I say you do not want details on why."

Aaron considers it a moment—and then they go back to arguing.

It's nearly twenty minutes later when they finally try Felicia's suggestion—and only ten minutes before Belion agrees. "This is perfect. First crew."

First crew, in this case, consists only of Kantina and Ila.

Ila takes my place in the bed, and while touchup turns him into stirfry, I wait for Felicia. "You need me? The oil is starting to congeal."

"You don't want to stick around?" Felicia asks it like there's a right answer and a wrong answer. "Kantina's got this way of making everyone else feel like she's just as comfortable naked as we are clothed."

I hold up both hands in surrender. "Pass? My arms are sticking to my chest."

Felicia chuckles to herself as she points to the front entrance. "Suit yourself, Will. Go shower off, but be ready in case we need to go again. You can do more than one shot at a time without a nap, right?"

"Of course I can." It isn't until after I'm in the showers that I catch her innuendo.

By the time I return to set, they're on take seven, and it sounds like someone is murdering Kantina with every take. I've elected to stay in Central Holding, because if she looks anything like she sounds, it isn't sexy, it's frightening.

"Will?" Sonia approaches me. She's wearing a leopard-spotted gray silk bathrobe that proves that what's hidden is so much more seductive than what's on display.

When I manage to tear my eyes off her, I stumble for words. "You showered too?"

She nods. "Don't leave that stuff on. You'll have zits everywhere, and I do mean *everywhere*."

"They're filming, and you're not watching the monitors?" I say.

She tilts her head toward me. "I could ask you the same."

Kantina gives the same wail she's made the last seven—or is that eight?—times, making me grimace. "That is not a noise I associate with a woman enjoying herself."

"Mixed with the score, you'll barely hear her. She's acting too reserved today. Something must be bothering her."

"I'm sure you'll figure it out. You two are something else, you know that? Is there anything you don't discuss?"

"You obviously didn't have any sisters." Sonia eases onto the couch. As she does so, the front of her gown falls open—and I look away as she ties it back. "All clear, Will."

I feel like I'm the one who should be apologizing, for a glimpse that feels more forbidden than anything we filmed. And since when did I act like a teen boy who'd never seen a grown woman? I take a seat beside her, humming to drown out the wails of fake pleasure. "Kantina. You were talking about Kantina."

"Are you thinking about her right now?" Sonia asks, letting her hand brush against mine.

"Definitely not."

"I guess I've still got what it takes." The smug grin on her face makes me wonder if the gown malfunction was an accident or not. "But yes, Kantina and I are more like sisters. I've worked every movie with her. Celebrated every birthday together. When she went to rehab, it was on the condition that I get the room next door, and I personally bailed her out the last time she got in legal trouble."

"Sounds like family. My brother and I aren't much different."

"Friends are the family you choose, Will."

I try to calm the feeling of weightlessness as I take a leap of faith. "Is that what we are? Friends?"

Her breath catches, and Sonia is dead silent. "Your brother—"

"Is happily married. Isn't me. Voted against us continuing production. You and I are two nobodies, Sonia. No one sees us, or cares, and if you and I had dinner, or breakfast, or lunch, it wouldn't make the headlines." I take her hand and hold on to it, willing her to understand.

She holds mine for a moment, then reluctantly draws back before shifting away. "If only it were that simple. I'm sorry, Will."

"Second crew," shouts Felicia. "Let's go again."

Sonia and I stand together, and return to film two seconds of fake sex that takes hours, with the woman I can't have. And don't want, I add mentally.

I don't make a habit of lying to myself, but there's a fine line between saying something because it's true, and it being true because I say it.

CHAPTER FIFTEEN

THE NEXT COUPLE DAYS OF FILMING STRIP AWAY ANY notion of romance that remained in film sex. I've hugged, held, lifted, and laid atop Sonia, and it's about as romantic as a trip to the dentist. But as we wrap one evening, Felicia isn't handing out shot lists. She looks at me as I wait expectantly. "Go home, Will. You have the rest of the week off, and I'll see you after Thanksgiving."

I blink. "But, Sonia said we'd film straight through the holidays."

Felicia raises one eyebrow and waits for me to realize Sonia isn't the assistant director. "It's a tradeoff. Less holiday pay for a few days' delay. Go home."

And that's when it hits me that I'm free.

It's Tuesday, according to my phone, and when I stumble through the door of Bradley and Tia's apartment, Tia looks up in shock from the counter where they're doing bills. "He does exist! Will, we were having debates about whether or not Brad imagined he had a brother."

"He's still on my list for voting against production." I've missed dinner, but at this point, I'll inhale anything in the fridge. "It's been hectic. We've been filming a single sex scene for days."

"Wow!" Tia gives me a wink. "That... is something I'd pay to see. What's it like?"

"Hot. Wet. Sticky." All of these are the truth she's looking for, and a lie, but who am I to shatter the illusion?

Bradley swings Tia into his arms and gives her a kiss. "What do you think? You and I could make our own—"

"Never." She shakes her head after kissing him again. "Not going to happen."

"Do I get a vote? I'm voting never, too." I say through a mouthful of meatloaf. "Videos like that get leaked, and there isn't enough brain bleach in the world to get that image out of my head."

Bradley sighs as he finishes the dishes. "You're just not romantic, Will. You doing the usual?"

He means, am I going to fall asleep on the couch in about twenty minutes. "Tonight? Yes. But tomorrow, when I don't have to be up at four in the morning? Probably not."

"Family Movie Night!" they say together, and I understand I don't get a vote.

"I have something to show you," says Tia, taking out her phone.

I know what it is in an instant—it's a sonogram picture. All of them look like those pictures of polar bears in a snow storm, and I can't make anything out until she points out the nose.

In a flash, the possibility that there'll be more to our tiny family becomes a reality in a way I just couldn't grasp before. I'm going to be an uncle. I'm going to be the best uncle ever. I don't care if it's a boy or a girl, I'll teach them to run every saw in the shop, and how to run the torch, and all the things that Tia and Bradley would say were much too dangerous for kids.

"Beautiful." It's all I can say as I wipe the tears from my eyes. And this baby will *not* arrive in chaos caused by me getting my brother's business blacklisted, no matter what. I lay down on the cold vinyl couch and cover myself with a quilt, and while the credits of some movie that I think is in French roll, the soundtrack is singing me to sleep.

AT FOUR THIRTY IN THE MORNING, I WAKE UP, JOLTING upright, gripped with fear. I'm late. I should already have showered, I should be packing my grilled cheese materials. I should… go back to bed, because I have today off.

But my brain is already on, and racing so fast it's leaving smoke trails, and ready to go for the day.

My phone buzzes, and I flip it over to read the text. It's from Sonia.

You awake?

I can't afford to let the excitement show. What sort of person would be awake at four in the morning willingly? I channel my inner grump as I type the reply. *I am not. Go back to sleep.*

The once-comfortable vinyl couch leaves creases on me when I lay back down, and I toss and turn. Also, I'm holding my phone and staring at it, waiting to see if she'll text again, which also makes it hard to sleep.

An agonizing minute later my phone buzzes again.

You awake now?

I count to ten to make it seem like I wasn't waiting, and get to six before I start typing back. *Why are you not going back to sleep?*

Can't. Awake is awake. You want coffee?

Might as well. Where do you want to meet?

A soft knock at the front door has me bolting upright again. I pad over to it and unlock the bolt and chain.

Sonia's standing there, dressed in a white tennis skirt with matching blouse and sneakers. Her pony tail is tied in sections that make it a tail of epic portions, and the white baseball cap she has completes the ensemble. She holds up a tray with two cups. "A week ago, I heard you say you liked the white mocha, but not the specifics. I brought one of each."

I'm wearing nothing but pajama bottoms, but given what we've shot over the last few days, it doesn't bother me one bit. Once she scans me head to toe, taking her sweet time, I accept the coffee, step back and bow slightly. "Come on in, but be quiet. My brother and his wife are sleeping, like normal people."

"You and I are actors. Actors aren't normal." She shuts the door and surveys the living-room that's served as my home. "It's nice. Homey. Not at all what I expected."

I take a seat at the breakfast nook and sip the coffee. "What are you doing here? We don't have to work. We don't have to run lines or put up with 'I am an artiste' rants or get turned into human salad dressing. So why are you here?"

Sonia doesn't answer until she's studied her coffee (cream, no sugar, like always) long enough to divine an answer from the swirls. "This business takes over your life. All my friends work on the lot. I woke up this morning and didn't realize it was a holiday until I was sitting in the parking lot."

"How did you find me?"

"Your address was on the contract you signed for Felicia." Sonia points to my coffee. "You're not drinking."

"So *why* are you here?"

"I was lonely," she says without missing a beat. "I knew you would ask. I asked myself the same thing the whole way over. If I know this is a bad idea, why am I doing it? And I kept thinking, 'It's morning. Where's Will?'"

A thought that's gotten me out of bed more mornings than I can say is that I would get to see her if I got up. But that? That's too close to breaking her rules, too close to saying I'd let someone hurt me again. "What about Kantina? Isn't she up meditating and trying to exist only on the first rays of sunlight at dawn?"

"Kantina's a vegan again this week, Will. And she's on her way to Europe, doing a benefit concert. Her flight left right after we finished filming. She'll touch down in a few hours."

"I'm surprised you're not going with her."

Sonia shrugs. "Not this time. She's my best friend—heck, I talk to her more than I do my little sister—but sometimes, it's like I can't tell where she ends and I begin. We have to do things separately just for our own sanity."

I nod, though I never had anyone that close. Tamara and I had our own lives that collided in sweaty nights and lazy mornings. I wave to the living room, with my suitcase tucked under the coffee table and my clothes hanging on the rocker. "It's not lifestyles of the rich and famous, but I'm welcome here, and I'm as close to happy as I can get."

"Big houses don't mean much if they're empty," says Sonia. "You know when Kantina built hers, she built one for me next door? It's six thousand square feet, and it looks like a playhouse next to hers. We share a swimming pool."

"You live in a smaller mansion behind a mansion?"

She shakes her head. "No. I live in an apartment I insist on renting. But I have the key and a code for her security."

"You own a mansion."

Sonia jingles her car keys. "Put some clothes on so you don't attract every stray woman on the street, and let's take a ride. I'll show you, it's not a mansion."

It's totally a mansion.

From the gated entrance to the security guard who waves us through, the difference is that behind a house I'd call a shopping mall, sits a smaller house that's larger than ten of Bradley's apartment. The ceiling is mostly glass, stone chimneys rise from either end of the house and the center, and the brickwork is covered in carefully trimmed ivy.

Sonia parks her convertible beside the pool and unlocks the front door, which opens to a wide living room with floor-to-ceiling windows and lush vines hanging from wicker baskets along the windows. The back wall is essentially one giant walk-in fireplace, and at the far end from the kitchen hangs a TV that's only technically smaller than a movie theatre. "Oh my God, Sonia."

"Stop!" She bats at me, then goes to the kitchen and opens the fridge. "Beer? They don't go bad, so I don't mind keeping them. Kantina and I watch movies here from time to time."

"How about breakfast? Do you have a cook?"

She checks the freezer. "I could call up to the house and have something made, but with Kantina on tour, I want this to be their holiday, too."

"I can cook with you." I survey the pots and pans hanging from hooks, most of which still have their labels attached. "Have you ever cooked?"

She slides up beside me as I test the gas stove. "I can boil water, and I can dial for takeout, and I can pour cereal."

"Can you order groceries?"

It takes her a moment to realize I'm serious, but this is LA, and we both have phones. You can order *anything*. Half an hour later, I walk up to the gate to accept two bags of groceries, which I carry across the manicured lawn, avoiding the mini-golf windmill.

"All right!" I say as I open the door. "Now we can actually cook."

Sonia's clicking the movie screen on to today's entertainment news.

"Well?" I say as I set the bags down. "I said I'd cook *with* you, not *for* you. You have to help. We have to wash up dishes first, since I'm guessing you've never used these."

Sonia searches through the cabinets. "I have a perfectly good pot at the apartment. I keep meaning to put these in the dishwasher."

"Never the cast iron," I say with horror. "Give me the scrubber." I make short work of the pans, show her how to turn on her fancy oven, and get the water going for gravy.

"You should do this shirtless," she says. "Women are supposedly sexiest when they clean house nude, and men when they cook naked."

I wipe a splatter of grease off my arm, ignoring the pain. "You want me to fry bacon shirtless, you take off your top, your bra, and stand right beside me. We'll suffer together."

Sonia takes one look at the sizzling pan and covers her chest. "Nope, nope, and also, let me think about it… Nope. Keep the shirt."

"Thought you might feel that way." A few minutes later, she's pouring orange juice while I deliver plates with biscuits and gravy. And when we finally dig in? She gives me the chef's ultimate compliment—a meal kept silent by people devouring food.

Afterwards, we stand shoulder to shoulder as I wash dishes and she dries, setting them on the rack. The scent of dish soap mixes with wafts of her perfume and sweet coconut shampoo. "What are we doing?" I say as we finish up.

"Now? Let's watch the news."

"Not that," I say, turning off the tap. "This. You showing up at my door. Me cooking for you. Us playing house. What happened to Belion and his threats? What happened to 'someone might see me' and 'I can't risk my reputation?'"

Sonia tenses, glancing around the room instinctively before she drops her shoulders and leans back against the counter, playing with a loose sprig of hair. "Belion went home for the holidays too. That means he's being annoying in some other part of the world, probably somewhere whinier and more petty. My family is on the other side of the country. My friends, the few I have, are busy with their own lives. I didn't come to you for a secret booty call. I needed a friend, and I thought maybe you needed one too." She steps closer, dangerously close.

I hand her the last plate. "What if Belion has spies?"

"It happened once, but it wasn't someone he asked to watch me. Just a co-worker who went to him on their own. I hope what he got was worth it. I'm barely human to Belion, though that does make me rank above you." She shrugs. "The only time anyone pays any attention to me is when they mistakenly think I'm Kantina."

I don't try to hide the shock or disgust that hits me as I momentarily loathe every man who's ever done that. "You aren't. You're your own person, a smart, beautiful, funny woman."

Sonia stops trying to drown her sorrows in orange juice. "You should tell that to everyone else. I can't get acting jobs on my own because I look too much like Kantina. The men who want to date me do it because it's easy to imagine me as her with the lights low."

That makes me shudder. "Seriously? Men want that? Those eyes of hers, it's like being stared at by an anaconda. I wouldn't be able to sleep next to her for fear I'd wake up and she'd be eating me toes first."

Juice spurts from Sonia's mouth and nose, soaking my shirt, and Sonia falls into a choking fit that has me pounding her on the back. When she looks up, her face is tomato red and there are tears in her eyes. "That burns so bad. Totally worth it. Oh my God. I can't wait to tell her that."

"You two aren't that much alike. Yes, I might have made a mistake once, but seriously, you're so different. Her skin is darker. You have thinner cheeks, and an actual chin." I study the lines of Sonia's face, then reach out to trace each feature as I speak. "Your eyes are narrower. Your nose isn't round like hers."

Sonia smiles and looks away, but she doesn't tell me to stop.

"Your shoulders are wider than hers, and I would bet all the money I don't have that you're taller."

"By a quarter inch. We have our hair trimmed at the same time so it's the same length when we're standing."

"Your hips—"

"You missed a couple of differences." Sonia drops her eyes. "Try again?"

"No. I am not studying your boobs and hers for comparison purposes. It's hard enough to not stare under normal circumstances. Not that I stare. Or that you're not worth staring at—okay, can we strike this entire conversation from the record?"

Sonia leans her head on my shoulder as she laughs. "Tell me something, seriously, Will. Why do you see me when you look at me, and not her?"

I know what she's asking, and the reality of it tears a hole in my soul as I imagine what it must be like to live in the shadow of someone you love, and yet can never out-run. "How could I ever see anyone else?"

The way she turns from me, I've hit a nerve I didn't mean to. When Sonia speaks, her voice is subdued, and the laughter is gone. "You know Kantina had a crush on you, right? All that waving and sashaying and finding a reason to talk to you? You thought all that just happened?"

"What?" I gently turn her to look me in the eye. "That's ridiculous."

"I'm not joking. She kept asking me what you were like, and what you said, and if you liked the outfit she was wearing. How could you not tell?" Sonia's eyebrows are raised, her mouth set.

"Well, most of the time I was around her, you were there. You eclipsed her."

Sonia's eyes are shining with tears, and remorse for whatever I said floods me. In one instant, I see a possibility of what it might be like if we cross—no, crash across the line between us. It would all begin with a kiss to those lush red lips.

Sonia hasn't stopped staring at me, but as I reach for her, her breath hitches. She steps away from me like I shoved her, and circles the kitchen to put the island between us.

If I've upset her, I might as well ask the hard questions. "The other day, Felicia said you should be behind the camera instead of in front of it."

"Felicia says a lot of things."

"She's an assistant director. She's fierce, and smart, and I'd bet money if she says it, it's probably true. So why aren't you?"

Sonia stares off into the distance, eyes unfocused, before she answers. "I couldn't do that to Kantina. She relies on me."

I'm not going to chase Sonia. The leather couch with its pull-out recliner seems like a better place, so I move to it, then kick back there before picking at this further. "She said that? It sounds selfish."

"Not in so many words," Sonia says, then adds, "It's an unspoken agreement."

"So you don't know."

The look of exasperation on her face as she stalks toward the couch would make me smile if the subject wasn't serious. "We discussed it, lots of times, at the start of her career, and after she got out of rehab the second time. Was I happy? Did I want to do this? Did I want her help doing something different?"

"Are you? Do you?"

"Most of the time, I like what I do." Sonia paces across the room, studying the ceiling, then drops into the seat next to me and kicks her feet out. "Every once in a while, I see a story and I think, 'I could tell that better. I could help them tell it in a way that would have everyone thinking about it.'"

"So why don't you? Are you protecting Kantina, or yourself?"

"Ouch!" She glares at me. "Just because I'm on the couch doesn't mean I need you to shrink me, Will."

That reminds me of something Tia said. "Friends are therapists you don't have to pay, or so I hear. I don't have many, and the few I do are back in Seattle."

"What about your brother?"

"Bradley's a great brother, but he's not a friend. Similar, but different."

Sonia rests her head on the recliner and closes her eyes. "I like to lay here and watch the sun on the pool. Early sun is the best sun."

"I'd go swimming every day if it were me. There's a pool at the apartment, but there's so much hair and scum in it, it's basically human soup. Even then, it's tempting."

"Go," she says, her voice half asleep. "'Tina doesn't use swimsuits, but there's a few for her guests in the cabana. From back when she still had guests." She nods her head toward the door, or maybe she's snuggling down. "Will?"

There's so many questions that brings up, but Kantina isn't the one I want to discuss. "Yes?"

"I feel safe with you."

I don't know exactly what to say to this, but I want her to feel safe. I want her to be safe. "I'm glad."

"I don't remember feeling safe." She tucks her head under my chin, and her breathing slows as the tension runs out of her body. At first I don't move, but after a few minutes, Sonia rolls over, and she isn't dozing—she's out and out snoring, in a way that would put Bradley to shame.

He claims I snore. I've certainly never heard it.

But the longer I sit here, the better the pool looks.

It's a short trip out the French doors and across to the pool cabana.

By cabana, Sonia meant a literal thatched hut. The door doesn't open without me unjamming it and just about forcing the lock. After minutes of fighting with the curtains, I give up and simply change. It's not like I have much modesty where Sonia's involved anymore.

The pool is saltwater, with a waterfall at one end that makes the water cold when I dive under. The California sun beats down, warming me when I float on top, so it's a mix of cold and hot I'd label Heaven. I can't tell you how many laps I do, letting the water leech away the heat. And when I'm exhausted, I roll over and simply float, arms spread, face back, drinking in the salt smell and the quiet trickle of water.

Quiet that is broken by the opening of a door, and light footsteps on the cobblestone. When I open one eye, Sonia's standing at the poolside, holding her phone.

I flick a spray of water at her legs. "Hey. You coming in?"

"Just enjoying the view. Kantina landed, and she wants to talk." Sonia covers the speaker. "Don't act weird, all right?"

"How am I weird?"

"You *don't* know she had a crush on you," says Sonia. "Because I *didn't* tell you. Now... K, can you hear us?"

"Of course I can, darling. William, it is so nice of you to be our guest. I am sorry I cannot be there to welcome you myself."

I put down my feet so I don't accidentally swallow water. "Thanks for having me. Your guest house is amazing. I mean, what I've seen of it. The backyard, mostly. And the pool."

"It is Sonia's house, not mine, though the pool is ours. I trust the swimsuit is to your liking?"

"Fits fine," I say, not fully understanding where she's going.

"William, next time, Sonia will disable the alarms before you go traipsing around. And should you wish to close the curtains, untie them from the sides. That way, the security cameras will not record you changing when an alarm goes off. Just a thought, darling."

I spin in the water and look.

Sure enough, small gray dots top the corners and ledges of the cabana. "Were those... on?"

"I have had many problems with stalkers," Kantina says, her voice rich and warm, like she's trying to stifle a laugh. "They are always on."

"And someone could have been watching?"

"Oh, no," says Kantina. "We do not watch them live, but I have on my phone an app, I will show it to you when I return. Sonia, darling, you can show him on yours."

"I don't need to see." In particular, I don't want to see that clip, with that woman. "Would you please delete that footage?"

After a moment she answers. "Of course, William. It is done now. How could I be so fiercely protective of my own privacy, and not honor yours?"

"Thank you." I swim over to the side of the pool and rest my head there. "Lesson learned. I doubt I'll be back, but if I ever were, I'd know."

"Do not be so hasty. Or so embarrassed. I have seen many men, and you have nothing to be ashamed of."

Sonia rolls her eyes and turns the phone around. "Enough of that. Tell me about the flight." She stops and turns her attention to me for a fleeting moment. "When you're ready to get out, if you don't want to fight the curtains or perform another strip-tease, second door on the right in my house is a guest bathroom you are welcome to use. Might want to check to make sure it has soap and towels and all that."

I take her invitation as an indication she won't be napping again, and by the time I emerge from a leisurely shower, Sonia's kicked back on the couch, headphones on, chatting. "Because I was lonely. What? You've never been lonely? I'm not going to show up at Aaron's door and invite myself in. Will's different."

My phone buzzes on the kitchen counter—and the moment I read it, my hands begin to tremble.

I drop it on the floor as my fingers refuse to move properly, and a surge of emotion rolls up my spine, knotting my shoulders as I fight to keep it in. Anger. Fear. Sadness. I'm not sure how I wind up sitting on the kitchen floor, but I'm still there when Sonia steps around the counter.

"Will? What's wrong? You look like someone died."

I shake my head and try to find the words. "That was the King County prosecutor's office in Seattle. Tamara— my ex—was arrested during a traffic stop this morning. They have her in custody now."

"Gotta go, I'll call later." Sonia eases herself to the floor, sitting cross-legged against the fridge. "How do you feel about that?"

Torn is the right word, as I grasp for the simple bliss I'd enjoyed moments earlier, the easy pleasure of being with someone who makes you relaxed and nervous all at once. This was a side I would never have chosen to show Sonia.

In my anger, my hurt, the dark days that came right after Tamara disappeared, I always imagined confronting her. Demanding answers. Finding some reason to believe it would make the pain less. But there's only one word for what I'm going through. "Terrified."

CHAPTER SIXTEEN

Sonia lets me sit on the kitchen floor for a good half hour before she speaks again. "You know, I have a table, and a couch, both of which are more comfortable for long term brooding."

"I'm sorry." It's the only thing I can think to say. I text Bradley a screenshot of the message I received, and ignore his call. If I wanted to talk to him, I wouldn't have texted.

"You want me to take you home?"

I nod, because what, really, is there to say? "Two years she's been on the run, and she has to ruin today. Why couldn't she have ruined tomorrow?"

Sonia tilts her head to the door. "If you feel that strongly about it, don't let her. Do what you were going to do. Relax. Go up to the big house and get some rum, get drunk in the sun. Will, you don't owe this woman another thought." She pauses and then looks back to me, her eyes narrowed. "Unless you want to."

"Never." I didn't expect the guttural anger that accompanies my declaration. "I don't at all. I've spent two years ashamed and guilty and asking myself why I didn't see through her sooner." The drive to move pushes me to my feet. "The show must go on, right?"

"That's usually used for plays, but I think we'll make an exception in your case." She stands as well. "When you say 'show', what do you have in mind?"

"We have a tradition in my family. Bradley and I have always eaten a lunch the day before Thanksgiving, and then we don't eat until the big meal. We're saving room for pumpkin pie. Tia cooks one for each of us." My stomach rumbles at the thought. "What time is it?"

"Nearly eleven."

That explains why Bradley's texted me half a dozen times. I check his messages.

We're at Reynas. If you don't want to talk, you can at least fill your mouth with food. We ordered enough tamales to feed an army. It's tradition, man. You don't mess with tradition.

I type out a reply, then tap my finger on the phone as I think. "Do you like tamales? Bradley pre-orders them from a hole-in-the-wall place that makes them for holidays."

Sonia shakes her head. "I wouldn't want to impose. We served them once on set and there was almost a war over who got the last one."

"Trust me, if we can eat the last one, they'll be taking us out on a stretcher. What do I do with my wet suit and towel?"

Sonia stops to think. "Leave it for the maid. I always take my suit home when I come to visit. This isn't home yet. It might be, one day, but for now, for my sanity, it's just a place to visit someone I love very much."

In the end, I hang it up to dry while Sonia honks the horn impatiently. She's wrapped her hair in a scarf and pulled the Volkswagen convertible top down.

"You should let the hair hang free. I bet it looks cool streaming behind you."

"That's the worst idea ever. I'd spend hours getting it untangled and removing the crap." But the moment I click my seatbelt, she removes the end of the braid and tosses it over her shoulder. "Where are we going?"

I bring up maps on my phone and set it on the dash. "Are those driving gloves?"

Sonia looks like a model from a nineteen-fifties ad, with dark sunglasses and white gloves on her hands. "Kantina bought me the sunglasses when she had hers made. You like?"

Like isn't the word for it. "I do."

She throws the car into reverse, and cuts the wheel so we slide on the gravel—and by the time we reach the gate, the guard already has it open. Her practiced ease in making a sharp left from the overhung drive says she's come here far more than she lets on, but soon enough we're zipping down the road, chasing the best tamales in town.

I should be angry.

I should be downright furious.

But to be that, I'd need to ignore where I am and who I'm with, and I won't give up now to brood on then.

Anger is patient, and it will still be there when I get around to feeling it, which won't be when Sonia's around.

The road out of town is clogged with traffic, but the sun is shining, the roof is down, and I'm riding with a beautiful woman in a Volkswagen convertible that rattles with every bump.

When we finally reach Reyna's there's a line to pick up, but as a long-time customer Bradley has a spot in the back. "Bro," he says as we thread our way through the narrow hallway that serves as a dining room. "Introduce us?"

Tia stands and offers her hand—a major step, since it took her a year and a half to stop spraying everything I touched with bleach. "Tia Mathis," she says to Sonia. "I've heard so much about you."

"You have?" Sonia and I say together.

"Sonia," I say, "Tia is Bradley's wife. This is my brother Bradley, and that thing on his face is his beard."

Sonia shakes his hand and then looks to me. "You had one like that. Is he good looking underneath?"

Tia answers before I can. "He's handsome always."

I'd kill to have someone look at me the way Tia and Bradley look at each other, with faith and trust and complete confidence. I wonder if I'll ever find that.

We take our seats at a wobbly Formica table, and before I can make small talk, Sonia starts off. "So what has Will told you about me?"

"Nothing," I say. Though there's more question in my statement than statement.

Tia leans forward because of the bustle and nearly shouts, "Is it true he mistook you for Kantina that first day?"

"True," Sonia says, with a smile. "Totally true. Oh my God, if you could have seen the look on his face…"

Bradley shakes his head. "Dude, have you figured out how to tell them apart now?"

"I have." This time, I speak with confidence. "The smart, talented, beautiful one is Sonia. The other one is Kantina."

Sonia was taking a drink, but she's frozen, and from the way she sets down her glass, I'm guessing she's surprised.

She shouldn't be. She should be used to being respected, adored.

"That's so sweet." Tia leans against Bradley. "Brad and I are huge fans. Huge. Huger. Hugest."

"She's coming to movie night, right?" Bradley asks, looking to me.

"I don't know. Sonia, if you're busy—"

"I'm not." Sonia says it quickly, like she was waiting. "But I have to know what movie in order to bring the right wine. What are we watching?"

"Something amazing," says Bradley. "It's a new film Tia chose for us to import. We bought the import rights and had it subtitled straight from Spain. We'll be some of the first people in the U.S. to see it," says Bradley. "It's called *El Grito Del Flamenco*, and—"

"You'll love it!" Sonia says, nearly bouncing up and down with excitement. Her hands are twitching, the smile on her face is nearly a manic grin. "That opening shot is worth the entire movie, I swear. It's like a microcosm of everything to come, and you don't know it, but you know everything you're seeing is important—and then, she unwinds the story like a ball of yarn…"

Sonia trails off as Bradley and Tia sit staring at her. "I'm in the industry. Studying this is like studying for a test, or taking apart a cabinet built by a craftsman to see how it's done. I can't wait to see it again."

"What kind of beer would you recommend?" I ask.

"Beer." Sonia says, the way I'd say 'lawyer.' "You don't pair beer. You swallow and follow—with another beer. Leave the wine picking to me."

Our box of tamales comes. We'll eat some now, freeze the rest, and thaw them out to give the turkey a break after Thanksgiving. But for now, we dig in. And only when we've eaten the first few does Bradley take a break. "So, truth time. We going to ignore the big news?"

"We are," I say.

Tia gives me a side-eyed glance. "Does this mean you're going back to being Mr. Broody-Angry-Silent Will? That version of you was a dick."

"Will? Silent?" Sonia looks at the two of them. "Where is this quiet version of Will and what did you do with him?"

"I'm quiet on set."

She elbows me. "And you practically never shut up off set. This morning, you two, I showed him my place at Kantina's house, and—"

"Guest house," I say. "She has a house of her own that's a monster."

"It's not that large," she says.

"It's huge. And she has a swimming pool, which she only shares with one other person."

Sonia raises an eyebrow as if to ask if I really want to bring that up. "Speaking of pools, Will set off the alarm when he opened the cabana, then stripped naked without closing the curtains, and Kantina had to delete the footage from the security camera after she sent it to me."

There's a moment of sheer panic before I whisper. "She sent it to you?"

"Before she called. Wanted to know why you were changing in there and I wasn't. Also, why you were bothering with a swimsuit given that we were alone."

Bradley and Tia haven't said a word during the exchange, but now they're looking at each other, and simultaneously, both begin giggling. Bradley looks back and me and shakes his head. "Oh, man. I just—you got me."

"Will?" Sonia says. "What are they laughing at?"

"Beats me." I cross my arms and give him my patented older-brother-glare. "Fill us in? What's so funny?"

Tia holds a finger to her lips. "I'm not going to ruin the fun. Brad?"

"Hell no," he says, arm around her. "But do go on. I think we stopped at my brother, naked on a security camera. Sonia, I'm so sorry for you."

Sonia scowls at him as she answers. "You? You didn't even see it."

"You did?" I ask.

"Only the first two seconds." She says, holding up her phone. "I'll show you the archives and my texts with Kantina. I deleted it, Will. Kantina finds private modesty funny, because she thinks you shouldn't have to worry about things like that in private. I don't."

"I believe you."

Bradley leans forward. "You actually talked to Kantina? Today?"

"Yes?" I say, trying to understand what he's getting at. "Dude, I work with her. See her on set. I wouldn't say we're pals, but she knows my name."

"She knows way more than that," says Sonia as she leans against me and takes another bite of tamale. "She had a crush on him when he first started working."

This morning, when she said it, Sonia was almost angry, or hurt. Now when she says it, the smile on her face reaches her eyes, and puts wrinkles at the corners. "Think about it—your brother could have been dating *the* Kantina."

"Excuse me?" I nudge her with mock offense. "I am a morally upright man of good upbringing. She's a heathen pop-star-model-actress with nothing to offer me but riches and fame. What makes you think I would have said yes if she had asked me out?"

Sonia thinks for a moment, then bows her head. "Please accept my most sincere apologies. I didn't consider your many virtues. If I have offended even a hair on your head, I will be eternally sorry."

"My hair is very offended," I say, twisting my head around. "It doesn't whip like yours, but see this one hair right here? That hair is extremely offended that you think a red-haired, green-eyed temptress could bat her eyelashes or swing her hips and win me over."

"Oh, but she could," says Sonia with a wink. "I hear she's very tempting. She definitely could."

Bradley and Tia are doing that thing again where they're staring at us.

"What?" I ask.

Bradley looks at Tia, then laughs at me. "I take it you're over Tamara?"

"Who?" I ask, then give him a wink. But the question knocks the fun out of me like a blow to the stomach. "Over, yes. Still angry with, yes. Ready to see her again, never. Ever. Forever."

"Do you have to go back to testify?" asks Tia. "Do you want us to go with you?"

She knows the answer before I give it. "I will. I have no idea how that fits into the filming schedule, but part of what got the prosecutors off my back was knowing they could reel me in at a moment's notice."

Bradley thinks a moment, then focuses on me. "How are you going to do that? You're in the middle of making a movie."

"I have no idea. All I know for sure is that it has to be done."

Sonia will know. She can ask Felicia. And thinking of Sonia is what clues me in to how she's sitting quietly, almost frozen. Her cap is pulled down, but she's watching someone or something at the front.

"Hey," I say, leaning closer. "What's going on?"

"Don't look up," she says in a whisper. "There's a guy at the front, orange vest, shorts, sandals. He pulled a camera out of his bag a moment ago."

"Like, 'Let's take a birthday picture'?"

"That's a telephoto lens," she says, her body completely rigid. "I have no idea if he already took something. My God, he probably followed us here. We left Kantina's house, right? She changes cars like most people change underwear."

If Sonia's voice rises any higher, she's going to have a panic attack. Scratch that—she might already be having one. I nudge Bradley under the table and text him the shortest summary I can think of.

Tia nods the moment she sees it. "Let me handle this."

"Honey." Bradley refuses to move. "Violence is sometimes the answer, but we promised the judge you wouldn't be back."

I raise my hands until both of them stop. "We are not punching anyone. Yet. As the designated adult in this group, I'm going to go over and explain to our friend the mistake he's made. He's going to go find the real Kantina. We're going back to eating tamales."

"You think they care?" says Sonia, barely speaking. "Will, you don't understand. It doesn't *matter* if I'm not Kantina. For legal purposes, it's better for them. All that matters is that it looks enough like her for people who want to believe it."

Tia's face is scrunched into a frown. "But you're not her."

"So the article says something like, 'This picture is barely recognizable as Kantina.' Or 'Is that Kantina sneaking around?'" Sonia stops, as tears roll down her face. "This can't be happening again."

"I'll punch him, you run out the back," says Bradley.

"Boys," says Tia, "sit. Watch how a woman handles this. Will, be ready. Sonia, it was nice meeting you." She stands up and winds her way forward to the front of the restaurant.

"She's going to punch him," says Bradley. "She's going to punch him so hard. I gotta go stop her, or I'll be out bail money again."

I wouldn't put it past Tia. My attention, however, is on Sonia, who has her head down on the table, and isn't saying anything. When a bus boy passes, I snag a clean table cloth from his cart. "Sonia, give me your car keys, and hold on to this."

She drops her braided keychain on the table, where I'm certain Bradley will collect it, then wraps the table cloth over her head like a hood, clutching the edges like a drowning man does a life preserver.

Bradley isn't small. Tia is short, but terrifying when she's angry, and right now, both of them are blocking the narrow aisle down the restaurant. "Let's go."

One moment we're there, the next, we're running past some extremely surprised cooks. Not even the dishes and chatter can hide the shouts behind us, but right now, I'm focused on adding another career to my resume: Carpenter. Stand-in. And now, magician.

My first performance? Making an actress disappear.

CHAPTER SEVENTEEN

Sonia follows me blindly with the tablecloth I stole wrapped over her head, trusting I won't hurl her into a wall. But rather than run down the alley, I test doors—and find one open. Inside, the heavy stench of carpet glue fills the air. It's a carpet store, and rolls fill the back room, stacked up on spools. "Pull that up so you can see."

Sonia does, and she looks like Red Riding Hood as she holds the tablecloth close.

"Hi," I say to the owner as I emerge from the back. "Your back door is unlocked."

He sputters an answer while I scan the roadway.

"Stay put until I give the signal," I say, leaving Sonia inside and ducking out to step in the path of a passing cab.

Sonia is right behind me when I throw open the door and shove a handful of cash at the driver. "Go."

Only after four blocks does Sonia relax enough to sit up, and even then, she clutches the table cloth and cries.

"It's okay. We got away."

"It's *not* okay," says Sonia, and then gives the driver an address I don't recognize. "I was enjoying the day. I was having a magnificent time."

"You want me to tell Bradley to tell Tia to go ahead and punch him?"

The tears on her face stop my questions. "I'm not mad at the paparazzi. I'm sick of this fear. It's not normal to panic when you see a camera, and now your brother and his wife—"

"Understand. You haven't seen Tia when her meds aren't working. They're not anyone to worry about." I gently put one arm around her and cradle her as she cries.

"When we're not filming, I go to a therapist three times a week. We worked up to her taking a picture and then giving me the phone to delete it."

"That's progress."

With a sniffle, she looks up. "One day, I won't be afraid anymore. I did this to myself, I can undo it, and sometimes, I'm *so* close to taking that first giant step, letting someone else take a picture without panicking."

"I'd be happy to help."

"You don't count. You'd never use it against me."

She's right about that. "What would it take for you to do that?"

Sonia doesn't answer for miles. "Something I couldn't live without. Something that would be worth the fear. But I'd have to want it more than anything."

When we reach her apartment building, I step out— and then stop as Sonia pays the driver to take me home. "Bring my car to work, okay?"

But I haven't forgotten what drove her to my doorstep in the first place. "You'll be stuck at home. What about movie night tonight? Why don't you come eat Thanksgiving with us? Kantina's gone, but we're still in town."

"I shouldn't." Sonia turns and waves to the doorman. "5C."

He opens the door for her without so much as looking at the card she's holding up.

"Sonia. Come eat with us." I don't want to make her, but I haven't forgotten a Thanksgiving in Seattle with an empty apartment and a case of beer. "You're welcome to stop by—even at five in the morning."

She doesn't answer—and I don't push it.

MOVIE NIGHT IS A DISASTER. THERE ARE ZERO FLAMINGOS in *The Cry of the Flamingo*, which, to my mind, makes the title false advertising. It is gorgeous, though, if you're into richly-done films with a visual style that grips you and doesn't let you go.

My mind is elsewhere, split between a holding cell in the Regional Justice Center of King County, Washington, and an apartment building that's actually *in* Los Angeles instead of on the outskirts.

What was Tamara thinking when she left me?

What is Sonia feeling, trapped in her apartment, afraid to go out?

Finally, I pick up the phone and tap out a message. *There were no flamingos. Were there flamingos in the version you watched? That would have made it better.*

Sonia replies after a minute or two. *You have got to be kidding me.*

What can I say? I'm a fan of shore birds with outrageous style sense.

A pause, and then, *Carlos says he remembers the zoo, standing at the flamingos when he was a little boy. He remembers how sad their cries made him, because they were the last thing he saw every trip, and he knew when he heard them, it was time to go. Then he leaves Estella so the cartel won't kill her when they catch up to him.*

I take a deep breath, lean back, and set the hook I've been baiting to lure her into conversation. *So that's zero flamingos in your version, too.*

The phone rings, and I answer it with sweaty hands. "I didn't know we had moved so far up the intimacy scale. From texting to actually talking, that's a canyon-sized jump."

Sonia snorts. "I was half naked and straddling you two days ago. We've got nowhere to go in terms of up when it comes to physical intimacy. Well, not far."

But emotionally—there, I can't say where we stand. And while I once bragged about how brave I was, now, asking would be a risk I don't want to take because both yes and no terrify me. "That opening shot—how many takes do you think it took to film?"

"Six. I count six light changes," she says. "And I'd bet it was filmed dawn-to-dusk. The beach looks different enough that I'd say it was the tide."

I'd only counted four changes. "Your homework ruined the way I watch movies. The dishes in Carlos's apartment drove me nuts. Different in every shot."

"I didn't ruin anything, I've improved the way you watch. The director filmed it at her own apartment, and her kids were running around between takes."

"So."

"Yes?"

I can't bring myself to ask her what's important. "My brother spent all evening trying to figure out how you've seen it. I checked, and it's only been shown—"

"Twice, in Spain. I was at the second showing. Kantina is old friends with the director, and we went to celebrate her opening."

"What happened to 'Kantina and I need time apart?'"

"Spain happened," she says, as if it's the most obvious thing ever. "I love the countryside, and the people, and the food. Time apart can wait for when we're not in Spain. London, for instance, she can have to herself."

"Is there any chance I can convince you to come eat with us? Tia's cooking a turkey overnight. She'll braise it every forty minutes on the dot. Bradley already made stuffing so it can sit in the fridge overnight. It's always better the next day." And I'd like to see her. "You'll be lonely tomorrow, too. You don't have to bring fancy coffee."

"Will, I'd love to."

She doesn't need to finish the sentence for me to know she isn't. "But. There's a but."

"But. I already took a huge risk. Kantina's going to come back from Europe to God-only-knows-what garbage in the tabloids, because of me. Again."

The guilt in her voice crushes the arguments I want to raise. "You think he got a picture of you?"

"I don't know. No. Definitely not."

She's lying, but it might be more to cope with the idea herself than because of me. "All right. You want to talk movies? Do you want to talk at all?"

"Talk. Please. I'm so used to being exhausted I don't know how to go to sleep if I'm not."

The truth is, neither do I. Sleep feels like it may never come. "Let's start with the basics. The non-negotiables. Popcorn: Butter or not?"

"You can get it without butter? What kind of monster would do that?"

"Congratulations, contestant, you move on to the next round!" I say, in my best gameshow host voice. "Biscuits: Gravy or Jelly?"

"Neither. Butter and jam."

"Oh, no." I'm doing my best to hide how much I want to laugh. "And here I thought you had a chance. Explain such poor decision making, please."

And she does.

It's not late by the time we finally hang up, it's very early. The conversation's covered everything and nothing, just like our idle chat while we wait onset, only now it isn't whispered and sandwiched in the moments between people shouting at us or humiliating me.

My phone has hovered at one percent battery for so long it's like a Thanksgiving miracle, and at last, we hang up.

Tia comes out to baste the turkey and sits down at the table. "Will, can I ask you a question?"

"If I weren't so tired, I'd tell you you just did."

"Smart-ass." She gives me the same glare that usually sends Bradley running. "What are you doing? You asked that woman to come over six times that I counted. If she didn't say yes the first time, she's not going to change her mind." While she talks, Tia scrubs the table in a circle, buffing it to a shine.

"Six? I asked her twice—no, three times. Maybe four." Though I'm so tired it hurts, I sit up and focus through bleary eyes. "You really think it was six times?"

Tia merely raises an eyebrow by way of response.

I exhale. "When Tamara left me, I spent a good two weeks in the house. Didn't go to the shop. Didn't even go to meet with the prosecutors. I was so ashamed."

"And?" The table will be buffed clean through the polish at this rate.

I watch as her hand moves in purposeful circles. "I didn't want to come out. I didn't want to get work. I didn't want to do anything, at first. But Bradley kept badgering me every day. One night I said yes just to shut him up. The rest, as they say, is history."

She sniffs. "You went from living on your own to sleeping on a couch."

I don't know exactly how to put it. "I went from drowning in debt to paying off my name. I went from staring at a storefront that wasn't mine anymore to working on someone's dream job. And you two put up with me when I wasn't exactly social." I shrug. "I've been that person, hiding alone in my hole. What I needed was someone to ask, and ask, and ask, and if I wouldn't come out, at least climb down into it to keep me company. You and Bradley did that for me. I want to do that for her."

"Go to sleep," she says, like anything short of an airhorn in my face could stop me. "Try one more time tomorrow."

If she says anything else, it isn't to me.

AFTERNOON HITS ME LIKE A CLUB TO THE HEAD, BUT IT'S a familiar feeling, waking up tired and heading straight for the coffee pot. Bradley's sitting at the table, looking at a tablet and talking quietly with Tia.

"What's up?" I ask as I pour myself the first of what I suspect will be many cups for the day. "Someone die?"

"Worse." Bradley turns the tablet toward me. "Your girlfriend is going to flip."

"Tamara and I are *not* together anymore," I say, a bit louder than I intended.

"I wasn't talking about her. Our friend with the camera must have been taking pictures while you two were driving."

Instead of protesting Bradley's proclamation about my relationship status, I snatch the tablet, and where I was starving a moment ago, now I'm ready to puke. That's Sonia's white convertible, and the shot of me is actually decent, riding in the passenger seat, though thanks to the angle it looks like I've got a ridiculous grin plastered on my face as I look at her. He must have been behind and to the left of our car, because all I can see of Sonia is her hair and those ridiculous sunglasses. *Red Hot Actress Starts White Hot Affair*, reads the title.

Bradley's right, and she deserves to find out from me, not at random.

I search for my phone, only to find I didn't plug it in, and the moment it finally turns on, it begins to buzz with one message after another.

Will.

Will, are you there?

Will, I need to talk to you.

Call me. Call me now.

I click through them, dial Sonia's number, and wait for the phone to ring.

After an eternity, she picks up. "Will, we're in trouble."

"I saw. I can't believe Kantina is flipping out. We went for a freaking drive, that's all."

"Not Kantina. Belion. He saw an entertainment website report and he went off on a rant during his interview on *The Final Cut*, talking about how difficult it is to work with Kantina, but he loves her so much he's willing to adjust to her." The way Sonia says it, he might as well have thrown acid on her.

"I don't see that happening on set. If anyone's adjusting, it's us, and to him."

It takes Sonia far, far too long to answer. "Kantina hasn't always been so down to earth. She goes through phases, and some of them are harder to put up with than others."

"You're saying she can be a pain in the ass?"

"I'm saying she's easier to get along with now. He's angry with her because he's still furious with you," says Sonia.

Disbelief makes me pause. "Over me calling him a talentless hack, an awful director making a worse movie? Didn't he already get his revenge?"

"No one carries a grudge like Belion. That and him knowing every time he looks at you that Eddie's sending him a message. Belion's not stable, Will, but he owns the rights to this franchise. He could quit and sink this whole production."

I can see it without even trying, Bradley and Tia sitting at the table, trying to figure out how they're going to make ends meet. It sends a shudder through me, and makes my heart race. "What does that mean, exactly? My brother doesn't get paid back?"

"No, and for Kantina—and me—that means something much worse."

Sonia's hinted at this before, but now, I feel like I'm in line to get a real answer. "What, exactly, is worse?"

"I don't have the right to tell you," says Sonia. "You'll need to ask Kantina, and she doesn't share her mistakes with everyone. You can ask her Monday morning."

"I'll do that." I change tacks and try to distract her the only way I know how. "Now, about Thanksgiving dinner. When we left off, you were on the verge of agreeing to not spend the weekend alone in your apartment. So—"

"No." This time, there's not a hint of regret, only iron determination. "Do something for me, please?"

"Name it."

"Don't ask. Don't call. Don't text. Don't go out in public, and don't answer the door or the phone. I'm going to wait for Kantina to get done with her show and then she and I will come up with a plan to contain this. I'm so sorry, Will."

"Me too," I say. I hadn't planned on seeing her over the holiday, but the thought of not makes it feel like something's missing.

"Bye, Will." Sonia hangs up, and I drop the phone on the coffee table—and almost into my now-cold cup of coffee.

"Not good," says Tia. "I don't even need to ask."

I lay back over and cover my head. "Not good."

My phone rings, and reflexively, I go to answer—until I read the caller ID, and see a name I've grown to associate with dread: Belion Androse. I listen to the voicemail message once it comes through. Belion's voice curls from the speaker, filled with quiet rage. "William. You think you can take from me without consequence? You can come into the cathedral of art I have built and sully my masterpiece? You are wrong, William. I will take much pleasure in teaching you this."

For the briefest moment, a war rages inside me, as a thousand answers fight to be the one I use to put Belion in his place. But I tried laying down fire and brimstone once, and I haven't forgotten how my mouth made everyone's lives more difficult. I let the end-call button answer for me, and ignore the subsequent ring. Let Belion think I'm too terrified to take his calls. As long as he keeps his rage focused on me, it's not on Kantina—or Sonia.

CHAPTER EIGHTEEN

My phone rings over and over throughout the day, but the best thing I can do for Sonia is not answer. While I honestly doubt anyone's remotely interested in me, I spend the long weekend stuffing myself with left-over turkey and whittling driftwood into a sculpture I call 'frustration,' which I intend to give to Sonia to memorialize our relationship. It's not the same as working in a full shop, but there's an elegance to following the curves of the wood and enhancing what I see within.

Monday morning, I'm at work at five thirty in the morning.

When I check in, the security guard takes a second look at my badge and points to a seat. "Wait there."

I don't have to wait long for the whine of an electric golf cart to approach. With every moment, the tension in my gut grows sharper—especially since I don't know who to expect.

"William." Kantina's voice makes me look up to meet her stare. "It is good to see you. Let us ride together."

"Where's Sonia?"

"She is not feeling well," says Kantina. "Perhaps she ate something that disagreed with her, so my friend Felicia is having the medics look at her. It is a convenient reason to keep Sonia out of the way." She beckons to me from the driver's seat like I'm some sort of puppy.

I eye her dubiously. "Do you know how to drive one of those?"

"You are stalling, William. What are you afraid of? That I will eat you, toes first?"

I wince as she mentions it. "I was joking with Sonia."

"Most funny." She pats the seat. "Now, you and I are going to solve a problem."

"Belion," I say, sliding onto the bench seat just before she guns the cart, heading off in the completely wrong direction.

"Yes. I wish to lie to him in a way that will involve you, but I will not unless you agree." She's not watching where she's going at all, instead keeping her gaze on me.

"Why?"

"To protect Sonia. Belion has a talent that is undeniable, but his fears make him a spiteful man, and I will not have him taking his insecurity out on her." She rounds the corner and dodges a troop of clowns, who are way, way more frightening than the guys dressed like werewolves we just passed.

"What's the lie?"

Kantina laughs. "We will show him what he wants to see, tell him what he wants to hear. But I cannot protect you, William."

"Do it. Are you still mad about the tabloids?"

"Mad?" The cart slows as she takes her foot off the pedal. "Why would I be angry? How could I be in Europe and in Los Angeles at the same time? Any fool would know it is not possible, but those who read such magazines and websites do not care."

"Then why does Sonia care so much?"

"That is my fault." Kantina's not looking at me, but judging from her tone, she's not far from tears. "I would trade all my fortunes to go back and make different decisions. Early in my career, I obsessed over what others thought. About what they said. Once, I felt threatened whenever the world looked at her and saw me."

"You asked her to keep to herself?"

"I meant only during that concert tour. I did not consider how she might take it, or the consequences. Some words cannot be unsaid, or their effects taken back. Even apologies from the heart do not heal all wounds."

I nod. "That I believe. But why is she so afraid of Belion?"

Kantina stops the cart, and we sit in pre-dawn darkness as she thinks. "We all make missteps along the way, William. Sometimes, the consequences follow us."

We've circled the lot, and now, down the way, under the purple and orange street lights, I see the side of Soundstage 52. "I'll take that up with Sonia. What's Belion got on you that you put up with his crap?"

Kantina looks at me from the corner of her eye and shakes her head. "Must I share all my mistakes? It is in the past, and almost done. Now," she says, focusing on the road, "we act, you and I. It is improvisation, William, which I have heard Sonia taught you. Please know that I am sorry if the lies you read have caused you distress."

I only read the article once. Okay, twice—twice in the morning and before I went to sleep. Every day of the weekend. "I can't imagine a downside. I'm a single man, allegedly having a torrid affair with the woman voted 'America's Most Beautiful' three years in a row. How is there a negative to this?"

Kantina floors the cart and swerves as we jet forward. "Then I'm glad you have enjoyed our time together, but fate has other plans. Your heart cannot belong to me, William, so we must break up."

I get a moment to wonder what she means—and then she swerves to the side, narrowly missing the makeup trailer—and the line of people waiting.

"*How dare you?*" she half-shouts, half screams.

"What?—Oh—Kantina, darling, please—"

Kantina swings off the golf cart and backs up to the crowd. "You think that because I amused myself with you, you have a right to approach me?"

The answer in improv is always 'Yes, and', but that's a statement I just can't agree with. "No." I shake my head. "No, I thought you *wanted* to be with me."

There's a crowd around us, one that formed so quickly I'm not quite certain where they came from. But in the front line stands Belion Androse, his arms crossed, his hands in fists that make him look like he's doing a superhero pose.

Kantina paces around the cart to stand in my face, so close I can feel her breath. Her eyes are wide and wild, her lips bared in a smile. "You are nothing. *I* am an *artist*. You may have set my body aflame with pleasures, but that is not enough to sustain true love."

"Please," I say, putting a tinge of fear and desperation into my voice. "I didn't mean it. We—"

"There is no we," she interrupts. "William, I will call Edward Geller myself at lunch. Perhaps he will agree to allow your replacement. Until then, you will speak nothing to me besides business. And you will never mention our time together. Do you understand?"

"Yes," I say, lowering my gaze to my sneakers and lowering my voice. "I'm sorry. I'm so sorry."

"Belion," Kantina says, pivoting to him so smoothly it's like she's on rails, "darling, walk with me. I need guidance." She holds out her arm. "I feel like only another great artist will understand."

"You were nothing when I found you," says Belion. "And look at you now. Magnificent. The Lady of the Manor in heart and soul. I cannot believe you soiled yourself with him."

"There is no inch of the man I have not seen," says Kantina. "This, I swear, is the truth. But I have made many mistakes in my life. One more can hardly be the end of me."

Belion holds one hand over his mouth. "No. Not yet. The fire of my anger cannot be contained. I must meditate and find the true meaning of art." He stomps away, ignoring Kantina as she pursues.

Felicia steps out of the crowd and turns her back on me. "People, I'm going to say this once. You have something to do and I'd better find you doing it. Nine, my office, now."

She walks right behind me like a prison guard the whole way there, then pivots and stares down the flock of production assistants trailing her. "Who wants to be part of this? You? You? How about you? I'll be out when I'm out."

"Ms. Slate?" One production assistant steps forward—Steph, the mousy blond Felicia pays more attention to. "The gaffers are claiming you didn't authorize the work for the feast scene. What should I tell them?"

Felicia glances back and forth, like she can't make up her mind. "Nine, leave that office and I will personally end you. Steph, take me to them."

I step into the production room, cold and lit only by the glow of monitors, and slam the metal door behind me with a metallic clank. How I'm going to explain this to Felicia is beyond me.

When I turn back to the production office, the screens light up Sonia's face, casting shadows behind her.

My heart leaps at my ribcage.

Sonia sits still, expressionless.

And from behind the desk comes clapping, soft and slow. "William," says Belion Androse, his voice hoarse and quiet. "It seems I was wrong on one minor account. I did not think a carpenter could be taught to act. Here I was, filled with rage, and then an assistant pointed out to me the most obvious detail."

Belion leans forward on the desk. "How is it that Kantina may have a trist with a carpenter while she is in Europe? I should have recognized this myself."

He looks at Sonia. "So. You have the loyalty of my most prized possession, but not the wisdom to avoid displeasing me. Is it not bad enough that Kantina will soon be done forever with my films, that you must go and dally with this man who mocks everything I stand for?" He shakes his head, clucking his tongue in disapproval. "Unwise, Sonia. I thought you were past unwise decisions."

"Belion," she says, "I thought that maybe if I worked with him, he'd understand your genius—"

Belion silences her with a single hand. "You are a better liar than I gave you credit for. But I have seen the pictures. How you look at him. How he looks at you." He shakes his head again. "Such a shame."

He stands from Felicia's desk, and strolls past me. "Enjoy the time you have left, Sonia. I cannot change Edward's mind. I cannot forbid you to work with this man. But it ends when we are done filming. You will not see him again, or even Kantina will not be able to protect you from the consequences."

"That's enough," I say, struggling to keep my hands relaxed when they want to make fists and beat him. "If I go to Eddie Gellar and tell him what you're doing—"

"Yes?" Belion says. "You wish to go to Edward? Shall we go together, you and I? Sonia, what do you think?"

"Don't," she says, the word dripping with desperation. "Please, don't."

"That decision is yours, one you will make every day. If I even suspect you of breaking my decree, I have only to make a call. To think you dared challenge me," he adds, voice dripping with scorn. He slips from the office and closes the door behind him without so much as a sound.

"Sonia, what was that?" I ask.

"The end of something good," she said, refusing to meet my eye. "Maybe even great." Her face shines with tears in the dim office, her jaw and shoulders tight. "I thought we'd get out of this last movie without him ruining anything else. But I was stupid. And wrong."

"He's blackmailing you," I say, leaning against the desk across from her. "With what?"

Silence is her only answer.

"With what, Sonia?"

"A cell-phone video," Felica answers from the doorway. She steps inside and then closes the door, throwing the deadbolt. "You can't trust anyone in this town, Will. Haven't seen it myself, but what I hear is that it features our favorite woman mouthing off about Eddie Gellar and his ability to pick bad movies."

"I was angry," says Sonia, wiping her face. "I was blowing off steam. I thought I was with people who were my friends. I had no idea someone was going to record it."

Felicia steps around the desk and punches knobs on a machine the size of small fridge. "Espresso? Gift from my assistants."

I collapse into the chair, my knees like rubber, my hands shaking. "How did *you* know?"

"Well, first off, unlike Belion, I do have a minor grasp of time zones. But mostly, it was because I was there the last time Kantina got into it with someone that made her that mad. It took three security guards to pull her off him, and he lost his front teeth."

I raise both eyebrows, not sure if I'm impressed or terrified. "Wow." I blink, clearing my head. "What do I do now?"

Sonia stands and wipes her hands off on her thighs. "I need to warn Kantina that he knows. If she goes off on him, we're all screwed."

"Nine." Felicia says the word as a warning as I turn to follow Sonia. "Don't move a muscle. The crew thinks I'm up here laying into you."

"You're not?"

She points to the chair Sonia just vacated. "You're going to sit quietly while I go over these orders, then, when I tell you, march out and look sad. The bus to the airport leaves in an hour, and you're going to have to ride with me."

"Bus? Airport?"

Felicia looks up at me like even raising her eyes that far takes a Herculean effort. "Don't give me that crap. I sent the email out two weeks ago, a week ago, and twice over the holiday… You're going to say 'What email,' aren't you?"

"What email?"

Felicia nods to herself, then lays her head down on her desk for a moment. "The good news is," she says, resurfacing, "that Mathew Allen, the guy you replaced, knows he was supposed to come prepared for overnight location shoots in Oregon. The bad news is, you aren't him."

I have so many questions, but the first one has more to do with what I've just seen. "I want to talk about that video."

"What?" Felicia cocks her head. "What's that you say? Why are there people on the set if we're not going to be here? Great question, Will. Not every scene revolves around Kantina or James. There's a speaking cast list of near twenty people. While we're freezing our asses off in Oregon, they're going to film the manor background scenes."

"Belion's threats—"

"I'm going through a tunnel, Will. You're going to have to speak up, because I can't hear you over the sound of how awesome I am," she says, without so much as looking my way.

"If you're not going to answer my questions, at least let me pack. My apartment is less than—"

"No, no, and no. You do not move." Felicia stands up and points like her finger can nail me in place. "Don't you even think about leaving my sight. I don't know what it is about you, Will Mathis, but if I let you step off this lot, there will be a seventy-car-pileup, or a volcano eruption, or a plague of locusts." She picks up a phone and dials it, then speaks tersely with her back turned to me.

"Good news," she says when she's done. "Everything's taken care of. PA Ben is packing for you."

"Can I at least go find Sonia?"

"Not a chance. You." She points that finger at me again, then at herself. "Me. Line of sight until the wheels are up. You're a stand-in, and you're paid to stand where I tell you. Stand there." She goes back to working. I go back to waiting, and wondering how actors travel.

ACTORS TRAVEL COACH CLASS.

Actors travel crammed in the middle seat between two people taller and wider than I am.

Stars travel on a private jet, which is where Kantina, Sonia, and I suppose James are, while half of this commercial flight is production crew. True to her word, Felicia has never been more than five steps away except at airline security, where she ordered me to wait for her, despite not having a bag or anything else.

We land in Portland a few hours later, and drive into the middle of nowhere, for absolutely nothing, except a roadside motel, where a flock of trucks wait. Any question related to Sonia, Kantina, or Belion is ignored, so I've given up, for now. But only for now.

"Did these guys drive here?" I ask Felicia.

"Down from Seattle. Up from California. I don't care so long as they get the job done," she says. "Everyone unload," she adds to the group, "then we head up to the lake and get set for filming."

I have nothing to unload.

I'm not certain I even have a hotel room, and interrupting Felicia to ask would be like walking into machine-gun fire to look for a napkin.

Only after everyone loads back in and we go bumping off do I finally get a quiet moment. "Where, exactly, am I sleeping?"

"My room, on the floor, if you don't behave," says Felicia without batting an eye. "Line of sight, Will. Line of sight."

We ride the rest of the way in silence .

'The rest of the way' leads us to a meadow that belongs on a postcard. Snow-capped mountains tower in the background, reflected in a lake so calm and clear every fluffy cloud in the sky lies mirrored in its surface. Brilliant orange maple trees dot the pines with color, and the grass is pale green. The air carries the crisp scent of frost even though it's noon, but the leaves haven't fallen. If you don't look toward the road or the lake, there's no evidence of civilization.

Down at the lake, someone's been busy. Tall towers of lights stand on the shoreline, and distant generators buzz, filling batteries that will keep the lights on while we shoot.

Moored to a small peg sits an actual rowboat, with the name 'Titanic II' stenciled on the side.

Before I can ask questions, Felicia's out of the car—and waiting, as a pair of tour-buses pull up behind us, black monstrosities that could carry the entire crew. From the first emerges James Becton, who surveys the area, then spots me and flashes me a friendly grin that makes me worry.

This might not be Hollywood, but these are Hollywood people.

From the other bus come a pair of angels. The dress Kantina is wearing is dark red and pleated so it reminds me of a kilt. Beside her, Sonia stands out like a dandelion in brilliant yellow pants and a jacket. The yellow brings out gold highlights in her hair I hadn't seen before.

The crackle of gravel precedes a town-car, which rolls up and disgorges Belion, dressed in a black coat that covers even his ankles. "Felicia, Kantina, James, we must speak."

"I have a shot-list ready," says Felicia as she heads over, "and we're going to stick to schedule."

They confer for half an hour while crews check wires and adjust lights, then Felicia comes back with a grin on her face. "We're good to shoot. Everyone in makeup."

She pivots and snags me by the arm. "I'm not going to follow you everywhere here, because I figure sixty miles from town, you can't run off. But don't attract any bears, and don't eat strange mushrooms."

"Yes ma'am," I say, giving her a salute.

"Cut that out, Will," she snaps good-naturedly. "Remember, this is all about mind over matter. We'll monitor your body temp in between shots. Union rules say we can't give you hypothermia." I can't tell if she's joking, until she looks up. "What are you waiting for?"

"What do you mean, hypothermia?" I hope my voice isn't revealing the jolt of panic that's run down my spine.

Felicia turns and points to the lake. "This is *the* lake scene. Where they're in *the* lake. And by them, I mean you and Sonia." She shrugs. "What do you want me to say? No pain, no gain? Gut up? Be a man? I've got half a dozen others, but essentially they're all ways of saying that you're going to be miserable."

Cold I can deal with. Miserable, I can deal with. Together with Sonia... That I'm going to have to find a way to deal with.

CHAPTER NINETEEN

Mɪꜱᴇʀᴀʙʟᴇ ɪꜱɴ'ᴛ ᴛʜᴇ ᴡᴏʀᴅ ꜰᴏʀ ᴡʜᴀᴛ I'ᴍ ᴅᴏɪɴɢ, ᴛʜᴏᴜɢʜ it comes with a heaping helping of misery. I'm wearing what I suppose is authentic Victorian clothing, but standing up to my waist in water so cold I'm not sure I can feel my feet. Actually, I'm not sure if I can feel anything below the waist.

If only the cold water could stop my thoughts.

The wind kicks up every ten minutes or so, turning a minor chill into a deep freeze, and in between lighting adjustments, I'm standing to the side, moving as little as possible to avoid disturbing the water.

The cold outside, however, can't touch the warmth I'm getting from Sonia. These scenes are *supposed* to be about two people coming together, admitting their attraction, but she *clings* to me between shots—partially to conserve body heat, but it's more than just that, based on how she looks at me when she thinks I'm not looking at her.

My secret? I'm always looking at her.

"Hold again," says Felicia. "Let's get a check on Nine and Sonia."

A medic in hip-waders makes her way out and scans our foreheads with a thermometer, then gives a thumbs up. "96 degrees and holding."

"Then get out of the way!" Aaron shouts.

I've heard him curse enough to know he's fighting the changing light and the water.

The moment the medic clears, he calls it. "Hit them again."

From the side, a production assistant wades in with a bucket—and dumps it over each of us, because, horror of horrors, we're *too dry*.

"How often have you done this?" I ask Sonia through chattering teeth.

"Water?" says Sonia, her teeth gritted so she doesn't shiver. "Never on location. In a tank, yes. With a towel and heaters waiting, yes."

Aaron has us step apart and turn. "Don't move. Felicia, Belion, check it."

Felicia isn't checking the scene, she's checking her phone and her tablet. "It's good. Let's shoot."

"No." Belion paces along the edge, smiling as he speaks. "This is wrong. We are rushing for time, we are not putting the effort in for great art. We must reset and do it again."

"That's a lie," Felicia says. "We're putting in the effort, but I can't stop the sun. And if those clouds keep rolling in, we're going to lose tonight."

The horizon carries a deep blue wall that promises rain, a Pacific onshore waiting to drench us.

"Move them closer, set the primary lights higher." Belion says. "Sonia, you will take two steps to the side. William..." He draws out the word like a knife. "Follow."

We dance our way to the exact point. Aaron adjusts.

Sonia's teeth chatter as she looks upward, imitating the longing glance Kantina makes look effortless.

"That will do," Belion shouts. "Second crew, to the side."

"But we need to get out," says Sonia.

Belion paces the shore as if he can block us. "You will not waste such time. Move out of frame. Hold position."

I'm almost ready to tell him where to go and what to do. But instead, I follow Sonia a few yards away, and watch as Kantina sheds her coat and steps away from the heater.

As they run the first take, Sonia lays her head against my now-numb chest. "Now I know what a penguin feels like."

I focus on Sonia to keep from thinking about the pain outside. "What does a penguin eat for lunch?"

She looks at me and squints. "What?"

"Icebergers."

She can't help laughing, shivering and shaking at the same time. "That was awful."

"How does a penguin build its house?"

"Will—" She stops and watches as Kantina begins another shot—and then whispers. "I don't know. How does a penguin build its house?"

"Igloos it together."

"Oh my God." Sonia huddles against me, sheltering from the wind. "I'm not sure which is worse, this shoot or your penguin jokes."

"This shoot." There's a pause as Belion shouts about passion—and I can't help myself. "I know you won't tell me what's going on with that video. Or Belion's blackmail. But what is going on with *you*? I love how relaxed and open you are, but my sense of impending doom keeps going off."

"You don't get it," she says, shaking her head against my chest. "I was so worried about how I'd convince you how I felt. That it wasn't about your brother, or the investors. Then I was worried about what would happen if Belion knew. But now, the decision isn't up to me." She snuggles herself against me. "You heard him. I may as well enjoy every moment I have."

Kantina and James clear the shoot and wrap themselves in blankets, but before we can set up, the medic wades out. And this time, she scans me twice. "Oh, that's a hold. Out of the water, over to the heater."

The groan from the camera crew echoes across quiet waters while the wind picks up. I don't move.

The problem isn't that they're upset. The problem is that I can't figure out how to make my feet respond. Sonia takes four steps and stumbles—taking me with her.

As we sputter and cough, the medic hauls both of us up and stomps out of the lake. "That's it, you're done for now. Stick these two in a slow-cooker and swap someone else in."

Felicia swears under her breath and scans the crew, then points to one. "Michael, I have an idea."

The camera man shakes his head. "You're turning blue. I don't know what your idea is, but I don't want any part of it."

Felicia immediately turns on her flock of production assistants. "I need two volunteers. Who wants to be my favorites?"

The low roll of thunder echoes—and breaks the discussion, as grips rush to disconnect everything and break it down.

That includes the heater Sonia and I are huddling underneath. Rain mixed with hail splatters and splashes, clinking on the lighting and the bus tops, the smell of wet dirt rising around us.

"Clear out!" shouts Felicia. "God himself is conspiring against me today."

I don't know which god she's offended, but the way it's pouring makes me want to offer a sacrifice or two. And then the hail starts, clattering against bus windows and production tents. Sonia makes a limping run for the nearest bus, and I don't see a sign of Kantina.

As the rain intensifies, I pick up cables and wind them into bunches. "Do you need help lifting?" I shout as Felicia rushes past.

Felicia glances my way, a look of horror on her face. "Will? Why are you not under cover? You can barely walk, and you aren't a licensed electrician." She continues her path of instruction, while a production assistant attempts to shelter her.

"William!" Kantina shouts from a bus window. "Come in, please."

I stumble for the bus and step up inside as what was a clatter becomes an unholy downpour. The sky isn't blue, it's black, and the bus shakes as the wind hits it.

"Do you not have the sense to come in out of the rain?" Sonia asks through chattering teeth. She's wrapped in a blanket, and what I can see of her legs shows terry-cloth pajamas.

"Sorry," I say. "I'm not thinking well right now."

Kantina is lounging on what reminds me of a psychiatrist's couch, except that it's built into the bus, and leafing through a magazine. "Sonia, darling," she says. "We care first, we question later."

Sonia rolls her eyes, but she looks back at me. "Strip."

"Excuse me?" I clutch my foil blanket closer.

"Human puddles are not allowed on Kantina's tour bus."

"Naked is fine," says Kantina, without looking up from her magazine. "I do not care either way. Such strange rules society sets, are they not?"

Sonia and I exchange a glance as I vigorously shake my head.

"But seriously," Sonia says, "get out of those. I'll get you a towel."

Using the stairs as a privacy shield, I shed my waterlogged costume, strip to my underwear, and accept the towel Sonia tosses my way. As heat slowly creeps back into me, the numbness turns to needles that have me cringing. Once I'm not dripping, I carefully take the last steps up—and realize just how bad the rental car was.

The soft mood lighting, luxurious leather seats, and wide aisle make it look less like a bus and more like a narrow apartment.

"Do not stand by the door," says Kantina. "The heaters are on back here."

When I approach, she looks me over, still covering myself with the foil blanket, and nods to the back. "If you do not mind, darling, I will lend you a robe. I have no clothing to fit you, sadly, but you will be more comfortable when dry."

"Is there a bathroom where I can finish toweling off?"

Sonia points back. "On the left hand side right before the bed. Robes are on a hook. Leave… whatever you're still wearing in there, please. You're dripping."

"I'm not—" I am, and there's no point in arguing. I head for the bathroom, and this time, I make sure I'm fully dry before emerging.

Sonia's sitting cross-legged on a couch, while Kantina continues her browsing. "William, there is cider in the kitchenette. You should drink."

"It hurts," Sonia says, then takes another sip of hers.

After retrieving a cup, I join them, taking the seat nearest the desk, which actually allows me to keep the robe lashed shut. "Movies suck."

"This movie sucks," says Sonia. "But it's almost done. We'll wrap up in January."

Another chill crawls across me as I realize I won't be seeing Sonia every day after that. Or ever, if Belion has his way.

"Will?" she says. "You look pale. Are you going to faint? I can call the medics."

Kantina slides sideways and stands, adjusting her navy blue pajama top before she steps to my chair. "You must both lie down. William, you will not argue with me on this."

"I might." But I don't, taking her place and letting my legs sink into the leather. It's heated, and the warmth is both agony and bliss. "How is it you get the fancy bus and we get a van?"

"I was thinking last week," says Kantina, "why do I own a concert touring bus, if I only use it twice a year? So I sent it ahead to meet us. I had planned for you to fly with me, darling, but that could not be."

"As long as Belion eases up, I don't care." I jerk my head up. "Did you just turn the heat up?"

Kantina dips her chin. "I am often cold after performances. Now, lie quietly. You speak too much for someone who should be recovering. Look at Sonia—she is not afraid to care for herself after such an ordeal."

"Worth it," says Sonia. "We're so close."

Without a word, Kantina silences Sonia—and then, somewhere, a bell trills. Kantina touches a button by the computer and speaks clearly. "Yes, what is it?"

"It's me," says Felicia. "Tell me, please, that you have Will. I can't find him, and I swear if he drowned I'm going to pose his corpse to finish filming."

"He is here, but I have forbidden him do anything but rest. How can I help you, darling?"

Felica lets out a sigh that says she's not happy. "You have Sonia there, too?"

"Where else would she be?" asks Kantina.

"You sure it's her?"

Kantina stops and glances to Sonia. "I do not understand."

"I'm alone in the car right now," Felicia says, her voice growing angrier by the moment. "And I just need to be certain you know where the real Sonia Bracewell is. Because the woman I know would never be *stupid* enough to risk a relationship with a man whose entire existence pisses off Belion. What are you *thinking*, Sonia?"

"Do not speak," Kantina says. "Felicia, darling, you have seen the papers and read of my dalliances."

"Don't bother trying to fool me," Felicia scoffs. "And Will, you're a great guy, but you're not that great. Not worth the consequences, especially not with us being so close to done filming."

"I'm an adult," says Sonia, ignoring Kantina's glare. "I do what I want to do."

"You are," Felicia states carefully. "But you don't get how happy Belion is right now with what he's planning. He's pissed about Kantina being done with her contract, he's pissed at Eddie, he's pissed at Will and frankly, you need to keep your head down and your mouth shut so he doesn't take it out on you in ways you can't control."

Sonia sits up, grimacing as she wraps her blanket closer. "I have the chance for something good here."

"And there'll be other chances, ones that won't cost you your career. Will, you know you're not her first on-set romance, right? In fact, I'd say you're her man-of-the-movie." Felicia says it like I should already know. "That's why she called you Nine, right? Eight movies, eight men, zero relationships that lasted past filming."

Sonia's face has turned red, and her eyes brim with tears as she answers. "That is *not* why I called him that. And I've made more than eight movies. When you were just a production assistant fetching coffee for Joel Anderson, Kantina and I had already made six full-length features."

"And how many of those did you date someone onset?" asks Felicia. "How many of those men do you still talk to, ever?"

Sonia grits her teeth as she answers, "None of your business."

"If you didn't have so much potential, I'd keep my mouth shut." Felicia hasn't changed her tone one bit, still cold and collected. "But you do, and you're pissing on yourself for something that probably won't last. Go ahead and be angry. But later, when you have what you've worked so hard for, you'll be grateful. Will, I'm sorry you're caught up in this, but if you're really a good guy, you won't let her throw away her career on a whim."

The speaker goes silent—and so does the bus.

I watch Sonia for some clue as to what she's feeling. My own feelings are as numb as my fingers were when I entered the bus.

At least, that's what I wish I could say. What I want to believe. But what I really want right now is the truth. "What happens if Belion follows through on his threat?"

"The same thing that happens to your brother's business if Eddie keeps his promise," Sonia says, without meeting my gaze.

I can't help but think about how Sonia looks when she talks about making movies. About how much she knows about the business. About how Felicia believes Sonia has more to offer the world than red hair and a spray tan. "Sonia—"

"Don't ask me about the other men."

"I wasn't going to," I say. "I don't care that you've dated other men. Wouldn't it be weird if you hadn't?" I shake my head, partly in answer to her statement, but also partly in denial about the whole situation. "I asked you once what made you happy. But I think this, this job, is what brings you joy." I watch her carefully as I finish my speech, willing her to understand. "I don't want to be the one who takes your joy."

I can't tell how many tears she's crying—they're coming thick and fast, a constant stream of sadness down her face.

"It's different with you, Will," she says through them, her voice soft, but sure. "I've always been looking for someone. Wondering if today was the day I'd meet them—but I wasn't looking when I met you."

I pull the robe tightly around me and head for the front of the bus. "I'll work with you for as long as this movie lasts. I'll be polite. I'll be professional. But I won't be a someone—something—you regret, Sonia." I nod to the driver as I reach the front, who seems shocked I'd be willing to go out in the rain. To Sonia, over my shoulder, I add, "I have enough regrets for the both of us."

It's still pouring when I step out into the mud, sloshing in my soaking wet shoes, wrapped in a bathrobe, but I can wait with Felicia.

As I slog past James Becton's bus, the door opens, and the driver nods my way. "He wants to talk to you."

I'm in no mood to tolerate assholes, and ready to set fire to something, so I step inside, ready to take out my frustration. James Becton's bus is a cheap rental, with vinyl seats arranged in groups, but he has a bottle of brandy, and a pair of shot glasses. He raises one to me. "Will, we haven't had much of a chance to talk."

"No," I say, taking the glass and downing the brandy to drown the cold—and the pain.

"That's because you didn't have anything to offer me," says James. "But I think that may have changed. Sit down, have a drink or two. Let's see if we can make a deal."

I sit, because I'm curious to know right now, just as I feel like I've lost everything, what James Becton thinks I still have to offer.

CHAPTER TWENTY

James Becton cracks open a bottle of whiskey to join the almost-empty brandy and pours himself a shot—then hands me the remainder of the bottle. "I don't have fancy robes, but I know what warms a man's soul almost as well as a woman's touch." He sits back and surveys me with a calculating gaze. "Now, Will. I thought you were firmly in the camp of the enemy, so I'm surprised you've come around."

"She's a magnificent actress." And I mean to make sure she stays one, even if the cost is my own heart.

"Didn't think you had it in you, to attract Kantina, but photos don't lie." He raises his beer. "To conquests."

I can't drink to that, even furious and hurt as I am. "What do you want? I can't influence Kantina, Belion hates me, and Eddie Gellar has me over a barrel."

James nods. "But you do have influence with someone important, whether you realize it or not."

"Sonia—"

"Sonia?" He raises an eyebrow. "I hardly think she warrants consideration. Your *brother*, on the other hand, is a major investor in this movie. Tell me, are you two on good terms?"

It's a toss-up between wanting to laugh at James and wanting to punch him.

Sonia avoided me because she didn't want the appearance of trying to influence Bradley. But James is going straight for the kill.

And Sonia will always warrant consideration in *my* heart. "Bradley and I get along well enough," I say with a slight shrug of a shoulder and a nonchalance I like to think comes across authentically.

"I'm a busy man, Will Mathis. I'm filming *The Man with A Dozen Deaths*, and it's clear that movie will serve my career, while this… disaster will be an unfortunate side-step that is blocking me from completing more important filming." He contemplates his now-empty glass. "But if production were shut down, your brother would receive the unspent funds, and write off the rest."

His ploy becomes clear as the shot glass between us. "And you would be free to film."

James nods in agreement. "I'd be happy to introduce your brother to the lead investor for UGM productions."

I lean back, posturing just enough to put some weight behind my words. "Little problem with your cunning plan, Becton. Bradley voted against continuing production, and was out-voted."

"True." James holds up his glass for a refill—and in return, I drink straight from the bottle. "But if your brother were more clever," he continues, setting the glass back down almost absently, "he'd know that one doesn't directly oppose Eddie Gellar. You want to go against him, you get the other investors together for dinner. Then, the conversation goes something like, 'I've heard some things that concern me.' And when the investors meet again, it isn't four to three, it's six to one."

It's a clever plan, one that might just succeed. But I know a little about business, and nothing in life is free.

"And there's something in it for you," James continues as though he's read my thoughts, and—in characteristic fashion—misinterpreted them. "Something I think you want very much." He runs a finger around the rim of his empty glass, contemplating its small depths. "It seems to me that your life can be divided into two phases. In one you're a successful artist with orders for your work longer than you can fulfill. In the other?" James twirls his hand around in the air. "You're failed stand-in whose primary talent is the ability to wait interminably long hours." That's when he leans forward again, eyes practically alight. "I can change that for you with one movie."

In one moment, I understand what he means. James Becton's films have always featured real products. Real work, working real miracles for the products that are featured.

He nods. "I see you understand the value of my offer. So, what do you think? A quick call to your brother is all it would take."

He's not lying—at least, I don't think he is, and in just a few words, he's awakened a hope I didn't believe could breathe again. If it were my work featured, I could reclaim everything Tamara took. Instead of living someone else's dream, I could reclaim my own. But of course, this is Hollywood. I smile wryly. "I think we don't have a deal. Promises you don't have in writing are worth toilet paper."

"You've grown smarter," he says, not entirely approving. "We are in complete agreement, Will. The details of a contract make all the difference. Take our red-haired friends, for instance," he says, glancing beyond me, out the window. "You do know why Kantina agreed to do this movie, don't you?"

I didn't—but I can put two and two together. "She's under some sort of contract."

"Correct." He taps his finger on the desk, twice, an impatient gesture. "Consider yourself fortunate Kantina dumped you the way she did. I wound up with three new teeth courtesy of Kantina's fists, but"—he tosses his head, and I can practically see the arrogance rolling off him in waves—"I insisted that she not be fired. Instead, she was forced to sign a contract that's a revenge worth taking. She's obligated to appear in Belion's films until he has another blockbuster, and his scheduling takes priority. That alone would make it difficult for her to make other movies, but add in Belion's games?" James shrugs. "It's a wonder she still gets any casting opportunities, given how many she's had to cancel on. And soon enough, she'll be thirty, with all the sex appeal of a month-old avocado."

The puzzle pieces finally lock into place, why Kantina and Sonia are so desperate to finish this movie. Why I haven't seen Kantina's name on more movie posters, why I haven't seen her on more red carpets. I can't help but pity them both, trapped in a cycle of bad pictures with Belion. "I'm surprised he doesn't schedule films just to mess with her."

"Oh, of course he does. You don't think there was ever a plan to shoot *Stardown Ranch*, do you?" James shudders melodramatically. "What a horrible concept. But it made certain that she couldn't appear in a sequel to *Blood Contract*." James laughs—and he's the only one who is. "You won't be celebrating alone if we succeed. I'll put all my resources to finding a way out of this that benefits us both. In the meantime, be thinking about how your work would best appear onscreen. It's easier for me to arrange, and something my fans expect."

"I'll put on my thinking cap," I say as I stand. The rain is only pouring now, instead of gushing, and right now, I need to be somewhere else—anywhere else.

"You do that," James says, snagging the brandy from where I left it on the table and refilling his glass.

I open the bus door as he toasts it at me, and step out into a the rain like I'm greeting an old friend. This time, I squish my way through the mud to the car I rode in with Felicia.

When I slide in, she looks over at me from the news she's reading on her tablet and nods. "Will. We're calling it for the day. We'll come back and film at dawn."

I grunt an acknowledgement.

"I'm sorry I hurt you, but not sorry enough not to do it again," she says without looking up from her reading. "You were going to get hurt one way or another. I just changed the timetable."

"Anyone ever tell you—"

"I'm a real bitch?" She flashes me a grin. "Every day, and proud of it. That's why I get to be director." Felicia leans forward and whispers to our driver. "We'll order in pizza. Surely there's pizza."

"You know about Kantina's contract, don't you?"

That puts a halt to her news consumption. Felicia sits stock still for a moment, frozen, then sets the tablet down. "James Rueben Becton, that bastard. I swear, he's going to regret opening his mouth. One of the rules was that he had to keep his mouth shut about it. The number of people who know *why* Kantina keeps the movie schedule she does would fit in this car."

I look around, counting seats. "But—"

"James would be in the trunk, after I hit him with a shovel." She glares at me. "I wouldn't hesitate to have you join him if you blabbed."

I think she's joking.

I hope she's joking.

I'm… not entirely certain she's joking.

"Kantina is super rich," I say instead. "Rich buys lawyers, lawyers can twist contracts into knots. And stars are *known* for being crazy."

"There are women being forced to work for men who raped them, thanks to contracts," Felicia says sternly. "Women working on terms that even I'd deem inhuman. Women"—she looks out the window, toward Kantina's bus—"whose careers are being held hostage." She shakes her head. "When Eddie said you couldn't be fired, it wasn't just because Belion pissed him off. It's because Eddie wants to see Kantina done with that ridiculous deal, too."

"But why would someone as smart as Kantina sign it?" I say, voicing the question that's been bugging me ever since Becton let the shoe drop.

Felica raises one eyebrow. "You say that like she had a choice."

Felicia taps the driver on the shoulder, and he shifts the car into gear. As we crunch up onto the road and begin our trek away from the lake, I try again and again to sort out the muddled mess of anger and sadness.

I've made the right decision, so Sonia doesn't get hurt.

It doesn't feel right.

But since I've already danced out on a tightrope once, I might as well do it again. "I think you and I want the same thing," I say to Felicia at last. "There's something you need to know, so you need to listen."

"Well, well, Nine. Sounds like your other testicle finally dropped. I like it." Felicia's giving me her full attention, something I thought only coffee received.

I ignore her comment. "James wants out of this movie. He offered to promote my business if I convince Bradley to work the other investors to shut it down. That way, James gets out of his contract without looking difficult, and I'm not breaking the letter of Eddie's orders. And Kantina stays trapped." And Sonia. I swallow. "I think he's got a solid shot at it."

Felicia is a small woman, but porcupines are also small, and when they're shaking with rage, a smart person moves further away. She holds up one hand, then looks out her window. And looks back, now bright red and trucking straight along toward purple. "Oh. My. God."

Self-preservation dictates I don't comment.

"One skill I've learned," she says, a single word at a time, "is how to work with someone you want to see murdered. I'm going to need that, Will. Delays?" She raises one shoulder in a 'what can you do' kind of motion. "Those I can live with. Delays happen. Sabotage, on the other hand, requires a response, unless you want to see your authority toppled."

"I'll leave that up to you."

Felicia fumes for a minute longer. Then, "Why didn't you take him up on his offer? Didn't you tell Sonia once that was your dream?"

The answer hurts to say aloud as much as it hurt when it hit me. "Maybe I found a dream I wanted more. Or maybe I just realized the cost of what I wanted was too high. James thinks he knows what I want. What I actually want is to make sure Belion Androse never makes another movie. I want to ruin his reputation so he can't get funding from anyone, anywhere, ever again."

"You're a sneaky, vindictive bastard," says Felicia, an eyebrow raised pointily. "I approve. But I can't subvert Belion directly."

I nod. "Right. But if anyone knows how to get rid of a director, it would be you."

With that, I lean back in the seat, and try not to think.

The steady tap of Felica's fingers as she works her phone form a ticking clock as I search for other options. At last, I crack one eye. "Is there any chance I can get Belion to drop his threats some other way?"

"I wish there was, Will. I really wish there was." She sounds sincere enough, and the sudden tiredness in her face agrees. "We need to get back to the hotel. I need to plan. One thing you might want to consider: Eddie taught me very early on that directors have to stay on top of things, or they lose the trust of producers. Belion has a taste for white wine and cherry juice boxes, and very poor impulse control."

I'm not exactly sure what she's suggesting, but I have nothing but time to think it over, and a supreme need to think about anything but what happened between Sonia and I.

THE HOTEL IS A MOTEL, AND IT'S NOT MUCH OF ONE AT that. Our production takes up most of it, and soon enough, the crew is kicking back and devouring pizza while they talk. The tour buses idle in the parking lot, diesel engines rumbling through the night as they charge their batteries and keep the heaters on. Despite Felicia's threat to make me sleep on the floor, I have my own room, my own pizza, and my own privacy.

The last thing I did before I retired was make a quick call from Felicia's phone, setting up a delivery that I hope will make tomorrow go better.

I spend the evening in the hotel bathroom, sitting in the bathtub. The motel offers a 'male-scented' bath bomb, which makes the water smell like a muskrat died in it two weeks ago, but it's hot, and relaxing, and I need time to think. Technically, time to feel, though from what I understand, I'm not supposed to be feeling this much.

Tamara left *me*.

This time, I'm the one saying it's over.

I always thought that would make it better, but experience teaches me now that it doesn't. I eat pizza in the bath while browsing my phone until far too late. Close to midnight, in fact, when someone pounds on the door—and I don't mean the hotel door.

"Go away."

The bathroom door swings open, and Felicia steps in. "Don't speak to your assistant director that way."

While I snatch a towel to cover myself, she appraises me like a chunk of meat. "Get dressed, Will, come with me. What died in here?"

"It's 'Winter Ox' scent," I say, reading the container. "And how did you get in here?"

"Got the key from the hotel manager. I told him you're an actor with a history of violence and med compliance issues, and that between the two of us, someone needed to do a health check." She holds up a keyring. "Move. We're filming at dawn, and I have no intention of being up all night."

Only after I'm sure she's left the bedroom do I wrap my borrowed robe around me. "Where are my clothes? I left them in the wardrobe trailer."

"Bad news." Felicia's voice comes from just outside. "Fairly sure they were mistaken for trash and thrown away. Also, PA Ben is fired because he took the bag with the gift for my sister-in-law's baby shower instead of the one that had a shirt and pants for you. My husband says you look good in the robe, so just put it on and get going."

"Your husband?"

"Happily married twenty years." Felicia opens the door and waits. "Head down to the lobby."

The staircase is cold and wet, and the night air smells of pine. At the lobby, Felicia stops and looks out. "See the yellow car next to Kantina's bus?"

"Yes. What's with the cloak-and-dagger?"

"If you don't shut up," she whispers, "I will strangle you with a cloak and stab you with a dagger. Head toward the car, passenger side. You do not want everyone to hear what we need to discuss."

The lights are on inside Kantina's bus, though the windows are tinted, so I can't see much more than that. My feet are way too tender for the parking lot gravel, but I pick my way across and try the door on the car. "It won't open," I say as softly as I can while still being heard over the noise of the bus engines.

"Try again," Felicia says. "Are you lifting up?"

I am. It's not budging.

She circles the car and gives the handle a pull. "Must be locked."

"Then unlock it."

She's laughing, quietly. "I seriously didn't think you'd fall for that. I don't have the key, Nine. It's not my car, it was just the closest one to—"

The bus. I turn as Felicia knocks.

The bus door opens—and Sonia's standing there. "Come on in…" She sees me, and her voice fades away.

"Hi," I say. There's so much more I don't have the words for.

"Hi," Sonia says, matching my speech-making ability.

"Can we move this awkward staredown inside?" asks Felicia, making shooing motions with her hands.

My feet move of their own accord, up the stairs. I don't know where the computer is, but the table's pulled out, and Kantina is sitting there, dressed in a brown tank-top that would leave her cold if she were outside. Sonia's wearing a blue version that might be a twin, except that hers has an undershirt, and her pant-legs go down past her knees.

"William." Kantina doesn't drag out my name in her usual method, or use her purring voice. "Thank you."

Felicia takes a seat across from Kantina, and I join her. "What is this about?"

"How we're going to get this movie made," says Felicia. "Our director is an incompetent asshole. Our leading man wants production shut down. If James finds another way to persuade another investor, it won't matter that Will said no."

Kantina purses her lips, drumming her glittery gold fingernails on the table. "I could call Edward and ask for a temporary shutdown. Though it gives James his desire, it also removes him as a threat."

"Any shutdown at this point will be permanent." Felicia looks like she's about to take a chunk out of someone. "I've seen Eddie watch productions go down in flames and light a cigar off the ashes. He's done it before. Given how he feels about this one, he'd do it again. He might want you to be done with your contract, but not at the cost of his reputation."

Sonia's gaze flicks to me, her mouth open. "Does Will know—"

"Not everything, but Becton"—Felicia speaks his name like it's spelled 'cockroach' —"told him the short version."

"You could have trusted me," I add. "I would have understood."

Felicia isn't with the rest of us, lost in thought. "If I go nuclear, and take Belion's incompetence to the investors, we will absolutely get shut down."

In the quiet that follows, it's Sonia who speaks. "The simplest way to handle it is to make the movie. Get it done. Finish principal photography and let everything fall out from there. How much do we really need at this point?"

"It's not that simple," Felicia says, her head in her hands. "I've already rearranged to leave James out. To finish the rest, I'd have to—"

"Pitch a streamlined, intense movie," says Sonia. "No fluff. No long shots. Whole thing is a flurry of gut punches, made mostly of what we already have. You can be convincing when you're angry."

"That might work." Kantina's lost her accent—or at least, most of it. She still sounds European, but not like she's some sort of were-cat. "Cut everything we can, pitch it straight to Eddie—Edward."

"I would, but that might backfire." Felicia is looking out the window. "He'll see it as me losing control. I swear this movie is some sort of test, and if I go back to him, I've failed."

"Then I will," Kantina says, back in what I thought was her normal voice. "He cannot deny me a phone call. I will claim I want to focus on the essence of Belion's art. You will speak of schedules and budget. Together, we cannot be denied."

"So in essence, we avoid being shut down by being done?" I ask.

"The story has to be airtight," Felicia says. "He can sniff out a con at fifty paces. You have to sell him on the whole 'artist who has a vision,'" she says, nodding at Kantina. "I'll be the bean-counter explaining how it makes financial sense."

Kantina rises and nods to Felicia. Together, they move to the rear of the bus, continuing their conversation in low voices.

And I'm left alone with Sonia. In the silence, the rattle and shake of the idling bus is deafening, and the smell of leather makes my nose itch. When the mood lights overhead dim, Sonia speaks. "Felicia told us what you're giving up. What happened to the Will that dreamed of going back to art?"

I shrug. "I don't know. But I've spent two years chasing the memory of a dream, and maybe I want to find a new one. Something that brings me joy." Some*one*, my heart says. "I want you to have that, too."

"What if being with you makes me happy?"

It's instinct, and desire that drives me to brush the strands of hair from her eyes. To wipe away the tear, and run my finger down her chin.

She—we—are standing in a heartbeat, my arms wrapped around her, her lips finding mine. Then she puts her head down on my shoulder and whispers, "Leave them. Take me to your room."

I want to, so much it makes my heart ache. "I don't want a single night in a motel, Sonia. I want a forever. If you can promise me that, I'll carry you there myself. But if you can't, I'd rather not spend the rest of my life remembering what we had."

"Will," she says in my ear. "Sometimes, you don't get forever. Sometimes, all you get is now. But we have now, and I don't want to waste it."

I think I've never loved her—I mean *appreciated* her more.

Where did *that* word come from? That thought—that feeling? Love takes *time*. You have to *know* someone to really love them. You have to go through pain and happiness, the boring, the exciting. It doesn't come from seeing them once at the supermarket, but from listening, laughing, sharing, living—

"What's wrong, Will?" Sonia asks. "You're barely breathing."

"Nothing," I say. *It's nothing,* I tell myself. She won't lie to me. But I'm not sure I'm ready for the truth, either.

"Would you two just bone and get it over with?" Felicia's standing a few feet away.

I have no idea how long Sonia and I have been embracing, or Felicia's been watching, but for now, I don't care. I move slowly, cautiously to kiss her, then ease back as she returns the favor.

How many times have I thought back to that first kiss? This time, the spark is present from the moment we touch, and this time, Sonia doesn't hesitate.

We know what's coming. We embrace it.

"Hello?" Felicia shouts over the engine noise. "You're taking up the aisle, and some of us—make that all of us— need to be up tomorrow to film. Come on, Nine. You're walking me back to my room."

"Not yet, I'm not." I kiss Sonia twice more, each time shorter, each time, leaving me wishing we were truly alone. Reluctantly, I let go.

Sonia's hands trail over me as she steps back and shoots Felicia an evil glare. "You are—"

"Tired," says Felicia. "But I seem to be the only person not thinking with my crotch." She glances back over her shoulder. "Maybe Kantina. Maybe."

I practically float back to my room. Almost fly away, out the bus, up the stairs, and back into my bed, in a dark, cold motel room. Oh, somewhere, deep inside, there's a rational part of me screaming that I should know better, but I've gagged it and locked it in the cellar. Right now, I saw how Sonia looked at me. How she felt as we kissed each other.

Sleep is the imp I can't quite catch hold of, because I feel like I'm falling, and I don't know if she'll catch me. If someone will catch me. If she will.

I jolt awake as the door swings open, and sit up, blinking as it slams shut.

"Good morning, Will," Felicia practically shouts. "Today, you've earned the highest honor I can bestow." She hands me a cup. "The surrendered coffee cup. It's yours, unless you don't drink it immediately."

I do, gulping it even though it burns my tongue. "I need to sleep."

"No, you need more coffee," she says. "What motivates you? Saving your brother's business? Getting revenge on Belion for the way he treats you? Getting Sonia out from under his thumb?"

All of the above. I drain the last of the coffee cup and toss it in the can. I throw the covers back and stand. "Come on," I say to Felicia. "What are you waiting for? We've got work to do."

CHAPTER TWENTY-ONE

Felicia and I ride together in a rental car from the motel to the lake, which bustles with activity. Sonia is dressed and waiting when I exit the makeup trailer. She give me a shy grin, then looks away as Belion stumbles up.

He's wearing dark sunglasses, and every time the lighting rigs rattle, he winces.

I've been the man with a hangover he is now; clearly he received—and enjoyed—my anonymous package.

During the morning scramble to get everything set up, Sonia pulls me aside, handing me a scene guide that isn't nearly so interesting as the woman who gave it to me. "Look like you don't understand this, Will. So I can explain it to you."

I throw the pages up in the air and shake my head, hands out, palms up. "This makes no sense."

"Little over the top," she says in the same voice she used to critique my face, my body language, my—

everything—during training. "Lean in. This afternoon, you and I are going to drag out filming so that Kantina and Felicia have time to convince Eddie Gellar their idea will work."

I lean in dutifully. "How, exactly, are we going to do that?"

"You?" Sonia bends to pick up the sheets off the floor, drawing out the motion as I try to not stare at her curves. "Will, are you paying attention?"

I grin. "Too much attention."

"No such thing." She pivots so she raises herself up in front of me, handing back the sheaf of paper.

Which is the only thing I was looking at, I tell myself. "Next time, I'll pick up any papers. It's warmer this morning, isn't it?"

Forget warm, I'm roasting.

"Good!" Sonia says, taking my hand. "Then a little cold lake water won't bother you a bit. Head down to the water, I'll catch up once I confirm our plan."

James Becton is waiting down by the lake, arms crossed, watching me as I approach. "Will, my man. Did you have a chance to think over our discussion?"

"I was up all night thanks to it." I don't trust James—or more precisely, I trust him to be exactly what he is: driven to act in his own best interests. While his needs aligned with mine, he would be reliable. But if the winds changed?

I'd sooner strike up a business relationship with Tamara again, and that will never, ever happen.

"And? Did you, by any chance, call your brother?"

"No." I wait just long enough for the displeasure to

reach his face, the downturn of his lips, the narrowing of the eyes. "I've never, ever, shown an interest in the business side of movies. If I come up out of nowhere saying I think he should cooperate with the other investors, how long do you think it will take Bradley to figure out something's going on?"

I give him just a blink before launching into my gambit. "Instead, I made a call. Had some wine delivered. And tonight, there will be a text, one that goes, 'You're not going to believe what I saw today. The director was hung over.'"

"Hmm." James jerks his chin in something that could be approval, or could just be him attempting to assert his dominance. "Don't fail me, and I won't fail you." He adds what I suspect is supposed to be an aggressive stare, but I'm not interested in bumping chests or whatever manly-macho display he has in mind. He probably pictures himself as the alpha male.

The word that actually describes him does start with an A, so he's not that far off.

"Second crew!" a PA shouts, running by me. "Second crew on set."

Filming a lake scene when it isn't even fifty degrees is utterly awful, but once Belion excuses himself to review cameras from the safety of a van thirty minutes in, the shoot shifts gears.

The moment lighting is set, Sonia and I are bundled with blankets, roasted under the heat lamp, and force-fed hot apple cider by PAs who seem to be competing to see who can best hydrate us.

It's not to say I want to take this up for a living, but it's the difference between being tortured for someone's amusement and doing a hard, cold job that no one else on this set is willing to do.

The water is freezing and murky, but Sonia is warm and open, and I could swim through a blizzard like this, holding onto her.

By the time we break for lunch, the water scenes are done. Sonia finds me as I emerge in dry clothing. She isn't quite running, but it's a speed walk, and behind her, PA Steph is following. "Ms. Bracewell? A moment?"

Sonia shoots me a warning glance and turns. "What is it, Steph?"

Steph glances to me. "Is he…?"

"Will's a good guy. What's wrong?"

"Something's off about Felicia. I think I might have made her mad. She's sent someone to the production van between every shot. And it's always someone different, and it's never me. I can fix whatever mistake I made—"

Sonia cuts her off with a shake of her head. "Steph, this happens. You get more of her time than anyone except me. You can't take it personally if Felicia occasionally decides to teach someone else."

After we leave Steph behind, I test my understanding. "Felicia is sending lots of people to check on Belion. Lots of people who will report that he's hung over and barely functioning."

"You're a good student," Sonia says. "The moment Belion and James are on site for the afternoon, Kantina's going to call Eddie Gellar and start ranting about how she wants to emphasize the art. Felicia's going to back it up with, 'Well, we technically could use most of what we have.'"

"That has a prayer of working?"

Sonia nods. "K can sell it like she means it, because she does. But only if we give her time. So no matter what happens, this scene had better take forever to shoot."

"Oh, I think I can help with that." I give her a wink. "Delaying production? Making small mistakes that ruin the setup? You couldn't have come to a better person."

"Imbecile!" Belion shouts, then scrunches up his face like his own voice is too loud.

I step back and look around, only now noticing the light I 'accidentally' kicked over as I stepped out of the brush. James will carry Kantina through the brush here, having just rescued her from a pack of wolves.

Said wolves are currently represented by a foam cooler, but I'm hoping that the magic of special effects will make it slightly scarier.

"I'm sorry," I say, kneeling and setting the light back up. Of course, it's pointing the wrong direction, but once they reset it I'll figure out a new way to screw things up. For the last hour, we've repeatedly shot me tromping through the forest, while James waits impatiently for his shot.

"Sir," says James. "I'd be happy to do my own light checks. I think we may be asking a bit much from our *carpenter*."

I never considered my profession profane, but he makes it sound filthy.

Sonia glances at her phone and frowns. This isn't the forever she had in mind, and barring attack by a rabid squirrel, we won't be out here another thirty minutes.

"You are correct. Set up, and let us run through," says Belion. "William, you are to sit at my feet and touch nothing."

I settle into the grass, still wet from yesterday's storm, and curse as James completes the light check without delay.

Two shots later, we're moving on to the final scene.

"Places," says Belion. "James, show us your fire. Save your lady, and prove to us your place as Lord of the Manor."

Sonia steps closer to him, and though James hesitates, he swings one hand under her legs and the other around her shoulders, lifting her with ease.

The pang of jealousy that shoots though me isn't emotional, it's physically sickening, especially to see the way she looks up at him. *It's an act,* I tell myself, but Bradley was right. A great actress makes you believe she's not acting, and I want to punch him in the mouth so much it's a need.

"Again," says Belion. "Do not let the lady sag into the mud. If you spoil Kantina so, we will never get this done."

James drops Sonia's legs, then backs away before she can gain her balance. I know her looks well enough to say I wouldn't go within ten feet of her if I were him.

Once she rises, she brushes the moss from her gown, a form-fitting green affair that hugs her curves and comes complete with a train that tangles about her feet if she takes more than two steps. Sonia dusts the dirt from the ends of her hair—and smiles.

A forced smile, I'd bet on it. I've seen her real one, and there's too much teeth in this one, too wide, too much like she's reminding herself of how important it is to buy Kantina time.

"Again!" Belion shouts. "This time, all the way through. Cameras ready for close up. James, be sure to turn at the end."

James grunts as he picks up Sonia.

She's not that heavy, I know. Once more, he half-carries, half-drags her through the tall grass—then stops where the grass is smashed down, and pivots. The camera is only catching his face, right up until he leans down—and my stomach does a triple flip off a high-dive as he leans over to kiss Sonia. While I should be appreciating how expertly she's hidden in his shadow, all I can appreciate is that I don't want *her* kissing him.

"And cut!" Belion shouts. "Well done, James. Well done."

James looks back to us, revealing the smear of red lipstick across his face. "That—did not go according to script."

Sonia stands and dusts herself off. "Hold eight seconds, that's the blocking. You can count to eight, right? Just imagine you're having sex twice."

"It matters not—Sonia, what have you done?" Belion sits up straighter and looks at James. "Makeup! Get us a makeup artist. We cannot shoot closeups with him looking so."

"He moved," Sonia says as she stomps past. "If he'd stuck to blocking, it wouldn't have been a problem."

A problem is what I'm having right now, reconciling the half a dozen ways I feel about what I've just seen. I know the difference between an actress and the character she's playing. My mind does. But does my heart? To be honest, it's not so certain.

Sonia comes to stand by me while Belion downs another round of migraine meds with sparkling spring water. "Kantina's going to have to make do with the time she has. I don't have any more tricks up my sleeve."

It's petty to feel this way, and I don't like being a petty person. "I could try what you just did. If I kiss him, I promise it will delay production."

"Oh, I'd like to do more than kiss him. I'd like to take one of those spotlights and shove it right up his—Will?" Sonia leans over to look at me eyes, her mouth an 'O'. "Are you *jealous*?"

"No." The word comes out much faster than I meant it to.

"Don't be." Sonia leans against me and picks grass from her hair. "I was just buying time. It's not like I enjoyed it, or like I'm looking forward to it. You have *nothing* to be jealous of."

I'm not jealous. Only sad, insecure men are jealous.

I may be just a *tad* sad and insecure, if I'm being honest with myself—but while honesty may be the best policy, it's a terrible coping mechanism. "It's fine. I'm fine. I'm actually feeling bad for you."

"Mmmm hmmmm." I'm guessing she doesn't buy it, but at least she lets it drop.

It's less than an hour later that we abandon the woods and skulk back toward camp. With every step, I watch for Kantina, for Felicia. For some sign that they're done with the call.

Belion looks around as his production assistants open water for him. "Where is my assistant director? I must review what she has filmed."

The crunch of gravel heralds a black town-car pulling off the road. When the doors open, Kantina emerges, one hand wrapped in gauze.

Sonia takes one look and bolts to the car, while I trail cautiously behind Belion.

"It was an accident," says Kantina, waving Belion away. "I cut myself on a broken glass, very minor. Two stitches only."

Belion stalks back and forth, pulling at his hair. "You have always been so clumsy. What are we to do now? I cannot have the Lady of the Manor wearing a bandaid."

Felicia cuts me off before I can whack him upside the head. "Makeup will cover it just fine. You won't have to change a shot. Come to the production van, I'll show you."

When I turn back to the car, it's Sonia I think needs restraining. The way her jaw is set, her fists clench, she's ready to jump in and defend Kantina, regardless of the consequence. "What happened?"

Kantina unwraps her hand. "It is a small cut, and I promise, truly an accident. But Felicia suggested that perhaps it would be wise to have a doctor examine it. Also, how convenient, that we should take time to call Edward while we were in town."

Sonia looks like she's trying to sniff out a lie. "And the reduced film, will that be because of your injury?"

"What a wonderful idea, darling." Kantina puts one arm around Sonia. "You are worried for nothing. This is not like last time."

Sonia's only response is a hug that looks like she's trying to break Kantina's ribs.

"Well?" I say, as they finally let go. "How was the call with Eddie?"

"William," says Kantina, like she hadn't noticed me there. "Edward was uncertain. But in the end, he did not say no."

"But they didn't say yes?"

"What did you expect?" Sonia asks, exasperation coloring her voice. "Movie execs never say 'yes' right away. The goal of any initial call is to not hear 'no.'"

"This is true," Kantina adds. "Edward has never agreed to anything on sight. He says it gives one a reputation for being hasty." She pauses and looks to Sonia. "Felicia received a call on the way back. Is it true that you ruined James's makeup?"

"True," Sonia says with a wicked grin. "What a shame they had to bring a makeup artist all the way up from camp to fix it."

At the mention of it, my stomach turns, and I can't help looking away.

"Will," Sonia says. "*Why* are you jealous of him? It was just an act."

I don't like that she can read me so easily. It leaves me vulnerable, and if I learned anything from Tamara, it was that when you're vulnerable, people will use it to hurt you. "My beard, my hair, everything about me is adjusted to look more like him. Whether it's money, fame, or power, there's nothing I have he doesn't."

"Not true. You know what you have that James Becton won't ever?" Sonia reaches over to brush my shoulder. "Look at me."

Something about her tone draws my gaze up to meet hers.

"Sonia!" Felicia shouts from the production van. "Answer your phone for once."

She doesn't flinch at all. "Didn't take it to the shoot. Be there in a moment."

"Now," says Felicia, heading toward us. "And how long have you had me listed as your emergency contact? There's someone from Saint Mary's Hospital trying to get ahold of you."

Sonia hikes up the dress and sprints to the production van, where she snatches the phone from Felicia.

I take one step to follow—and Kantina grasps my arm with a grip that's deceptively strong. "Wait, William. I know her well enough to say you should let Sonia decide when she is ready to speak to us."

Sonia finishes talking on the phone and hands it back— dropping it in the process. Felicia waves up the hill for us—and then shakes her head as I come. "I didn't mean you, Will."

"Sonia?" I say, ignoring Felicia. "What's wrong?"

"My dad fell this morning in the grocery store." Her answer comes devoid of tone or feeling. "They took him to the hospital by ambulance."

"Darling." Kantina starts—and stops. "Is it as I fear?"

"His cancer's back. Has been for a few months, but he conveniently forgot to tell me because he knew we were going to be filming." Now an edge of anger creeps into her voice. "And he says he's not going to do another round of chemo."

"Then change his mind." Kantina puts both hands on Sonia's shoulders and turns her. "Go home, darling. I would never order you, but I am asking you please to consider, what if you do not? You and I are young. Now is not the time to collect what-ifs. We have too long to consider them."

Sonia's not even trying to stop the tears that roll down her cheeks. "I can't abandon you—and Will, he and I might not have—"

"I'm willing to just about kill myself to pay off the debts Tamara left me," I say quickly, firmly, "but if Bradley or Tia were hurt? Those debts would have to wait." I shake my head. "Don't let this be something you regret. Kantina is right. We're too young to collect what-ifs." I let her go, physically, emotionally. "You have a phone. If you need me, you know how to get in touch."

Sonia doesn't hesitate. She pivots and heads toward Kantina's bus.

Only after she's gone do I have time to grasp what just happened. What I said, and the gaping hole it's left.

"William," says Kantina. "We will work together, you and I, so her absence is not a concern. Do you agree?"

"I'll do it for her." I've done harder things already today.

"If you asked, she would have stayed. I believe this."

I lean my head against the van and close my eyes as I sift through the rubble of what almost was. "Belion told Sonia if she has any contact with me after filming, he'll give Eddie the blackmail film."

"So I have heard, and I have no doubt of it."

"I didn't want to tell her to go. I thought for sure she'd know how I feel."

Kantina's answer comes quietly, so the flock of production assistants coming to prepare her for the next shoot can't hear. "Perhaps you are a better actor than you think."

CHAPTER TWENTY-TWO

SONIA IS GONE WITHIN MINUTES, DRIVEN BY A PA TO THE hotel—and we're not done filming. For the next four hours, it's nothing but hard work and harder waiting and worrying. The last shots are time sensitive, requiring sunset or sunrise, and if we don't nail them the first time, we're stuck another night.

"Have you heard anything from her?" I ask Kantina as we stand face to face. The angle of the shot will take the setting sunlight and use it to light her right side. I, as usual, will not be visible.

"William, I tell you once more, when Sonia arrives safely, I will let you know."

"And roll film. Action!" Felicia shouts.

Kantina stares through me, seeing God-only-knows who. "Where once I could not bear your presence, now, your departure is the essence of my pain. Do not leave me so."

"I must," I say, wondering what kind of idiot the Lord of the Manor is. "But let this settle the matter in your heart, and answer me in the morn."

"Return quickly. My heart will not beat again until you do." Kantina looks slowly down, and to her left, so the shadows consume her face.

"Cut!" Felicia shouts. "What do you think?"

Belion rubs the soul-patch on his chin as he looks. "Shoot it again and again until we lose the light. I will do the rest in editing."

He leaves us—and in fact, a few minutes later, his town-car pulls away from base camp, leaving a small film crew alone on the hillside, while everyone else disassembles and packs.

By the time we're done, what was a thriving campground is now a lonely, trampled area, with Kantina's bus looming over the film crew's trucks.

"Will," says Felicia, as we head to her lone town-car, "we missed the flight to LA, but if we head to the airport, we can be home by ten."

I'm weary, and worried, and can't help watching Kantina to see if she's reading her phone. "Tomorrow I'm going to be near useless."

"Perhaps not." Kantina says from just behind me. "Felicia, darling, William chooses to return with me."

"I do?"

"He does?" Felicia says, raising one eyebrow. "And Sonia's okay with that?"

For one, brief moment, Kantina's face clouds with something I'd call anger. "I would never hurt her so. Never."

"Fine." Felicia shrugs. "Will, as far as I'm concerned, There wasn't a seat on the flight home for you. Bus it is. K, any word?"

"Sonia landed during our final shots. I worry for her. I should not have let her go alone."

"K—" Felicia's voice is laced with worry. "That's a very, very bad idea I see swirling around in that brain of yours. I can use Discount-James here for most things, but I can't make this movie without you. Sonia will be fine."

Kantina's giving off storm clouds, which matches the worry I can't help feeling. "If you need someone to go keep her company, I could…"

Under a pair of withering gazes, my idea looks less and less smart by the moment. "Never mind."

"Sonia does not mix this world and that of her family," says Kantina. "It has not ended well in the past. I cannot say even I would be welcome, and I have leverage you do not."

While Kantina and Felicia discuss who's going to contact Eddie next, I wander a short distance away, pick up my phone, and call my brother. Kantina's mention of leverage has the wheels in my head spinning.

"Will?" Bradley says. "What's up?"

"If Tia's there, put me on speaker."

"Done." Bradley's washing dishes, if the clink in the background is any indication. "You going to come home for dinner?"

"No." I pause—Kantina and Felicia are cackling, and I have zero idea why. "I'm keeping a promise. You know how you said I'm not cutthroat enough to run Hollywood deals?"

"That's an understatement." Tia's voice comes from further away.

"Maybe I was just never motivated before." I take a deep breath. "James Becton tried to buddy up with me. Suggested that if you heard from me how crazy things were on set, you would want to shut down production and recover your money."

Bradley swears under his breath. "Eddie would never allow that."

"If you went to all the other investors first? And they turn on him together?"

There's a moment of silence—and then it's both of them cursing so much the air curdles. I wait for them to finish. "The problem is, if James is trying to get to you, he's probably *trying* to get to the other investors. So you have to decide: Do you want to lead the revolt, or be the person Eddie remembers as having his back?"

They're mumbling to each other, or maybe Bradley's covered the phone. After long minutes, Bradley speaks. "What do you think, Will? Is it a disaster, or a mega-hit in the making? If I get out now, we won't be sunk if it's a failure."

Now it's my turn to be silent. Time to count the strings attached to my heart, and ask myself if I really have any business saying what I feel. Brad and Tia have their own life, their own family, and I need to protect them. "I think I'm too close to trust my own advice. I think I'm letting my own relationships get in the way of making the best business decisions. Sonia said she didn't want to use me to get to you. I don't want to do that either."

"What do you *want* us to do?" asks Tia.

"I want you to call Eddie." I don't even need a second to think about it. "Tell him what's going on. Tell him Felicia's got a handle on it. Tell him everything." My heart slams against my chest; I hope I've done the right thing.

"Thanks for being honest, bro." Bradley says. "Tia and I need to talk it over, and then any way it goes, I've got calls to make. And Will, one more thing?"

"What?"

"Just because you're close to someone doesn't mean you can't see clearly. Sometimes, it's what lets you see clearly after all."

Bradley hangs up, and I trudge back onto the bus, passing Kantina and Felicia on the way, both of whom are still laughing like it's the best joke ever. Without Kantina present, I don't hesitate to kick off my shoes and sink into one of the lounge seats. A moment after I sit down, I realize they're heated, and perfect for burning away the chill of the mountain air.

I unlock my phone and text without thinking. *Hey. I hope your flight wasn't awful.*

Sonia replies in less than a minute. *Are you on a plane home?*

I'm on Kantina's bus. We didn't wrap until dark and they're still outside plotting.

This time her reply takes a little longer. Is she typing a long message, or just thinking about how to respond?

They'll rehearse every detail. Enjoy the bus ride. K wanted you to ride down with us. If she asks if you want a pedicure, say no and everything will be fine. You're getting along just fine without me, Nine.

Without is the operative word. I'm as empty as the bus. There's an echo in my soul, but I can't bring myself to tell

Sonia what I'm feeling, not when she needs to focus on her family.

Instead, I text, *Felicia told me you don't let us horrible LA folk visit anymore.*

It takes no time for her to begin her answer. *You're not horrible. LA hasn't gotten to you yet, but I promise you anywhere is better than here. My step-mom is supporting Dad not going through chemo.*

I'm sorry. Don't give up. You can be very persuasive.

Another pause. *You know I can. Heading to bed, Will. You might as well settle in for the evening. Blankets are stored under the beds. Lift up.*

I roll off the bed and try—sure enough, the heated portion of the bed swings up, revealing fleece-lined blankets which must weigh twenty pounds each. It's like being hugged by a polar bear once I'm curled up under them.

I wish I was on a plane, but not to LA.

And wishes are kin to the dreams that come, dreams of holiday dinners when I was a kid. Of Mom and Dad screaming at each other when arguing wasn't enough. I don't have a family besides Bradley and Tia, but in my dreams, I still sit down for dinner with them. And in my dreams, if Sonia's there across the table? That's my secret to keep.

I WAKE BECAUSE THE BUS IS MOVING—OR MORE precisely, because it isn't anymore. Judging from the light, it's morning. As I sit up and peer through the windows, I recognize the outskirts of Los Angeles.

"William."

Kantina's voice nearly makes me jump from my skin. Despite what Sonia implied, Kantina is dressed, though her skin is completely bare of makeup, and her hair hangs in a loose mess that looks like she just woke up.

I don't recall leaving. I don't recall anything other than warmth and sleep. "Morning. When did we finally leave?"

"Far too late." Kantina gestures to the back of the bus. "Darling, would you like something to eat?"

My stomach rumbles, reminding me that dinner didn't happen. "I would, but we're late, aren't we? Where's my phone?"

It turns out, the uncomfortable lump under me is my phone.

"We are not late. I have asked our driver to take you to the beach, and then I will continue on to the studio." Kantina rises and sashays to the back, working her robe like a runway gown. "What do you think? I am considering this for my next premier outfit."

"Too tame for you," I say without thinking. "To top what you've already done, you'd need to wear a dress made completely of live ants and throw your hair over your face so no one can see you at all. Then don't say anything to anyone. They won't be able to see a bit of you, and it won't matter at all."

Kantina purses her lips as she thinks. "It must be wild. Each outfit must defy what the world expects, so I am the only one defining me."

"Except the hair. Everyone expects the hair, so you don't get a choice there, do you?"

Kantina halts her procession to the back of the bus, and for just a moment, I think I might have gotten to her. The even-wider-than-normal eyes, the downright scowl on her face—then it melts away, she's just her cool collected self. "I am uncertain about the ants. Sonia will of course wear the same dress she always does. It is bright green, like a lime."

"She goes to premiers?"

"I insist. Her fear cannot be allowed to rule every aspect of her life, and no photographer wants to ruin the color balance with that dress. We stay at opposite sides until the screening starts." Kantina holds her hands out in a gesture that makes me think it should be obvious. "You should get dressed for the sand, William."

"Wait—What did you say about the beach?"

"That, I will leave to Felicia for explanation. You should call her." Kantina looks to my phone, like I needed a reminder of how or what to use.

After a short shower break, I reluctantly dial the number on my phone which came with a text saying, *Call me when you wake up, Nine.*

I dial the number, and wait patiently.

"Will, it sounded like there was a bear under the covers when the bus pulled away."

It's nice to know Felicia hasn't lost her sense of humor. "Why am I on a bus to the beach?"

"Funny story, Will. Funny story. Once, there was a set carpenter who was innocent and sweet and clueless. Then one day, his testicles dropped, he grew a spine, and the son of a bitch developed a brain to go with it, and his brother—out of nowhere—clued in our producer about problems on the set." I'm not sure if it's anger or admiration in her voice, so I keep quiet.

"Eddie just had a come-to-Jesus moment with James Becton, and let's just say it's not safe for you to be on the same set with him. The man with a million tomorrows is the man with a hundred reasons to lose a fist fight with you."

Panic wells within me as I consider the consequences. "But Eddie said I had to show up *every day*."

"Will." Her tone says she has a plan.

Maybe that's just my desperation.

"You belong to me, and I'm loaning you out to a friend. He's shooting another *Swords of Justice* movie and needs eye-candy extras. You're going to show up every day, like Eddie said. Just on a different set. I'll let you know when you're clear to return."

"And Eddie Gellar's okay with this?"

"Once he stopped laughing? And once he stopped coughing from the laughing? He said it was my decision to make. Get off the bus so Kantina can actually show up and film my movie. I'd better not see a hair of your head around here."

With that, Felicia hangs up.

As the bus door swings open and the smell of salt water and the cries of seagulls filter in, I grab my phone, give Kantina a nod, and get to work. If Sonia were here, nothing would keep me from being near her for as long as I can. But without her, I have to focus on keeping Eddie Gellar happy and protecting my brother's business. Swords in the sand, here I come.

AND THAT'S HOW I WIND UP STRIPPED TO A LOINCLOTH, carrying a fake sword, with my face painted with a dozen blue Celtic runes, one of a screaming horde of warriors running down a beach. Well, walking slowly until we're told to run. Then running for a short distance, turning around, and repeating it.

During one break, I sit with my phone, texting. *Guess where I am. Guess what I'm wearing. Guess who I am.*

Sonia replies, *Will Mathis. The looney bin, and a suit of armor. Not in that order.*

Wrong on all accounts. Location: I'm on the beach, wearing a crotch-rag and carrying a sword.

Her answer takes minutes to come back. *Will, what's going on?*

I'm not Will right now, I text. *I'm a Gandarian Warrior. My job consists largely of trotting through the sand and screaming. Also, in the afternoons, I'm whoever the Gandarians are fighting. The difference is our face paint is red, we run the other direction, and I scream in a slightly higher pitch.*

I give her an easier version of what brought me here. The official story I picked up from listening to a podcast is that James didn't want to be shown up by Kantina, who is doing her own light checks.

Felicia sent them a picture and they snapped me up, I text Sonia. *Though they seemed disappointed I didn't have a tattoo.*

…What made them think you have a tattoo?

No idea, but I have one now that they painted it on. From what I can tell, these armies never actually fight, they just engage in beach calisthenics. Every day is leg day.

Sonia sends an eye-rolling emoji and the message, *Dad and I are driving to the beach for a walk the way we used to. I'll think of you the whole time. Also, I leave and you go and get your big break! You'll be a star by the time I get back.*

When will that be? I reply.

She doesn't answer.

After ten minutes of obsessively checking my phone, the warriors are called back to action. I tuck my phone away and return to screaming. She's on a beach somewhere, and as they signal for us to run, I do—if only because I'm imagining Sonia waiting for me.

$$\sim\!\heartsuit\!\sim$$

CHAPTER TWENTY-THREE

Filling in as a faceless extra is an easy way to pass the time—days of it—before Christmas. I text constantly with Sonia in between shots, since no one seems to be concerned with the fact that barbarian warriors are wearing flip-flops and carrying cell phones.

This film is crazy. Today they changed the script to add a scene where we're meeting Garg.

Sonia's always on her phone, and she answers immediately. *Garg? I've seen every Swords movie, and I don't know Garg.*

No one knows Garg, but he's 'Killion's most trusted advisor.' If he's the most trusted advisor, why wasn't he in any of the other films? Or at least the first half of this one?

In answer she sends me a GIF of women running in bikinis. *You're thinking too hard. It's not that kind of film, Will. More this kind.*

There's no emotional arc, I text back. *I got a copy of the script and read through, and as best I can tell, Killion really needs a hug and some therapy, not a sword battle on the beach.*

This time, a crying-laughing emoji accompanies her message. *It's DEFINITELY not that kind of movie. The point of this movie is hot shirtless men moving in slow-motion. Are the women wearing bikini-armor?*

There are no women, I reply. *No, I take that back. There are two. The love interest he sleeps with at the beginning of the movie, and the evil temptress he sleeps with in the middle. Damnit, both of them are wearing bikini armor.*

Welcome to Hollywood, she says.

After the next take, I fill her in on the real dirt.

The actor who plays Garg is a cocaine addict. The dude is currently passed out in his trailer. I swear, this makes me miss Lady of the Manner.

You miss Belion? Dang. Swords really must be an awful set.

*I miss *you*. How's your Dad?*

She doesn't answer until late in the afternoon. *Better. Still won't agree to see the oncologist, but I'm working on him. How's my favorite barbarian?*

Tired, hot, and my throat hurts. We've been filming fight scenes, and everyone has to shout something. I'm shouting, 'Doom, doom on you all.' The guy next to me is yelling, 'Cheese pizzas.'

Now that's something worth fighting over, says Sonia.

Not really, I reply. *We had it for lunch. The food on this set is better, though Garg is still crazy. He laid down on the beach and passed out. Makeup splashed some fake blood on him and we filmed around him like he was dead.*

Sonia replies, *Your dedication is a credit to actors everywhere.*

And so for a couple of weeks, my nights consist of checking in with Felicia to see if I'm allowed back, and texting with Sonia until I'm so tired I can't keep my eyes open. My days are spent screaming 'Doom,' though with hard work and my decent tan, I've worked my way up to being the nameless barbarian on Killion's right.

At lunch, I pick up my phone to find a text from Sonia. *Will, I saw set photos from Swords. Guess whose arm was in one?*

Kantina's? I reply.

Very funny. Also, I found you in a barbarian horde. You said you were at the front.

Only in closeup shots. Garg was hauled off by an ambulance today. He came out of his trailer high as a kite, charged into the middle of a scene, and tried to cut the heads off of everyone with a sword. Want to see my bandage?

Oh my god, Will. Are you ok?

It was a rubber sword. The bandage is on my knuckles. I split them when I punched him in the mouth.

Felicia was right, Sonia texts. *You are a walking disaster. Ice the hand.*

It was reflex! I protest. *Someone swings something at my neck, I'm going to duck and punch them. We caught it on camera, it's probably going to be a fantastic blooper reel. How are things there?*

There's a pause, a little longer than the short message that comes through warrants. *I'll call you tonight. Do you ever sleep?*

Anticipation flushes through me at the thought of a phone call, but all I say is, *Do you?*

Of course, when she calls me that night, I'm waiting at the table, phone fully charged. "Sonia!"

"It's good to hear your voice," she says. There's an edge in hers that tells me I've been right to worry. "How's the city of angels?"

"Missing one of its angels. I hear I'm back on set after Christmas break. We're wrapped on *Swords*, so I don't have to work, and LA is celebrating the launch of their newest star." I can't help the grin. "Guess who got a speaking line in *Swords*?"

"Will!" she shouts. "That's awesome. What happened?"

"They decided to use the footage of us being attacked. I mean, they're going to dub over the part where he's screaming that aliens ate his dick, but me punching him? That's part of the movie now. That was Fake Garg, an imposter sent by Haxor the Ruthless. I'm Real Garg, who has been biding my time to lure him out and protect my leader."

Sonia pauses. "Did you go out to celebrate? Does Kantina know? Does your brother? What was it?"

"That's a ton of questions, but: I went to McDonalds, ate a quarter-pounder and fries for lunch, no, no, and do you want to hear my line?"

"I can't wait," she says. "Please?"

"Doom," I say, in a deep voice. "Doom awaits all who oppose you."

The phone goes silent for long enough that I have to check to see if it's still connected. "You there?"

"You know I was kidding about you being a star when I get back, right?" Sonia's voice has a somber tone I didn't expect. "I really wish I was there to celebrate with you."

"Me too. Something's wrong, though. I can hear it in your voice. Are you upset that I pronounced doom on someone?"

"No, I'm happy about that." Sonia pauses, then lets out a long breath. "Sometimes I forget what it was like growing up here. In LA, I've got Kantina, Felicia, Aaron… People who get what I do."

"Is it really that bad?"

The time it takes her to answer tells me exactly how bad it is. "I wait for you to finish filming so we can talk every night."

It's not panic in her voice. At least, not yet. I think it's despair.

If I can't give her comfort, I can at least give her gossip. "Did you see movie news this week? Script rewrites on the zombie western they're filming one block over."

"I did! You want to know why?" Sonia launches into a lengthy discussion of who is screwing who, who's getting screwed, and how screwed up the whole process is.

I'm not sure when, but the conversation has turned to dog breeds when Sonia stops short. "Will, did your phone buzz?"

"Yes. I ignored it. I'm on a very important call right now, and I don't know the number."

"What time is it there? Seven?"

"Six thirty," I say. "Why?"

"Kantina wants you to come on set, right now. I told her about your part. She's insisting on a celebration dinner."

"Not happening. As I said, I'm in the middle of a very important call with my favorite actress—"

"Will. You know what would make me happy?" Sonia says it slowly, like there's a right answer and a wrong one.

And I know what it is. "If I appease Kantina—"

"No," she corrects. "If you could *say yes to my best friend in the world*, who wants to throw you a celebration dinner, *that* would make me happy. Please. If I were there, you would come."

If she was here, I doubt I'd leave. "Fine. But it's going to take forever without someone to carpool with. Tell her she better not leave."

I don't remember the last time I went out and celebrated. I don't remember the last time I had something to celebrate that didn't come with a heaping helping of doom associated.

It's not that I don't want to be having dinner with a beautiful, red-haired, green-eyed actress. It's just that I'll have to settle for the superstar, when what I really want is her best friend.

By the time I reach the studio and the soundstage, most everyone is gone home. Most everyone, however, does not include Felicia, who is heading back inside as I walk past.

"Nine," she says, stopping. "You're back on set after Christmas. You heard, right?"

"Yes, ma'am. Did Steph not show you the note I signed saying I understood?"

"Never hurts to confirm. Also, heard about the role, Garg. Doom!" She gives me a salute, ignoring my sarcasm. "You did good work, and I'm pleased. We'll be done within two weeks. For that matter, I wanted to wrap with what we already have, but I lost the argument."

That makes me freeze. "As in, done filming?"

"We cut a quarter of everything we film," Felicia says. "The movie that shows will only be distantly related to the one that's shot. I know what you're worried about, Will. You can't change it. You can't control it. You can only survive it. Have a good dinner."

With that, she disappears into the soundstage.

Kantina is waiting by her trailer door, fanning herself in the humid evening air.

"William, darling, congratulations!" Kantina gushes as she wraps her arms around me and then lets go.

"Thanks." It's getting easier to meet her gaze without either feeling star struck or curious how she can see at all. "It's not really that big a deal."

Kantina frowns and draws herself up, chin out as she speaks. "Do not dismiss your successes, William, embrace them. I am sorry to say I have lied in part to Sonia. I did not call you here only to celebrate. I called because I am worried for her."

"Then *tell* me where she is," I say, fighting to keep my voice level, "and I'll surprise her." I turn as an idea breaks on me. "Felicia knows where she is. Felicia will have her address."

"Stay. Eat. Felicia could give you Sonia's address," Kantina says, swishing up the trailer steps. "But I could give you something you desire more."

I meet her gaze head on, unafraid. "What's that?"

"My approval," she says, her emerald eyes wide and appraising. "You are aware, perhaps, of what it means when a woman's best friend approves? Or how disastrous it is if she does not?"

"You have my full attention." I'll keep my idea as a backup plan, but for now, I head up the stairs into Kantina's trailer, determined to not only pass her test, but to smash it.

CHAPTER TWENTY-FOUR

I FOLLOW KANTINA, BECAUSE THE GIRLFRIEND CODE IS unbreakable and I can respect that, and Kantina is definitely Sonia's best friend. "What's the deal with Sonia and her family?"

"First we must celebrate." Kantina stops and looks back at me. "Otherwise, what I told Sonia would be a lie. A bottle of wine is in order."

"I don't think that's a good idea. Tomorrow's Christmas Eve, and you—" I catch myself, remembering I read once in a magazine how she doesn't celebrate. "Why don't you go out for the holidays yourself?"

Kantina tilts her head. "You seem so eager to leave. Am I such awful company?"

"You're not awful," I say, shaking my own head in response. "It's just that I haven't spent enough time around you to be immune to the 'Kantina reality distortion field.' I'm always wondering if I'll say the wrong thing and offend you." I wait to see if this will set her off.

Kantina nods as if she's not surprised. "This is not my intention. How can you dream of being with my best friend, and not be comfortable around hers?"

She's got a point. "That's one of the reasons I'm here. I'm working on it."

"Good," she says, putting one hand on my cheek, I have seen how you look at her. Once, I hoped it was me you looked at that way, but the heart decides as it will. You know, Sonia's family feels much as you did. That those of us who make our careers here cannot be trusted."

"Even now, I can't tell you *why* I believe Sonia feels the way I feel. I know what I feel, but I can't begin to explain it."

"You want explanations for everything," Kantina says, with a slow shake of her head. "This is what makes me think you are not yet right for her."

"I am." I blurt it out faster than I mean to. "Since when does wanting to be sure make me not?"

"Eat with me. Listen to me. Perhaps you could change my mind." Kantina leads the way to her trailer and when she opens it, the smell wafting out is pure heaven. "Do you eat chicken?"

"Do you? I thought you were a vegetarian." I raise both eyebrows. "Personally, I eat anything that doesn't eat me first." I take the stairs two at a time, my mouth watering.

Moments later, we're sitting around a table while she takes dainty bites and I devour a seared chicken breast. After a few gulps, I lay it out the detail I should have caught immediately. "All right. You said 'yet.' I'm not right for her *yet*. What does that mean?"

"Forgive me asking," Kantina says, concentrating on cutting a tiny, precise cube of her chicken, "but I must be certain. Are you over the woman who hurt you?"

I ponder the answer before I give it, because I want to be absolutely clear. "I'm still hurt by what she did, but I don't want to fix that relationship. It's as dead as the orchids in the garden set."

Kantina gives a perfunctory nod. "Good. And yet, you are not right for Sonia, because she desires adventure. You are not an adventurous man, William. You are a quiet, safe, careful man. I do not believe Sonia can be happy without adventure."

"You've got to be kidding," I say before I can even think my response through. That doesn't make it less true, though; if anything, it makes it more true, because I'm speaking from what I've seen, from what I know in my gut. "The woman's so cautious it kills me. She's the only one more reserved than I am."

Kantina raises one eyebrow. "Now, perhaps. I have known her long enough though to understand that Sonia desires to take risks, but only with one who she can trust." She shakes her head again, firmly. "You may be trustworthy, but you are too set in your ways. The pain of your past has squeezed the sense of adventure from your soul."

I sit back and mull over my options. How I can convince Kantina that she doesn't need to worry. That I'm everything that Sonia could ever need—and she's all I could ever want.

Then I sit up as the realization strikes. "You have something in mind, don't you? That's the point of this." I narrow my eyes at her. "You probably already have it planned."

"Perhaps," Kantina says nonchalantly. She picks up a tablet. "Tell me where you would be, if you could be anywhere right now."

'With Sonia' isn't the answer she's looking for, I guess, even though it's at the top of my list. "I can't afford to travel."

"If you wish the chance to be with Sonia, you cannot afford not to. Let us agree it would be my treat." Kantina leans back in her chair and watches me. "Tell me of a dream of yours."

I inhale, deeply. I have the feeling that I only get one shot at this. It's now—or never. "It's Christmas," I begin. "At least, it is for me and a bunch of other people. I can't have Christmas dinner with a big family, so I guess I would love to be in a cabin, with snow and fire and a bottle of wine." And someone in particular to share it with me.

Kantina studies me for what feels like an eternity. "I am not convinced, but perhaps we can make an agreement. You will go on an adventure. I cannot, because I must see to the opening of my art gallery, but you will go. If you embrace this, I will consider it proof you are at least willing to try." She taps a few places on the screen.

"What exactly do you have in mind?"

She shakes her head. "Travel is the heart of adventure. When I was young, I would go without knowing where I was headed. I would meet people in places I never imagined. I did not know where I would sleep or what I would eat. Travel cleanses sorrow and frees the soul."

I tense, then try to hide it, keeping my voice light. "I have to be back for filming in three days, and Felicia says we're almost done. This is not a good time for me to drop off the grid."

Kantina's not listening. "Ah, here we are, this will do." She hands me the tablet, where I'm looking at a nightly room rental. It's less bed-and-breakfast and more 'spare-bedroom-complete-with-spiders.'

"Vermont?"

"There is snow, as you asked," she says. "And look, it says Christmas dinner with the family."

"I meant *my* family…"

That look on her face says I might as well shut up.

"What if these people are freaks who want to sell my organs on the black market?" I say instead.

Kantina takes the tablet back. "It says nothing about organ harvesting, only picturesque views and a Christmas dinner." She eyes me thoughtfully. "You must learn trust, if you are to abandon yourself to adventure." She clicks something on the tablet, and gives a decisive jerk of her chin. "It is settled, then. I have your number. I will call to check on you."

"How did you get my number?"

"From Sonia, of course." She scans the new screen that's popped up on the tablet. "There, your room is reserved for three nights. We have only to call you a cab, and I will book you a flight to Vermont."

"Can I ask you something serious?" As much as I know appeasing Kantina's whims might be crucial, the concern that ties me in knots isn't for myself. "I appreciate all the effort and attention, but have you talked to Sonia lately? I'm worried about her."

"It is always like that when she goes home. Sometimes, our relationships are best from a distance." Kantina nods to me. "Sonia showed me pictures of your work. Were your parents proud?"

Once, I couldn't answer that without the sadness crushing me. But the truth is, all those ideas I had as a kid of the perfect family were no more real than the movies. "Bradley's the only family I have left. He doesn't really remember Mom and Dad. I remember too much of the way they fought. But he and I stick together. I know no matter what, he's in my corner. Sonia needs someone like that."

"I see." Kantina studies the tablet, her brows knit together in thought. "Do this, and perhaps you can be that person."

"Deal." It's not even really a decision. I push back from the table. "Thank you for dinner, but I have to go pack."

"Oh, darling," Kantina says, "there is no time. You are already late for the flight—or you will be. By the time a cab arrives, you will be fortunate to make it."

"But—"

"Go with what you have. Find your way. Adventure." She takes out her phone and dashes off a message, then rises and hands me an envelope. "Do not open this until you arrive. When I was young, I hitch-hiked, but if you do not come back, Sonia would be most disappointed. You will find a ride to the address. This is your confirmation code for the reservation. Come back only if you have succeeded."

"Oh, I'll succeed," I mutter, stashing the envelope in my back pocket. "I have no clue what your crazy scheme is about, but I promise you, I will succeed."

"One more thing, darling," Kantina says, holding out her hand. "May I see your wallet?"

I hesitate for a second, but it's not like there's much to steal. I hand it over.

She takes out my driver's license, which still shows me brown and bearded, and hands it back to me. "Take nothing else."

I meet her eye. "What do you have planned?"

For one moment, I'm not looking at some ridiculously famous celebrity, but simply a woman—one who loves and cares for her best friend. She wraps me in a hug and says, "Something marvelous. Now, prove me wrong, William, so that I can trust you. Go have an adventure."

And God help me, I will.

THERE'S A CAB WAITING AT THE FRONT OF THE STUDIO lot, and an extremely agitated gate agent waiting to hand me a ticket and usher me onto an overcrowded plane at the airport. Any dreams I had of flying like a celebrity get crumpled up like used tissues. I'm stuck in the corner seat at the back of a flight that is mostly grumpy babies.

By the time the flight lands, it's three in the morning, local time. I'm bleary from lack of sleep, exhausted, and my phone battery is nearly dead. Plus I'm on the wrong coast, in the wrong time zone and it's like stepping into a deep-freeze when I get off the plane.

My phone chimes with a message from an unknown number. *William, I hope your flight has landed safely.*

Kantina.

We're on the ground, I reply. *Did you arrange a cab?*

That would deprive you of the adventure. You may open the envelope. I'm going to bed, but I will check on you tomorrow, when I have slept.

The envelope she gave me contains cash— the flash of green brings a smile to my face, but it's not hundred dollar bills, or even twenties. I count nineteen dollars, mostly in crumpled ones.

Nineteen dollars, an address that according to my phone is thirty miles away, and a confirmation code for a room reservation.

Kantina's idea of adventure sucks.

Outside, snow is falling, and I'm wondering what ever made me think snow was so great. It's icy and cold, and the blast of air every time the airport door opens just about gives me frostbite.

With the last of my battery, I book a ride with a Pakistani man who drops me off at the base of a hill. At the top is a three-story house I recognize from my brief glimpse of the listing. At least they left a porch light on.

I crunch through the icy snow, painfully aware of how unprepared for any place with winter I am. The wind slices through my breezy LA clothing, each breath burns, and it's only a few steps before snow fills the sides of my tennis shoes. At the door, I fumble with stiff fingers to push the doorbell, and settle instead for a knock. Moments later, another light comes on, and a woman with silver hair cropped close to her head answers the door.

"I'm here about the room rental," I say, holding up my dying phone to show her the code.

She waves me inside, keeping her floral robe wrapped tight. "What are you doing out here without a coat?"

"Long story," I say. "I'm still on Pacific time."

She offers me a hand. "I'm Susan May. Just call me May. My husband Earnest is asleep, but I'll introduce you tomorrow. Maybe I should go wake him up."

I offer her a half-frozen hand for a pitiful handshake. "Good to meet you, and no rush on introductions. I probably won't be up until noon. Is it late or early?" I step out of wet shoes, shivering despite the warmth in the house. It smells like hardwood oil and cinnamon inside, bringing back memories of my parents.

"A little of both." She shows me up the stairs to a wide room with hardwood floors and a stone fireplace. From the rows of boxes stacked to one side, to the mismatched furniture and frayed rug, it's clear they've converted a storage room into a rental. "We'll be cooking Christmas dinner tomorrow afternoon, but there's always food downstairs. Mr. Mathis, right?"

"Call me Will."

"Will it is. You know, we didn't think we'd get a taker this close to Christmas. My husband was tickled pink that his idea of pulling up another chair at the table worked."

I smile politely. "Any table with friendly people's better than one without."

She chuckles and nods on her way out. "Good night. I'll try to keep the house quiet, but no promises once everyone arrives."

With only one pair of clothes, getting ready for bed is easy, and soon enough I'm nestled down in a four poster bed, looking at silver moonlight streaming in through the window and across the floorboards. This isn't the adventure I wanted, but it's the key to the one I do. I dream of red hair and green eyes, and wicked laughter that usually comes at my expense.

When I wake up, it's not morning. In fact, it's probably closer to evening, based on the light. My phone has charged, and I have so many new text messages my phone has stopped even bothering with numbers.

The first five are from Sonia:

Hope you had a great celebration.

Will, how's the hangover?

Kantina says you're thinking about one of her trips. Call me. Now.

DO NOT GET ON THE PLANE. She sent me to Canada once without a passport.

Will, wherever you are, call me. We can fix it.

Then one from Bradley:

Be sure to water my venus flytrap and if you get a chance, check on Mrs. Chan's cat.

The rest are from Kantina, wanting to know if I'm alive, if I arrived, and so on. I type out a quick reply. *I'm alive. I'm here. I'll have you know, I'm adventuring.*

She replies almost immediately. *Excellent. You will call me tonight and tell me everything.*

I send Sonia a brief text. *I'm ok, still in the country, though I'm about as far from home as I can get.*

Sonia replies, *I'll call as soon as I'm back. I love K, but these stunts she pulls are going to give me a heart attack.*

I send Sonia a smiling emoji and put my phone away. Right now, priority one is filling my stomach. I put my one set of clothes back on and stumble down the stairs to find a small kitchen. Mrs. May is cooking there, stirring a pot of simmering potatoes.

"Well, good morning, Mr. Sleepy Head," she says. "I don't know how you slept through the ruckus. The family's out getting the fixings for dinner."

"Long days and sleepless nights," I say. "Is there anything to eat?"

She points to the fridge. "Anything in there you're welcome to. Bread's in the drawer. It's not fancy, but it's filling."

Under her approving watch, I proceed to make myself a sandwich that is almost too large for my jaw. "I haven't eaten in—well, it feels like forever." Starvation is definitely not adventure. And speaking of adventure, I'm going to prove my willingness to Kantina, starting immediately. "What's to do around here? I've got six dollars burning a hole in my pocket."

"There's a liquor store on fifth," says Ms. May. "I could have one of the girls run you into town tonight."

I did say I wanted a bottle of wine to go with Christmas dinner. "That would be great. In the meantime, you mind if I just sit out on the swing and listen to the snow?"

"You're welcome to for as long as you can stand it," she says, in between testing sips of broth. "Borrow one of Earnest's coats and hats, or you won't have fingers when you come back in."

From the closet, I pull a heavy, full-length coat the likes of which I've never needed in Seattle or Los Angeles, and a brown fur hat that looks like it originated in Mother Russia.

They're warm, though, and from the moment I shut the front door, silence falls across my world. I always loved pictures of snow growing up, and the way the cold has a sharp fresh scent all its own. Snow drifts cover almost everything, and what little they don't is crusted with icicles that catch the sun and split it.

It's only been a few minutes when a rusted orange van comes crunching up the lane, driving so fast I worry about if it'll be able to stop. It roars up the hill and slides into the driveway—and five people leap out and begin to unload.

All of them are dressed for winter, and all of them are carrying grocery bags. Mrs. May bursts out the front door, waving. "About time you're back. Earnest, come meet our guest!"

Earnest is a thick, short man with stocky shoulders and white hair where he isn't bald—which is most of his head. He shakes my hand with a firm, respectful grip. "Good to meet you. What's your name?"

"Will," I say. "Do they need a hand?"

He glances over his shoulder at the commotion as the others bicker over who's helping with what. "Make them pull their weight. May, I need to start the cornbread."

He heads into the house.

May points to the first woman coming up the stairs. "This Tara, our youngest. She just graduated from college, got a degree in advertising."

Tara takes off her hat, revealing short, golden hair and nods. "Dad's going to be insufferable. He kept saying he'd make money with the spare room. Now that he's been proven right we'll never stop him." She squints at me and then smiles. "I know you from somewhere, don't I?"

"I'm sorry," I say with a shake of the head. "I don't think so."

"No… I've definitely seen you." She pauses, lost in thought.

And it hits me. "Acting fails video? Me telling off a Hollywood producer?"

The grin that spreads across her face is infectious. "I knew I recognized you. Though I swear it was from somewhere else." Tara takes her bags and heads inside.

"These are the twins, Ricky and Bobby, they'll be back for Christmas dinner tomorrow afternoon." May stops them both and makes them shake my hand, even though they're competing to see who can carry the most bags at once.

"That straggler is Earnest's daughter," says May.

The woman climbing the stairs has her hair in a single braid that flails as she climbs the stairs, and it's red in a way I recognize, a way I know better than my own hair. The chill that runs down my spine has absolutely nothing to do with the snow or the ice.

Sonia takes one look at me and drops her groceries in the snow. She cycles through emotions so fast it makes me dizzy. One moment surprised, the next delighted, and the next, with tears. "Will?" And then she runs to embrace me.

I don't have time to think, but it's okay, because everything I need to do comes from the heart, not the head. I wrap my arms around her as she buries her head on my shoulder, and breathe in the scent of her skin. I didn't know I missed it until now. And for a time, we simply hold each other, while the world spins on around us.

CHAPTER TWENTY-FIVE

Sonia's on the phone with Kantina. I know this, because everyone in the house knows this. It's a small house, the walls are thin, and, also, Sonia's shouting so loudly I could hear her from the porch outside. Now I'm no longer cowering outside in the cold, but sitting at the dining room table as she rants.

"You don't *do* this sort of thing, K. It's not funny. No, it's not. I said it's not funny. No coat? No money? It's dangerously cold here. Was there even a moment where you thought to yourself, maybe this wasn't the best idea ever?"

I don't know what Kantina says in answer, but at least Sonia's voice drops to the point where the walls can muffle her words.

"You're from California," says May. The awkwardness now has congealed to the point where I don't think I can move from the table. Earnest hasn't looked my way once since the shouting started. I don't blame him. Lizards have used this as a survival skill for a thousand years, and if he can avoid conflict by blending in with his recliner, more power to him.

"I'm from Seattle. I moved to LA to live with my little brother."

"One of those *actors*." She pronounces the word like what she means is 'dead skunk.'

Despite the despair clinging to the room, that makes me smile. "Not if I can help it. I used to think I was going to be a wood carver again, one day. Now I don't know what I am."

May perks up and looks at me. "You mean you make fancy wooden stuff?"

"I used to. Sometimes, I make functional things. Salad bowls. Salt and pepper shakers. I would make these jewelry boxes I carved from a single piece of wood. Box, drawers, everything, from one piece. At least, I did." I've failed at running a business, picking a partner, a girlfriend, being a stand-in, and now, apparently, at forming any sort of normal relationship with Sonia.

Earnest opens his mouth to answer—and then turns his attention to the staircase as Sonia comes trotting down, her eyes red. "Will, come on, we need to drive into the city and get you some winter clothes."

"Honey." May steps between us. "Don't you get traffic alerts? The interstate's closed due to that overturned truck. You could maybe make it into town, but I don't think a t-shirt from the dollar store is going to make a difference."

"Fine." The way Sonia says the word, it isn't. "I swear, Kantina is in so much trouble when we get back. May, Dad, this another one of Kantina's adventures."

"Like our trip to Hawaii?" asks Earnest, perking up. "That was something else. I tell you, we saw a real, live, volcano."

I shrug, because I'm trying to focus on what would make the holiday good for Sonia, not me. "If this is awkward, I'll leave. Surely there's a hotel in town. I'm good for the money once I get home to my wallet."

"Now, now," says May. "Your reservation is paid up for three days, and she's a guest in my house just like you. I'll be the sayer of who goes and doesn't, and no one's going before Christmas dinner."

May takes one look at the way Sonia's nose is crinkled up and glances to her husband. "Earnest, could you give me a hand? Boys, give your sister some space."

After they leave, Sonia flops on a worn couch and motions for me to join her. "You have zero idea what's going on here, right? You've really never seen one of Kantina's movies?"

I take my place, tossing aside a thread-bare purple and gold pillow. "Bradley keeps telling me I need to."

"So that's a no to *The Accident* or *Three Days*?"

The way she's watching me, I feel like there's a right answer and a wrong one. "What am I missing?"

"*Three Days*," says Sonia. "Our favorite friend with long red hair and a single name hires a business associate to come home with her for Thanksgiving. Awkward meet-the-parents, terribly embarrassing conversations with siblings, hijinks, romance."

"Never seen it." Though I'd love to star in the real life version, with someone else with red hair, but with three names, even if Margret isn't one she uses.

Sonia puts one hand on her head. "*The Accident*. Millionaire's helicopter malfunctions, stranding him. He rents the perky, green-eyed love interest's spare bedroom for the night. Cue the hot sex, romance, love, dinner."

"In that order?"

"No," says Sonia, to my relief. "But you see the point. She's putting us through one of her movies. I wouldn't be half surprised if we get a baby delivered to the doorstep tomorrow, like from *The Unexpected Delivery*. You know, so we can fall in love while putting aside our differences to care for her."

"Her? Our baby is a her?"

"I've changed diapers," says Sonia darkly. "Kantina has not. That's the only reason she could even possibly consider it romantic."

"She's being ridiculous." Now's as good a time as any to stretch and put my arm around her. "You can't create romance by re-enacting scenes from famous love stories. I mean, you and I might as well make some pottery, or go dirty dancing, or jump out of a building with a fire-hose tied to us while the building explodes."

"Not *Die Hard* again?" The way she crinkles her nose reminds me that she doesn't consider it romantic.

"I know!" It's time to change the mood, and see if I can pull off another magic trick—bringing back that laugh of hers I love so much. "We could re-enact the T-Rex scene from *Jurassic Park*. Your parent's cat can be the stand-in dinosaur." I rise and pull her toward me, staring at the cat with eyes wide. "Don't. Move. A muscle. If you don't move, he can't see us. Also, don't hold on to catnip, and don't crinkle foil."

Sonia yanks back her hand, then swats at me playfully. "There's nothing romantic about that movie. Or sending someone into a snowstorm with no coat."

I shrug. "You can't blame her for everything. For instance, I think we can assume Kantina's not responsible for the overturned tractor-trailer. Or if she is," I add thoughtfully, "I want to move very far away from her and hope my name never comes up in your conversations again." I glance toward the kitchen. "So what now? This is your house, your home. I'm the guest and visitor."

Sonia shakes her head, then answers softly. "May and I got along about as well as any grieving teen and her step-mom ever did, but this is her home, not mine. I need someone who'd take my side no matter what. I'd say 'Let's make the best of it and pretend', but that's *exactly* what Kantina had in mind, and I detest it when she meddles in my relationships. You would think after the last time, she'd know better."

I have some ideas of what to do that I don't think anyone will expect, but before I can bring them up, May leans around the corner. "Dishes time. Mr. Will, we clean up before we eat, or we don't eat, so if I can borrow my daughter—"

"I'll help." I shrug and head for the kitchen. "I believe the ad said I could join the family for the holiday. Seems like sitting around and letting everyone else work isn't exactly joing the family."

May beams a smile my direction. "Tara's on scraping, Sonia, you wash, and Will, I hope you're decent with a towel. Many hands make light work."

I take a worn dish-towel from a hanger on the wall and stand at attention as Sonia takes her place, pinning her hair on top of her head so it doesn't fall in the sink while she washes.

Tara, the short blond who passed me by earlier, bumps Sonia aside and stands by me. "Hello, mystery model."

"Evening, ma'am." I nod to her to be polite. "No mystery about me, and I'm a carpenter, not a model."

"Uh-huh." She looks up at Sonia. "First you're Mom and Dad's surprise renter. Or maybe, you're Sonia's almost-boyfriend who surprised her. Then I realize where I recognize you from."

"The fail video?"

Tara steps back and looks at me. "The poster. The promo material for that movie Sonia's working on? It's hanging in my bedroom. Come on—"

"Will isn't going anywhere near your bedroom," says Sonia, her tone a few degrees colder than the wind outside.

"Calm your tits, sis," says Tara. "Be right back."

When she returns, she unrolls a set of posters.

Some of them I recognize. Belion, standing at the rowboat, looking like he's giving a speech. James Becton, in formal attire, staring at the camera like sheer desire could melt it. Then she flips to the next one—and my jaw drops.

"Where did you get this?" The photo is me, from the bedroom shoot—but I never looked like that. My skin isn't that dark tan, my muscles simply can't bulge that way and I do not have a tattoo of any sort, though now it's starting to make sense why people expected one. "Sonia? What the fresh hell is this?"

She takes the poster from Tara and stretches it out. "Oh, God. This was from a lighting test. It probably got mixed up with the set photos for the promo package."

"Mixed up?" I draw myself up to full height and cross my arms. "That's seriously edited. I don't look anything like that and you want me to believe it's a mix-up?"

She bites the side of her lip and nods. "When it comes to promotion, advertisers don't care who's in the photo, they care about the message it sends. Tara's got a minor in marketing, she can tell you."

"Oh yes," Tara says, looking at me like she can see my abs through my t-shirt. "What matters is what people think when they see it, and this picture says, 'Hey, girl. I may be a set carpenter, but I'm *very* handy with my tool.'"

"That's enough," says Sonia, snatching the poster and rolling it up. "Will, you want this?"

"It's mine," says Tara, making an attempt to take it back. "It's been on my bedroom wall at college for a month. Will's been my fantasy boyfriend. I didn't know his name was Will. I was calling him 'Matt,' but now—"

"*Tara.*" Sonia says the name like a threat.

A threat I need to defuse. "So, you know… what I look like. I know nothing about you. Your mom said your name was Tara. You're blond and probably need a stool to climb into bed, but that's all I know. Perhaps you could tell me a bit about yourself?" I lean back against the sink.

"Oh. Right." She throws herself into scraping a dish. "You're like her, deflecting attention."

"Showing interest in someone else isn't deflecting," I say, even though I was totally deflecting.

"Sis, spill it." Tara hands Sonia a dish—and a stare. "What's going on here? Who is he?"

"A good person caught in one of Kantina's schemes."

"If you don't give me a straight answer, I'm going to come up with my own ideas. Oooh," Tara continues. "Did his car break down and he's forced to spend Christmas with us?"

"No." Sonia offers nothing else, plunging a plate into the dishwater with a little more force than strictly necessary.

"Did you pay him to pretend to be your boyfriend so Mom will stop bugging you? Oh my God. Are you two falling for each other even though it's just a business arrangement?"

"No!" Sonia swings the towel overhand, smacking her little sister. "It's nothing like that."

"Will?" Tara steps between us, bumping me with her hip to make room. "Is she pregnant with your baby, and you don't know it's yours?"

"If she's pregnant—"

"I'm not," Sonia adds with a glare.

I don't grin back, but I can feel my eyes sparkle. "It's not mine, sadly."

Tara nods and leans closer to her sister. "He's a billionaire, isn't he? His helicopter can't fly in the snow and he's bought the bedroom for three nights… but can he afford your love?"

"No," says Sonia, throwing her head back. "Will's not my pretend boyfriend. He's not my secret lover from some passionate night of sex."

"Maybe not with you." Tara leans over to me. "Your secret is safe with me. Do you have a helicopter?"

It takes time for me to answer, because I can't help the feeling this whole conversation is a landmine. "My brother bought me a tiny remote control one for Christmas, but it's in LA, and unless you're a cricket, you can't ride on it."

Tara leans closer. "If my sister isn't interested, could you *pretend* to be a billionaire trapped in a snowstorm? I know where some of my brother's old suits are, and we could entertain ourselves—"

"Tara?" Sonia says with a cold, still voice that makes the wind outside feel like a furnace. "Do you remember how I used to lock you in the cellar?"

"Yes."

"Unless you want that to happen again, you will *not* proposition Will. Think carefully. It's cold and dark down there."

Tara puts one arm around me and draws me close. "That's exactly what I used to warn men about her. It's cold and dark down there. Also, I like you way better than the last Hollywood guy she brought home. He was an asshole."

Sonia freezes, and from her lips, a single command spits. "Shut up."

"What, he didn't know?" Tara, looks from Sonia to me. "How could you *not* know about her old boyfriend? It was in the tabloids, my sister and the Super Spy?"

"James?" The thought hits me in the gut, with a pang of jealousy I have no right to feel. The thought of her and him wrings me into knots I can't begin to explain. "James Becton?"

"The one and only," says Tara. Her face twists. "Mr. 'You should all be honored to know me. Here I am, slumming it with the commoners. Look at my wine I brought, which costs more than you make in a month.'"

I back away from the sink, swirled by confusion and feeling more lost by the moment. "You were *dating* that asshole?"

Sonia doesn't answer. Her face is as red as her hair, her mouth is open, her eyes blank.

"More than dating him," says Tara, either oblivious to Sonia's distress or else plain uncaring. "Way more than dating him. I'll find you some tabloid photos after dinner. They're in Mom's scrapbook for Sonia."

I turn to ask Sonia if her sister is joking—and she's gone.

She's not upstairs in her room, she's not *anywhere*. So I do the next best thing, once I'm in my room: I take my phone and dial Kantina. Supermodel, super actress, and in super-deep trouble.

"Darling," she says, without even saying hello, "I was wondering when you would call."

"Sonia was dating James Becton?"

After a pregnant pause, Kantina answers. "What of it?"

"You don't see anything wrong with this? Okay, let's start with the fact that you dated James as well. Women *don't* date each other's ex. I know that rule, and I don't even have a sister."

"James and I?" Kantina laughs, a bitter, forced sound. "You know this how?"

"I saw it on the news..." Now—and only now—does it occur to me that what I know and what happened might be different.

"And according to the news, you and I had a passionate affair, but I believe that you know better than that. I could not tolerate James personally. My only mistake was believing that just because James and I could not find happiness did not mean Sonia and he could not."

My cheeks are hot and I answer without thinking, "Because he's an asshole."

"I have been an unpleasant person at times. James is charming and caring, except when he is not. He was often tender with Sonia, and perhaps they were meant for each other."

"They weren't." It comes out angrier than I mean for it to, but perhaps it's just that I'm stunned. "Did you not think this might come up when you shipped me out to surprise her?"

"I am sorry, William." Kantina takes a deep breath. "If you want to leave, I will not ask you to stay or hold it against you."

"Leave? Not without finding Sonia and fixing this—this mess." I hang up without waiting for an answer.

Tara's waiting for me as I open the door, not even being subtle about listening in. "If she's doing the usual, I know where she went. I'll grab the keys and get the car warmed up. You're going to need a coat, Mr. Hollywood."

I steal the same coat I wore before and head out into a night so bitterly cold it hurts.

Tara's already scraping the van's windshield. "I have to ask, Will. Are you certain you're not a millionaire whose helicopter won't fly?"

There's only one thing that would make me feel like a million bucks and leave me flying, and that's not going to happen.

"I'm about as poor as they come," I say. "I don't have a paper airplane, let alone a real helicopter. I'm sorry."

"Figures," Tara says. "Sis has no idea what's been going on around here for the last year, so she's probably up over the ridge over there." She gestures with her head.

Ridge is a low hill, barely enough to count.

"What's there?" I ask as we get into the van.

We crunch down the hill from the house, tires sliding in the snow, barely missing the ditch. "Now? Sixteen luxury town homes. When we were kids? That's where she'd go to sit by the pond when she and Mom were fighting."

Tara drives through the dark in a way that says she might have learned from Sonia—which is to say, full speed ahead, snow or not. As we come up and over, I spot a familiar form walking along the road, avoiding the drifts thrown up by the snow-plow.

I lower the window as Tara pulls to a stop. "Sonia, it's freezing out here."

"Below freezing," she answers without looking over. "I grew up in this area. I'm used to it."

Sure she is, clutching her thick coat, head bent over. I step out and open the van door. "At least come in out of the snow. Please?"

Sonia stops shuffling and looks to me—then reluctantly takes my hand, sliding into the first row seat. I switch places and sling the door shut, cutting off the smell of crisp snow. "I know how it is to need to get away. When I was in our fourth foster home, I must have spent six hours a day outside, rain or shine."

"What am I supposed to say?" Sonia asks. "I let myself be fooled. I knew what kind of man James was, and maybe I just wanted to believe it wasn't true."

Tara coughs something that sounds like 'stupid,' but she's at least got the good sense to keep her eyes on the road as we head back to the house.

"I know a thing or two about mistakes," I say as I hold her close. "I just didn't think—I don't know. I have no idea what I thought."

"You thought," says Tara as she guns the van to climb the ridge, "that my big sister wasn't dumb enough to go glacier skiing with an A-lister. Or for picnics in Hawaii. Or was it London?" She sniffs. "People do stupid things when they're in love."

Sonia jerks her head up. "I wasn't in love with him. Ever."

"Could've fooled the world," says Tara. "Will, you mind taking the keys?" she adds as we pull up in front of the house.

I slip out of the van and circle to meet Tara. "Thanks."

In answer, Tara leans over—and kisses me as I step back, hitting the open door.

Now I know exactly what a stage kiss is supposed to feel like. There's no spark, no fire, only a sloppy wet fizzle that I can't help jerking back from, even as I'm thinking about what the timing for this would be if it was a scene.

Tara wipes her lips and gives me a wistful shake of the head. "I thought that was going to be a lot better. Wall-Will's got you beat by a mile." But she whistles as she skips up the steps of the house.

And Sonia is still in the van, where I rejoin her, taking the seat beside her, listening to the snow brush the van roof. "Your sister is an awful kisser. I wouldn't wish her on James Becton."

Sonia relaxes, leaning her head over against me. "If you hadn't said that, I would feel honor-bound to lock her in the cellar. You know it all now, don't you?"

"All what?"

"Everything. I was dating James. He liked to buy me dresses. Makeup. Makeovers. Anything that made me look more like Kantina. But I avoided public attention because of the rumors it would start. So one day, he surprised me with a photoshoot. Paid some paparazzi to ambush us."

Her voice breaks, and she doesn't speak for minutes, just holds me, her head buried on my chest.

"That's the time you said you didn't remember how you got home?" I say at last, running my fingers over her hair in what I hope is a comforting manner.

"Right. Kantina was furious when she found out. We were filming *Many Times Over* and all I can remember is her hitting James over and over. Knocked three of his teeth out. Broke his nose."

More of the puzzle falls into place, what Felicia told me about Kantina and breakups. "James mentioned that."

"Eddie Gellar had security sit her down. Told her she was going to sign a contract or she was never going to film again. After she did, he turned on me. Said it was *my* duty to keep her in line."

I blink. "You can do that?"

She shakes her head against my chest. "No one can do that. I was out drinking that night with some friends. I might have been angry about being made her keeper. I might have said exactly what I thought about Eddie Gellar."

At last, I understand. "Someone was taping?"

"Someone who went straight to Belion, asking how he could best use it." She turns away. "So, now, Will Mathis, you know all my secrets. Kantina wasn't thinking at all. You know what's going to happen if Belion finds out about this trip. He'll explode. He'll derail the production. You'll lose a job. Kantina and I? We'll lose a lot more."

"That's on set," I say, reaching for her hand. "We're not on set. I was wrong before, and I asked too much of you. If I can't have forever with you, then at least let the next three days—"

Sonia turns to me, tears on her face. "No. I don't *want* three days. I want a forever. I don't want something I have to hide. I want something I'd stand in front of the world with and say, "Look at me.""

"I want that to be me and you."

Sonia takes my hand in hers and wraps it up—then reaches up to kiss me.

Her lips burn mine, and we twist and turn to get closer, until she slides across the seat into my lap. With one hand, she's pressed on my chest, while the other traces my ear and chin.

This is what I've imagined from the moment she first kissed me—a frantic desire to explore balanced with the delicious thought of savoring every moment. As she rocks against me, her hair falls in a curtain that surrounds us— and when she pulls at my shirt, I can't get it off fast enough to let her trace patterns on my skin while I plant kisses down her chin, then her neck.

There's no spotlight on us, or camera men, or makeup people waiting to spritz us with cooking oil, just Sonia and I, alone together and lost in the moment.

This time, she doesn't pull back.

The van door swings open—letting frigid air in. And chilling the fog on the windows.

Tara stands there, a wicked smile on her face. "Dinner's ready. Come eat."

Sonia's shaking as she answers, though I think it's frustration I hear. "We were *busy*."

"You mean *getting* busy. You left the car door open, the dome light is on, and Dad says that's bad for the battery. We've all been watching, and while your awkward foreplay is entertaining, we're hungry, and you know Mom's rule about eating without everyone at the table."

I jerk my head away and look over Sonia's shoulder. There, in the picture window, stand her brothers, waving and giving me thumbs up.

Embarrassment threatens to flood over me—people watching us, *again*. But Sonia gives me a little knowing smile as she climbs down and straightens out her hair—and her clothing—so I turn back to the window, and give her brothers a wave.

It could be worse, after all. They could be threatening to kill me.

CHAPTER TWENTY-SIX

DINNER THAT NIGHT IS AWKWARD, TO SAY THE LEAST.

"Dish!" Sonia's step-brother Bobby shouts as we sit back at the table, having eaten more than one helping. "Tell us about someone famous."

Sonia pauses. "What have I said? It's not polite to tell secrets."

"But you know them. You're the woman who knows the secrets. I bet you could tell some real stories." He waits, motioning with his hand the way Sonia does when she's prompting me for a line.

"I can tell a few." I lean forward, looking to each person as I try to come up with a whopper to turn my outburst into a genius idea. "Anyone here seen *Swords of Justice*?"

Richard stops and stares. "You… you were in that?"

"You didn't recognize me?"

When he stammers, Sonia cuts me off with a glare. "Will's not in the first one, and besides, all the men in those movies are the same."

"Smooth? Clever? Dashing?"

"Overconfident," Sonia answers. "Easy on the eyes. Sorry, boys, but Will's sticking to the code of honor. No set stories. *Right?*"

I don't need any more warning. "What I meant was I *could* tell some stories, but it would be wrong. No stories from the set. But, you want to hear about what happened when I visited Kantina's house?"

"No, they do *not*," Sonia says, faking a gag response. "My brothers definitely do not."

Tara taps her water glass. "I'd love to hear, Will. Tell me."

Sonia raises one eyebrow as she tilts her head.

I can't tell if she's warning me or Tara. "I... went swimming. That's all."

"See?" Sonia says, looking to each of her family members. "Hollywood stories are boring. Tell me about the year. I really have missed you all."

This moment, the way they talk and laugh—this is what Bradley and I always dreamed of. And I know the way they look at her, just drinking in every word.

May heads to her room and comes back with a scrapbook. "Time to update this. You have pictures?"

Sonia stops and glances at the book, her eyes wide in horror. "May—"

"I just want to show your boyfriend." May pushes the book across the table.

It's separated not by years, but by movies—and I had no idea Sonia was in so many. "Woman Number Three? I didn't know you were Woman Number Three. And Woman on Cell Phone. And..." I find the tab labeled *The*

Bride Becomes Her, and just after that, *The Man With A Million Tomorrows*. "You were in that?"

Sonia slams the book and pushes it away. "I could do with a little less Hollywood right now."

Before I can move, she picks up a plate or two and heads to the kitchen.

"Leave her be," says Richard. "You look like a chaser. Give sis some time to cool down. Why don't you come out back and let us show you our gun collection?"

By the time I make it back in, Sonia's keeping her distance, or, more accurately, being kept at a distance. Both her brothers have playfully suggested after all that they'll bury me in the snow if I lay another finger on her.

Her dad makes certain we don't spend time alone, and apparently she's not allowed to 'disturb' the guest anymore. Still, on Christmas morning, we sit together on the swing, noses freezing, while she holds my hand, and savor the few minutes of being alone.

"You know," Sonia says, "I don't have a gift for you."

I squeeze her hand gently. "You already gave me a smile. Let's talk about anything. It doesn't have to be about me and you."

"I don't mind it being about us," she says, untangling her fingers so she can run them across my palm instead.

I stare at them, memorizing the way they move. "Kantina told me I wasn't adventurous enough for you.'"

Sonia sighs. "I love her, but her advice is what she'd want, not me. Plus, she doesn't know when to stop. Stay right here." She gets up and goes inside, then comes back with a bundle and hands it to me.

It's a baby.

At least, a baby doll. A remarkably lifelike doll with perfect weight, and skin I swear is warm to the touch. "Where did you get this?"

The eyes pop open and fake-baby lets out a blood curdling shriek that results in me hurling it end over end into the snow.

"No!" Sonia's already leaping to pick it up, cradling it, rocking it until the unholy noise it's making dies down. "Will. You just threw the daughter you didn't know we had face-first into a snow bank."

"It surprised me," I say, not sure where this defensiveness is coming from. "I didn't throw it—"

"Her."

"Her. I dropped her."

"Twenty feet away?" Sonia asks as she pats the demon-doll on the back. "Forget carpentry, you should have been a major-league pitcher."

"I *may* have been surprised. Where did you get that?" I reach for the doll, but Sonia turns away.

She doesn't speak until the baby goes back to lurking. I mean, sleeping. "Special delivery, arrived before sunrise this morning. I swear, we filmed that scene six different ways."

"She's got your eyes, and my… lithium ion batteries." I peer more closely at the baby, then glance up at Sonia. "Seriously, she has green eyes and red hair, tan skin. How long has Kantina been planning this? And where was she keeping her?"

"I'm guessing she ordered it overnight, and you do not want to know how much these dolls cost. I told my parents it was a gift to help Tara remember birth-control and snuck it into her room. She's been up since dawn trying to calm it down." Sonia turns the baby over and presses a switch on the back. "This thing we're doing? The banter, the laughter?" She shakes her head. "That's what Kantina was aiming for. Will, I don't want someone else pulling my strings. I want to do things in my own time and in my own way."

I take the baby-doll from her and kiss it on the forehead. "Have a good nap, Charity."

"Shellie," says Sonia. "Her name is Shellie Marie."

"I like Charity. Charity Meredith."

Sonia pulls back the blanket covering the dark red hair and brushes it. "You didn't give birth to Shellie, so you don't get to name her."

"Neither did you."

I could pop popcorn on the glare she gives me. "What I mean is, of course you can name our fake daughter. You get to name the first one, I'll name the next five."

Sonia returns to the swing, still cradling the now-silent doll. "We are not having six." At six, she winces and shakes her head. "But, we're not having one, either. She needs a sister. Someone she can feed spiders, and lock in cellars, and tell secrets she doesn't want kept."

I stare at the lines of her body as she wraps it around the doll, soft and strong—and safe. "You'll make an amazing mother someday."

"I hope so, I had two as examples. Even though I gave May a hard time, she taught me more than she knows. More than I would admit." Sonia continues to rock the doll—and then hands it to me.

"Tell her," I say as I accept the baby. "I'm a big fan of telling people what you feel or think instead of expecting them to just *know*. Like the Lord in *Lady of the Manner*. If he would sit down for ten minutes and talk it over—"

Sonia isn't listening; she's bent over, shaking. "Oh, like it's that easy."

I hug the baby close, almost instinctively. "I didn't say easy. But important, yes."

"You want me to tell you what I'm feeling?" she asks, her voice fraught with warning.

This I have to think about, because the answers could hurt. But it's better than not knowing. I have to believe. "Please."

"I feel like I've lost control of my own life. I love what I do, but I can't bring myself to do something I'd love even more. I want a relationship that lasts, but it feels like all I find is hurt." Sonia looks up at me, and the laughter that had welled up from her is so far gone. "Kantina is always there for me, and she's my best friend, but she has these expectations, and every time, I feel like I'm failing her and me."

"Like what?"

She looks back down as she answers, and with each word, she picks harder at her nails. "Like I'm going to quit being a stand-in and fetch coffee for a few years, so I can have a moon-shot at becoming a director. Like I'm somehow going to wake up and not be afraid of attention."

I put one arm around her and hold her as she leans in. "I believe you will. In your own way, in your own time."

The huff of anger she lets out isn't what I expected, nor the way her mouth bends down in a frown. "Some days, I think I'm there. My therapist says I am, but she's not the one having to do it. Mom and Dad don't say much anymore, but it comes up at least once a visit. Am I *still* just standing around on movie sets? Am I *still* afraid of having my picture taken? Did I ruin *another* relationship?" Sonia sits up and slides to the far edge of the swing, putting all the space she can between us. "If I knew what to do, I would have done it already."

We sit in silence as I consider what she's said, her staring silently at her fingers, or the snow-covered yard, me still rocking our not-child. "After Mom and Dad had their accident," I say slowly, "Bradley and I bounced around between foster homes. Some were good, some were bad, but there was one—must have been a year after the funeral."

The pain is dull now after so many years, but it's always present, an ache like the hamstring I tore playing baseball. "We had one foster mother who used to say, 'Some things you can't know your way through. You just have to feel your way through them.'" The baby's green eyes flutter open, and I cradle it closer, tickling its chin. "Maybe this is one of those things."

"Maybe." Sonia looks through me, into the distance. "You sound like Kantina. The heart, the head, the remote control. She has a saying for everything."

I flip my scarf over the top of my head, clear my throat, and attempt the deep purr Kantina uses. "Never once has the head won. The heart always pushes it down the stairs and locks the cellar door, darling. That is why you should not go there, Will-I-am, of course."

"You are terrible. And, you sound nothing like her." Sonia wipes the corner of her eyes.

"But I must, darling. It is the only way."

"You know why she talks like that?" Sonia raises one eyebrow, as if to say she shouldn't need to tell me. "She's nervous. So she speaks slowly, and pauses, and adds in words to give her time to think. There's a video on the internet that's her before she came to America. Listen to her then and now."

"I don't want to talk about Kantina, or Kantina's movies, or Kantina's videos. The world—my world—doesn't revolve around her." I lean over and fake-whisper to the baby, "Unless, of course, Shellie-The-Demon-Baby is recording our conversation and relaying it to her. In which case, I love Kantina. She's the best."

Sonia leans over and adds, "If you're listening, K, you're in big trouble. Now, Will, if you don't mind, I'm going to return Shellie to my sister so *she* can have her Christmas vacation ruined."

"That's something you do?"

"It's something I do. You want to stay on my good side." Sonia gives me a wink.

"What's your naughty side look like?" I ask as I stand up, savoring the cold we never get in LA.

"Will!" She elbows me with mock offense. "I am a morally upright woman. I'm offended. My hair is offended."

"Does your hair have a naughty side?" I ask as I follow her into the house. I shout up the stairs after her, "Does it?"

Sonia doesn't answer, and while I wait for her to return, I take a seat in one of the chairs by the fire.

"You two look right for each other."

From the other side of the fire, the chair turns, and Earnest is sitting there, covered in a blanket.

"She's special."

Earnest tilts his head side to side. "That's one word for it. She's a firebrand, just like her mother. Every time I look in those eyes, I see her."

"That's funny. I don't think Sonia's anyone but herself."

He eyes me thoughtfully. "You seem like a nice boy."

Anytime someone says that, there's more behind it. Or more to say. "But?"

"Just take care of yourself, that's all." Earnest's lips are drawn tight like there's more he wants to say, but won't.

I shove my hands deep into my pockets and watch him for some sign of what I'm missing. "I am. Something in particular I should be on the lookout for?"

The fire crackles and pops, and logs shift before he answers. "I can't tell you how happy I am she came back to see me, but that girl and her step-mother are too alike to get along without killing each other. You get along with yours?"

Over time, I've learned how to tell the truth and lie at the same time. "We haven't fought in years."

"You should have taken her home to meet your family," says Earnest. "I have a diagnosis, not a death sentence, and if it means that much her, I'll go see the doctor. Cancer might not get me, but keeping May, Sonia and Tara from killing each other might."

"Sonia met my family at Thanksgiving."

There's a twinkle in Earnest's eyes as he looks up and gives me an appraising nod. "So that's how it is."

"We'll see." The fire's warmer than I like, now that I think about it, and I nod to excuse myself, then head upstairs to find Tara and Sonia together in a room that looks like a glitter party exploded in it. "Hey," I say, tapping on the doorframe, "got a moment?"

"Wall Will, meet real Will." Tara points to the poster, which I've decided isn't me.

"He looks fake." I turn my back on Hollywood's version of me, surveying the glitter wallpaper walls, neon pink and purple bed sheets, and tattered movie posters covering the walls. "When was this room last redecorated? 2010?"

Tara spins and flicks a light switch, adding an actual disco-ball to the mix. "How do you think she managed to sleep in here?"

"Sonia?" I glance to her. "This was your room?"

Sonia turns away, her face taking on the slightest tinge of red. "I was younger. We can talk in your room."

Tara crosses the room to a mound of micro-VHS cassettes perched precariously on a bookshelf. "You think any of your old home movies are here? We could show Will the first movie you ever made. It stars a little sister who gets attacked by a monster. The monster's a furry pillow case, but I look good on film."

Sonia's mouth falls open and she shakes her head vigorously. "We don't have anything to play them on. They're old analog tapes."

"Mom and Dad kept the camera somewhere, we can hook it up to the TV," Tara says, rummaging through a drawer. "Seriously, Will. You've got to see some of these. And her fashion shoot one. The soundtrack's played on a cassette player, and the spotlights are flashlights my brothers held. I bet Mom still has that swimsuit in the attic. Sonia doesn't need to stuff socks in the top now, though. And I *know* we have your college projects somewhere. Mom's always bragging about them."

Sonia isn't saying a word. She's standing there, alternating between looking like she's going to strangle her sister—or shove me out the door. Which brings me to my exit plan. "Hey, I need to talk to you about something. Something serious. Outside."

"Close the van door this time," says Tara. "See, this is the power cord for the camera," she adds, dangling a three-foot-long black cord in the air. "It's got to be here somewhere."

Sonia follows me outside, out the front door, and into the snow. "What do you need to talk about?"

"Nothing, I was just thinking how nice it might be to get out of that house."

"Me too." Sonia reaches into her coat and jingles something, then nods. "Come on."

We walk down the hill from her house to a mound of snow—and Sonia starts digging. Soon enough, she's uncovered a car. "My rental," she says as she opens the passenger door and climbs through to sit in the driver's seat. "Come on. I'll show you the town."

Getting out of the snow is an experience all of its own, but she drives like she's done this her whole life, and soon enough, we leave country Vermont behind, trading it for small-town Vermont, which is like country Vermont, but with more beer-barns.

"That back there was pure, undiluted embarrassment," says Sonia, as we crunch along the road.

"I don't know. It was kind of cute. Except the part where your Dad thinks I took you home to meet my family at Thanksgiving for something more serious than tamales. Also, he thinks you're just going to fight with your step-mom." I adjust the heater to something that won't leave me with memories of the lake scene.

"That's Dad, all right. You know, he paid my rent the first five years I was in LA? Sent me money for the car when the transmission went out. Flew in overnight when I had my appendix out. May's not evil by any stretch, but she never forgets the mistakes I've made, and she never lets me forget, either." Sonia keeps her focus on the road, but she's not hiding the hurt. "Welcome to the family, Will. Soon enough, May will give you her 'Watch out for Sonia, the girl can be flighty' speech."

We ride in silence. She's not pointing out the sights because there's not much to see. We rode through a town that wasn't much more than one main street and a couple of almost-alleys, and from there, it's all gentle, rolling hills and fields. "Family is hard. Tara obviously idolizes you."

That gets her attention. She gives me the side-eye glance. "Right."

"Seriously. She has posters from all your movies. She knows what you've been up to, and you told me you don't talk much. Your brothers are half-convinced they're related to movie royalty. Your Dad obviously adores you."

"This?" Sonia waves her hand. "This was Kantina's idea, too. Embarrass me. Get us talking about our pasts. Tonight's going to be even more awkward, and tomorrow, breakfast with the cousins is going to be worse."

The idea strikes me out of the blue. "This is a rental car."

"Yes?"

"Do you have to return it to the place you rented it from?"

Sonia pauses. "No, but... Will, I can't," she says, catching my drift.

"Go back and get your suitcase, say goodbye. You've already seen your family, and spent time with your dad. He told me he's going to at least see the oncologist once. You had Christmas morning and Christmas dinner with them. There's nothing stopping us from leaving *now*."

"What about your stuff?"

I shrug. "Kantina said packing would ruin the adventure. I don't even have a change of clothes."

Sonia only takes a moment before she relaxes back into the seat. "Screw it. We're going to the airport. Tara can ship my suitcase back."

She's so close. "I have a better idea. You said you wanted to feel like you're in control of your own life, right?"

Sonia looks my way, a hopeful smile at home on her face. "What do you have in mind?"

I smile, hoping beyond hope that I've read the situation right. "Get us to the interstate, and I'll reveal everything."

CHAPTER TWENTY-SEVEN

We've been on the road for three hours, driving from Vermont to Los Angeles. In theory, it's a forty-four hour drive. But we don't need to be back immediately, so to say it's the scenic route would be a lie, in that it implies we have a route beyond 'south' and 'west.'

"If you're so smart," says Sonia, as she relaxes in the passenger seat, "you come up with an idea for a movie."

"Romance?" I think a moment. "Southern Baptist Texan moves to New York City and takes over a sex-toy shop. Falls in love with the Girl Next Door."

"Never do romance again. How about Horror?"

"Way ahead of you." I wasn't, but now I'm going with the first idea I can come up with. "Vampire snakes. Vampicondas. They were buried under an ancient Incan convenience store since the nineteen fifties, when an atomic bomb woke them from their slumber. Now, they're out to suck your blood and devour you whole."

"Why? Why suck your blood if they're going to devour you?"

"Why eat the filling from an Oreo first?" I ask. "They're vampire snakes. They don't give explanations."

"Not even remotely scary," Sonia says, laying her seat back. "Come on, you can do better."

"New idea: Single woman. Five foot six inches, green eyes. Red hair down past her butt. She's alone in the house, late at night. She's standing in the bathroom, staring into the mirror, when she feels an itch. She scratches—and another itch. And another. And another. She looks in the mirror and finds… lice."

"Oh my God!" Sonia shouts, sitting up. She scratches her head. "That's not funny at all. That's terrible."

"You might say *horrifying*." I grin.

She scratches more instead of responding.

Six loops through my phone's playlist and one gas station stop later, Sonia finally speaks, careful to avoid looking my way. "What are we going to do when we need to sleep?"

"No idea. I left my wallet in Los Angeles."

"Not that. Trust me, I can afford a hotel." She darts a glance at me. "Separate beds? Separate rooms?"

That gives me more than enough to think on. "It's hardly fair to expect a morally upright woman like you to have to resist my smoking body and sizzling-hot looks. Separate beds are a must. Rooms—I've been told I snore."

"I'm the green-eyed, red-haired temptress, remember?" She cocks her head at me and bats her eyelashes. "If anyone's morals were to be corrupted, it would be yours."

"That's assuming I had any morals to begin with. If I

didn't, I would lie about it and call myself morally upright."

"Same," she says. She shakes her head. "It's not that I don't trust you, Will. It's me I don't trust."

"Same." I hope I've hidden my disappointment. "When are you going to call your parents and tell them you won't be home?"

"When I've figured out an excuse. Also never. Or tomorrow."

That makes me want so much to have a way out, but the only one I do is a subject I'd rather not bring up. "What if I had a way to explain it?"

She doesn't answer, but she's listening.

"Hand me my phone." I can't take my eyes off the road, but I can unlock it and hand it back. "Go to messages. Bradley. Zoom in on the picture. That came in the mail two days ago, and Ms. Chan mailed it to him in New Mexico."

Sonia reads it and remains silent. "Your girlfriend—"

"She's not." My stomach churns at the thought, now.

"Ex-girlfriend. She took a plea bargain?"

"Looks like it. She'll do time, but the difference is, it won't be for decades. Check the last paragraph."

"Oh." Sonia pauses. "Do you *have* to go to Seattle to testify?"

"There are two answers to that. One gives you an excuse for why we needed to leave immediately. The other doesn't."

"Will, did you read this?" she says, looking at me over the edge of my phone.

"Enough."

"So you didn't read it all. Pull over."

When we're sitting by the edge of the road, I reach for the phone, but she clasps it to her chest, and any attempt to recover it would be awkward, to say the least. "What is it?"

"You *didn't* read it all, or we would have been having a minor celebration. Recovery of assets, Will." She tilts the screen toward me. "It means she didn't spend all the money. In fact, if she was really living in a motel on the highway, she barely spent anything." Sonia reaches out to lift my chin so I look her in the eye. "You don't owe anyone anything. They'll get their money back now. You're a free man, Will Mathis."

I've carried the guilt over what Tamara did for so long I don't know how to feel now that it's no longer mine.

"You know what this means, right?" Sonia says softly.

I wipe my eyes, which are not filled with tears, no matter what anyone says, and nod to myself. "When we get back, and I retrieve my wallet from Kantina, *I'm* buying lunch."

There's a moment, a quiet moment where it's only the passing cars rocking our car in their wakes, and it feels like we've always been this way. Like we always will be—and then reality hits me. "I'm free, but you aren't."

"What if I could be?" Sonia says it softly, almost under her breath. "What if we just didn't go back? Not forever, just… long enough that they had to finish without us? Long enough for Belion to move on to torturing someone else?"

"No." I take her hand and wrap it in mine. "You have a brilliant future, a great career, and a talent you *have* to share with the world. As much as I'd love to pull in at the next motel and just party for a month, we can't."

Sonia stares out her window as we pass yet another shuttered hotel, dark and empty. "It was just an idea."

"Bradley bet his business on this movie, and he and Tia have a baby on the way. If I didn't come back, who knows if Eddie Gellar would be pissed off enough to take it out on my brother? We started something together, Sonia. We're going to finish it together. And I believe we'll still be together a week from now. A month from now." I put the car in gear.

"Will, I've seen the shot lists Felicia sent out. We only have one more major scene to shoot. You know what Belion said. If he finds out I'm seeing you afterwards...." She drops her gaze to the floorboard, unwilling to finish the sentence.

It's good that I haven't pulled out yet. "Honestly, how likely is it that Belion is really going to care what you do after we're done filming? It's just an empty threat, right?"

The car shakes as trucks blow past, and the French fries we bought hours ago make my stomach sick, because it's taking far too long for a simple yes or no.

"I never mattered to him before. But now, given everything that's happened—I don't know."

She knows. When someone says they don't know that way, what they mean is they don't want to answer.

"So...that's it? He wins? He gets to say what you do or don't do with your life?"

"Not if I'm willing to give up everything I've worked for." Sonia stares out the window, eyes expressionless. "This isn't fair."

I'd rather crush my heart than kill her dreams. "It's not about us. We're going to do what we have to. For Bradley's business. For Kantina's contract. And we have to trust that somehow, we'll find a way for us, too."

"Once Belion no longer has Kantina to work with, no one will listen to him, right?"

I think she's trying to convince herself, not me. "I don't listen to him now."

"Some days I don't know if I want to kiss you or smack you," she mutters.

I grin. "You might want to get used to that."

THE DRIVE HOME ISN'T AS MANIC AS I FEAR. IT'S NOT desperation keeping me at the wheel, but determination. Determination that I'll see this movie finished. That I'll tell Eddie Gellar where he can go and what he can do when he gets there.

Belief plays its part as well. I believe Kantina deserves to be free of her ridiculous contract. I believe Sonia deserves the chance to do whatever she wants.

I choose to believe that includes doing something with me.

The next day, we finish our drive back. Kantina's waiting at the rental drop-off for us. She stands beside a black town-car, wearing a red tube-top and torn skinny jeans that only serve to make her look thinner. "Sonia, darling. William."

Sonia gives her a hug—and then takes two steps back, pointing at Kantina. "Never again. Promise me, never, ever again. You can't fix *yourself*, so what makes you think you can fix me?"

Kantina looks Sonia in the eye and nods. "I give you my promise I will not interfere in your relationships again. I only want to see you happy."

Sonia shakes her head. "I know. But this is something I have to figure out on my own. When I need something from you, I promise, I'll ask."

"There is nothing I would not do for you, darling. Are you tired?"

"Yes. No. I'm worried about shooting tomorrow." She doesn't mention that tomorrow is the last day of filming. That tomorrow we'll be done. That after that, being seen together will be enough to trigger Belion's blackmail.

Kantina waves to the town-car. "I wish to apologize to William privately. Do you mind?"

"As long as the apology doesn't involve lips," Sonia says, raising her eyebrows.

"Darling, when have I—" Kantina stops. "Ah, yes. I promise, words alone."

After Sonia closes the door, Kantina pivots to stare at me, but either I'm becoming immune to her charms, or Sonia just makes Kantina look like a shadow. "I am sorry, William. It is good that you went there."

"It was an adventure," I answer, shrugging. "I won't wait so long to take the next one. Now, I need something from you. I can't do anything about whether or not this movie is a blockbuster. But I know a way to get Sonia out from under Belion's blackmail. I think it's the only way."

This makes her beam at me. "What do you know that I do not?

"I know Belion's a terrible man. It doesn't matter what he says, he's never going to stop using this against Sonia. If it's not me, it'll be to get you to act in one of his movies. The only way out is for Sonia to go to Edward and tell him herself. Show him the video. Explain. Take Belion's power."

"But—"

"Sonia has a gift, you have said so yourself. Eddie's promise was that she wouldn't act again, but acting isn't what she wants to do with her life. It's just what she's doing now."

Kantina thinks for a moment, then nods. "You should tell her this."

"The problem is, there's no way she'll risk everything for a chance."

"Not for me. But if you ask her?" Kantina says, leaning in. "Tell her what you feel, not in quiet words, but before the world. William, let her know she will not be alone, come what may. Then she will have the courage she needs to take action."

I frown. "This doesn't feel right. I think Sonia needs to do this her way. Let it be her decision."

"No bird ever left the nest on its own, William, but the choice is yours. If you are willing to risk your chance with her, then do nothing. Wait. Hope. But if you desire a life with my best friend, you will consider what I tell you."

I'd risk anything at this point, so I nod with a certainty I'm not sure I feel. "Tomorrow, then. I'm going to lay it all out."

"Of course," Kantina agrees. "It is your only chance. Now, I may not interfere, but I can offer motivation, so listen." She puts on a stern expression, and I'm not sure if she's acting, or if it's real. Either way, it doesn't affect me like it once might have. "If you fail to win Sonia over, I will never speak to you again, ever."

She may be losing her shine, but Kantina still believes the world revolves—at least in part—around her. "Go home," I say. "Get some sleep. If I fail, I doubt I'll have anything left to say to you anyway."

Failure. Even considering it leaves me shaken, jaw aching from clenching my teeth. I can't fail. I won't. I've always been a quiet man, but it's time to shout. I've avoided the spotlight, but tomorrow, I'll step into it gladly for something I didn't know I wanted—and now, I don't know how to live without.

CHAPTER TWENTY-EIGHT

On the final day of filming, I finally give up any hope of sleep at four in the morning. Belion told Sonia she wouldn't be seeing me after this movie ended, or he'd end her career.

I spent half the night thinking about what I need to say and the other half how. I'd bet more than my life I know what it is—I'd bet my heart.

When I reach the soundstage, though, I'm struck by the number of additional vehicles lined up outside, including an actual limo.

Felicia nods to me as I pass her in the morning darkness. "There he is, Mr. Gellar."

"Will!"

I stop and turn. There, in the shadows, sits Eddie Gellar, looking no better, but at least no worse.

He takes a deep breath of his oxygen before offering me a hand. "Came out to see the last day of filming myself, Will. You made it. And I have a surprise for you."

"Sir, this job has been more than enough—"

"Don't flatter me." Eddie's look says I could easily be in trouble with him if I don't shut up. "I had you by the short-and-curlies, but you did good. I'll make sure Mathis construction gets more work than they can handle. And you." He turns his gaze to Felicia. "You pulled it off. I was betting against you, I'll have you know, but you did it."

"Well, we're close," she says. "Close doesn't get movies done, sir. I'm going to check and make sure we have everything ready. Will, get to makeup."

"Not yet," Eddie says. "You can wait on him just a bit." He turns to me. "Walk with me, Will, figuratively speaking. I need to talk with you."

The subtle glance from Felicia tells me I shouldn't argue, even if I wanted to. So we stroll and roll down the side of the soundstage and around the corner until we reach the spot where he and I used to eat lunch. "How can I help?"

Eddie raises one eyebrow and looks at me over his glasses. "That's my line. I make a point of rewarding people who do well. There's such a thing as good consequences, and what I've learned in life is that you never, ever let the opportunity to help people go by."

"What I want isn't yours to give."

"I doubt that. I could get you a job. Let you skip making coffee and head right into making movies. Or make sure you get a role that shows more than your shoulder. Those marketing photos were genius." He pauses, watching me. When he speaks, his gruff tone is softer. "It's about the woman, isn't it?"

"Sonia."

"You need a romantic night on the town? Getaway? Someone to feed you romantic lines via ear-piece? That's common enough."

After considering his suggestions, I have to dismiss them all. "I just need to tell her how I feel about her, and I have to do it now." I can't say more about Belion without endangering Sonia.

Eddie thinks in silence. "I felt the same way about my fifth wife, you know. She was another soulmate, and I would have done anything, anywhere to prove I'd love her forever."

"I didn't know you were married."

"She divorced me ten years ago," Eddie says. "Sixteen months wasn't the forever I had in mind, but it was worth it. The point is, I've been you. And all I can say is, do what you have to. Take the shot, kid."

"Thanks."

"Can you tolerate the tiniest bit of gossip?" Eddie asks, looking up at me with innocence in his eyes.

"Go for it."

"I don't interfere in productions unless it's life and death—and by that, I mean, going to cost me my reputation. But I hear Belion has exactly two hours booked in the soundstage, and an appointment at an all-day spa at eleven." Eddie nods to me like I know exactly what that means.

I have zero clue. "We only have one scene."

"I don't know what that munchkin has planned, but I'd bet you only have one take. Given what I've been hearing about him, I think Belion is preparing to say goodbye to his career. If you have to do it here, say what you have to say the first chance you get, and make it count." He offers me a hand to shake—and I return it.

Rumors. Get enough PAs seeing Belion passed out or with a hangover… and I bet there were a ton of them. "I have to get to makeup, and wardrobe, and—"

"Go. I'll be watching."

I go. At the door to the soundstage, a production assistant hands out sheets of paper.

"Today we will film the heart of the movie," it reads. "Only the words of creation may be spoken within the soundstage."

Only the lines of dialogue Belion has somehow regurgitated.

"Second crew!" Felicia shouts from deep within the set. "Let's make it count."

I intend to.

The set which once held a fake tree is clear now. The cameras are on metal railings that hold them far above us.

Aaron is pacing off the set as I arrive. "Ok, primary rule of today is you do *not* look up."

The scene will be shot overhead, with the viewer seeing only the tops of the heads, and the space between the Lord and Lady as he gives his speech—and they come together at last.

Sonia's waiting, dressed in white with plastic beads and a train—and the look on her face is sheer panic. She's sweating, and it's ruining her makeup. She sees me, and at once, she smiles—and looks like she's about to throw up.

"No words which detract from the heart of the movie!" Belion shouts. It's not clear if he's talking to Kantina, who's standing at the side of the set with James, or Sonia, or me, or… everyone.

The set is packed with people. Even Eddie Gellar has a spot just out of view of the cameras, and his own detail of hulking security guards.

Felicia points to my spot. "Nine, you ready?"

"I am." I step up and wait for Sonia to follow my lead. We're only two feet away, but it could be a thousand miles based on how she's standing. *"Breathe,"* I whisper.

"Cameras, ready," says Belion. "We will do a live running test. William, look at your audience. You have never performed before with so many people listening to your every word."

Maybe he means to upset me. To make my tongue refuse to work. But today, I'm performing for an audience of exactly one. Everyone else might as well not exist.

"Belion," Felicia says. "Could we cut the games and just do a light test?"

"This is my set." The way he speaks, it's a threat. Maybe a promise. "You are not the director, Felicia. You are, at best, my assistant. I will run it as I see fit."

Felicia looks to Eddie Gellar, and when he remains silent, throws her hands up in the air. "You heard him, people. Cameras roll for the light test. Whatever. Nine, Sonia, first positions."

Sonia reaches her hands out and clasps mine. Her hands are damp and cold, and she clings to me like she's about to drown.

"Lights?" Felicia says.

Aaron answers. "Ready. Cameras are ready."

"Action!"

The weight of a thousand different things to say comes and goes. What I want to say is, "I love you. I trust you. I'll be ready when you call." But that's the coward's way out, isn't it? It's hardly a grand gesture, something that says what she means to me, or how I feel.

"Action, Nine. You can go," Felicia says, gently.

I know what the script says, I've learned my lines. But I also know what it feels like to be a man desperate to win the heart of a woman, and when the words finally gush out, they come from deep inside. "Listen to me, Sonia. Love isn't bubble bath fights, or horseback rides, or haughty dinners where no word has less than four syllables. It's bone-weary mornings and long afternoons. It's prop-room practicing, penguin jokes in the freezing water. It's lazy holiday mornings in the sun, when you could be anywhere, but all you want to be is with that someone. It's Thanksgiving tamales and awkward Christmas dinners, and convertible rides where you don't care where you're going, you only care about where you are and who you're with."

Sonia stands stock still, her eyes so wide I can see the edges of her irises, her mouth softly open.

"Felicia said you were looking for a career, and I believe that. You have talent, so much more to offer the world than red hair and the ability to stand in one place for hours. Kantina says you are looking for adventure, but adventure doesn't have to mean being stranded with no money in the middle of nowhere." I tighten my grip on her hands, and her gaze at last focuses on me as she takes two steps closer.

Now we're so close I can feel her breath as Sonia gazes up at me. "Love is an adventure. One you don't ask to go on, or plan, or even know it's coming. It's a trip you only realize you're taking halfway down the road. I didn't want any of it. Travel. Adventure. Love. But now, I'm ready to take that adventure, if you're with me. Travel that road, if you're on it too. Sonia Bracewell, I love you, and if you say you love me too, we'll make it work, because if you love me… then nothing else matters."

"And that's a wrap," Belion shouts. "We are done, ladies and gentlemen."

"What?" I can't see Felicia's face, but I can hear the shock in her voice. "We don't even have Kantina or James—"

"It does not matter. From above, no one can tell the difference. We will dub James speaking over the music. The shot is done, the movie made."

"Sonia," I whisper. "Talk to me. Say something."

"Not one word which is not the language of creation!" Belion approaches, but he's not talking to me, with his voice so quiet it doesn't carry. "Edward is here, Sonia. If you speak, I speak. Tell me, are you ready to have this discussion?"

"Sonia." I can't read what's going on inside her, but I know the way I know the sun comes up that I love her, and I believe she loves me too. "You want to be a director, not an actress. That's your dream. That's your passion."

Belion laughs, and I can barely resist the urge to punch him. "What could a carpenter know of passion? Principal filming is over, William. That means we are done. That means you are *fired*." He turns to the crowd. "Get him off my set. Throw him off the lot. Keep the costume, William."

Now I know why security is standing by. It wasn't for Eddie Gellar. It was to get rid of me. "Please, just give her time to answer. Sonia, I can be patient. I can wait, if I know I'm waiting for you."

Belion steps forward as a guard takes my arm. "And destroy her life's dream? For a man who believes himself smart, you do not seem to realize. If your dearest Sonia were going to reply, she already would have."

I don't know if we're on the same planet. She hasn't spoken. Hasn't moved. She's frozen, staring blindly past me. I would fight the guards, but my strength drains away, and the rumble of arguments behind me becomes a distant buzz as I flounder.

Belion was right.

I failed.

I go quietly as guards march me out. Outside the soundstage, Eddie Gellar and Felicia are engaging in a one-sided shouting match, her shouting about how Belion can't do things like this, Eddie nodding as if they're just discussing the weather.

"Boys!" says Eddie, rolling over to block our path. "What's going on?"

The guard on my left answers. "Director's orders. He's fired, and to be removed from the set. You want us to do something different?"

Eddie pauses, eyes closed, his face scrunched up. "You still have my number, Will?"

Shock is the only thing keeping me functioning, so I nod.

"Call me, if you need a favor, or just want to grab breakfast. For what it's worth, kid, you swung for the fence in there."

I try to tell him thank you, but the grief inside me is drowning everything, so I nod.

Eddie looks to one of the guards. "Let him get his things and walk out on his own. And get me Belion Androse in a private room. Now."

Felicia's next to approach me, clutching her tablet and biting her lip so hard I think it will bleed. "Will, I'm sorry."

"She never answered me." That's what I regret most. 'No' would hurt, but not so bad as not knowing. And now, I'll never see Sonia again.

I walk away from Felicia without another word, because what else do I have to say?

There's a cab waiting when I reach the front gate, I'm guessing thanks to her.

I get home, and Bradley and Tia are both still at work, so I sit in the empty apartment and listen to the silence.

I can't tell you when I decide, or how, but once my feet start moving, everything makes more sense. I leave a note—and my phone—on the bar.

Bradly and Tia—

Thanks so much for letting me stay with you. For giving me a home when I didn't have one. For helping me find my way. I did it. I went for everything. I lost. Don't worry, I'm not going to find a bridge and jump, but right now, I need to get away. I need an adventure.

I'll call you when I land on my feet. I know you'll be great parents.

Love, Will.

I leave LA on the wings of a plane, on the first flight to anywhere but here.

I doubt I'll ever be back.

ADVENTURE ISN'T EVERYTHING IT'S CRACKED UP TO BE. Kantina didn't mention that, but it's true. It's cold and wet, and hot and humid. Mosquitoes in Alabama suck the grief out of me, and I've now seen the Grand Canyon and ridden a burro down part of it.

But it helps me find the distance I need. The space to grieve. The time to heal. And eventually, I find my way back to Seattle.

I find work as a carpenter, building houses.

I set up a table at the local summer fair and sell driftwood I carve into whimsical shapes.

But I don't forget what happened, and on Friday nights at the bar, none of the women make me smile. I even have a few recognize me, from videos or that awful promotional poster. None catch my eye, though sometimes they make me laugh. It isn't until September, when Bradley flies in for a conference, that I realize how the months have gone.

"Bro!" he shouts across the terminal at SeaTac airport. "Brown hair, lost the beard. Almost didn't recognize you."

"I had black hair for three months. I've had brown hair for two decades, and you don't recognize me?" I shake my head. "How's Tia?"

"Huge, miserable, and planning on spending the next few weeks with her mother. She's got a month to go and I swear she's carrying an entire baseball team. She says she wishes she could go to the premier."

His words hit me like a club. *Lady of the Manner's* premier, which I'd done my best to forget about. "I'm sorry. None of us will be attending."

We walk in silence to my car, a second hand hatch-back with mismatched fenders and no back seat. Once we hit the highway, Bradley can't contain himself, fidgeting the way he used to any time he was in trouble. "There's this thing, Will. I kept meaning to tell you, and I—I didn't want you to think I was making it up."

"What? Whatever it is, spit out. I'm offering pre-forgiveness."

"She showed up at our apartment three days ago." Bradley reaches into his pocket and pulls out an envelope.

"Sonia?" I hate the note of hope in my voice.

"*Kantina.* For real." The excitement in Bradley's voice is impossible for him to mask. "Tia talked with her for like thirty minutes, mostly about her pregnancy."

"Tia? What were you doing?"

"I—I couldn't think of anything to say. But she brought me this, and said I was supposed to make sure you read it. Also, she said she never breaks her promises—but she wants to talk to you."

I take envelope and tuck it away for when I'm not driving. "Did she sign you an autograph?"

"No." Bradley reaches over to try and retrieve it. "You're not going read it?"

I try to ignore the way my pulse is skipping over thoughts of what it might contain. "Later, when I'm not doing sixty miles per hour."

"*Now.* I'll read it for you. Please. It's killing me. Tia and I have been betting on what it says ever since."

But it's only after we reach my studio apartment that I draw out the envelope with trembling hands.

No one will ever accuse Kantina of having good penmanship, but that's probably my name on it. When I unseal the envelope, what slides out into my hand is a set of plastic cards—and a pair of tickets.

The handwritten note is to the point.

William—

I keep my promises. You stayed through filming. Your brother and you will be my guests at the premier. Also, you have something of great value to me. Please return with it.

K.

I read it and nod to myself. "You and Tia can go in my place. And as for what she's wanting, I know exactly what that is."

Hanging by the door, on the hook where I keep the keys, is Kantina's jade frog. I didn't realize I left with it, and keep it now as a reminder of the most painful—and happy—time in my life.

"Even if she were in town, Tia isn't going to the red carpet looking like she is. I'll ask, but I can't get her to go to the grocery store, let alone anywhere with cameras. What do you think? Tuesday's not far off."

I hold out the keys. "I have an idea."

"No." Bradley stands up and dusts himself off. "You want to know how many *weeks* it took for your phone to stop ringing while you went on some sad-ass voyage of self-pity? Tia read the messages at first, until I made her stop because it was too depressing. What's wrong with you?"

"What do you *mean*, what's wrong with me? Did you not read the note? Do you not get it? I threw myself out there. I made my best shot at convincing Sonia I was worth the risk. That my love was worth it. I was hauled off the lot by security, and she never even answered my question." My chest hurts as I reach back into memories, and every muscle in me tenses as I go through the hope and the devastation of that day once more. The anger, the hurt, they're still raw in ways I didn't expect. "And I don't want to fight. I want to remember the good."

Bradley doesn't look like he's done, but my brother must know when not to push me. He turns on the TV and flips the remote. "We need to do something."

"There's beer in the fridge. Let's throw a few back."

"Not that. You made a promise too."

"I did?" Then, as I watch him select movie rentals, I finally understand. "I promised Kantina one day I'd watch her movies. Let me make popcorn, and we'll do it."

"No butter on mine."

"You're a monster." But he's my brother, too. And as we sit down to watch, I can't help wondering if Sonia is doing the same. Her movie is probably in French or German or Ugandan, and it probably doesn't have any flamingos in it.

And I wish, even as I hate myself for it, that I was sitting with her now.

The Bride Becomes Her is a masterpiece. That's the only word I can use for the two and a half hours of a story that's told more by the way the Bride reacts to everything than by what's said. And the imagery is a story of its own, stark and visceral, grounded in a way that leaves me watching every shadow and every ray of light.

Belion Androse is a self-serving bastard who deserves to walk down the stairs in socks filled with legos, but he's also an incredible director, if you ignore the dialogue. While I'd heard so much about how the movie featured

Kantina naked, it's hardly the scandalous soft-porn I'd expected, and even then, the shadow of her curves is the focus of the shot, rather than the bare flesh.

And after it's done, I watch every name, every line, every thanks, and nod to myself as Sonia's name scrolls by.

"What did you think?" Bradley says.

"How many times do you think they filmed the well scene? The camera's rotating, and moving upward. The equipment must have been moving too, and yet, you don't even see—"

"The movie." Bradley says. "You've finally seen one of Kantina's greatest works. What do you think?"

"I think it wasn't her in more shots than I imagined."

He looks over his glasses at me. "What?"

"Give me the remote." Scene by scene, shot by shot, I back it up. "That's not Kantina here. Not there in the stable, either. That's Sonia at the dinner table, when you see her silhouette, and those are her hands exchanging wedding rings."

"How can you tell?" asks Bradley. "It's like, two seconds at most."

He can't understand. How I spend the empty minutes, late hours, early mornings remembering every word. Every moment, look, touch, or laugh. The answer comes from my soul. "I'd know her anywhere."

CHAPTER TWENTY-NINE

MY RETURN TO LOS ANGELES IS WITHOUT FANFARE—OR anyone waiting besides Tia. She is so very, very pregnant, but not so much she can't drag me down to hug me. "Will," she says. "We've missed you. Tell me you're coming back to LA."

"With a baby so close?" I look her up and down. "There'll hardly be room for the three of you. And don't worry, I didn't go all mopey and sad. I traveled. I cried. I drank a lot of tequila, and in the end, I picked myself up and went back to work."

She gives me that same appraising look she's always had. "Tell me one thing, Will. Why did you run?"

"I didn't run. I gave Sonia the distance we both needed. I made it easier on us. I told Bradley you could have my ticket. You two can go—"

"Like this?" she says, waving her hand in front of her belly. "I want to be able to enjoy the movie. Right now, I can't sit through a commercial without needing to use the toilet twice. Besides, Bradley told me you have something to do.”

“Something to return.” And, I think, something to say, at last. “I do have an idea, though. No red carpet for you, but how about a hotel? Room service? Rest, and relaxation?” I pull out the cardkeys. “I checked online. They’re from the Mondria. One night there is more than I make in two weeks. There’s an in-room spa. You could get a massage without setting foot outside.”

Tia looks at the keys like I’m handing her gold. Nothing makes me happier than seeing someone else smile these days, and when she looks to Bradley with a grin, I know I’ve got her. “If you’re not going to…”

I shake my head. “Someone should enjoy it. Why not you? I’m going to relax. Bradley, we can meet at the premier, say, around five?”

Bradley pauses, thinking. “Earlier. This premier’s all kinds of messed up. Normally, people just go in and watch the movie. This time, there’s a party in the lobby. Media junket, interviews. I’ve never heard of this happening, ever. I think they’re trying to start the awards circuit.”

“Earlier it is. Four?”

He pulls at his beard in thought, then nods. “Zeke’s Pizza is just far enough down the street to not be mobbed. See you there.”

“You two better pack in a hurry. Every minute you’re here, you’re not there.” I sit on the couch, my long-time bed, and watch them scurry as fast as a heavily pregnant woman can.

When they finally are packed, Tia begins her waddle to the car while Bradley checks the phone and hands me the key. “Bro, can I ask you something, something real?”

"Always."

"You're not going to get pissed off at me?"

"Normally, when you ask that, you already know what you're going to ask will piss me off. But I want you two to go enjoy this." I point to the door. "So ask, and then go."

"Are you doing this because you want us to go, or because you don't want anyone to know you're in town?"

His question makes me want to punch him, and I just promised I wouldn't. "Why would I do that? I was trying to do something nice for you and Tia. You two were a godsend to me."

"Okay, okay. Sorry, Will. It's just that… I think you're afraid to see Sonia again. I think that's why you left your phone, and that's why you ran away, and that's why you want us to go spend a night at a hotel you will *never* be able to afford." Bradley puts one arm around me. "You're afraid she'll show up at the door. Or in the lobby. Or somewhere."

"That's the stupidest suggestion I've heard in a while. What would I possibly have to be afraid of? Memories? You think I don't remember every day?"

Bradley picks up the suitcases and shrugs. "Because if you're still in love with her, you might forgive her. Are you, Will?"

"I don't know," I say, sharper than I intend.

Bradley nods. "You should figure that out. Your old phone's in the silverware drawer. Chargers are on the counter. See you tomorrow."

And Bradley walks out, leaving me with a host of fears where before, I'd had none.

What if he's wrong, and I see her at the premier, and she's happy? Smiling? Vibrant?

And what if he's right?

THE MORNING OF THE PREMIER FINDS ME AWAKE BEFORE dawn, something I haven't done in ages. The town creeps into you, or so I'm told.

The entertainment sites say Kantina will be filming again next month. She's got three new films lined up and just finished filming one.

By ten o'clock, I'm pacing the apartment—and finally take my old phone out of the drawer. The screen's still cracked like a spiderweb. The power button still doesn't work when I trigger it the first time, but after a few minutes on the charger, it glows.

The number of notifications makes me shudder.

The number of text messages even more so.

The last few still show on the screen.

My heart skips as I see Sonia's name.

Will, I know you're in town. The hotel called us when you checked in.

Will, call me. Even if it's just for a minute, I need to talk to you. I know you hate me.

Tell me you'll be at the premier, Will. I'll look for you.

My answer takes so much longer to write than it should, because it comes from deeper inside of me than I usually look. *I know you want to talk. I'm not sure I have anything to say. Even now, part of me even wishes we could go back to the way we were, but I'm not the man that walked off the studio lot that day.*

I don't hate you. I never did.

I'm not bitter, or angry, even though I am sad. But I don't think you and I will work. I've changed, grown, learned. I don't know if you have. I don't know if I'd believe you if you said you did, or what it would take to convince me.

I'm sorry.

After clicking send, I turn it off and drop it back in the drawer, probably forever.

AT FOUR O'CLOCK, I'M WAITING IN A BLACK SILK SUIT AT the front of Zeke's Pizza to meet Bradley. He sees me down the street and whistles. "Wow, when did you get that?"

I smooth the lapels of the suit coat. "It's a rental, and I have to be careful, or I won't get my deposit back. Did I really need a suit to sit in a theatre and a watch a movie?"

Bradley whacks me on the back. "You could have *asked*. I told you, there's normally a party somewhere else afterwards, but this one's all kinds of messed up. The director—"

"Belion?"

"Him—insisted on a meet-and-greet." He shakes his head. "It's weird. It's not how this business works, Will."

Memories that used to make me angry or frustrated now make me laugh. "Not even remotely the oddest thing Belion Androse ever did. Someday, I'll tell you all about him, every last detail. On a scale of one-to-Belion, this is downright normal."

Our tickets let us in through the front, but Bradley wants to see the stars arrive. He wants to see what madness Kantina will have cooked up for the red carpet.

Personally, I'm hoping it's the faceless mop look and the dress made of live ants.

"Bradley, listen to me. You are going to help me, do you understand?"

He isn't paying attention. We didn't arrive early enough to get a good place, so we're pushed to the middle of the line—but at least we're right by the rope.

"I came here to return something," I continue anyway. "I don't want to see the movie, because I lived it. So while everyone is doing their meet-and-greet, I'm going to do what I came to, and leave you to figure out which shots have my left shoulder, or my ear, or my hair in it."

Bradley rolls his eyes, but doesn't comment.

"At any party, Sonia and Kantina will be on opposite ends of the room. At least, I hope they will be. That way there's no one taking pictures of Sonia. She's going to be easy to spot—she'll be the only one in neon green."

"You want me to go get her for you—"

"No!" I attempt to silence him with a glare. "You will keep an eye on her. If she starts to come over, tell me."

"Why?"

I give him the honest answer, the one he deserves. "I survived losing her once. I don't know how I'd do it again."

The first people to arrive aren't even people I remember from filming, but given how the press takes pictures of them, I guess they must be at least mildly famous.

Belion Androse arrives in a flurry of photos and flashes. His leather gloves are grey that matches the dye-job on his hair, and he still looks like he should be playing an organ while a monkey holds a tin cup.

If he recognizes me in the crowd, if he even knows I'm there, he shows no sign.

Felicia Slate and her husband come in next with almost no fanfare. I point her out as a hundred and ninety pounds of ambition, and give her a sharp salute to make sure she sees me.

She stops for a brief moment, her mouth open wide, and then smiles back before heading inside.

James Becton, taking a break from what must be the fifth installment of *The Man With A Million Tomorrows*, greets almost everyone in the crowd—except me.

I know he saw me. I wonder if we were both thinking of throwing a punch.

Then a sleek, black limo pulls up and stops. A hush sweeps across the crowd, and I stand, hands folded, watching and waiting. The crowd's pushed in so close they could open the door if someone was having problems, which I'm supposing they are, because no one gets out.

Photographers keep shooting picture after picture of the car door; it's got to be the most interesting limo door in America at this point.

"Something's wrong," says Bradley. "You think the door won't open?"

The barrage of pictures slows to a trickle—and then the door opens. First to emerge is America's favorite security guard. I don't know who he is, but he's almost as popular as the limo door, if we go by camera flashes.

Kantina emerges, followed by another guard—and I understand.

I can't help and wouldn't bother stifling the gut laughter at how her red hair is pinned forward, making her faceless. But instead of live ants, she's wearing jewels, and not much else. I don't mean a diamond bracelet; it's more like a bikini made of precious stones and gold. There's more jewelry wrapped around her than in all the safety deposit boxes in Hollywood, with diamonds, rubies and emeralds, and white gloves that reach her elbows that match thigh-high boots.

I can't tell if the stones are glued on or stitched into a netting, but this is insane, even for a woman known for flamboyant red-carpet style. She poses at every step for the cameras, drinking in the attention—and then she sees me.

At least, I think she does. It's hard to be sure when you can't establish eye contact, but I'm looking at the place where her eyes would be. I hold up the jade frog, ready to hand it over—and she moves away, strutting through the crowd, swimming through silver light as she surpasses even the limo door in popularity.

"Oh. My. God," Bradley gasps. "Did you *see* that dress? How many million dollars do you think it's worth?"

"That's the point." It's time for me to use our tickets, so we join the line. "We look at what's outside and focus on that without caring about the woman inside." What little of the outside there was. I saw this woman naked last night in *The Bride Becomes Her*, and still that outfit makes me blush.

From the limo, I catch a flash of lime-green as the door shuts on the other side. "Sonia comes in through a side entrance. Find the neon-green dress. Keep an eye on her."

There's hardly a single photo shot of Bradley and I as we hand over our ticket and step into the lobby, which is unfortunate for him. I wanted him to have at least one souvenir.

The lobby is obviously not meant to serve as a gathering place. Normally people go in, they sit, they watch, they leave. Oh, and according to Bradley, afterwards they party.

Nothing else has been normal, though, so I suppose it's more in keeping with the rest of this movie.

Belion is bragging to a set of reporters about how he touches the depths of the heart—and how his next film will be independently filmed, so his art isn't restrained.

Felicia is chatting with Aaron and his husband—and there, in the far corner, I catch the briefest glimpse of brilliant green. "There she is—" My heart catches in my chest. "She *cut her hair*."

"The word you want is 'butchered,'" says Bradley, aghast. "I would have done a better job with kitchen scissors. Is that in style, looking like a kindergartner is your barber?"

The question of why leaves me completely confused—until I remind myself it's not my right—or place—to question her decisions. I roamed the world. She cut her hair. Maybe we both changed.

Kantina has set up a sort of court on the other end, flanked by guards and shining with every camera flash. And though I want to go the other way, I work my way through the thickening crowd to see her.

She stands in the corner, nodding as a fan gushes about the meaning of life, or love, or something—and then she looks to me and beckons with a single hand.

I step out of the crowd, unafraid of her at last. I stand close enough to be heard, and hopefully far enough away that the guards won't think I'm after her jewelry. "Hi. I got your note, and I know, you keep your promises, so you won't talk to me, but that's okay. I don't need you to talk, I need you to listen. I have something I need to tell Sonia, but I can't, so you are going to do it for me. Nod if you understand."

She does, gracefully, slowly, so her hair waves like a willow's branches.

"Tell her she changed me for the better. Tell her I can't watch movies the same way anymore. I have to see every credit, every name. I dissect every shot, listen to every line. Tell her I hope she finds happiness. That she deserves to be loved. Tell her I'd do it all again, even knowing how it ends. Tell her that one day, I'll be watching a movie, and I know I'll see her name under the director's credits, and I'll say to everyone, 'I knew her before she was famous. I was in love with her, once.'"

I hold out the jade frog—and she takes it, wrapping her gloved hand around mine. "Will."

It's dead silent in the lobby, even though we're surrounded by people, as my heart skips so many beats I might fall over.

It's not Kantina.

It's Sonia.

CHAPTER THIRTY

MY BRAIN GOES INTO EXTREME MELTDOWN WHILE MY HEART does a gymnastics routine. Sonia, standing in front of me, in front of everyone. "How—"

"I saw you when the limo pulled up. We swapped dresses and I cut Kantina's hair with the scissors she uses to remove plastic from water bottles. I knew after that text this morning you would come to her. I knew you'd avoid me."

She isn't wrong.

"Listen to me, Will," Sonia says, pulling back just enough hair so I can see her face. "I've tried to reach you. I called your phone. I sent you actual, physical mail. Kantina had this crazy idea with mercenaries and kidnapping you, and a flight to South America. I went to your brother's. I went by the hotel last night. I flew to Seattle and went to the address you had listed on your contract."

"Why?"

"Because I made a mistake. I was afraid, afraid of change. Afraid of taking a risk. Afraid of being hurt. But life is change, and missing someone you love hurts even more."

"But, what if Belion tells—"

"I had breakfast with Eddie this morning. Showed him the video myself. I'll never act again as long as he's alive, but I don't *want* to act." Sonia wraps my hand in both of hers and pulls me closer. "I couldn't answer you when you asked, because I needed to decide on my own. Then I let shame over what I did keep me away for months, but please, understand. I'm wearing eleven *million* dollars' worth of diamonds, so if I take a step toward the entrance, the guards will tackle me, but I *swear*, Will. If you leave, this time, I'll chase you down."

The murmur of the crowd reminds me we aren't alone, a murmur that grows louder by the moment.

"I love you, Will. I'm ready for that adventure with you, if you still love me."

It's not about what I know, or what I remember, or what I think.

It's not even a decision.

Kantina was right. The heart always wins. The tears in my eyes don't bother me for a moment as I lean over to whisper, "I'm going to make a distraction. You do whatever you have to do to get out of that dress without getting arrested. I'll find you."

"No," Sonia says. "Kiss me. Here. Now."

"But—"

"This is it, Will. This is something I want the world to see."

And so, heart pounding, the sound of the crowd ringing in my ears, I part the hair pulled over her face with both my hands, and I kiss her amid a growing chorus of clicks and flashes.

We aren't alone, before an audience, before the world, but while her lips are on mine and her arms are wrapped around me, we might as well be.

If you're wondering how long it takes to get out of eleven million dollars' worth of diamonds, the answer is, about six minutes, if it's done right.

If you're wondering how long it takes to get to Sonia's house, that's twenty two minutes… if it's done right.

What comes next, away from the cameras, when we can finally, finally be alone?

That can take *hours*. If it's done right.

ONE MONTH LATER

IT DOESN'T MATTER WHERE YOU LIVE: IN HOLLYWOOD, traffic is a constant. In the pre-dawn darkness, Sonia and I ride together in her convertible, belting out a classic from the late nineties at the top of our lungs. The humid air, as it always does, smells of burning plastic and wild-flowers, but life is sweet when you've got someone to love. Sonia reaches across to mesh her fingers in mine, since using a turn signal is pretty much against the law in LA anyway.

Early mornings don't bother us at all now, because they're just an excuse to sneak off to bed that much sooner. But today is special. Today marks the start of something good, maybe even great. "How are you feeling?" I ask.

"Like I'm going to puke," she says. Her hair falls to her shoulders now, and no further. Somewhere, there's a kid or two with incredible red wigs.

"You're going to be awesome."

"I'm going to get yelled at." Sonia stares out the passenger window as she toys with the door locks. "Felicia warned me the first month is nothing but getting cursed at all day."

"Felicia exaggerates." At least, I hope she does. "You are going to be the best assistant director ever."

Sonia sighs heavily. "Not an AD. Not even an assistant-assistant director, or an assistant-assistant-assistant. Who ranks lower than everyone else, but higher than a production assistant?"

"Goldfish. Probably the potted plants outside the soundstage." I run a thumb lightly over her cheekbone. "You are amazing. I'll come by this evening. If you need to work in production, I'll make you coffee."

She reaches over to run a single finger down my cheek—and a shiver down my spine. "What are you doing today?"

"Building a drawbridge. It has to look like weathered oak, hold the weight of six horses, and burn like crazy when lit on fire." I shrug. "Pour enough gasoline on it and everything burns."

"Oh, last night I made some adjustments to your schedule for next week," Sonia says. "Don't book anything without running it past me."

"My *work* schedule?" Sonia's got a real gift for arranging scenes, but when it comes to lumber deliveries, pickup and drop off, that's all me.

"Bradley's dying for a reason to get back to work, and you're going to be shooting in the desert. *Swords* is getting another sequel, and they want a certain barbarian back."

That makes me roll my eyes. "We're too busy. Plus, I

told the casting director no a month ago, three weeks ago, and twice yesterday. How many ways could I possibly pronounce doom on something?"

"That's why you have *two* lines this time. Come on, Will," she coaxes. "Scott Francis asked for you personally. Felicia owes Scott. I convince you and Felicia owes me."

My lips twitch, but I'm not giving in just yet. "And me? What do I get?"

"I'm sure we can work something out." Sonia bats her eyelashes at me. "I can be very convincing."

"Doom it is," I say, and lunge in for a kiss like the barbarian I apparently am.

As she slides out the door and joins the throng, I wrap my warms around her and squeeze her until she wriggles loose with a playful laugh.

From the rear-view mirror, Kantina's jade frog hangs. It's been a good luck charm for Bradley and I as we expand his business. I tried giving it back to Kantina, but she said it wasn't important to her. That I had something that *did* matter to her—the heart of her best friend.

As I signal to turn out of the lot, I can't help but smile.

This is Hollywood. The sets are fake, and so are some of the people who act on them. The stories they tell, those are as real as the audience makes them.

But the romance? The happy ending?

That's real.

THANK YOU!

Thank you for buying this book!

When you buy an Inkprint Press book in print, we like to thank you by offering you the ebook for free. Please head to:

https://www.inkprintpress.com/jc-nelson/hearts

and use the coupon SIHEARTSPRINT to download your free copy in both .mobi and .epub formats. (The coupon will only work once.)

ABOUT THE AUTHOR

J.C. NELSON is a 40-something author living in the rainy Pacific Northwest, with an ark's worth of animals and four kids. J.C. has written the popular *Grimm Agency* series of urban fantasy novels with a fairytale twist, the stand-alone paranormal police mystery *The Reburialists*, and another sweet romance under the penname Jaycee Nelson.

You can find out more about J.C. at
http://authorjcnelson.com

TOYS: CHAPTER ONE

MY FIRST CHANCE AT LOVE CAME INTO MY LIFE IN THE FIFTH grade and rode out of it in the cab of her dad's moving van five years later. My second chance at love, I blew because I was afraid to take a risk. I like to think that wasn't entirely my fault. Dad always told me "You don't get second chances at life," so I never saw it coming.

Men like me want to believe that when life's about to change, we'll get a warning. Some sign from the gods, like a flock of seagulls or crop circles or maybe the ghost of Patrick Swayze warning us that squirrel suits are itchy and hard to remove on your own. What do I get? A shoplifter. Matilda and I watch him for at least twenty minutes. He's sixteen, maybe seventeen, with his cap pulled down so low he'll need eyeholes if it goes much farther, and his puffy coat zipped up. Frosty the Snowman might be under there and I won't be able to tell. But I know he's up to something. Heck, I saw him across the street and knew. The way he studies our sign, looking away every time someone gives him a sidelong glance?

I've seen it before.

I let Matilda keep an eye on him while he browses the selection of adult magazines that line our far wall. I can't actually see the other side of the shelves, but Matilda has a clean line of sight and infinite patience. And I'm so close to falling asleep before my break, the tension from watching him is the only thing keeping my eyes open. He waits until fifteen minutes before my dinner break to make his move.

One moment he's researching the pages of "Jugs," the next, he's a blur of oversized coat slamming into the door. The sign on it reads "Pull" for a reason, but he's no longer interested in reading material beyond that he grabbed from the magazine rack. As he flies out the door, his fist dips into a box of condoms, scattering what he doesn't grab.

I'm not strong. Not particularly fast, unless I'm being chased by a zombie, a bear, or a mobile phone salesman. What I am, however, is used to this particular scenario, and desperately in need of something to keep me awake. I don't bounce off the door, and I don't waste seconds dodging the newspaper stand, and I damn near catch up with him at the corner. "Stop! Hey!"

He glances over his shoulder and darts out into traffic. If his goal is to catch the bus nose first, he misses by half a second.

I give up at the corner. My lungs are heaving, gasps of air coming out as white puffs in the chill night air,. "Idiot. You forgot the lube."

"Evening, Les. You got another shoplifter?"

One of our regular beat cops stands a few yards back. Give his portly stature, I don't figure he'll be able to chase down a runaway donut.

I cram the packets of lube I grabbed back in my pocket and lean against the post to recover. "Fourth one this week."

"What'd he get? You wanna file a report?"

I shake my head and heave a sigh. "He took a handful of condoms I get free from the clinic and a copy of 'Jugs' from 1967. I keep the cheap stuff by the door so that's what gets stolen."

My friendly neighborhood policeman proceeds to turn fifty shades of red. "Why were you chasing him?"

"I felt bad for him. Those clinic condoms have to be manufactured from recycled truck tires. You won't catch a disease with them, but you could build a fire by rubbing two together."

"You look exhausted. You want some coffee?"

"Thanks, but if I drink one more espresso, my sweat will be give people the second-hand shakes." I tip my head to him and head for the warmth of the shop. With the sun set, the neon sign outside my shop lights the night with a golden yellow glow. "Sense-You-All," it reads in fluid cursive that might have been meant to be seductive. "Toys!" reads the other, flashing sign. Our neon is the only part of the shop that projects sex appeal. The mannequins in the window I personally rescued from dumpsters. The red lights inside our shop remind me of emergency lighting. Like most people, what makes Sense special isn't on display.

I push open the shop door and flip my sign to "Closed for Dinner, See you in an hour!" Once I lock the door, I can relax.

"Matilda? Anyone try anything while I was gone?"

My lead mannequin, still painted as a crash test dummy, thankfully doesn't answer. I'll check in with her later. But what I need most at the moment isn't food, and it isn't a drink. It's sleep. I started my shift at six in the morning, and given that I hardly sleep, the hours are stacking up. With my front door locked, I make my way back behind the counter, where a cracked vinyl recliner waits with open arms. From the display rack to the side, I steal a Bouncy Betty doll. You can only call Betty anatomically correct if the anatomy it represents is that of another Bouncy Betty, and even that's iffy. We sell them by the dozen, and they might last ten, fifteen minutes, according to our customers. Fortunately I have more gentle plans for this Betty.

Sense's previous owner taught me early on that Betty makes a far better pillow than a companion. So I stretch back in the recliner with Betty's back under my head. There's a customer coming, an important one. But It's not like I can help her when I feel like one of the living dead and probably look worse.

So I set my alarm and tell myself I'll hear when she knocks. I blink.

And the shop is lit up like daylight.

"Mac, sleeping beauty is awake," a bass voice booms a few inches from my face.

I blink a few more times to clear the sleep from my eyes. "What are you two doing here so early? And why'd you turn on the backup lights?" Sense's front room has backup lights for a reason. I can barely avoid banging my shins, let alone do inventory under the normal ones.

The man looming over me could be a model. I mean that literally, because Rand Nalley's day job—when he works during the day—is as a print model. At night, he and his husband, Mac, run the Wild after Dark program at Sense. "Where's Mac?"

Rand gives me a hand, pulling me to my feet, and puts a heavy palm on my shoulder. "We need to talk."

My college roommate can put on quite a show when he sees fit, and if a little drama floats his boat, I can do that, but not in public. I glance to the door that leads to the back of Sense. The sequin sign on it reads "Special Services Department."

Old customers headed straight through.

New customers always gave it the eye. The eye is a look that imagines that I keep a midget with no teeth behind that door. That's ridiculous, because midgets are people. If I employed one, our dental plan would pay for dentures, and I sure as heck wouldn't keep him in the back room. I'd have him watch the front so I could sleep.

Through this door steps Mac Nalley, my other college roommate. Like his husband, he's easily four inches taller than me, but with a shock of blond hair and blue eyes. I've known Mac since back in elementary school, and living in NYC fits him way better than Arlington, Texas. When he smiles, his eyes smiles to match now. He flashes said smile in my direction, though I suspect it's actually aimed at Rand more than me. Then the smile flees as he focuses in on me. "We need to talk, Les."

Whoa. Drama from both of them at once? "Listen, you two: I didn't eat your turkey. Ok, maybe I did, but I'll replace it from the deli tonight."

Mac crosses his arms and glances to Rand, who leans against the counter while he glares at me. "When we showed up, Mrs. Zimmerman was waiting outside."

A cold bolt of fear shoots through me. My alarm is blinking. I must have slept right through it. "What time was it—wait—what time is it?"

"It's nine-fifteen, but tonight we don't start festivities until eleven." Mac sidles up to Rand. "And as for your other question, it was seven-thirty. Rand handled it, sold her a me-go-ah, the new model with the random remote, plus a new seat for her swing and a few more sundries."

The pent up tension in me flees, using a sigh as its getaway vehicle. "Thank God. And thank you—"

"Les." They speak as one, then smile and squeeze hands.

"We love you," said Mac. "We love Sense. It's a good business, doing good things for good people, twenty-four hours a day. But we think running a shop fourteen hours straight is a little much for one person."

And here it is, or there it went, depending on which way you look at it. "I don't need help. You run the shop until six in the morning. I run it until eight at night. We're good."

"We're not," says Rand. "Matilda stays awake better than you do, but she has a lousy personal touch. Could we please just discuss this? Hiring help is a normal part of a growing business. It's your shop, so you need to handle this."

"If it's my shop, I get to decide—"

"No." Mac's tone of voice could ice my coffee. "You don't. You need help. You need a girlfriend, too, but my particular contacts can't help in that realm."

A woman. That's the last thing I need. I haven't gotten over the previous one, or the one before that, and my therapy sessions really can't handle me adding another ex to the list of issues keeping me awake at night. "It's not that easy. I can't just hire someone off the street."

"You mean," says Rand, "You couldn't just hire someone hanging out in front of the shop? Because he'd applied for a job next door and been rejected?"

Mac gives him a high five. "Or do you mean you couldn't just die and leave the shop to that person after three months?"

Some days I really hate living down the hall from those two, but they are my best friends. I was the best man at their wedding. Or maybe the maid of honor. Since it was just me, I can't really be sure. At least with the two of them, I can be honest.

"I haven't hired anyone because I care about our customers. Men…you've met the sort of men who want to work in Sense. They're hoping some lonely woman will walk through that door and let them put the service in 'special services.' And a woman? Let's see, how long do you think it would take to get a sexual harassment suit filed? I'm guessing the first purchasing day."

I stand up and grab a cheap plastic dildo, holding it out. "Let's see how a normal question might end badly. 'Oh, Ms. Employee, what do you think? Would you mind feeling of this and telling me if it's too hard or not hard enough?'"

The two can't resist cracking a grin, because they know I'm right. And men from Mac and Rand's crowd don't even consider working here, because of what I insist we term an unfortunate accident. But that doesn't stop me from driving it home.

"Of course, if you've got a friend or two—"

"Nope." Mac's tone says it's still a sore subject. "Your squirrel suit poisoned that well."

"Then it's settled." I dust off my pants and rise from the recliner. "You two saved my bacon. I'll buy you breakfast, and we'll consider this matter closed, right?"

The look that passes between them could blister paint, but I take it for good. Rand opens his mouth and then shuts it twice. The third time, he squeaks out, "We need a new toaster. Can't serve bagels and cream cheese on cold bagels."

Rand's bad luck with kitchen appliances is going to bankrupt me. "What happened to the old one?"

"An accident," says Mac. "Involving a that new pirate sword prop. The good news is we definitely shivered her timbers. The bad news is the toaster's missing a plug. And most of the cord." He reaches under the counter, then raises his right hand and holds up the toaster like a rodent.

Great. A fifteen-dollar prop sword for a thirteen-dollar toaster. I seize the toaster from the counter, tuck it under my arm, and spin to make a speedy exit. "I'm going next door to see if I can break even."

"This discussion isn't over," says Rand. "This is the third time in as many weeks you've fallen asleep. You *need* help." His tone says he wants to be heard.

My body language says I'm not listening.

I duck through the front door, snagging the help wanted sign they hung in the window as I go. Help wanted at a sex toy shop. I am so screwed.

Keep reading!
www.books2read.com/toys

www.ingramcontent.com/pod-product-compliance
Lightning Source LLC
Chambersburg PA
CBHW060949190726
48286CB00005B/1495